From the minute Matt Aymer enters Montauk University in 1969, he is confused, energized, and educated by the social, moral, political, and personal unrest of the '60s all around him. The university lurches from unity to chaos as Vietnam War protesters, Black Power militants, and women's rights activists shut the school down unpredictably. Drugs are as available as if they were legal.

Matt's openness and good nature draw a motley band of friends who are eager to educate him. With the urging of Dorman, a drug-fueled androgynous upperclassman; Lana, the gorgeous political radical; Wit, the dorm's army veteran; and Nicky, a romantic, wounded gamine, Matt learns about himself in ways he never anticipated. Matt realizes that he is truly free—free from his parents, free to express his sexuality, free to determine what he stands for, and free to control his life. It's like jumping off a cliff.

But the people who leave the deepest mark on Matt are two women more than 50 years apart in age—Bonnie Williams and Mrs. Devin. Bonnie shows Matt that a commitment to politics doesn't have to be boring and that sex doesn't have to be hidden. Mrs. Devin, the 70-year-old dean of students, shows Matt and everyone else in the school that being an adult is not a foreign country or a forbidden substance.

Matt is drawn into the student government, which is dominated by the student body president, Joe Kashman. Kashman is either deeply committed to the welfare of the student body or a drug dealer whose only interest is power. He presides over the chaos on campus as if it is an opportunity.

Matt and his friends decide they can either sit by and let the school cease to be an oasis for growth and discourse or take action to stop the deterioration. They choose action, hatching a clever plan to restore the campus to a place that ferments learning rather than conflict.

The issues brought to the forefront in the '60s are still with us six decades later and still as confounding as they were then. Whether you are a baby boomer or Gen Z immersed in today's culture wars, you will find the quirky and irreverent engagement with authority, morality, and malevolence surprisingly current.

EVERY THING IS POSSIBLE

A NOVEL OF FREEDOM AND CHAOS

Walter Bode and David Mauer

Momentum Ink Press

NEW YORK

Published in the United States by Momentum Ink Press, New York.

PUBLISHER'S CATALOGING-IN-PUBLICATION DATA
provided by Five Rainbows Cataloging Services

Names: Bode, Walter, 1950– author. | Mauer, David, 1948– author.
Title: Every thing is possible : a novel of freedom and chaos / Walter Bode [and] David Mauer.
Description: New York : Momentum Ink Press, 2022.
Identifiers: ISBN 978-1-7358893-3-7 (paperback) |
ISBN 978-1-7358893-4-4 (Kindle ebook)
Subjects: LCSH: College students—Fiction. | Drug dealers—Fiction. |
Nineteen sixties—Fiction. | Long Island (N.Y.)—Fiction. | New York (N.Y.)—Fiction.
| Bildungsromans. | BISAC: FICTION / Coming of Age. | FICTION / Historical /
General. | GSAFD: Bildungsromans. | Historical fiction.
Classification: LCC PS3602.O34 E94 2022 (print) | LCC PS3602.O34 (ebook) |
DDC 813/.6—dc23.

www.momentuminkpress.com

For information about special discounts available for bulk purchases, sales promotions, fundraising, and educational needs, email walterbode5@gmail.com

Book design by Kathryn Holeman

To Carmela, who makes everything possible.
—Walter Bode

To Freddi and my children:
Without their love and support, this story would not have been told.
—David Mauer

PROLOGUE

HE COULD FEEL the anger all around him. There was an edge that hadn't churned the other rallies at Montauk University against the war. Matt tried to get the image out of his mind—a teenage girl at Kent State crouching over a boy's lifeless body—but he couldn't. No caption was needed to feel the abject horror on her face and the utter senselessness of it. Four kids shot dead by the Ohio National Guard. The Vietnam War was now brought home.

The four dead at Kent State. The secret bombing of Cambodia. The weekly body count's sickening rise. The threat of dying in a hot jungle 8,000 miles away. All of that was fuel for the crowd's desperate rage, all the lies and the betrayals. But it was stoked too by the equally desperate hope that they could change an adult world that seemed useless and disappointing and disillusioning.

Matt's own anger came from inside as well as outside. The student body president, Joe Kashman, was getting the crowd worked up, telling them to take back their school, stop all war-related research at the university. Matt knew what most of the others didn't. Kashman was as angry as a fox in a henhouse, a sex maniac in a whorehouse. With each pointing finger and fist pump, he was getting a step closer to what he really wanted, chaos. Kashman pointed to the line of police that loosely ringed the quad. "Why are *they* here?" he yelled. "Get the pigs off our campus!"

Kashman was still ranting, urging the crowd to take over the library, when a big Black guy grabbed the microphone from him. "I'm with you, brother. Fuck the war!" His clenched fist shot in the air and he yelled, "And fuck racism and fuck segregation." There were cheers and shouts of "Right on!" Raising the other fist, the Black guy yelled, "I can't walk where I want to, I can't say what I want to. Some places I can't even piss where I want to!" Both fists came down on the podium. "Well, I'm pissing in the streets now, brother. This campus should shut down until we have equal rights, Black teachers, and a Black studies program. *We're* going to the library and sit until the university gives us what we want and deserve!" The library was the central building on campus, fronted by a large patio where students gathered en masse. It was a perfect spot to shut down all activity on campus. It was the most valued ground for demonstrations and the brothers weren't going to give it up to the anti-war protesters.

Kashman moved to the side of the stage, whipping up the crowd while three women students jumped on stage. They ripped the microphone from his hands before he could resist. "We hate war too," one said, "and it's time you stopped subjugating us! Discrimination doesn't stop at our skins. We want equal pay for equal work! *We* will control our bodies, not a bunch of old white men! We are not second-class citizens. *We* will take over the library."

All three groups were rousing their followers, hoisting them up on different parts of the stage, but there was only one library and they all wanted that to be the site of *their* demonstration to shut the school down. What had started out as a rally turned into a demonstration that turned into a mob, with its leaders fighting over which group would take over the library. The stage became a riot scene, with the three factions fighting for the microphone and dozens of students jumping on stage to support their cause. People were wrestling each other for the microphone and two women were on the back of a big Black guy who really didn't want to hurt them but he was having a difficult time keeping his balance while fighting them off. The sheer weight of the two women brought him to the ground and you could hear him yelling at them, "Stop fighting with *me* and start fighting for the *cause.*"

Matt thought, *If this weren't so serious it would be downright com-ical. Just work together and split up the buildings for chrissake.* Then he thought, *This is the world I live in—factions splitting the country and now the school to pieces. If the country is so divided, how can we actu-ally end up a better place to live? Or will we tear it apart in the process?* Kashman was back at center stage, giving the police the finger. *He's hoping they'll charge us,* Matt thought, surprised by how much he hated him at this moment.

The cops, as surprised as the students by the power and intensity of the thing that was gripping all of them, advanced on the crowd, and the kids just seemed to mirror the provocation without knowing why. An acrid, biting smell filled the air and attacked the crowd as some of the police launched tear gas. The cops became a target, first for insults, then for rocks. Matt started to feel sick. Would Montauk become another Kent State? Is that what Kashman wanted?

Matt's breath was turning raspy and he pulled a handful of ban-danas out of his back pocket and offered one to his roommate Mel. "Here, wrap this around your mouth and nose. It'll help a little with the tear gas." Neither of them were militant anti-war guys, but it was hard not to be part of this thing that had taken over campus once everybody knew about Kent State and the bombing.

"Better if they were wet. You always carry some bandanas in your pocket?"

"Just since Washington." People were choking and scrambling to escape the gas, which was pretty much hopeless, but the wind blew the gas back at the police. Not all of them had gas masks, so they were almost as tortured by it as the students. There was hardly any more room on the stage as students kept climbing on to join their leaders. And then just as the shouting reached a crescendo, the stage broke in half. People on either side of the crack slid down, crashing into each other. The stage was only three feet high, but in the confusion, people couldn't figure out how to get out of the hole, so they were grabbing arms or legs or whatever they could lay their hands on. Sometimes it was broken planks, and that made some of them scream even louder.

"We have to help them," Matt said. There was no reason the night should have come to this. The insanity seemed to have a life of its own. None of it had to happen. It was nobody's fault and everybody's fault.

There was more screaming when the fires started. Some of the guys were burning their draft cards and throwing them in the garbage cans, but the anti-anti-war protesters had ripped up protest signs and posters and thrown them into the trash, which caught on fire, which was blown onto the broken wood of the stage.

Mel tensed. "We're not really equipped. We don't know shit. The emergency people will be here soon."

Matt looked back at his other dormmates. "Lurch, Fish, Brain, you too." Everybody had a nickname. Matt, six foot four and 175 pounds, was Ribs. Mel, five seven and the shortest and fastest on the dorm football team, was Munchkin. They heard people yelling for help. "Come on, you're the premed," Matt said to Mel and started to work his way through the crowd. "Now's your chance to use those skills," he yelled back over his shoulder. "What're you waiting for?"

As they worked their way up to the stage, they heard sirens. "That's the emergency people," Mel said. "The cops probably have rescue teams available too. So there should be some real doctors soon." The crowd in front of the stage had thinned a little but some people had fallen to their knees and were crying.

The first person they saw was flat on his back looking up at the dark sky. He was shaking convulsively, but it was hard to tell if he was conscious. Matt saw something sticking out of his arm and realized that it was bone. His stomach heaved. "Open fracture," Mel muttered. Matt turned to a dormmate, "Fish, see if you can find an ambulance. This guy needs immediate attention."

They saw a lot of bleeding foreheads and a couple of sprains, but no serious injuries. "It could have been worse. Here come the medics," Mel said as the quad cleared.

"Yeah," Matt agreed. "We could be in Vietnam. 'S funny, I thought I could avoid this kind of shit by being admitted to college."

1

"WHAT DO YOU MEAN, I'm not admitted?" Matt stared at the brunette behind the registration table whose smile had just given him a heart attack. "Of course I was admitted. I got the letter. This is just a bad dream."

She looked down and then back up. "I didn't say you weren't admitted. I said you're not on my list." She frowned at the papers on her table as if they had betrayed her and pursed her lips. "Aymer, right? A-Y-M-E-R?"

For a second Matt hoped he had gotten his own name wrong. Maybe he was really Matt Smith or something, but when he realized how idiotic that idea was, he had to laugh at himself. "That's how it's spelled. Maybe I'm under 'Matt'?"

She raised an eyebrow. "That would be a different registration table, M through R. You could try it." She gave him a half-smile, indulging his confusion. "Hey, Matt, relax. Do you have your acceptance letter?"

Matt could just about taste the relief he felt. He let his duffel bag fall over and took off his backpack. "Right here," he said, doing everything he could to appear calm on the outside but his mind was racing about everything bad that could happen.

She waited a second, then said, "Could I see it?"

"Oh! Sure! Here." He heard impatient noises behind him. The girl smiled again and took the letter. Matt smiled back, but she was already reading. She looked good, reading. She had on a dark green sweatshirt that was so big it was sliding off one shoulder and she had a nice collarbone, Matt thought. "This is obviously fine," she said. "You know, it's probably just a screwup."

"Is that an official university category?"

She tried to hide a smile, which made her mouth do interesting things. "More or less. The university is moving to doing things on computers this year, so everything is entered on punch cards now. You know what I mean, punch cards?"

"Sure." Matt nodded. "We saw a movie about computers last year in a class." He thought a second. Bad move. The demons got him again. "Wait, what if they admitted the wrong person because somebody punched the wrong card? You know, the guy is sitting there punching thousands of cards. His Milky Way bar is melting and it messes up the card so that they admit me instead of the person they wanted to admit."

The girl shook her head and laughed. "More likely somebody punched the hole for like a 'z' instead of the 'a,' and presto! You're Matt Zymer. Pleased to meet you, Matt Zymer." She reached up to shake his hand.

Matt shook her hand, which he thought was warm in a really nice way, and said, "So what happens now?"

Her answer was lost because a guy in the next line over was banging his hands on the table and screaming. The guy behind the table just laughed, which made the new student yell some more and start to climb over the table. A few people shouted, and Matt instinctively walked over and put a hand on the table-jumper's shoulder. Since Matt was six feet four, their heads were at about the same level. "Do you think that's a good idea?" he asked.

The guy was taken aback, but recovered enough to say, "What's it to you, asshole?"

"Well, I was having a problem registering and I thought maybe you were too, and maybe two heads were better than one. What's going on here?"

The guy climbed down off the table while he growled, "Well, asshole, *this* asshole—" he jabbed a finger at the registration assistant, "—says that there's no record that I paid the tuition and fees for this semester. But I *know* I paid them. I worked all summer and I wrote the check, so I damn well know that I did. And *this* asshole—" more finger-jabbing—"laughs and says some shit about how I probably wasn't good enough to get in and, and I thought he should shut his piehole!" The guy was shaking mad.

Matt looked at the registration assistant. "You said that?" The guy nodded. "I'm surprised. Why did you say that? What's your name?"

The assistant fumed. "John. And *this* asshole—"

"Wait," Matt said and turned to the new student. "What's your name?"

"Randy Silverstone."

"So, John, it's really not your responsibility to know what happened to Randy's check, is it?"

"Fuck no."

"So Randy, John's really not responsible if there was a problem with your check. Somebody else is and there's no reason to hassle John about it. He can't help you. Let's find out who can."

Randy was pale under his already fair skin, and his face started to crack. "We goddamn better because my father doesn't even want me going to college because he never graduated from high school and he thinks he did just fine. And if they didn't get my check . . . I can't . . ." Randy bit his lip.

"Hey." The girl Matt had been talking to called out from her table. "You, table-climber. When did you write the check?"

"Last week," Randy said.

"There's your problem. Takes them at least a week to process. I worked there last semester. Just go over to the business office and make them go through the mail for a change."

"Hey, what's goin' down here?" A ponytailed guy wearing painter's pants that had never seen paint and a blue workshirt walked up to the group. John looked away, Randy looked annoyed, and the girl smiled some. Matt thought it was a little tentative.

"Oh, hi, Joe," she said. "Look, it's all fine now. There was a little misunderstanding, but this freshman, Matt Aymer here, helped calm things down. Joe, this is Matt Aymer, he's registering"—Matt raised his eyebrows, but didn't say anything and she went right on. "Matt, this is Joe Kashman, he's the student body president. And this is Randy, who's also a freshman and this is . . ."

"John."

"John, who's working here."

"Cool meeting you all," Kashman said. He held out a hand to Matt. "Matt Aymer, it was outta sight how you took control of things. Perfecto. It's easy to cause trouble but only a few people can end it. It takes a really big person—" Kashman looked Matt up and down— "no pun intended, hah!—to do something like that. I really admire it."

Matt was a little overwhelmed. Nobody had ever said anything like that to him. He opened his mouth, but Kashman wasn't finished.

"I was coming over when I heard the yelling, but you did the job. Hey, don't let that title fool you. The student body president is really just the servant of the students. Look, if there's anything you need, just say the word."

Matt was trying to figure out how to explain his problem when the girl said, "It's nothing, really, Joe. There's a little screwup, probably just a computer error. I'm going to take care of it." Matt's eyebrows flew up like sparrows, but he was too surprised to say anything. He kept smiling because he didn't know what else to do.

Kashman folded his arms and looked at the girl. "Well," he said, "if anybody can take care of things, it's you."

Somebody from Matt's line yelled out, "What's going on up there? Can we get moving?" At almost the same time, a big guy smoking a cigarette came up behind Kashman and grabbed him by the shoulders. Kashman looked behind him and said, "Grizzly! Man! How's it hanging?" He turned back to Matt and the girl and said, "Looks like it's time to get back to business. Great to see you, Bonnie." He looked at John and Randy. "Nice to meet you ... guys. And Matt, I hope I see you again some time. We should talk." The big guy put an arm around Kashman's shoulders and they marched off.

The girl turned back and told Randy where the office was, and John managed to squeeze out an apology, and Randy squeezed one back and left. The noises from the line were getting louder.

"Joe can kind of be a busybody, but he's right. You really cooled old Randy down. You didn't have to do that," the girl said. "But I'm glad you did. I'm off in about an hour. Give me a little time, I'll look into it. The bureaucrats were kind of expecting some chaos because of the new system, so there's someone I can talk to." She thought for a second. "Go over to B dorm. Tell the RA I sent you. His name is Wit. He'll give you a room."

"Wow. I mean, great." Matt tried to smile again, but his face hurt. "I, I really appreciate it." She smiled and nodded, saying she'd catch up with him later. Matt turned around, trying to remember where he should go now in these unfamiliar surroundings, and immediately bumped into the guy behind him who was pushing to get around him to the table. Matt apologized but dropped his backpack on the guy's foot. He apologized again, bent over to pick it up, and hit his butt on the table where the girl was sitting. He sometimes forgot how tall he was. He'd grown four inches in the last year and they still felt new.

He turned around to apologize to the girl, but she was already dealing with the impatient guy, who was smiling and leaning into the table over her. Kind of looming, really. She leveled her pencil at him to make a point and he backed off. Matt headed out the door and looked around for a campus map but couldn't stop worrying. *What if it's not just a mistake?* he thought. *What if I'm really not a student?* He worried some more. He had a room, at least for now. Maybe he could barricade the door with the bed and the desk. *They'll have to rappel through the window*, he thought, remembering *The Guns of Navarone*.

He found the map and located B dorm. He dreaded the idea of

calling home. He'd insisted that his father just drop him off, and the whole thing was awkward. His mother hadn't come, saying that she didn't want to cry all the way there and back. His father didn't know how to say good-bye and had never been entirely sure that college was the best thing for Matt.

If he was out, his mother would be upset and worried. His father would be annoyed and tell him he'd have to get a job. Then he'd bring up the army. He'd joined during World War II but wasn't in combat and talked about it like it was the experience of a lifetime. Get him riled up and he'd bring up joining the military. "They'll take you as far as you can go." *Yeah, right, Southeast Asia.*

Matt had a huge fight with his dad just before leaving for school. His mother was in tears as the fight got really ugly. Matt was really agitated. With uncharacteristic anger he shouted at his dad, "Is it okay if I get killed in the war?" His father didn't quite answer but said everyone had a duty to defend the country.

Defend the country, from a country 8,000 miles away?

Matt had never really paid much attention to the world outside his neighborhood, so the war was kind of an abstraction to him. But when his father didn't say definitively that he wanted to protect his son from harm, Matt went apeshit. He yelled and pounded the table. His father shook his finger under Matt's nose and it turned into a fist. His mother cried for hours and for the first time Matt saw her yell wildly at his dad.

That's when he knew he had to get out of the house. Matt didn't really care where he went to school, had barely the slightest idea what he wanted to do with his life, and just wanted to go. His grades had been fine but not outstanding. He was a good pitcher for his varsity baseball team but not scholarship material. When he got into Montauk, he celebrated mainly because it wasn't within walking distance of home and would keep him out of the draft. The campus was only five years old. The school had been started by a bunch of rich heirs to a shoe fortune who wanted to foster the study of the liberal arts, primarily psychology. It was barely a university—just one graduate-level course, in psychology. Matt's incoming class had fewer than 1,000 students, and the entire school was under 4,000. Now, walking to B dorm, he wanted more than anything to stay there.

A line of people wearing skull masks and white T-shirts with peace symbols were making their way steadily up the path. One was wearing an American flag like a cloak. *Must be hot under that*, Matt thought. There were about twenty of them, all carrying signs, mostly anti-war, some with four-letter descriptions of what should be done to Richard Nixon, some with just more peace symbols. One with an aura of tightly curled black hair surrounding his mask held a burning joint and looked more like he was dancing than marching. "Jones!" one of the other marchers yelled. "Get in step! You're fucking up the march!"

The dancer took a hit off his joint and looked back. "Up yours, Appel! This is how a brother marches!"

They went on their way. Some people waved and cheered, some people booed. There were a bunch of big guys standing in a circle, chanting what sounded like "Oh, gee, em, oh, gee, em." Matt noticed Kashman standing behind them, cheering them on. Matt wondered why, but since he couldn't understand the chant, he was at a loss. He was standing next to a girl who looked like an upperclassman, so he asked her, "What's O-G-M stand for?"

The girl looked at him. "Are you serious?" She made a face. "They're saying 'Ho Chi Minh.'"

"Oh." Then, "So what's Ho Chi Minh?"

She rolled her eyes. "He's just the leader of North Vietnam, supposedly our archenemy. I think you need to do some reading about this before you get drafted. I don't have to fight but you may have to give it up for Uncle Sam." She put a hand on her hip. "You must be a freshman."

Matt felt really dumb. He hated feeling dumb. "Not as fresh as I'd like, I guess." The girl looked like she might actually smile, so Matt tried again. "So who are those guys making all the noise?"

She wrinkled her nose. "They're Zoomen. Neanderthals. Anti-anti-war. They just like to cause trouble."

"Is that the student president behind them?"

"I don't know." She looked again. "Yeah, I guess it is. Jeez, you can't go anywhere without seeing him." With that she went on her way.

Matt continued walking to B dorm, surprised at all the construction going on. The campus was in a rural part of Long Island but was basically a mud pit while buildings were being erected to handle a presumably growing student population. The *New York Times* called the architectural style of the first buildings neo-penal. There were no tall trees, no ivy, no statues of great people. It had no air of privilege, no I-have-been-here-for-hundreds-of-years-with-rich-traditions feeling. The plus side was that current students could be pioneers in forming the culture for future generations of students, if you were into that.

Since there were relatively few dorm buildings on campus, Matt found B dorm without any trouble. When he walked into the entryway, a guy poked his head out of a first-floor room. "Hi," he said, "I'm Wit Thomas. I'm the resident advisor here. You moving in?"

"Um, a girl at the, uh, admission, um, thing said to come here and ask you to give me a room. I, I wasn't on her list."

Wit nodded. "Bummer. Brunette? Good-looking?"

"Yeah, I'd say."

"Sounds like her. Be cool. You have an acceptance letter?" Matt nodded, and Wit gave a grunt of satisfaction. "You'll be okay. They can't throw you out if you've got an acceptance letter." He receded into his room and then came back out looking at a piece of paper. "Why don't you take room three fourteen? There's another freshman there. Name's Mel something."

"What's he like?" Matt asked.

Wit shrugged. "Okay. Nice enough. A little intense, maybe. Hey, if you don't like him, you can always ask for another room. They'll give you a choice once they've confirmed you're a student." Wit laughed. "That is, a choice between a cramped, bare room in this dorm or a cramped, bare room in another dorm."

"If they confirm I'm a student."

"I told you, don't worry. You interested in football?"

"Huh?" Matt wasn't sure what he was talking about.

"Football. Touch football. The school doesn't have a varsity team, so touch football is a big deal around here, and this dorm almost won the league last year. But we lost our quarterback. Can you throw a football?"

"I've thrown a football. But I was a pitcher in high school. Baseball."

"How'd that go?"

"Pretty well. I won eight, lost one senior year." Matt stopped himself from talking about the dismal state finals.

"Okay, I'll tell Barry. He's the coach. He's on the third floor, too." He looked Matt up and down. "Being tall is an advantage. And you've got big hands." Matt smiled tentatively, still not convinced he was in the school at all. "Tryouts are tomorrow afternoon," Wit said, as if it was decided. "After the welcoming speeches to you guys."

Matt carried his duffel bag up the steps and opened the hall door from the stairwell. He stood in the hall wondering which way to 314. The next thing he knew he was on the floor, having been rammed by a fat guy on a tricycle.

"Hey, man, sorry," the fat guy said.

"'S okay, mostly hit the duffel—" Matt started, but was interrupted by a roar.

"Fat Frank! Pull that shit again and you're off the team!" The roar turned out to belong to Barry, the coach, who helped Matt up while Frank struggled out of the tricycle, apologizing again. Barry pointed Matt to his room and asked him if he played football. Matt said he was a pretty good pitcher but hadn't played much football.

"Hey, why is intramural football such a big deal? I can understand a varsity team having a great following, but intramurals?"

Barry looked at him like he was offended by the comment. "First, it is *because* there is no varsity team that it is so important. This is the only activity that brings our student body together. Whether you are pro-war or anti-war, for or against a Black studies program, teacher evaluations, pass/fail grading, women's rights . . . ," he took a breath. "Shall I go on?"

Matt said, "I get it."

Barry continued, "Everyone agrees that the intramural program provides just a bit of relief from the constant warring among the factions. And everyone knows someone who plays. Now, the program isn't without conflict or should I say competition. We play in the dorm league utilizing only players from our dorm. The independent league can choose their players from among all students. We are the superior dorm league team and the Zoo is the one to beat in the independent league. We hate each other for reasons that go beyond last year's defeat. This year we must win. Does that answer your question?"

It does, Matt thought. *Who is this guy? Vince Lombardi's son? And why does everyone seem to hate the Zoo? Kashman seems to like them, so they must be somewhat okay.* He thanked Barry and headed for room 314.

The guy named Mel something was at his desk in the room, filling out forms. Matt introduced himself and learned that Mel's last name was Lender. They exchanged demographic information until they ran out of gas. There was silence for a while and then Mel asked, "What's the matter?" Matt sat down heavily on the bed. Matt told him the story as far as he knew it. "That bites," Mel said, getting up and sitting on the bed across from Matt. "Total bummer. But look, it's probably like this girl said, just a mistake, like a clerical error. What was her name, anyway?"

"I don't know." That made him feel even worse, and once again really dumb, not even getting basic info on the angel who helped him.

Matt flopped down on the bed and put his hands over his face. "But the RA must know her. At least it seemed like it."

"Well, if she's doing registration, you can find her there. Or in the main office or something. Is there anything I can do?"

"Such as make me a student?"

"Get you a beer?" Matt shook his head. "Hey look, they're not going to send you home."

"Because it would be too embarrassing to admit the mistake?" Matt stared at the ceiling for a while.

Mel said quietly, "Really, if there's anything I can do, I will. You talked to Wit, right? What did he say?"

"Same as you."

"Oh." Mel said he wanted to finish up his registration packet and then maybe they could go look for the girl. The fact that Mel was already working on his registration packet made Matt feel even more anxious. *Everyone will get a jump on signing up for classes while I sort things out. Crap*, he thought.

Matt said he wanted to lie down for a while anyway. "Good idea," Mel agreed. "Maybe your girlfriend will show up in the meantime."

"Not my girlfriend. Probably Wit's," Matt grumbled and rolled over. The feeling that there was a plan, or something that might lead to a plan, let him relax a little, and after a while he started to drift. There weren't any sheets, which seemed to fit the situation. He'd walked onto campus that morning with a floating sort of feeling. It was great being on his own. He didn't know what he was going to do, but for the first time in his life, it didn't matter, at least for a few days. He had felt free. *Yeah, now I'm even freer and I'm screwed.* Once again, he thought about talking to his parents. Wit would know where he could find a phone. *I'll just lie here for a while before I tell them*, he thought.

He dreamed he was on a train, but he didn't know where he was going. He decided he had to get off the train at the next stop, but he couldn't move. Then he heard his name and opened his eyes and the girl from the registration table was standing in the door and smiling at him. "Matt Aymer?" she said. Matt tried to remember where he was and pulled himself up so that he could sit up at the side of the bed. He pawed at his face to rub the sleep out of his eyes.

"Hi, Matt Aymer-not-Zymer. Remember me?" She was leaning against the doorjamb, arms folded, still in the big floppy sweatshirt with the cutoff sleeves, one foot on her other knee, a flip-flop on the floor. Her dark brown hair hung to just below her chin and curled up at the ends to frame her triangular face and a big, mischievous smile.

Matt batted his curly hair out of his eyes. "Sure, of course, I'm sorry, I just fell asleep a little. I was going . . . going to . . ." He trailed off, not knowing where he was going.

She put both feet on the ground and leveled a slender index finger at him. "You're going to college, that's where you're going." Matt opened his mouth and then shut it. "I went back to the registrar's office," the girl said, walking into the room. "Oh, okay if I come in?"

"Oh, of course, I'm sorry, please, I . . ."

"No need to be sorry," she said. She slipped off her flip-flops, and sat down on Mel's bed, folding her legs up under her Indian-style. "Okay, so I went back to the registrar's office and looked into the files for the freshmen. Your file is there, so you're admitted. I don't know why you weren't on the list. I told somebody that you should be."

"Um, wow." Matt was suddenly awake enough to understand what she was saying. He stood up and stared down at the girl. "I mean, that's outta sight! So cool." He paused and felt silly standing up so far above her. He sat down and put his hands on his knees. "And weird, I guess."

"Yeah, sort of." She leaned forward. "That stuff isn't supposed to happen. So it happens all the time."

"Okay, I'm about three-quarters conscious now." He shook his head again.

"That's a lot of curls you've got."

"Yeah." Matt held down his hair with both hands. "They've loosened up some. In elementary school, the kids called me Bozo the Clown for a while." Matt had truly suffered through that period. Cut his hair as short as possible. "The taller I got, the less I heard that nickname."

"I can see why. You do have a presence. They're not so bad, the curls."

Matt stood up again, feeling that the room had suddenly become too small. He walked around the room, but it only took him a couple of strides to come to the end of it, and he turned back to the girl. He wanted to hug her. Instead, he said, "I don't know how to thank you . . . I'm sorry, I don't even know your name."

"Bonnie." She was still leaning back on the bed, and she shook her head to send her hair flying back on either side of her neck. She smiled her heart-shaped smile. "No need, Matt Aymer. All in a day's work. And by the way, I really liked you talking the crazy guy down off the ledge or should I say table. Not many freshmen would have done that." She went on, "And . . . the guy in the business office said it would be done tomorrow, they do a new list every day." She stood up and Matt felt that her flip-flops hopped gratefully back onto her feet. "So you should try again tomorrow and it should be cool."

Matt's face fell. "That's really so great, I . . ." Now that she was leaving, Matt felt like he and this girl had shared something, but it was pretty obvious she didn't feel that way. He felt a little foolish. She stood in front of him, the top of her head about even with his shoulder, and folded her arms again, waiting. Matt threw caution to the winds. "I'm glad to be in your school, Bonnie."

She smiled and ducked her head to slip past him. "Not my school. Or, your school too. Got to get back to work." She glided out of the room into the hall, then turned on one foot. "But about how to thank me . . ."

"I'd like to."

"I may think of something. Stay tuned." She was gone.

"I'm a radio," Matt said to the empty room. He looked around as if something would appear if he looked hard enough. He reminded himself that he should be happy, and decided that he was, and then kicked himself. *I didn't get her* last *name. Again. Jeez.*

He wasn't a complete rookie when it came to girls. He'd dated Jill for more than a year in high school and Jill was a knockout, long blond hair, good body, smart. They were king and queen of homecoming. He'd done the whole corsage thing for the prom without even hurting himself. But when she was accepted to UCLA—*with a scholarship*—they both knew they weren't going to spend their lives together. *Snowball's chance* was the way Matt thought of that.

Matt decided that Bonnie was not a freshman. She was too self-assured and relaxed. *Probably has a boyfriend*, he thought, *Wit. But wait—was she or was she not flirting with me?* He decided he would unpack, pulled his transistor radio out of his backpack, and turned it on. *That dorky song about Guinnevere. Not exactly a sing-along. What's that shit about pentagrams anyway? Isn't that for witches?* Matt figured that if Bonnie said he was in school, then by god, he was going to believe her.

Mel got jammed up at the door carrying a bunch of cardboard boxes, one of which fell on the floor. "Hey, I saw this girl walking out of the dorm. I tell you, she was—"

"A total babe," Matt finished for him.

"A total—yeah, do you know her?"

Matt shrugged. "She was the one working at registration. The good news is that she found out why I wasn't on the admissions list and she fixed it. So I'm officially enrolled at Montauk. For sure. At least, as of tomorrow."

"All *right!*" Mel and he slapped palms. "See, I told you it would work out. Shit, this place would probably have admitted you late anyway. They need all the help they can get." From down the hall, Matt could hear "Talking 'bout my generation . . ." coming from somebody's stereo. Loudly. "G-G-G-G . . ."

Mel listened for a minute. "I think it's sick he wants to die before he gets old. You ready to get something to eat?"

"Almost. I haven't finished unpacking my duffel bag." Describing the duffel bag as "packed" was giving it a lot of credit. Matt stuffed his good jeans and a bunch of T-shirts into the bureau drawers and hung a couple of button-downs that no one would call dress shirts in the closet. That's what he had and from what he could tell so far, that seemed to be enough. When winter came, he would bring back more from home, if his father would let him in the house. Montauk wasn't the epicenter of fashion. A friend's older brother had told him that if you had a few sweaters you made the best-dressed list but if your clothes were clean you could get thrown out for impersonating an Ivy Leaguer. He figured he didn't need to bring his suit, the only one he owned and which he had worn only to Grandpa Aymer's funeral.

Clothes stowed, they left for lunch. It was still gloriously sunny, the air still warm with a fall freshness instead of the suffocating summer blanket. A Frisbee sailed past them, and a dog leapt up and caught it effortlessly. *How come no one ever says, "As graceful as a dog"?* Matt thought. A stocky guy nearby said, "Good catch, Captain! Here!" The dog trotted over and the guy took the Frisbee while the other players called or whistled until the dog's owner threw it back. Mel and Matt slowed down to watch. The dog was good. The Frisbee went around the horn until the stocky guy said, "Cap!" and once again the dog waited, positioned himself, and caught the Frisbee. The guy said, "Cap! Frisbee!" and again the dog trotted over and gave it to him.

Matt motioned for Mel to get going again and when they were a few yards past, Matt said, "I think that guy was blind."

"He—what?" Mel turned back to look.

"Don't be so obvious," Matt hissed. "See, the other guys call out so that the blind guy knows where they are. When it's their turn, the guy with sunglasses calls the dog's name so that he knows to catch the next one."

"You know, I think you're right," Mel said quietly. "I wonder if he plays football."

"The guy or the dog?"

2

THE NEXT MORNING, there were bagels and muffins and drinks in the quad for breakfast. Special for freshmen and Matt and Mel pigged out. They were lying down in their room digesting when Wit popped his head in. "Time, guys. The auditorium is across the quad, left turn. It's big. You can't miss it." There was a meeting for all incoming students, an introduction by the president of the university, but Matt wasn't sure he could go. Mel stood up, but Matt flipped his baseball uncomfortably. "What?" Wit asked, and Matt reminded him of his registration problem and whether he'd be allowed into the president's meeting. "Look, my man," Wit said, "you're out in the world now. You can do what you want. You take what you can get and you get what you can take."

"Nobody's going to shoot you," Mel laughed.

"They might." Matt threw the baseball to Mel.

"So you'll say you don't have an ID yet because admissions fucked up your registration, but you gave 'em hell and they're getting their head straight by tomorrow." Mel dropped the ball into the crook of his elbow, bounced it back up into his hand, and backhanded it to Matt.

Wit shook his head like he was waking up. "Nobody'll even ask. Don't forget about the football practice this afternoon."

Matt and Mel walked over to the auditorium for the president's introduction of freshmen to the campus. The fall weather had held off and the quad was still everybody's outdoor living room. "I'm free," Pete Townshend sang from a speaker somebody had put in their window.

The inescapable Frisbee game was continuing on the quad, including the dog and his blind owner.

"Just a minute," Matt said. "I just can't believe that guy." He walked over to the blind guy. The dog came and sat by his leg, looked at Matt, and made a noise in his throat.

"What is it, Cap?" the guy asked. "We have a visitor?"

"Um, yeah," Matt said, "I wanted . . . I was just wondering . . ."

"How a blind person plays Frisbee?"

"Well . . . plays so well. It's amazing to watch."

"Oh, it's mostly the Captain here. He does all the hard work." The guy bent down and scratched the dog's neck. "Right, Cap?"

Matt introduced himself and the guy said his name was Sam. "How do you know where to throw it?" he asked.

"I just listen. People make more noise than they think. And these guys know to help out," he added, gesturing to the other players. The Captain saw a Frisbee coming and tracked it down with a leap. He brought it back so that Sam could keep the game going. "It's not so bad for me, with the Captain," he said, "but I really feel sorry for the people in wheelchairs or even the guys on crutches. They put those pieces of plywood up if you ask them to, but mostly the stairs are like the Berlin Wall. Dividing people from . . . people with handicaps."

Matt nodded, then realized Sam couldn't see that, and said, "Wow. I see what you mean. I mean, I get it." Sam laughed and said Matt didn't have to watch his language. Matt said he was glad they met and went back to Mel, who had heard most of the conversation.

Mel pulled out a pack of Marlboros and offered one to Matt, who refused. "Thanks, no. My father always smoked in the house, and I got kind of sick of it. You smoke a lot?"

Mel lit up and exhaled. "Sometimes. I mean, I don't smoke all the time, but there are times when I'll go through a pack a day. I can do it in the lounge if it bothers you."

Matt considered this. "Well, um. Yeah, I guess I'd appreciate that. If I do anything that bothers you, you can tell me."

"You snore?"

"I don't think so. My sister never said so."

Mel stopped in the midst of a double take. "Your sister?"

"Yeah. We shared a room up until a few years ago."

Mel stared. "You *shared* a *room*? How does that work?"

Matt shrugged. "It wasn't a big deal. That's just the way it was. We lived in an apartment in Queens and didn't have enough bedrooms until we moved a few years ago. It's not like we had sex or anything. My friends understood. You can close your mouth now. Flies are getting in."

"How'd you, like, get dressed?"

"Oh, well, we mostly got up at different times, and . . . ," Matt thought for a second, "and we—I guess we just worked it out. Eventually we moved and we each got our own room."

Mel laughed. "Well, I'll be damned. That's a first, as far as I'm concerned." He thought for a second. "I guess you know all about girls."

"Don't be a jerk. She was my sister, not my best friend. We didn't spend any time there. We went out and did our own thing. Come on, we're going to be late. There's the auditorium over there."

"Hey, there's another guy from B-3." Mel nodded toward a pale guy who wasn't anybody you'd pick out from a crowd. He was about five eight and had brown, straight hair neither short nor long. He wore a blue button-down broadcloth shirt, chinos, and penny loafers.

"How do you know?"

"He helped me bring my stuff up."

Just as the guy reached the double doors to the auditorium, he stopped, turned around, and looked steadily at Matt and Mel until they got to the door. "Hi," he said without smiling. "B-3, right?"

"Yeah, I'm—"

"Mel. I carried your lamp up. That's Matt, right?"

"Right, Matt Aymer. How'd you know?"

"Wit has a list. I know everybody's name on the floor." He didn't look at them directly.

Mel was right, Matt thought, *a little strange*. "I just got here. I had a little problem at registration."

The guy reached out and shook Matt's hand, not smiling but not unpleasant either. "John Riley." Then he shook Mel's hand. They stood there for a second. Matt was surprised that Mel didn't have a comeback as usual. It was like Riley sucked conversation out of the air. "Okay," Riley said. "Let's get seats."

The auditorium was a little like a movie theater, Matt thought, except it was a lot wider, the upholstery of the seats was still new, and there wasn't a popcorn smell. "Where do we want to sit?" he said to no one in particular.

"About a third of the way up," Riley said. "Middle of the row. That's the best sight line and auditory focus."

Mel opened his mouth, looked sideways at Riley and then at Matt. "That sounds good," he said and leaned over to whisper in Matt's ear. "What did he say his name was? Spock?" Riley pointed to a row and started to slide down to the middle. Mel turned to follow, flashing the Vulcan greeting back to Matt.

As they settled into their seats, picking up a mimeographed program, Matt saw Kashman leading a parade into the room. At least the people seemed dressed for a parade—their bell-bottoms were really wide, and some of them looked like they were made of sails and others like pajamas. Their shirts were either skintight or billowing, falling as far down as their knees. Some wore leather jackets with several inches of fringe and others wore fringed belts. A couple had American flag shirts. Their hair fell to their shoulders on both the men and the fewer women, when it didn't bloom out around their heads in a kind of aura that was lit by the sunlight coming from behind them from outside. The sound of small bells accompanied them, and a slightly cloying aroma. There were a few jeers from the other students and catcalls and some shouts of "Right on." The group walked across the front past a couple rows of older people who were obviously faculty or staff or something like that, until they got to the opposite-side wing of seats and occupied the entire first row of it.

Matt looked across at Mel and Riley. "Are they freshmen? What are they doing in an orientation?"

Then the downstairs door opened again, and a clown walked in and waved to everyone. He had an explosion of red curly hair, his face was painted white with a red mouth, and he had the too-big pants and floppy shoes to match. He carried a horn with a big red bulb on the end, which he now squeezed to sound the thing with a *honk!*

"What the shit?" Mel said.

"Clown—" *Honk!* "—test," Riley muttered.

"Wait, there's a test on being a clown?" Mel snickered.

"No." *Honk!* "*Protest.*" Two men in matching dark blue polo shirts with logos on them converged on the clown and began an earnest, if one-sided conversation. Riley continued, "There are some people who think students were treated like idiots, so this guy decided to dress up like a clown in protest." The clown kneeled down and kowtowed to the men, who continued to talk until the clown held out his horn to them as if offering a tribute. Laughter rippled through the auditorium, and some shouts of "No! Keep it!"

Mel looked at Riley. "How do you know all this?"

Riley shrugged. "Saw him yesterday," he said, as if that was an explanation. Mel just nodded.

The clown sat down in front and leaned forward with his head in his hands. A light went up on the podium on the stage and a man in a dark blue suit walked out of the wings, smiling and waving to the auditorium. He reminded Matt of the guy running for state assembly whose motorcade had driven past Matt's apartment building in Queens. Matt couldn't remember if he got elected. The older group, probably faculty in the front row, started to clap and the students dutifully, if uncertainly, followed.

The man reached the podium and tapped the microphone, which he thumped, and woke up a guy in front of Matt. "Good afternoon . . . ," the man began and then waited for the feedback screech to die down and be adjusted, ". . . and welcome to all our new students at Montauk University. I'm Lane Thomas, president of the university, and I'm delighted to have such an accomplished and eager group." He stepped from behind the podium and began to applaud the audience. The older people in the front row all stood, turned to the audience, and also began to applaud.

President Thomas put on some half-glasses and looked down at the podium through them, then looked up over them and surveyed the audience. "These first few days may be the most relaxed days you will spend on campus. And at the same time, they may be among the most structured. That is, we have a schedule of events that will occupy most of your first three days here, if you choose to take advantage of them all. They will give you a complete introduction to the campus, to student life, and to the opportunities—academic, cultural, social, and athletic—that are available on campus and nearby. We hope you will enjoy these three days."

Mel leaned over to Matt. "Now we're going to hear how hard college is."

"Because after these days," the president continued, "you will find that college is challenging in ways that you have probably never experienced before."

Matt congratulated Mel with the two-fingers-down sign, a swish in basketball. Mel sat back as if his work here was now complete and he could take a nap. The president elaborated on the challenges of individual education, and a bunch of other stuff that sounded familiar. Matt counted the number of times the president used the word "journey." Twenty-five!

He was beginning to regret the second helping of bagels and cream cheese and starting to nod off. Mel was sitting with his eyes half closed, playing the drums lightly with his fingers on the armrests. Riley was sitting with his arms folded, staring ahead with eyes wide open. He was either listening intently or practicing Transcendental Meditation like John, Paul, George, and Ringo—although Matt wasn't so sure about Ringo.

"The greatest challenge you will face," the president was saying, "will not be from the academic hurdles of Montauk, however formidable they may be . . ." he paused a second, ". . . but from the forces of disruption, inside you or invading from without. Last year, the terrible turbulence in so many of our major cities was a tragedy. The country was speared through the soul." The president paused for several moments now. Matt realized that the president knew the silence would get the audience's attention. Then he started again, evidently satisfied he had it. "You must stand up for your beliefs, but I ask you to examine them carefully. The university exists to provoke that kind of thinking, that kind of self-examination. Know not only what you believe, but why you believe in it. Then make your stand."

Matt loved the idea but he couldn't see how any institution could keep this philosophy from boiling up into chaos, not the way things were now. *Who decides whether someone is stepping on another's rights?*

Thomas was now done with his talk and he evidently didn't expect applause. He looked down at the ponytailed guy who led the parade into the meeting. "Mr. Kashman, will you stand?" Kashman uncurled from his seat and turned to face the audience. "Let me introduce the president of the student body, Joseph Kashman," President Thomas said, "who will say a few words."

Kashman looked around to make sure the president had finished and then stepped up to the podium. "Thank you, President Thomas. That was a fantastic introduction to Montauk. I'm sure we'll all think about it for a long time." He turned back to the students. "Welcome, everybody. I won't take much more of your time. We're going to tell you all much, much more about your student government in two days. At Montauk the student government—we call it the Polity—is incredibly active in campus life. We fund the campus newspaper and radio. The student government manages the activity fee that you all pay and it adds up to hundreds of thousands of dollars. We are in charge of important campus activities, like bringing you some of the biggest names in rock and folk in the country and important lecturers like Timothy Leary and Muhammad Ali—" Somebody from Kashman's group shouted "Yee-hah!" and some others clapped.

Kashman went on, "We provide funds for intramural football, mixers and other parties, and various other great things here on campus. Last but not least we have organized major programs off campus to help those in need. As two examples of many, the Polity was instrumental in establishing a women's shelter only a few miles away from the U, and our people have been to the south to help register voters. So, come and hear about what the Polity does for you and the community. *Do not* miss the meeting on Friday. I can't say more here today, but it will open your eyes and, I promise you, blow your minds."

The president reclaimed the microphone. "Now our dean of students, Mrs. Devin, will help guide you through the wilds of Montauk with tactics and strategies for survival. It will, no doubt, be much more immediately useful than anything I can say. I recommend that you listen to her with the utmost attention. Thank you, and good luck for all your days at Montauk." With that, he stepped from behind the podium and applauded the audience, who responded similarly.

As they waited for the next speaker, Mel said, "I don't get it. Was he telling us that we should protest and march and shit?"

"If that's what you believe," Riley said.

"But only if you really know why you believe it," Matt added.

Mel rolled his eyes. "*I* believe he's full of crap. How's he going to keep control of things if he's encouraging people to go on strike and 'do their own thing'?" Mel fumed, air quotes dripping from his voice. "I came here for an education, not a four-year demonstration."

"That's your thing," Riley pointed out.

Matt was puzzled, however. He liked the idea that he could do anything he believed in, but that meant he had to ask himself the question *What do you believe in?* For the first time in his life, maybe, he realized he didn't really know. He'd seen the TV news about the protests and remembered how his father had sneered at the campus protests. He'd been outraged at the protests around the Democratic convention. Went ballistic.

Mel said, "What was up with that Cash-'em-in guy anyway?" Matt shook his head. "With his little ponytail. Seemed like he was hiding something, to me."

A woman stepped up to the podium. Mrs. Devin looked close to 70. She was maybe a little more than five feet tall. She had to stand on a box to be seen over the podium, and she pulled the microphone down as low as it would go. Her hair was silvery grey and although it was neat, it didn't look like it had been styled. In fact, nothing about Mrs. Devin looked styled, but she looked just right.

"Good afternoon, ladies and gentlemen," she began. "Dr. Thomas has given you information about the school and it is very important information. However, only part of your education takes place in the classroom. In your years here," she paused to interrupt herself. "I hope you will stay four years and I hope the government will allow you to stay four years. But in any case, in your time here, you can learn a great deal about who you are as a person, and that will be the most difficult and worthwhile education of all. I am not here to talk about your academic life. You'll have plenty of resources for that. I am here to talk about life outside the classroom. While I cannot tell you very much about rock and roll, I can tell you some things about sex and drugs." People looked at each other as if to say *Did she just say what I think she just said?* There was some murmuring. Mrs. Devin ignored this and added, "Then I will tell you about the most dangerous, and most exciting, pleasure of all." This time, no one looked around while they tried to figure out what she was referring to.

Matt thought, *She already said sex. What else is there?*

"First, sex." Snickers rippled through the room but didn't stop her. "I am reliably informed that all of you have either a penis or a vagina." The snickers died a thousand deaths. "I can reasonably conjecture that you will use your personal organ in sexual intercourse.

"Universities evolved from monasteries and I assume that even the most religious of you will acknowledge that debauchery existed in both places. I like sex and I know you do too, so let's talk about how to handle your new opportunities. A lot has changed just in the last two years. I am not condoning premarital sex, but it is unrealistic to think that no one in this room will have sex while in college. The decision to have sex is a serious one but we shouldn't pretend we have no desires—it is a natural act and as responsible adults we should discuss and understand the consequences of having sex. This institution is committed to having an open dialogue on all the issues that face your generation and our country.

"I can say that, with depressing predictability, thirteen percent of you will contract a sexually transmitted disease. We have a health clinic that will discuss contraception with you and practices that will help ensure that you do not contract a venereal disease. Gentlemen, it is not only your partners' responsibility in this area—it is yours as well. The clinic will dispense condoms and birth control pills after a thorough discussion with you."

There was rustling in the audience as a male student in the middle of a row attempted to crawl over those seated. Mrs. Devin paused, as someone from the audience yelled, "Hey you, where are you going?"

The guy trying to exit said, "I'm going to the clinic, where else?"

The auditorium exploded with laughter, as much from relief of tension as comedy. Mrs. Devin smiled and laughed along with everyone. "I'm glad that someone actually had the balls to break the ice," she said, and the audience laughed harder. "I want to thank you for being proactive but why don't you wait and listen further. It might be useful."

"Good idea," he said, and went back to his seat. More laughter.

"Gentlemen, I urge you to visit the clinic after this little talk and take a supply of condoms if a woman has made it clear to you that she wants to have sex. Ladies, I caution you not to ask a man if he has a condom lest he take that as permission."

A woman raised her hand and asked, "Mrs. Devin, how can we stop a man from forcing us into sex?"

"An excellent question." Mrs. Devin nodded. "Electrical shock is effective but technically difficult to manage. Some ladies have come up with extraordinarily inventive ways to emphasize their resistance to nonconsensual sex. It is possible to acquire small cans of pepper spray, but I have been told that pepper itself can be quite effective." There was a noticeable pause in the audience chatter as the men considered this possibility. "There are also," Mrs. Devin continued, "small horns that you can keep in your pocket or purse that can produce

quite significant auditory defenses. Men often have difficulty main-
taining an erection with a fire alarm going off in their ear. See me, if
you're concerned, and we can discuss this privately so that the surprise
will be complete."

Mrs. Devin paused a moment, as if she were considering what to
say next. "Now I would like to speak about homosexual sex." The quiet
in the room was like a blanket. No one knew where to look, so they
looked at Mrs. Devin. "I would like to speak to each and every one
of you about homosexual sex, not just those of you who enjoy it. As
you may know, humans have practiced homosexuality for as long as
we know. For the men of ancient Greece, it was as natural as breathing." She smiled ruefully. "Unfortunately, we do not know whether the
women of ancient Greece found equal freedom, since their preferenc-
es were not recorded. Which is to say, we know more about ancient
Greek homosexual men than about heterosexual women. A great pity.

"You may know about the Stonewall demonstrations in New York
City this past summer. Our laws about homosexuality, the so-called
sodomy laws, are gradually changing, and I think those demonstrations will accelerate that change. Legally, then, those who are intoler-
ant of homosexual sex are being, shall we say, emasculated.

"But what I want to focus on is not your behavior in private but
your behavior in public. Some of you may feel that homosexual sex
is immoral, a sin, unchristian, a stain upon the human race. It is your
right to feel that way. It is not your right, however, to force that opin-
ion on other people. Freedom of speech is a necessary part of our society and guaranteed by our constitution. Freedom to degrade, debase,
and humiliate are all, I believe, immoral, sinful, and stains upon the
human race. Or as the legal people say, your right to swing your fist
ends at my nose."

Mrs. Devin looked at the audience for a long time, seeming to
search out each pair of eyes and look into them. "Have I made my
point clear?" There was a general murmur that sounded like assent.

"Very well then. Sex can be addictive—and the clinic can also
counsel you about that problem, but the more pervasive forms of

crippling addiction involve drugs." Some in the audience reflexive-
ly checked around for narcs. "In the last few years, the use of drugs
throughout the country and our campus has gotten out of hand. I
believe that even a moderate amount of drugs—indeed, almost any
amount—will be harmful to you. I will even go so far as to say you
should abstain completely. However, as with sex, I would be a dimwit
to forbid you to take drugs."

Her voice took on a new note, one of deep concern and urgency.
"When use of drugs takes over your life and you can no longer accomplish what you came here to accomplish, then you have gone over the
edge. I implore you not to let drugs take over your campus life. If you
find yourself tempted to the point of being out of control, please seek
counseling immediately. You have probably heard the horror stories
but let me assure you that I have seen them. I have seen the screaming
and weeping, the vomit and the inert bodies. Do not become one. I
am not going to say any more about this, but I hope you will come to
see me if you would like to talk about anything I have said here.

"Next, I want to talk politics with you. I witnessed what happened
on campus last year and I am concerned that the demonstrations that
occurred last year are likely to get more frequent and more violent.
We take seriously our responsibility to protect our students. I am not
here to tell you what causes you should support. But I am here to say
that we must let all sides express their point of view. Free speech is
everyone's right and the basis of our democracy, but violence is never
acceptable. A great part of your college experience comes outside the
classroom, learning who you are and what you believe. But I urge
you not to blindly follow the crowd or even your friends. Think for
yourself and remember that you are responsible for your actions. Your
decision to act or not act is your choice. Take responsibility for your
actions.

"Finally, as I said, I want to talk for a moment about the greatest
and most dangerous high." The audience sat up in their seats expectantly. Mrs. Devin waited a moment and smiled. "I have actually talked about it indirectly several times today and one of the reasons it is so

dangerous is that it is subtle. You are not always aware you are taking advantage of it. You are not always aware when you are not taking advantage of it."

"How long is she going to make us wait for it?" Mel whispered.

"Maybe it's served at intermission," Matt said.

"This thing you risk," Mrs. Devin went on, "this thing you enjoy, this thing you can never have too much of until you can't handle it, is freedom." She had her audience in the palm of her hand, surprised, skeptical, amused, or enthused. "For most of you, the kind of freedom you're experiencing here at Montauk is a first. Oh, no doubt, you could decide what you were doing on Saturday or Sunday, what you would wear, who you would talk to. But the context, the frame you were in, was provided for you. You may have thought it imposed on you or given generously to you, but in either case, it's no longer there. Some of you may take that as a chance to, ah, let it all hang out, to take liberties with your life. And yes, it is a gift. But it is a dangerous gift." Someone had raised a hand to ask a question. "Yes."

"But we still have to take classes," a guy in a white shirt and chinos said. "We still have to live in the dorm. Unless you're a commuter, I guess."

Mrs. Devin looked pleased. "Thank you. Yes and no. You have to sign up for classes. You have to have an address on campus. No one, except perhaps your closest friends, will rouse you out of bed and tell you to go to class. There will be no bed checks at night. You are free to use your time—and your bed—however you want and with whomever you choose. You can drink all night or study all night or have sex all night." She paused, but there was nothing but silence in the auditorium. "Until the consequences arrive. Until you flunk out. Until you pass out. Until you burn out."

"Until Daddy takes the T-Bird away," Mel snickered.

"So wear your freedom lightly." A couple of dozen people checked with their neighbor to see if they'd heard right. "Freedom is a great richness, and like the air, it is always there. Like our other dangers, it would be foolish of me to restrict your freedom. But I do ask you to be aware of it, partake of it but do not drink too deeply all at once.

"Lastly," Mrs. Devin said, "let me say that I am interested in each and every one of you. Talk to me. You will see me around on campus. Do not assume that you will be interrupting me, whatever I am doing. Thank you."

The room exploded with applause. Mrs. Devin smiled but looked thoughtful. Matt wondered if she knew something no one else knew. *Probably.*

"You're going the wrong way!"

Mel stopped in the middle of the field in frustration. The linebacker covering him was so surprised that he fell over backward. "You're supposed to cut to the sidelines!" Barry yelled. He seemed to treat these touch football tryouts as if they were the Super Bowl.

"Does he have any volume lower than maximum?" Matt said to the Black guy walking over to him.

"Puts it out on the field to the limit. Can't turn down the volume," laughed Jones—"just Jones," he'd said. He was the only Black guy on the team, so Matt didn't have any trouble remembering his name. He was the one with the huge Afro who was in the anti-war march that Matt had seen yesterday. Jones seemed an okay guy, but he kept apart a little.

"I had him beat in the flat," Mel said between clenched teeth.

"I don't give two bull farts where you were beating him off," Barry said. "When you play on this team, you *execute* the *plays*. This isn't eighth-grade gym class." Barry made a note on his clipboard as if scheduling Mel's execution. "Come on, huddle up again."

Matt looked at the list of plays that Barry had given him. He was still surprised that Barry had made him quarterback for this practice, but he was beginning to like it. It was kind of like being a pitcher. You were always in the middle of the action. He could never play real tackle football given his skinny frame.

The other guys had introduced themselves, but Matt immediately forgot most of them aside from Lurch, who was as tall as the butler in *The Addams Family* but about four times wider. Matt had been impressed, almost overwhelmed, at the organization. They started with ten wind sprints across the field. When they were done with the wind sprints, Fat Frank, the guy who'd run into him in the dorm, gave out playbooks to everyone and they devoted thirty minutes to going over pass routes and blocking assignments. There were fifteen plays in total while each one had at least two different formations. And then a student carrying two large duffel bags ran onto the field. He breathlessly told Barry that the uniforms were here. Without much fanfare, Barry started throwing jerseys and sweatpants to each player.

This is unreal, Matt thought. *Each jersey has the player's name and number. How did he know the sizes and get it done so fast?* Barry had the #1 jersey and Matt was #10. *What am I getting into? Is this the B-3 military? But I do really like the jerseys!*

In seven-man touch football, the defense was two or three guys who stayed on the line to rush the quarterback, two others on the line to cover the offensive ends, and two defensive backs to cover anybody who got loose. Everybody was eligible to catch a pass, even the center. It was a surprisingly rough game. No helmets, no pads. Touch was a bit of a misnomer. Touching often became very rough grabbing and slapping. Tackling was forbidden. The only other no-no was leaving your feet to launch at the ball carrier.

The game was mostly passing, and when they were warming up, Matt was happy to see that he could still throw a perfect spiral as far down the field as anyone. Farther, in fact.

There were a lot of people watching, even a lot of girls. Matt wondered if Bonnie was there but couldn't really look. The sky was overcast, but it didn't feel like fall yet. Somebody had a wheeled cooler and was selling hoagies and sodas out of it. Doing pretty good too, it looked like to Matt. Wit said that there was some betting on the teams, although one team, the Zoo, was much better than anybody else. "People figure out creative ways to bet," Wit said.

As Matt walked on to the field a guy with white-blond hair stood up and yelled, "Hey, stringbean! You're doing too many uppers! I've got some 'ludes to chill you out and some grass for munchies. First one's free!" The whole group laughed hysterically.

"Don't let him bother you," Mel muttered.

"Doesn't bother me," Matt muttered back. "I'm not really sure what he's talking about. Everybody's always laughed at how skinny I am. They'll forget about it."

Matt discovered that his height really was more of an advantage in football than in baseball. He could see over almost everybody except Wit and he could throw to him. He completed a short pass to Wit. A running play was broken up. On the third play, one of the linemen missed a block and Matt found himself the target of somebody coming at him like a torpedo.

Matt took off to his right and saw that the defender on Mel's side of the field was coming in. He threw the ball over the defender's head, hoping that Mel was on the other side of him. He was and he was alone. Mel ran under the high arching pass and it dropped right into his hands. Touchdown. The group with the white-hair guy all stood and cheered. His teammates were incredibly impressed as well, but intentionally not showing Matt how they really felt. That one pass, however, said it all. B-3 had its starting quarterback.

As he glanced around at the crowd, he could see a guy with a ponytail, surrounded by a number of students, raise his arms in the touchdown sign.

He thought the guy looked familiar and then he realized that it was the Polity president, Kashman, who spoke at the president's welcome speech.

Matt was feeling pretty good about himself and took a deep breath and looked around while the defense was on the field. It wasn't a bad crowd, considering. There was that gaggle of girls around the blond guy, but there were groups scattered throughout the stands, and they seemed to be surveying the workouts pretty closely. There were guys with clipboards and even a few girls with clipboards. Matt asked Wit what they were doing.

"Scoring the new male talent," Wit said. Matt felt he had to ask again. "The girls come here and look over the new freshmen, rate them on looks and build. Did you think they were here just because they love touch football?"

At the end of the scrimmage, Barry came up to him. "You throw a pretty nice ball. Twenty completed out of 35. The longest was 30 yards, that high arching pass to Mel. Nine passes were over 20 yards. Six were between ten and fifteen yards and five were under ten. You set up pretty well, but you need to get rid of the ball faster. Study the playbook and be ready for next practice."

It took Matt a second to realize he'd been given the job, and by then Barry had turned away. "Uh, thanks," he said, but Barry ignored it and walked off. *All in all*, Matt thought, *a pretty good day*.

3

MATT WAITED NERVOUSLY in line to register. He looked to see if
Bonnie was working the table but didn't see her. If he was for real
registered, he was supposed to make an appointment with a counselor,
sign up for courses. He'd never really thought about what he would
study at college. In fact, he hadn't thought much about anything beyond staying out of Vietnam. He didn't want to get killed or even shot
at. But if he wasn't registered, his father would expect him to go if he
was drafted. Hell, he kind of expected to go if he was drafted. It wasn't
like he wanted to go to Canada. He was an American. Suddenly he
was at the head of the line.

"Name?"

"Matt Aymer. Look, man, I know that there could be a problem,
and I—"

"Spell it."

"A-y-m-e-r. But I mean, yesterday, I was trying—"

"Aymer. Okay, fill out this information sheet. You can do it over there
and drop it in this box." He tapped an inbox next to him and gave Matt
a smaller card. "Fill that out for temporary identification. Your number is
on it if you need that for anything, but everybody's pretty laid-back the
first few days. You'll get an ID card by the end of the week. It's all just
basic stuff, name, home address, blah blah, if you have trouble, see the
help desk over at the end of the gym. Over there." He waved his hand in
the general direction of one side of the gym. Matt looked that way and
saw a few kids standing around another table. Then he realized.

"You mean I'm registered? It's done?"

"Yeah, wha'd you expect? You're stuck here until you graduate, flunk out, and/or get sent to Nam."

Matt felt a little dazed and the student behind the desk could see that.

"Sorry, man, just a little Ho Ho Ho Chi Minh humor."

Why does everyone know about Ho Chi Minh except me? Matt stepped aside to fill out the card, thinking he ought to thank someone or do a little victory dance. But he'd feel stupid doing it all alone. There were some chairs to sit in, but they were all occupied, so he just stood at a table and started to fill in the little boxes, always too small for his handwriting. He concentrated on squeezing in the letters and numbers.

"Looks like everything worked out." Matt startled and yelped in surprise.

"Oh, hey, I'm sorry," Bonnie said with a grin spreading across her face.

Matt stood up straight, feeling his face getting warm. "Hi! Yeah, I'm glad to see you. Thanks again." He looked down at the card. "Without you, I wouldn't have the opportunity to write down my home address, next of kin, doctor. But I'm having trouble with my blood type. I was thinking of using 'B Cool.' Do you think they'd believe me?"

"Are you sure it's not 'O no'?"

Matt grinned. "I guess you're A plus."

"So you're registered," she said, peering behind him at the paperwork. Matt nodded. "Great. I'm glad it worked out." She pulled a strand of her brown hair off her cheek and looked up at him, waiting. She was dressed in jeans that she'd clearly worn before and a grey T-shirt.

Matt recovered enough to say, "Yeah. Wow. I mean, I feel like celebrating."

She nodded. "Any reason to celebrate is a good one, right?"

"Yeah. So, you work here? For the school, I mean."

Bonnie ducked her head and came up smiling. "I do, yeah, for the administration. Part secretary, part go-fer, part ambassador to the world. At least the student world. It's part of my financial aid, but it's really like the best thing that ever happened to me. I meet all kinds of people and I get to see how the system works." She laughed. "But believe me, 'works' is an overstatement. You aren't the only one who's gotten lost in the ozone. There are kids who are still wandering around from last year."

Matt blurted, "Well, I'm glad you found me." Bonnie made a little comma with her mouth and Matt wished he had fallen into a ditch. "I mean . . ." *I need to stop saying "I mean" and just say what I mean.* He looked down. "I mean, what are you wearing on your feet?" *Damn.*

She looked down. "They're called espadrilles. They're French."

"Did you get them in France?"

She wrinkled her nose. "They're kind of hard to get here." She leaned back against the table and looked out at the crowd. "So you did the president's talk yesterday."

"What's up with that Cashin guy and the government? Does the Polity rule the school?"

"Kashman. He's, um, an interesting guy." She seemed hesitant, something Matt hadn't seen in her yet. "He knows a lot of people, and he's really smart. Smart about people, at least. Too smart, maybe. I am sort of concerned that he's lost sight of why he wanted to head the Polity. His work outside the campus is what attracted me to the Polity in the first place. The ideas for improving Montauk are great—organizing protests against the war, teacher evaluations, curriculum upgrades, more power to the students—all right on, but we seem to have stalled out a bit. Sometimes I think the change has become the focus, not the ideas." She stopped short and said, "Well, I am going on and on. Time to stop! Let's leave that for another day."

"You sound like you know him pretty well. Are you involved? Are you a PoliSci major?"

She nodded enthusiastically, a light in her eyes. "Well, I will be.

International Relations, actually. And yeah, I'm on the Polity, hoping to keep the 'revolution' on track."

Matt had another flash of feeling out of his league, and then a mock-deep voice over his shoulder intoned, "Beware, Big Sister is watching." Matt turned. "Hey, Wit. I didn't see you."

"Yeah, us elves just sneak right up on you. Hi, Bonnie."

"Wit, cut out the Big Sister crap. Anyway, I'm not watching *you*."

Wit laughed, "Sorry, couldn't resist. Believe me, the last thing I want is for you to be my big sister."

"I'll let you slide this time," she smiled and the air seemed to clear. "How's things. Taking care of business?"

He shrugged. "Just tryin' to lose these schoolyard blues."

She looked him up and down. "I see you're dressed for combat." Wit was dressed in camouflage pants and heavy-soled boots. Matt hadn't noticed before, and he wondered where Wit would have gotten camouflage. Unless he had been in the military. A part of Matt's stomach contracted.

"Always ready." He grinned at her. "You should try it some time." She laughed sarcastically, but didn't say anything, so Wit asked, "How does it feel to be a sophomore?"

Bonnie stood up. "'Bout the same as it did for you, I guess. Are you taking Woodbell's class this year?"

Wit smiled. "Yeah, I couldn't put it off anymore. I hear he's kind of a dick." They launched into a conversation about a course that seemed to be about politics or history, or politics and history, talking over each other, comparing what they'd heard about the professor, Woodbell, and how hard he made the course, which was why they'd avoided it even though it was a 100-level class. Matt didn't have anything to say, and he knew that he should finish filling out that card, but he didn't want to end the conversation with Bonnie, even though he didn't know what to say to her either. He shifted from one foot to the other and then he noticed a pale guy with long blond hair walking up to them. He was wearing loose paisley pants and a T-shirt with a color that matched the background of the paisley. Matt thought he looked familiar.

As the guy got close to the group, Bonnie noticed him and her mouth dropped open. "Dorman!" she said, or something like that, and he wrapped her up in a big hug that nearly lifted her off the floor. Wit looked exasperated.

"Hey, gorgeous," the guy said when he let Bonnie down. He looked at Wit and Matt and then back to Bonnie. "Am I allowed here or are you only talking to tall people today?"

Bonnie laughed and tossed her head. "You can talk to me any time, Dor. You know Wit, right?"

The guy nodded and said, "I have had that pleasure, but not in the Biblical sense." Wit rolled his eyes, and the guy punched him in the stomach. Wit didn't flinch.

"And this is Matt Aymer," Bonnie said. "Newest recruit to the best and brightest." Matt felt absurdly pleased for some reason. "Matt, this is the freakiest freak on campus, Dan Dorman. Also known as Doorman, or just Dor."

Dorman half-bowed. "I open the doors of perception. Matt, I am pleased to meet you, rising touch football star that you are. I would love to shake your hand except that I broke my fingers on this guy's abs. I better take something for it."

Bonnie gave him a half-smile. "On top of what you're on now?" Dorman feigned shock. "Dan's biggest problem," Bonnie said to Matt, "is that he forgets which pharmaceutical he took last."

Dorman looked hurt, but then drew himself up to his full height, which was around five ten. "On the other hand," he said proudly, "I can fly."

Bonnie laughed and slapped him on the shoulder. "Matt, don't take him seriously." She looked around at the registration lines, which were getting longer. "I should get back to work, and we should let Matt finish up his registration card so that he can officially become a student and see guidance about his schedule. But it was outstanding to see you guys again." She hugged Dorman again and held out a hand for Wit to slap. "See you in class," she said to him, and turning to Matt, poked him in the stomach. "I haven't forgotten that you owe me, Matt Aymer."

Matt wondered if he was turning red and didn't care. "Me neither." She waved and was gone before Matt even remembered that he didn't know how to find her again.

Dorman watched her go and then saluted Wit and Matt. "I'm away as well. I think I see a dealer I know over there." He walked away with a kind of lope, his clothes flapping in the breeze he created.

"Shit. Crazy bastard," Wit said, shaking his head. He folded his arms and stood with his feet slightly apart, his weight balanced. "I mean it. Watch yourself around that guy. He's a nice guy—a great guy, in a way—but like, he does a lot of poppers, among just about anything else. And he really does think he can fly."

"Like fly in an airplane?"

"No, like fly." He unfolded his arms and stretched them out to the sides, waving them up and down. "Like a bird." He folded his arms again. "Broke his leg last year jumping out of a tree." Wit twisted up his mouth. "I guess you could say he really was out of his tree."

"Ho-kay." Matt sighed. He went back to the dorm to prepare for the guidance meeting.

"What do you want to do with your life?"

Matt had been asked this question, or variations on the theme, so many times in the last year that he had an answer ready for the guidance advisor. "Well, I don't really know." He smiled, knowing she had heard this a thousand times.

She smiled back as if she had heard it a million times. "Okay," she said slowly. "Do you want to go into the army?"

Matt practically jumped out of his seat. "No!"

"Okay, now that I have your attention," she said, dropping the smile with a thud, "maybe you can start figuring it out." She shuffled some papers on her desk and handed one to Matt. "You must have seen this before," she said. "This lists the required subject areas you should fulfill by the end of your sophomore year." Matt looked at the list, which he had ignored when it was sent to him over the summer.

There weren't any surprises—math, history, English, science—but the number of semesters was a little different in different subjects, and there was a long and completely confusing list of substitutes that would fulfill the requirement, or partially fulfill the requirement. Some requirements required two semesters of classes and they had to be taken consecutively, but some didn't.

The counselor handed him a course catalog. The ink smelled fresh. "You can decide which courses you want to take when, but I suggest that if you're interested in business, say, you take the required math courses first. Or if you're interested in journalism, you should do the English classes. So it kind of depends on what you're thinking about for your future." She tapped her pencil against the desk and smiled. "Or you can just roll the dice."

Matt smiled back. "Um, okay." He flipped through the catalog. "When do I have to tell you?"

She leaned back in her chair. "This week would be good. But technically, you can sign up for a course up to two weeks after it's started, or later if you have the instructor's written permission. You can drop a course up to six weeks into the term, with or without the instructor's permission. There are a lot of sections of the 100-level courses—the required courses—so you shouldn't have a problem with scheduling. Here, here are some scheduling cards. Take a look at the catalog and fill out a card. I'll give you a few in case you want to try out different arrangements. When you decide, bring the card back to me and I'll sign off on it."

Matt thought for a second. "What about international relations?"

"What about them?"

"I mean, are there any courses in international relations?" Matt was getting excited now. "That I can take?"

"Oh, those would be upper-level classes. 200, maybe 300."

"Oh." So much for that.

"You would start with the prerequisite courses. One of the popular ones is a European history course. Professor Woodbell." She snickered. "It's called Revolution Now! Starts with the French Revolution."

She snickered again. "I guess there are a lot of you who would like that."

"I'd like that." This was not true. He'd spent high school learning how to throw a curve ball, not protesting. He'd been stunned and even a little outraged at the Chicago riots during the Democratic convention, but just because both sides seemed kind of stupid anyway. He thought Abbie Hoffman was a clown and Tom Hayden totally boring. But it was all kind of scary. Maybe the kids were out of line, but the cops —vicious. He even went to a candlelight vigil in the park for Bobby Kennedy—mainly because Jill insisted that they go, and it was a beautiful warm June night. He admitted to her that the light of all those candles was out of sight, though he'd worried all night that someone would drip hot wax on his pitching hand. Wasn't Nixon going to end the war anyway? Maybe he was making a mistake taking a course with a tough professor and with two people who knew more about history than he did, but maybe he could sit by Bonnie.

"Okay?" the counselor asked. "Anything else I can do for you?"

"Oh! Sorry, I was just . . . thinking." Matt stood up, stuffing the schedule cards into the catalog.

"That's good! Keep it up. It'll come in handy someday."

Matt thanked her and found his way out of the office, passing by a hallway of similar offices with similar advisors and students. There was an energy there, though, a sense of expectation that made him wonder if his counselor was kind of a dud. *Well, I probably won't see her that much.*

After his guidance meeting, he was heading toward the dorm looking at the catalog when he almost ran into Dorman again, who greeted him enthusiastically, which made Matt a little uneasy. Dorman asked him where he was going and when Matt pointed toward the quad with the dorms, Dorman said, "Great! I was going that way myself."

"It looked like you were going in the opposite direction," Matt pointed out.

Dorman laughed. "That depends on what you mean by 'opposite.' No matter what direction I was going, I would eventually have been going in that direction, wouldn't I?" He pointed behind him toward the dorms. Matt was puzzled. "Eventually, I say," Dorman added, as if that explained it. "The curvature of the earth requires it. However you go, you will *eventually* get where you've been." Matt thought about that and tentatively agreed that was possible. Dorman took this as encouragement. "Wherever you go, there you are. And then in addition to that, there's the question of where was I going in the first place. Just because I was walking in this direction, that doesn't necessarily mean I was *going* somewhere in that direction. I could have been *going* anywhere! Think of that. We are free."

Matt nodded again. "Where *were* you going?"

Dorman scratched behind his ear. "I don't remember. Anyway, let's go." And he turned around, beckoning Matt to follow, as he continued with barely a hesitation. "What a gorgeous day. All this sunlight. Isn't it amazing that this light that's drenching you left the sun only eight minutes ago? That and a billion billion more photons that you can't see. And you still can't look at that light directly. And eight minutes later, it will reach Saturn, where you can look at it. Think of that. You could stand on Saturn and watch the sun sail across the sky." He shook his head frantically, as if the idea were too big and trying to get out. "What have you got there, a catalog? You picking courses?"

Matt, overwhelmed by the jet-fueled chatter, said yes and started to admit that it was all a little confusing. Dorman grabbed the catalog and said, "Here, let me help. I worked this out last year. You want to get the requirements out of the way, of course. But not all at once—it's too boring. Do you like science?" Matt pursed his lips and started to shrug, but Dorman said, "Okay, skip that for now. Everybody's more laid-back in the spring. So look, take English this first semester, it's pre-req for a lot of things and they don't expect you to actually be able to write since you're just out of high school. Look for Professor Harris—he's super-cool. I smoked a lot with him last year and it was very mellow."

"Smoked . . . ?"

"Yeah." Dorman looked modest. "He's become a regular customer, actually. Some downers too. Do you need anything?"

"Need . . . anything?"

"Sure. Weed, uppers, downers, MDMA, acid. Have you ever tripped?"

Matt thought for a second. "Been to Chicago with my family."

Dorman looked at him sadly. "No, man, that's not what I mean."

"You haven't met my family."

"No, it's—oh, I get it. It's a joke. Ha-ha!" He laughed as if he were trying to catch up. "But anywho, you should try my windowpane!" Dorman started to walk faster and Matt stretched out his stride to keep up while Dorman rambled on fast and faster. "Open the windows of your mind. You'll see a new real in reality. Tripping squares the circle and circles the square. There are dimensions we . . ."

"No, really, it's all right . . ."

"It *is* all right on the night." Dorman stopped for a minute and looked around. "Ah. Be here now. What do you see?"

"Well, there are some students walking around, and of course all the buildings." Matt wondered if there was a point to this. "And yes, the sun, and the trees and the grass . . ."

"And it's all beautiful," Dorman nodded. "How about that girl over there. What do you see?"

Matt figured he was being set up. "She's got brown hair, jeans, a flannel shirt."

"And?"

"And she's carrying a book . . . and a purse . . ."

"And?"

"Um, I don't know. Could maybe lose a few pounds."

"You missed the most important thing."

Matt frowned. "What's that?"

"*She's not wearing a bra!*" He stopped again, turned to the girl, and waved both arms above his head. "Hi! Beth!" he yelled.

The girl turned toward them and smiled. "Dor! How're you doing? What are you doing this weekend?"

"Tripping! You want to come along?" Matt tried not to show that he was shocked that they were shouting to each other about drugs in the middle of campus.

"Yes! Save me a tab. I'm good for it. Gotta go."

"Cool. See you there." They waved good-bye to each other and Beth went on her way.

"Ah, Beth," Dorman said, looking wistful. "A bright and bubbly girl with a seductive tang of sadness underneath it all. Lana's best friend, oddly enough. No pair more unexpected on campus, I'd say."

"Who's Lana?" Matt was getting a little tired of being thrown into the middle of a conversation without being given any rules.

"Ah, Lana. Indescribable. Come to the party at the dorm—when is it? God, I can't remember anything. End of September, like that. That dorm over there. We modestly call it the Taj Mahal. A stately pleasure dome. I'll introduce you. Be there or be square," he laughed. He turned around as he walked off. "And take one of the eastern religion courses. They show you the path to your essential nature." He walked a little farther, then turned back again. "And life drawing! Everybody should draw. Besides, naked women and men. A dio."

Matt watched him go, feeling as if he had briefly visited a foreign country without a passport. He walked aimlessly along a path that was lined with small trees. Dorman wasn't like anyone he'd ever met and not because of the drugs. Matt had tried some marijuana in high school. Maybe it was just all the paranoia around it, but he didn't particularly have a lot of fun. It made him feel weird, but also sleepy.

There were more students around now, striding across campus like they had a plan or drifting aimlessly in groups, littering laughs here and there. He heard Simon and Garfunkel toast Mrs. Robinson: "We'd like to know a little bit about you for our files / we'd like to help you learn about yourself."

He thought about the last scene of the movie, with Dustin Hoffman and Katharine Ross sitting in the back of the bus looking a little lost. Mrs. Devin had made freedom sound like a scary prospect, so maybe that was messing with their minds. Still, if he was sitting next to somebody who looked like Kathy Ross, he'd be looking at her. This reminded him that he wanted to see *Butch Cassidy and the Sundance Kid*, which was supposed to open soon. Then he wondered where he would go to the movies around here.

He wondered what Jill would have said about Mrs. Devin. She would have loved her of course, but it wouldn't have slowed her up. "Okay, let's get to work and have some fun!" How many times had she said that to him? Jill was always on—on top of things, on the go, onward and upward. It had been a little exhausting, but she was really popular and Matt always felt like he had won something to have her as his girlfriend. He wondered if California would make her laid-back. He didn't think so.

They'd almost had sex once, but Jill made them stop. Matt had once calculated that he had thought about sex for 189,216,000 seconds though he couldn't be sure that he was thinking of sex during the first Super Bowl of 1967. He reasoned that even though the game was long, it probably didn't change the calculation that much—so he was okay with it. Bonnie was so—*why am I thinking about Bonnie?* She was too popular. But still, she said he owed her. But she was probably just kidding or playing around. She and Wit could talk about international affairs—*affairs, hah*—and she liked Dorman. He needed divine intervention, he decided. *Not likely.*

———————

"Don't take that European history course," Wit advised him. "You have the psychology course for the social sciences requirement. What do you need with all that extra reading? And Woodbell is a dick." Matt had complained about all the reading he would have to do this semester, and Wit was trying to help, but Matt couldn't help wondering if he wasn't also trying to head off competition for Bonnie. *In your dreams*, he thought, and realized sardonically that was literally true. Matt insisted that he was really interested in the course, and that the French Revolution was very relevant to real life today, and that even though he hated to write, Napoleon really interested him. "How could such a short guy control all those people?"

Wit laughed. "Hey, that's what the military is all about. Taking ordinary people and turning them into sheep. Sheep that can kill," Wit sneered. His disdain for the military ran deep, but it was also informed. Wit had started college and been in ROTC, then dropped out and joined the army. "I was a brainless kid then," he said, in the same sneer he offered about Napoleon. "Looking to be a hero. So naturally they posted me to Berlin to break my spirit. Berlin was a dead end for me. Nobody really did anything. Guys had snakes for pets—they were easy to feed and didn't need to be walked. But I studied war as part of my training, and also because I'd never realized that there were actual strategies, planning, logistics. That was Napoleon's downfall, as you may know."

Matt said he didn't know, and Wit explained the basics of Napoleon's Russian campaign. When Matt felt he'd had enough, he asked, "So you weren't in Vietnam?"

"No. I feel lucky about that and I feel like shit."

Matt waited, and when Wit was silent, filled in. "So, practice is in an hour, maybe—"

"A couple of the guys I knew in basic were sent there and died," Wit said in a monotone. "I mean a bunch of guys were sent there, but I knew a couple who were killed. They were even sent in the same unit, and they were all happy as shit about that. Sure, better to fight with somebody you know than a complete stranger. So they were able to die with somebody they knew—they went together, in an ambush. One of them, Oliver, that's his helmet over there."

Wit fell silent, looking out the window at the sky. At least that's where he was facing. "Jeez," Matt said. "I'm sorry. I never knew anybody who died. Got killed, I mean."

Wit's head sagged. "No. Well, practice is in an hour. You should get your ass in gear." Matt let out a breath. Wit's mouth tightened, but into a smile. "No, there's nothing to say. You'll understand if it happens to you. Stay out of Nam if you can. Pray for a high number in the draft. Stay in college. Let's play some football."

4

AFTER SEVERAL GRILLED cheese sandwiches and a plate of French fries, Matt and Mel walked over to the quad for the Polity rally. Music that sounded live started while they were walking, competing with Santana talking about changing evil ways. It wasn't much of a competition, though, and when they got there, they saw why. The band included a kazoo, a washboard, a fiddle made out of a few pieces of wire, a broomstick, and a wastebasket. There were the usual tambourines and bongo drums. The one thing that was actually an instrument was a saxophone, pressed to the lips of an African American guy. He was creating a slightly scary series of squeaks and honks, as well as the occasional arpeggio just to show he could actually play.

"At least they're not pretending to be professional," Mel said.

Matt nodded. "The question is, what are they pretending to be?"

The stage itself was pretty clearly built with more enthusiasm than expertise, two-by-fours and a lot of nails. But it had what looked like a real sound system, a microphone on a stand, and speakers. There were upright poles on the sides that were strung with Montauk U. pennants and banners and some posters that were totally unrelated to the school but added a lot of colors. There was a heavy cable strung from the archway at the entrance of the quad to a stanchion at the back of the stage that seemed neither decorative nor functional. Across the back of the stage, somebody had painted a big mural, mostly in red, of people trucking and smoking fat joints.

"So far, so-so," Mel said. But the quad was filling up, and there was even a kind of excitement in the air, a party atmosphere ready to boil over. Wit ambled up with some of the others from B-3. Some of them were freshmen, not all. Matt turned around and saw that John Riley—everybody was calling him "Neut," for neutral—had joined them without anybody noticing.

Clouds had come across the sky, which kept the sun from burning them up. That was good, because the campus was so new that there weren't many trees for shade. Some had been planted but they weren't tall enough to offer shade. About fifteen minutes after one, the saxophonist stepped to the microphone alone and blew a middle C into it. People covered their ears, and the guy simulated surprise. "This thing on? Damn!" He tapped the microphone and then looked over the crowd. "Okay, then. I'm Kingman." There were some jeers from the crowd. "No, man. That's my *name*. Kingman." There were some cheers.

Kingman boomed, "Now we gonna have some talk from the people running the show, at least the student part of the show, around here. They got something to say, so if you don't listen, you lose." He turned away from the microphone toward his fellow musicians.

Matt looked around at the others. "Well, that was short and . . . well, short." Lurch snorted and raised his hands over his head to clap. "Give that man a cigar!" he yelled. The other guys from B-3 started a rhythmic clapping and chanted "Cigar! Cigar! Cigar!" until the energy died out. Fish, who was a swimmer, yelled, "Play the saxophone!"

That seemed to get Kingman's attention and he walked back to the microphone. "Now you're going to hear from the student government president. Be cool."

Kashman walked up to the microphone. He was wearing tan chinos that managed to look casual and expensive at the same time, an open shirt whose collar spread across his clavicle, puka shells around his neck, and sandals that Matt could hear squeak. Real leather. "Good afternoon, and welcome to all students, new and maybe some old. I'm Joseph Kashman and I have the honor of being the president of the

Polity, the student governing body of Montauk University." He took the microphone out of its stand holder and began to stroll across the stage. Leaning forward, he held out a hand to the audience, palm up. "Don't for a second think of the Polity the way you thought of your high school's student council, or whatever you called it." The hand snapped into a fist. "The Polity is the power on campus. We make recommendations to the university about classes and about how the system is organized and overseen. We control the student administration fee that the university collects from you in those quarterly payments."

The fist opened up again and swung back and forth to include the whole audience. "That all goes back to you. It pays for extracurricular activities on campus, including intramural sports teams, concerts, and guest lectures. It funds the newspaper, *The Blowing Wind*. You may not need a weatherman to tell which way the wind is blowing but you need *The Wind*. With *The Wind* and the campus radio station, WMU, we will keep you fully informed of what's happening on campus and what the Polity is doing to give you the freedom and power you need to take control—control of your university, your classes, and your life! You make the Polity work and the Polity works for you!"

There was a cheer, and Matt felt energy running through the crowd. *He's really pretty good*, Matt thought, and *I wonder if Bonnie is here. I can see why she's involved if it's everything he says it is.* He thought about that again and wondered just what her relationship with Kashman might be.

"You might be wondering," Kashman was saying, strolling from one side of the stage to the other, whipping the microphone cord around behind him, "how I got to be the president, but you freshmen never had a chance to vote for me. In order to provide continuity—and to prevent the lame-duck seniors from hogging all the money—elections are held in the middle of the year. That means that in January you will have a chance to vote."

He paused and looked searchingly at the crowd. "And not only vote! But run! Nominate yourself to be on the Polity, to make the college work for you, to hold the power! If not you're not part of the solution, you're part of the problem, and you can become part of the solution by being part of the Polity!" He raised a fist, opened it and lowered his hand, palm out toward the crowd. It wasn't exactly the Black Power salute from last year's Olympics, but it was close enough. A bunch of the crowd mimicked the gesture, holding a fist up to the stage.

Kashman had the crowd responding. Matt felt like pumping his fist too, but he looked around. "I'm not the problem," Mel huffed. "I'm not so sure about this guy."

"I'm going to hand off the mike to our vice president, Jack Appel, who has some really ballbusting ideas about our academic program for the year. Everybody listen up! Jack!"

There was polite applause for a guy with what seemed like yards of curly brown hair snaking down his back, a "Stop the War" T-shirt and jeans. In fact the rally was like a walking billboard for anti-war sentiment and the many movements of the time. Matt saw signs and T-shirts—"Drop Acid Not Bombs," "War Is Not Healthy for Children and Other Living Things," "We Shall Overcome," "Jim Crow Must Go," "Stop the War on Women"—there was no shortage of protest factions.

Kashman had put the microphone back in the stand and Appel pulled some slightly wrinkled pieces of paper, creased in half, out of his back pocket and unfolded them. "Hi," he said tentatively into the microphone. "I'm, uh . . ." Somebody called out for him to speak louder, so he leaned closer in the microphone. "Is that better?" Something like agreement rippled through the crowd. "I'm Jack Appel," he started, and then launched into a description of how the Polity would work to give students a voice in the selection of the faculty, choices of courses, and other workings of the mechanics of the bureaucracy. The plan seemed more theory than reality but Matt thought trying would be worth it. The crowd got restless, and Mel said, "This guy couldn't convince a mouse to eat cheese."

Wit said to give him a minute. "He's not a good public speaker, he's more of a doer—a leader by example. He worked to register voters in the summer and he accomplished a lot, from what I hear. Took some guts."

Even Appel seemed to realize that he was losing his audience. "But most important," he said, suddenly changing topics and tone, "most important is that we are going to be demanding equality. Equal rights *and* equal power." The murmuring subsided as his voice grew stronger. "Why should we be the ones being judged? Why should we be pigeonholed, made to compete with each other by this system of letter grades?" A few people echoed, "Yeah, why?" which gave Appel some energy. He shook his head. "No reason!" he said. "We're going to demand that all classes be pass/fail. No grades *per se*."

Mel muttered under his breath and Matt could tell it was not praise. "Who's Percy?" Lurch smirked.

"He's bringing the beer," Fish said.

Appel was gathering momentum now, like a VW van going downhill. "Not only that! We're going to judge the teachers. We will institute a system of grading for all the professors and the results will be published in *The Blowing Wind*." That drew a cheer and Appel paused to enjoy it.

"House organ," Wit said. "Entirely controlled by the Polity."

"Last summer I was down south, trying to get people to vote." Suddenly it felt like Appel was talking, not speechifying, and there was something compelling in his voice that made Matt pay attention. "I saw people whose lives were . . . were *hard*. I couldn't believe how hard. People who worked twelve hours a day and still had nothing they could call their own. Children who didn't have shoes and houses that didn't have beds, much less televisions or air conditioners. Some of them didn't have toilets. And these people had never voted. They'd never had the chance to vote, not really. Even if they did, they didn't see that it would make any difference."

The audience was quiet now and Appel seemed to draw strength from it. "And I think that you, a lot of you at least, feel the same way. That there's nothing you can do, that people somewhere else have control over your lives and no matter what, you'd be stuck in whatever rut they want.

"But it's not true!" Appel said, as if he were personally wounded by the idea. "I know that it's not! And I know how different you can feel when you take charge of your life. Yes, it's hard. Yes, it takes time, but god yes, is it worth it! We want to make you want to make it yours."

Matt had a strange feeling in his stomach, but he wasn't sure what it was. All Appel's awkwardness had disappeared and Matt felt like he should go somewhere and sign up for something.

"Finally—" Appel began.

"Way too late," Mel groused.

"—we will institute a series of alternative courses that will educate us about the real history of the United States, its alternative voices, and its colonialist, hegemonic strategies around the world. How to end war. About how to bring peace!"

For no obvious reason, a chant of "Peace now! Peace now!" began to grow in the crowd, and Appel took it up. Kashman came back out, thanked Appel, and began to introduce the next speaker, but nobody was paying him much attention because a tall, slender woman with two or three feet of luminous black hair and legs that were even longer was striding across the stage. "Stride" was only an approximation of the way she walked, which was something like what a cheetah crossed with a willow tree might do.

She came to a halt about three feet from Kashman, who finally turned to acknowledge her presence, ending with, ". . . social/consciousness coordinator, Lana Harananinan!"

"Thank you, Joseph," Lana Harananinan said, "and thank all of you for attending our meeting this afternoon. We are nothing without you." She smiled, and every man in the crowd smiled back. "I would like to invite you to involve yourselves in activities that will expand your horizons, your circle of friends, and your consciousness.

This is how we will change society because, as you know, the personal is the political. Our groups, which you might have called clubs in high school, are called circles, because everyone is equal in a circle. We join hands together."

"I'll join," Lurch said. People shushed him.

Lana Harananinan went on to name a list of circles that left Matt dizzy. There was a self-actualization circle that had activities like falling into other people's hands. There was a wilderness survival circle made up of people who evidently thought spending a weekend in the woods with only a knife and a book of matches sounded like fun. There was a witches' coven, but only white magic was allowed. There was a politics circle, and a personal exploration circle, and, Harananinan said, "Yes, we have a chess circle and such things that you are no doubt familiar with in other realms of your life. There is a list of all the circles available in the student government office, and I encourage you to drop by and we can discuss all these activities personally."

"Definitely need to discuss that list," Fish said.

"Me first," Lurch said.

"She paint that T-shirt on?" Boomer, another footballer, asked.

Neut spoke up. "Got the shadows right."

"And now," Harananinan said, her voice like a bell, "Mr. Dan Dorman will tell you everything about our entertainment! Thank you for listening."

"She's pretty entertaining," Wit pointed out.

Lana Harananinan was looking up toward the back of the quad until she nodded and smiled, and then walked quickly to the side of the stage. Things were quiet until the big cable above them moved, and someone yelled, "Geronimooooo!"

Dorman—it had to be him—literally flew over the heads of the crowd, holding on to a wheel with handles that was rolling down the cable toward the stage. As he got lower and closer to the stage, people in the way ducked and scattered, and Dorman picked his legs up until he threw them down onto the stage, which quivered unnervingly while he tried to keep his feet under himself. The wheel rolled into a backstop at the back of the stage, Dorman fell over in a heap, jumped up, and yelled, "Aiyeeeee! What a trip! Wow!" He shook his head to clear it. "Oh man. Wow. Okay." He looked at the crowd. "You have *got* to try that! All of you!" He ambled around the stage for a minute, shaking his head and muttering, "So far out, so far out.

"Okay!" he finally said to the audience. "We're gonna have music that will shake your soul and make you shake your ass." A few people in the crowd hooted and offered examples of ass-shaking. One guy, who didn't seem entirely sober, fell to the ground and everybody around him laughed. "Sly and the Family Stone! Big Brother and the Holding Company! We're trying to get Janis for the spring!" Dorman yelled. He went on to list some of the most famous rock groups in the country as well as Joan Baez, Pete Seeger, and others who were as known for their activism as their music.

"They actually get some of those," Wit said. The crowd was cheering and Kingman had reappeared along with three others who seemed to be real musicians—lead and bass guitar and a drummer—because they launched into a song that had real rhythm and had people beginning to tap feet and sway in place. Dorman also listed some speakers. Matt hadn't heard of some of them, and some of the others—Stokely Carmichael and the inevitable Tom Hayden—weren't really his bag, but there were more cheers and chants. "Jane Fonda!" someone yelled. There were some boos. "Only if she comes as Barbarella!" There were some cheers.

"Thank you all!" Dorman concluded. "Be here now! Enjoy and come see us! Sex, drugs, and rock and roll!" Kingman came back on with a couple of guitarists and a drummer and they launched into an up-tempo version of The Band's "The Weight," which was actually pretty good. Dorman started to dance and so did some of the audience. Lana Harananinan joined him and they twined themselves around each other without ever actually touching. It was a mesmerizing performance.

"Okay," Mel said with relief, "free at last, as a famous person said."

But Kashman was back on stage. "Actually," he said over the

murmuring of the crowd, "we have one more traditional happening in the Polity's presentation. We want to have one of the freshmen remind us of what that first moment on campus is like, give us this year's first impression. How about you there!" He pointed in Matt's direction.

Matt confidently assumed he was pointing at someone nearby and he looked around. He was a little surprised to see Mel standing directly behind him, and he noticed that everyone was looking at him, not whatever luckless rookie had been picked. "No, you," he heard Kashman say. "Matt!"

Matt turned around to see Kashman pointing insistently at him. Mel pushed him from the back. All the other B-3 guys were cheering and waving him on. Wit put a hand on his shoulder and said, "Go on, go on. Don't worry. Nobody will ever remember anything you say."

Matt stepped forward, as Kashman pointed to some steps at the side of the stage. Matt stepped up, tripping on the last step onto the stage. His arms pinwheeled but he was able to stay upright. There were laughs and cheers. Matt looked out at the audience looking back at him and thought of his last baseball game, the state finals. He'd lost but the crowd cheered anyway. *Can't be worse than that, can it?*

Kashman, waiting for him in the center of the stage, lowered the microphone and shook Matt's hand. "Just tell us how it felt," he said quietly, "good, bad, indifferent, no matter."

Matt thanked him and took the microphone. He thought for a minute. "Time's up!" someone yelled. More laughs. "I've been told," Matt started, "by an undoubtedly wise man, that no one will remember anything I say." Some laughs among the B-3s. "I'm counting on that." More laughs. "There'll be a quiz at graduation. No right answers allowed." Applause.

Now what? "I guess there aren't any right answers up here either." He paused. "Okay, the first thing that happened was that the university lost me—lost my registration, I mean. Or that's what I thought." There was a soft groan. "But it was all right. A nice girl helped me out." Scattered applause. "Then I saw a blind guy playing Frisbee with his dog. I guess if he could do that, I should be able to get through my first day in college. Then I met a guy who offered—who said he could fly." Matt looked around and pointed to Dorman. "And he can! Then I heard the university president tell us we should be sure who we are and take a stand about it. Sounded like he was okay with protests!"

A shout from the crowd asked, "Is that what he said?" and there was some laughter.

"I think so," Matt said, to loud applause. "The coach of the football team gave me a playbook that looked like a calculus textbook." All the B-3 guys chanted "B-3" and clapped as loudly as possible. "Then I heard about a professor smoking with a student and I don't mean Marlboros." The crowd yelled, "Dorman, Dorman!" "A seventy-year-old talked about sex and warned me that I could get pepper-sprayed." The crowd chanted, "Mrs. D, Mrs. D, Mrs. D!"

"And the student body president said I—we—should take charge. Then he gave me the microphone." He turned to Kashman, whose eyes narrowed, but he bowed. "And all that has happened in forty-eight hours before classes even started." Matt laughed, "I guess all that's left is to take over the university!"

"Power to the people," Jones said in a deep and quietly penetrating voice. The crowd was quiet.

"That was a joke, really. Anyway, I can't imagine what a year at this place will be like. I better go take a nap." Matt looked around. "Thank you for listening. Okay. Oh, thanks, Ka . . . President . . . uh, thanks." He started to walk off the stage, heard someone say his name, and realized that he was still holding the microphone. "Oops." He handed it to Kashman and saw Bonnie at the back of the stage, her hands held palms together in front of her face, half-bowing. Kashman took the microphone and immediately turned to the audience, yelling, "Thank you! Thank you! There's a list of times of circle meetings and Polity meetings being handed out! Take one! Thanks! Have a great year!"

When Matt got back to the group, Wit shook his hand. "You're in for it now," he said. Mel said he was going back to the dorm, but the others all had other things to do, so Matt and Mel walked back to the dorm. "So," he said to Mel, "it was kind of a circus, huh?"

"You were fine," Mel answered, "but I always thought student government is like your dog. It was nice to have around, you could pet it, sometimes you'd play with it or take a walk with it, but mostly it kept to itself and slept a lot. I really don't want a student government that thinks I'm the pet and it's going to do things to my life without me having a say. They're trying to turn college into something else."

"Or maybe they're trying to turn college into what it was original-ly—a place where people got together and learned things and talked about them. Like the Greeks, you know."

"The Greeks didn't have to get into med school. They just, like, stabbed a snake and called themselves doctors."

Matt laughed and nodded. "Getting into med school is that tough, huh?"

They entered the quad, and Matt could hear "Marrakesh Express" playing in someone's dorm. Some people were dancing to it on the lawn. It had been the song of the summer, free and easy, sounding like sunlight and vacations in warm places. Summer now seemed distant. "It's worse than tough," Mel said, and he seemed to be almost smiling. "You go through hell for four years as an undergraduate and then you go through hell for six years in med school and residency." He turned and looked at Matt straight in the eye. "But if you can make it that far, you know you've got what it takes."

Matt was fascinated that Mel looked almost eager for it. "What if you get a low number in the draft and have to go to Vietnam?"

"I'd volunteer first," Mel said. "Better to go the way I want to than just letting someone else make all the decisions."

Matt was impressed and a little overwhelmed at this guy who seemed to have figured things out so definitely. "Well, that's cool," he said, "I guess."

Mel laughed. "I'm . . . I just need to have a plan, that's all. I don't feel comfortable when things are left vague. Like this grading thing.

I mean, I've heard that med schools have no interest in transcripts that don't have grades. It may be a myth, but I'm taking no chances." He shook his head as if someone was arguing with him. "But even if I weren't going into med school, I'd want to know how I stacked up. Makes me work harder. It's just the way I am. And what about that grading of teachers. If you get a bad grade, do you then give a bad grade to the teacher? Is it the teacher's fault?"

Matt kicked a rock off the sidewalk. "I hadn't really given much thought to it. You know yourself a lot better than I do."

Mel shrugged his shoulders. "I could say the same about you, I'm sure."

Matt blinked. *I wish that were true*, he thought.

5

IN THE DORM, Matt heard a commotion in the lounge. Mel liked to stir up these nighttime bull sessions, so maybe he was there. Matt wandered down to the end hall lounge to see what the ruckus was. A bunch of the upperclassmen were drinking beer and eating pizza from open boxes. The air was a pungent mix of incense, farts, and pizza and the guys were dressed accordingly—tees, shorts, sweats. They were talking, of course, about the war and the draft and how to avoid both.

"Hey, this isn't difficult for me," one of them said. "We have to fight Communism over there. I don't want those gooks coming here. If one country falls it's only a matter of time before the rest fall. I believe our government. This is really serious and we have to stand up for it." Somebody threw a pizza box at him, and he batted it away.

"Willie, you are out of your fuckin' mind," another guy said. "I don't believe anything those guys say and need I remind you that the French were driven out of Vietnam after a gazillion years of fighting? If we 'win' the war, whatever that means, we will be like the dog that finally caught the car. What will we do when we win? And by the way, do you know what this war is costing the country, not just in dollars but what it is doing to the great USA here at home? I can't even talk to my father anymore, not that my relationship was so great to begin with. And my mom cries all the time thinking that I will be coming home in a box."

Another guy jumped into the fray and he looked deadly serious. "I'm a senior, so this is major shit for me. I'm applying to med school, so I don't want to move to Canada. I am leaning to declaring myself as a CO."

Matt had wondered about becoming a conscientious objector. "How do you do that?" he asked. "Excuse me, I don't know your name, but don't you have to be, like, a Mormon or part of a church that is against war, to become a conscientious objector? I heard that was very difficult."

"Well, not exactly. I'm Arty by the way," Arty said. "You have to show that you have a longstanding commitment. It's difficult, but my father knows someone who can coach me and, like, get letters from people that will vouch for my serious opposition to war and violence. While this would solve the biggest problem, a lot of med schools are like prejudiced against COs. So, if I can get CO status my future may not be very bright. There are not a lot of win-win options."

"Well, I'm not applying to med school or any other school," a guy said with a mouthful of pizza. "If my lottery number is low I am going to Canada."

Arty snorted. "Hey, shithead, for how long? You can't come back for god knows how many years. Are you sure you want to do that? And, Howie, if you step inside the U.S. good chance you will spend years in prison. Are you ready for that?"

"Hey, I'm ready. I'm learning Canadian."

"Jerkoff, they speak English there. Most places."

"You guys just don't have a clue, you know that?"

"Oh, John, enlighten us."

"I've almost got it figured out," John said. "There are still a few last details."

"Okay," Willie said. "Don't keep us in suspense. What's the silver bullet?"

John nodded. "Precisely, it involves a bullet." He lit a cigarette.

"What? You going to kill someone?"

"Of course not. That would be stupid." He blew out a long trail of smoke. "Not a person. A bald eagle."

"A bald eagle? You are fucking crazy, man."

"Hear me out. First, if you are convicted of a felony you can't serve in the Armed Forces of the United States. I found out that it is a felony to kill a bald eagle. Killing a real person is bad shit for obvious reasons. But killing a bald eagle, how much time could I really get? And when I'm convicted, I have a criminal record, so they can't draft me." He flicked some ash off his cigarette and studied it. "But here's the part I can't quite figure out yet. I've never fired a rifle so I am not sure how hard it will be to actually shoot an eagle. I'm also not clear on how to find a bald eagle. I know there are none around here, so where do I go to find one?"

"'S easy," Arty said. "You can learn to shoot and get a guide to take you to bald eagle land."

"Right." John pointed a finger at Arty. "But how do I get a U.S. marshal to see me actually shoot the eagle? I can't say 'Hey, Mr. Marshal, come with me and the guide and watch me shoot a bald eagle.' That's the part I still need to work out."

There were groans all around. All the guys started throwing everything they could find at him, laughing hysterically.

"Hey, can we talk about anything else but the war?" Willie complained. "What about the insanity of our student government? I hear they're talking about no grades, teachers getting graded by students, students deciding what classes are offered. What do you think?" The conversation went into a million directions.

"I heard they were going to go to honors, high pass, pass, low pass, and fail," John said. "Big fucking deal. Seems like you don't need to be in the CIA to decode A, B, C, D, and F. Doesn't sound like a breakthrough."

"Teachers getting graded by students and thrown out for poor performance—now that is an idea worth pursuing," Howie said. "I got a few candidates."

"No way the powers that be will let that happen. But look, even if it doesn't really happen, the chaos will still affect the campus. Kashman likes stirring things up and rallying people to challenge anything and everything. How many times will the protests shut the school down this year?"

"But he's on our side," Matt said.

"You running for office to fill the freshman spot?" Willie asked.

Matt shrugged his shoulders. "Haven't really thought about it."

That stopped them for a second. Then Arty said, "Speaking of the Polity, we need to compare notes on Lana. I went out with her a few days ago. We had a lot to drink and I thought it was a really good time, but she doesn't want to go out again.

"I got two dates and got nowhere," Arty said. "I didn't even get a kiss. Frigid, that's what she is."

"Why, because she doesn't want to go out with you again?"

"Maybe she's a lesbian," John offered. "She hangs out all the time with that dumpy girl."

"I never thought about that."

"How does that work, two women?"

"That's easy to understand. The hard part is two guys."

"The two guys are hard, jerkoff." Willie giggled at his own joke.

"Who's the guy and who's the girl?"

"I am not even going to dignify that."

There was a pause. Matt decided it was his chance to work his way out of this. "Have any of you guys seen Mel? I'm looking for him."

Arty looked mock-shocked. "I didn't know you swung that way, frosh."

Matt rolled his eyes.

"He doesn't," John said.

"Wit told me he's got the hots for the Ice Princess."

"Bonnie?" Arty scoffed. "No way. She is way too cool for a freshman. Besides, I hear she's got a boyfriend stashed somewhere else."

Matt was getting seriously uncomfortable now. He had no idea he was the subject of so much discussion. "She just helped me out when I first got here."

"Oooooo, Matt has a crush on Bonnie." They all laughed.

Matt turned red. *Is this grade school?* he thought. "Like I said, I was looking—"

"Oh, someone wants to change the subject."

Matt realized it was a no-win situation. "I'm outta here. If any of you see Mel, tell him I'm looking for him."

———

Matt liked his classes and for the most part he could keep up with the work. He was blown away by not having classes every day. The sense of freedom he felt was something he hadn't contemplated. The first day of classes he woke up at 7 a.m. and realized he didn't have a class until noon. *Fucking A*, he thought, *this is amazing*. He was really on his own!

The profs were treating them like grown-ups, assigning tons of reading and moving at least twice as fast as high school to cover the material. It was a lot of work, but he loved the flexibility even though it challenged his organizational skills.

In English 101, they were reading *Julius Caesar*. "In a democracy," the professor, Ms. Meadows, said, "we can change our rulers by popular demand, so to speak. The Romans didn't have that option once Caesar took power." Matt had a hard time keeping the names straight, but he hadn't expected to be confused about who were the good guys and who were the bad guys. Despite having about a yard of straight chestnut hair and an amazing body, Professor Meadows could read Caesar's lines with a baritone that Otis Redding could appreciate. "But Brutus is an *honorable* man," she crooned, surrounding the acid dripping from "honorable" with honey.

In the second week, a girl sitting next to him said, "I don't see why we had to start with a political murder."

"Don't you like politics?" Matt asked. She made a face. He tried to sound knowledgeable. "What would you prefer? *Romeo and Juliet?*"

"Oh, for sure," she said. "Suicide beats murder any day." Then she grinned so mischievously that Matt had to laugh. She said her name was Nicole, but she preferred Nicky, and they agreed that Shakespeare had more deaths in his stories than *Dragnet*. After that, when Professor Meadows would launch into poetic descriptions of Shakespeare's language, Nicky would mutter, "Just the facts, ma'am," because she knew Matt couldn't keep himself from laughing, then trying to choke back the laughter and snorting at the attempt. She had short, straight blond hair and blue eyes and Matt decided that English wasn't so bad.

Anything was better than calculus, which was taught by a professor named Wolf, who had a personality to match. There was no textbook. Professor Wolf would lecture as he faced the green board and cover it with equations. He wouldn't turn around for questions or comments until the end of the period, when he would look out over the heads of the students and say, "Well, that about does it for today." Four or five students who had sort of kept up would then throw out questions, and Wolf might answer one of them before the bell rang. When it did, he put down his chalk and walked out of the room. After that, everybody stayed in the room and asked each other about things they didn't understand, except for a group of Chinese or Japanese or something kids who always sat in the front of the class. They just followed Wolf out of the room.

A bright red flannel shirt stood out in the class, and Matt saw that it was Beth, but he thought she probably wouldn't remember him. They hadn't really talked. And she was tripping that second time. But she seemed to be following Wolf and taking notes feverishly.

But in more ways than one, the hardest class for Matt was Modern European History. He always sat with Wit and Bonnie, Wit on one side of her and Matt on the other. Since it was known to be a tough class, there were fewer students than in any of his other classes, and there was a chance for give and take with Professor Woodbell, who always had on a fitted sport jacket, no tie, and had black wavy hair that he parted in the middle and let fall to either side.

"The nineteenth century starts with the French Revolution," Woodbell began, and continued enigmatically, "and the nineteenth century was largely about crowd control." Matt wasn't used to abstract ideas that were being used metaphorically, but that wasn't nearly the hardest part of the class for him. The hardest part was keeping himself from turning to ask Bonnie what some pronouncement meant—or just turning to look at her. When he did, Wit was always right there one seat beyond. He assigned them to read parts of a book called *The Crowd* by a French guy. Just for a second, Matt thought maybe Wit had been right about dropping the course. Except for Bonnie.

Matt was on a steep learning curve with the football team, but he was climbing it. The first regular season game was against a pretty average team known as the Big Dogs. They were neither particularly big nor particularly dogged, but they scored twice in the first quarter. The quarterback shocked everybody by actually running the ball. Whether he wanted to or not wasn't clear, but all his receivers ended up on the right side of the field and so did all the defenders. He ran to the other side of the field as if dogs were chasing him. The defense took a lot of ribbing about that.

Matt was at least four inches taller than any of the Big Dogs and probably 40 pounds lighter, so he just kept throwing. It was so easy to throw to Wit that the Dogs started to double-cover him, and then Matt could throw to Mel, who came out of the backfield into any open space. They scored four times and then ran a play they called "Double Flanker Criss-Cross," which basically involved the receivers crossing past each other in the middle of the field. It worked every time they used it.

Late in the game, Matt hung in the pocket till the last second and released a 30-yard pass that he never saw completed because three guys fell on him. At about the same time, the receivers crossed and the defenders ran into each other. Wit caught the pass for an easy touchdown. Lurch pulled Matt up off the ground and said, "How do you like your watchit blockers?"

"What? Watchit blockers? What do you mean?"

"When we can't hold the opposing team away from you, we at least yell, 'Watch it!'"

So thoughtful, Matt mused.

After the game, Matt turned around to find Nicky standing next to him. "Are you okay? You were doing great until you fell on your ass!"

"I had a couple of asses on top of me," Matt pointed out. "And we scored." He tried to brush the grass stains off his shorts.

"It's pretty obvious that you can score," Nicky said. She leaned back and folded her arms in front of her. The weather had turned fall crisp and she was wearing dark blue sailor pants that hung on her hip bones and a light blue work shirt over a pink sweater. "Almost like you could do it anytime. How are you coming on that essay for Meadows?"

Matt looked as pained as he felt. "You had to bring that up just at my moment of triumph?"

Nicky instantly looked contrite. "Sorry! Really, I was just making conversation." She pulled a strand of blond hair and picked at its ends. "If you're having trouble, maybe I could help. I did pretty well in English in high school, in Huntington."

Matt realized that the conversation had shifted, and he wished he weren't standing there in shorts and blood oozing down his leg from the cut on his knee. "Yeah! Well, I should work on it, that's for sure."

Nicky tossed the offending strand of hair back. "Great! I'm in D dorm," she offered, naming one of the girls-only dorms. "Just check at the entrance with the RA. Tuesday would be a good night for me, but just come when you have time," she grinned and started to walk away backward. "It's right across from B dorm, you know. Maybe one day they will even name the dorms after somebody famous. Oh! Sorry!"

She'd walked into Kashman, who put a hand on her back to keep her from falling and said, "It's okay, I'm fine. No damage done." Nicky straightened up and Kashman put out a hand and introduced himself. "Hi, I'm Joe Kashman. Student body president." Matt thought he sounded like he was still running for office.

Nicky giggled. "Yes, I know. Joe. I'm pleased to meet you, student body president." Nicky introduced herself as Nicole Watkins and Kashman asked, "What do you think of the new quarterback for B-3?"

Matt said, "Just the facts, ma'am."

Nicky grinned and said, "Oh, he stands out."

"I agree," Kashman nodded. "We're hoping to get him on the Polity." He looked at Nicky for a second. "Maybe you'd like to come too. First of October at 7:00 in the student center. You'd be a great . . . addition." He smiled.

Nicky started backing away. "Oh, I have an English paper due." She raised her eyebrows at Matt. "Sorry, I should go or I'll be late. Nice to meet you. See you later, Matt." She turned around and broke into a canter.

Kashman watched her go, then turned and shook Matt's hand. "Great job, Matt. Even with those three Dogs in your face." Matt said he was still learning the game but Kashman went right on. "But I like the way you kept your team together. You have a sense of command. They looked like they were having fun, even. That's great, Matt."

"Well, it's just football," Matt said. "We're here for an education, a degree."

"Ha. Ha," Kashman laughed artificially. "You can't say 'just football' on this campus. Intramural football rules the fall, believe it, and the people who rule football, *dominate*." He paused and looked around. Matt wondered if he should say something, but then Kashman leaned into him and looked up. "But what happens after the fall, Matt, that's what it's all about. Like you say, we're here for more than football. Maybe a degree, but while you're getting a degree, there's life to live." He stepped back. "That's why I'm on the Polity, to make a difference in the life of the campus. Well, I may have said that to you already—I talk too much! But I mean it. I really hope we'll see you at the next Polity meeting. Anyway, think about it. Later."

Matt said good-bye to his retreating back and just stood there on the sidelines to catch his breath. Mel came up and shook his head. "Wow, what was that all about? Is he *on* something?"

"High on life, I think he'd say. He's really pushing for me to get involved with the Polity."

Mel laughed. "Yeah, you do that. Then you can get me a date with your, uh, friend. Speaking of which, who was the lollipop?"

"The who? Oh, you mean Nicky. She's in my English Lit class."

"Well, she looked like she wanted a lick of you. Jeez, how about sharing the wealth?"

Matt could feel himself turning red. "I'm taking a shower," he said.

"Oh, it's that bad, huh? Look, if you want some privacy in the room to, you know . . ." Mel added the appropriate hand gesture. Matt threw the towel at him and strode off as Mel, laughing, ran to catch up with him.

6

IT'S NOT HARD to figure out where the party is, Matt thought, not as sure now that this was the right place for him. Music was roaring out through the windows of the dorm everybody called the Taj, short for the Taj Mahal, and rooms were either dim, dark, or flashing. "Kashman's dorm," Wit pointed out, "and we used to call it a mixer." Kashman had proposed that each dorm have its own party in the first weeks of school. "It was supposed to be more personal that way," Wit said. "People would be more relaxed. Everybody agreed the gym was a piss-poor place to have a party, so Kashman and his allies won the vote. Somehow, this is the only one so far. Funny thing."

Matt walked up the steps to the entryway, where there was a table holding a keg and stacks of plastic cups. One person offered him a beer and said, "Hard stuff in the common room," and another person offered him a hit on a joint and said, "Rolling on the second floor." Matt took the beer and declined the joint, saying, "Not right now."

He started down the hall, which was dotted with people and doors, some open, some not. It was the first time Matt had been in a different dorm, but there wasn't much obvious difference. The common room was at the end of the hall, just like B dorm. The big difference was the air. Matt was used to smoke from grass and tobacco floating through B dorm—hell, his father smoked all the time, one big reason Matt never had—but the air in the Taj was so thick he felt he had to push it aside. It didn't smell like either tobacco or marijuana or even a mix of the two, but a conglomeration of smells that wrapped around each other without ever combining—sweet, pungent, woody, spicy, and others he couldn't identify.

He wove past people down the hall into the common room, where he was hit by a wave of bass that began "In-a-Gadda-da-Vida," never exactly his favorite song, and caromed into a denser mass of bodies, some of which might be dancing. It was a little hard to tell. Then he heard "Matthew!" and a shriek and suddenly Dorman was slapping him on the shoulder. "Come on over here," he shouted over the music that was almost but not quite so loud that no one could hear. "You got a beer, good. Meet some people." Matt threaded through the crowd behind Dorman, who was wearing, as far as Matt could tell, a dress. It was white, with a gold embroidered rectangle that dropped down from the shoulders, and the whole thing fell straight to the floor, though he could see pants underneath it. *Okay*, Matt thought, *some Eastern kind of thing.*

The music stopped for a minute and Dorman stopped in front of the woman they had seen on the quad the other day. "Matt, you remember Beth, one of my best friends in the whole world."

Matt said hi and Beth looked up at him and said, "Hiiiiiiiiii." Her eyes were little pinpoints and her smile was beatific.

"Beth is in a very good place right now," Dorman said.

She nodded enthusiastically. "Very bright and fine. Sort of a mellow gold. Dor is so bright, but I can see through him." Dorman smiled. Black light flashed and he turned incandescent.

"That's cool," Matt said. "I saw you in the meeting with Mrs. Devin too. You asked a smart question. Were you taking notes?"

Beth frowned and closed her eyes. "Ohhh noooo, I don't want to go there." Dorman took her head in his hands and held it, whispering in her ear. She smiled again. He turned back to Matt and leaned into him.

"We want Beth to enjoy the journey she's on. When she goes into a dark place, it's not fun. Take it from me."

"Oh, sorry," Matt said back to him. The music was loud enough that Beth didn't notice them talking. She was swaying slightly as Iron Butterfly went on with an extended guitar solo. "This is a lot longer than I've ever heard this song go on."

"Seventeen minutes," Dorman said. "They say that Doug Ingle drank a gallon of wine to write this song and he was so bombed that when he sang 'in the garden of Eden,' they heard it as 'In a Gadda da Vida.' So that's what they called it."

Matt laughed. He was starting to feel a little high. *Just breathing the air is enough*, he thought. Then two arms wrapped around Dorman and the tall, dark girl from the Polity meeting bent down and kissed him on the cheek. "Daniel," she cooed. "Greetings. I love your abba." Dorman melted into her embrace, and she rubbed his hair and laughed. As soon as she let him go, Beth took her place, reaching behind Lana Harananinan's back and pulling her down into a very extended kiss. Matt felt a little embarrassed and explained it to himself with, *She's tripping*. Lana broke away from the kiss and put her arm around Beth's shoulder, noticing Matt as if for the first time. "And who is this tall gentleman?" she asked, smiling at Matt.

It took Matt a minute to remember to speak. She was wearing a white silk blouse that flowed over her body and glowed in the black light that came on and off, and scarlet slacks that shimmered. She was almost as tall as Matt, which he wasn't used to in a girl, and stretched out one leg as if to emphasize how long it was. It didn't need much emphasis.

"This is Matt," Dorman yelled. "Do you remember him from the Polity rally?"

"Oh yes, our freshman speaker!"

Dorman started and then stopped. "Matt, did you tell me your last name?"

"Aymer," Matt said, looking at Lana. It seemed impossible not to.

"And you are a high aimer, I am told," Lana said.

Matt laughed. "I don't know about that. Turns out I can throw a football."

"Sometimes that is enough around here," Lana laughed. "But you seem to have an ability to make people like you."

"Oh, he does," Beth agreed. Matt reminded himself again that she was tripping.

Matt said to Lana, "You spoke very well at the Polity rally."

"I could not fly like my friend Daniel here," she touched Dorman's arm briefly, "but I have a strong belief in commitment. People must take part. As they say, if you are not part of the solution, you are part of the problem." Her eyes focused on his. "What are your politics, Matt Aymer?"

Matt was speechless, but then he heard himself say, "I believe in teams." Beth and Dorman seemed to have suddenly retreated into the background of bodies.

Lana's dark eyes flashed. "Spoken like a true American. But teamwork is not politics, only tactics."

"I'm against the war."

Lana made a comment with her lips alone and dismissed this with a wave of her hand. "To be for the war is to have the consciousness of a turnip." She turned slightly and looked at him sideways. "But it is not enough to be against it. Do you believe that the United States is a colonialist hegemon?"

Beth said tremulously, "My head is beginning to hurt."

Lana was instantly apologetic and she wrapped her arms around Beth and rocked her. "My poor baby. I'm so sorry. I will take care of you now." She looked up at Matt, not unkindly. "We will continue this conversation another time?"

Matt nodded, "Yes, sure. I'd like that." But he felt incredibly small in her presence. *I have to really start digging into politics if I want to hold up my end*, he thought.

Lana looked behind Matt and then said to Beth, "He is coming. Let's go."

Before Matt could say good-bye, a hand on his shoulder turned Matt around. Kashman was standing there smiling. "Matt. Good to see you here. Dorman. How's it hanging?"

"Straight up and down, man." Kashman and Dorman grasped fingers, entwined thumbs, and slapped palms so smoothly Matt thought they must have practiced. Kashman turned back to Matt.

"And you've been quite a standout among the freshman class. Football is not a small thing around here and your flair for public speaking is refreshing in these times." His hair was tied back and he was wearing jeans and a T-shirt that had a lot of colors and shapes and some letters that looked like they had melted. Matt made out "The Grateful Dead."

"What's that on your shirt? It's not the Rolling Stones."

Dorman intervened. "The greatest psychedelic band in the world, Matt. You should hear them, man, if you haven't. But you should be properly prepared." He produced a joint from a pocket somewhere and offered it to Matt, who waved it away. "That's okay, man, later. Yeah, later." Dorman lit the joint and took a long drag, then offered it to Kashman, who did the same and gave it back.

"Mexico?" Kashman asked, smoke pouring out of his mouth and nostrils.

Dorman took another long drag while nodding his head emphatically. He held the smoke in for a while, then let it out in a long, thin stream. "Yah," he said thinly and coughed. "Brought it back this summer."

Kashman nodded and said, "But seriously, Matt, I'm glad you came tonight." Matt wondered when they hadn't been serious so far but put on his listening face. The music came back up in a screech of "down on me" that made you feel that the singer didn't give a shit about what people thought of her. "Those guys on B-3 are a tight group, I know. You're lucky to be a part of them." Matt remembered his beer and sipped it, letting Kashman stay on his rap, whatever it was. "Did you play football in high school?"

Matt shook his head. "Baseball. I was a pitcher."

"Good?"

Matt looked around, suddenly a little embarrassed. "Yeah, pretty good. I was eight-and-oh senior year. Regular season. We made the state finals."

Dorman made an impressed face. "Did you win?" Matt shook his head.

"Aw, that sucks," Kashman said. "What happened? You pitch the finals?" Matt winced and nodded. The room had gotten quieter, and the people dancing were just swaying around each other while Janis told everybody to help each other even if they didn't like her. Kashman leaned in and said, "Bad day, huh?"

Matt looked at him and nodded, unwillingly remembering the line drive that had nearly taken his head off. After four solid innings, he suddenly lost everything after that, and after a while all he could remember was how baseballs flew out over the infield and the opposing team was making the bases look like a merry-go-round. Back in the dugout was one of the few times in his life he'd ever cried around people outside his family.

Kashman was watching his face so hard Matt felt like he was being interrogated, but then he said, "Man, I think it's just so great that you're trying out something new"—he paused to inhale and hold it, then released a puff of smoke—"football, I mean—and not letting the past take control." Matt felt his face relax before he even realized it was tense. "And you're so good at it. Man, that is cool. You know, sometimes I wish I had that kind of talent. You know what I mean, Dor?"

Dorman looked surprised to be called on. "I'd like to fly," he said quietly.

Kashman clapped him on the shoulder. "And you probably will. You probably will." Looking at Matt, he continued, "Like our man Matt here is flying on the football field. I was never much of an athlete, not me. In fact, I never stood out in any way, really. And it bothered me. It really bothered me." His head sagged and his face turned dark, or the lights went down, but then he looked up at Matt and his eyes widened. "You heard Janis. She's right. We've got to help each other and do what we've got to. You just have to find out what that is."

Matt said, "Yeah, I was thinking about that today. What did you find?"

Kashman chuckled a little and shook his head. "Well, it's funny. I got involved in the student government in high school and I discovered that I really liked doing things for other people. I liked getting people together and getting them organized to make something happen."

"Like a team."

"Right on, like a team. So you see I absolutely understand why B-3 can be so cool. But the only thing is, you know, that like when football season is over. And I, we get to move on to other things, make new teams and find new successes. Sure, we like to party and have fun and get high. But we're part of the world. And we want to make it a better world."

"I guess," Matt said. "Hey, what's with that name anyway?" He pointed to Kashman's shirt.

"The grateful dead," Dorman said, his pride showing, "are people who died but couldn't afford their own burial. But then somebody else pays for it, so the dead are grateful to them."

Kashman shrugged as if it was all the same to him and held out a hand for Matt to shake. "So Matt, look around a little. We have several worlds here at the Taj Mahal, as we like to call it. There are some people upstairs who do Transcendental Meditation, if you're into that kind of thing."

"And there are really good drugs on the third floor," Dorman said enthusiastically. Kashman smiled, then said to Matt, "Seriously, check the Polity out. The first meeting of the year is in a few weeks."

"I'll mark my calendar," Matt said, trying not to sound overly enthusiastic and wishing he had a calendar to mark. Someone came up to Kashman and whispered in his ear, or rather talked loudly into his ear over the music. Kashman nodded and signed to Matt that he had to go and held up two fingers to Dorman. "Peace," he mouthed.

Dorman seemed to have faded away. Matt turned around to get another beer and noticed Neut standing against a wall, talking to someone with long, stringy hair. That guy was talking very earnestly, from the looks of it, and holding out his fingers as if he was counting something. Neut was listening intently, but his eyes never stopped moving and finally landed on Matt. Showing no surprise at all, Neut said something to the long-haired guy and then raised his cup in Matt's direction.

Matt returned the salute and ambled over to them. The long-hair looked around nervously, but held his ground. "Nice to see you," Neut said to Matt, holding out a hand to shake. Then, "Matt, this is Mr. Blue, as he likes to be called. Mr. Blue is a businessman. Mr. Blue, meet Matt Aymer. He's in B dorm too. B-3, to be exact."

"Oh!" Mr. Blue said. "Yeah, okay. Here's my card. Got it. Nice to meet you, Matt. You having a good time tonight?" Matt realized that he was having a good time and said so. "You need anything?" Mr. Blue asked. Matt wasn't sure what he meant. Mr. Blue tried to clarify. "I mean, you know, do you *need* anything?" and pointed upward. Matt made a confused face. "Jeez," Mr. Blue said, exasperated. "Do you want to get high?"

"Oh," Matt said, turning a little red in the face. "No, I'm okay." Mr. Blue frowned. "Maybe later."

"Okay. That's cool." He turned to Neut and said, "So anything you need, just let me know. I gave you my card, right? Okay. Peace, man." He picked up a briefcase Matt hadn't noticed and slunk away.

"He's very organized," Neut observed. "He may look a little strung out, but he says he and his business partner have a lot of customers on campus, and more where he lives, in Hicksville."

"Really?" Matt said. "Who's his business partner?"

Neut said he didn't know. Matt wasn't sure he was telling the truth, but gave him a pass. Neut went on in his monotone, "He offers more than twenty different kinds of marijuana, hallucinogens, stimulants, and depressants. The pills and such are where the money is. Since everybody can get grass, he can't command premium pricing on it. But it is high volume." Matt couldn't tell if that was a joke or not, since Neut's expression never changed. "He says he's mostly paid for college with his business." Matt asked what Mr. Blue was studying. "He's going for an MBA," Neut said. "Naturally."

Matt laughed and they stood and listened to the music for a while. It was the first time Matt had actually talked with Neut, and now he didn't know what to say. He asked Neut if he'd thought about a major, but all he got was a vague idea about sociology. The Rascals were insisting that it was easy to see that people had to be free, and Matt wondered if Bonnie was at this party. She seemed like the last person who needed a mixer, but if she was on the Polity, maybe she would come. *Her civic duty*, Matt thought. *Maybe I should look around*. He asked Neut if he had been upstairs yet.

"Sure, I looked around. There are different things going on. You should take a look." Neut said good-bye and faded into the crowd, headed for the door. *Kind of a strange guy*, Matt thought, *in an okay way. And he seems to know a lot about the school.*

Matt wandered down the hall. Mostly the doors were closed. One of those closed doors was holding back noises that made Matt pretty sure that they were having sex. He hoped it wasn't Bonnie. Another door was open, but it was dark inside. There were four or five inert bodies on various surfaces. Occasionally someone would describe what they were seeing in their head, and someone else would respond, though not necessarily about the same thing. That Indian guitar-like music was playing in the background. That was probably the room of good drugs that Dorman had mentioned.

He went up another floor, where it was even quieter than on the second floor, although the bass beat of the first floor still reverberated through the walls and inside Matt's head. He saw Beth sleeping in Lana's lap and he recognized Jack Appel from the Polity rally holding court. A coffee table held a bottle of Southern Comfort, a bottle of vodka, and a couple of other bottles Matt couldn't immediately identify.

"Now that the trial has started," Appel said, "there will be protests outside the court. There's going to be a revolution in Chicago. You know they just blew up that statue in the city, right?"

"Let's go to Chicago!" the long-hair said enthusiastically. He didn't move. "Off some pigs and shit. Look at what happened in

Paris last spring," he went on. "It was just like the French Revolution, overthrowing the fat cats, the dictators. That's what we need here. Organization. We can take down the ruling class if we have that."

"That is very inspiring thinking, Charles, and I admire your passion," Lana said. "But it is an entirely different story in this country. The French have a long tradition of socialism. And, as you say, they have the revolutionary tradition. And they also have the pompous ass Pompidou. He is a target as big as a blimp."

"Americans are the original revolutionaries," Charles said pugnaciously.

"Two hundred years ago." Lana smiled benevolently.

"We brought down Johnson," the guy pointed out.

"Yes, and you ended up with Richard Nixon. And now Kissinger. He is even more devious than Nixon. The two together are the dynamic duo of deviousness." Everybody laughed at this and Lana triumphantly raised her glass and drank.

Jack said, "I just don't want to go halfway around the world to get killed in the jungle."

"Matthew!" Lana warbled as Matt walked forward toward the group. "I am glad to see you again. Please come in, sit down. Would you like a Black Russian?" she asked, raising her glass again. "If you can't beat them, drink them. This is Charles, or Chaz, as he says, and perhaps you remember Jack."

Jack said, "I liked your speech. You should join Polity and see what can be done on this campus," he said earnestly.

Matt was getting really annoyed. "I'm not very political. Some of the things that are happening—you know, like the riots, Watts, Detroit—I mean, I'm glad I wasn't there. Scary. Scary and awful."

Jack shook his head. "Matt, if there's one thing Montauk isn't, it's Watts. Watts was like ground zero of oppression. So is Detroit. Long Island isn't ground zero of anything."

"That's the problem," Chaz said.

Jack snorted. "New York might be ground zero if Nixon starts a war with Russia. The madman theory fits him, all right. He's crazy enough to actually use the bomb. The Doomsday Clock is down to a minute and a half."

"The Soviets would start with the NORAD defense system," Chaz offered. "You saw *Dr. Strangelove.*"

"Um, I was a little stoned."

"So was I." Everybody snickered and took a drink.

Lana finished her drink and jumped up. "Matthew, where are my manners? I will get you a Black Russian, yes?" Matt nodded, not sure what he was agreeing to, and Lana went to a side table and started mixing a drink for Matt and another, probably for herself, while she talked. "But you see, Matthew, the Polity, here at this place, it is not politics. Or really, it is the politics of life. Life is politics. If you were a woman, you would know this because your body would not be your own. Other people you will never meet make you part of their agenda."

Matt looked a little confused, so Jack whispered, "Abortion."

"But here it is different, the Polity is different. We are not a distant, faceless, relentless machine. We work together to solve problems for the students. And sometimes we can call attention to things not yet understood to be problems. The Polity is just you and me and Chaz here—"

"And Kashman."

Lana turned around and looked at Matt for a time. She seemed to decide something. "Yes, and Kashman. The president has many faults, but also perhaps some talents. He can be persistent—"

It was Matt's turn to snort. "That's one word for it."

Lana brought his drink over and sat down across from him. "He can also be authoritarian. And maybe that is exactly the reason that we need to make sure he is surrounded by people whose better nature can take control. I will admit that before you sat down, we were discussing whether Polity had lost its way under Kashman's presidency. Many of the ideas are really breakthrough but we can't even get the factions together to discuss an action plan. Joe says he will speak to them but already we've had demonstrations and classes cancelled. How do we organize to achieve serious goals? The unrest is the focus, not the ideas."

Matt nodded. It was only a month into classes and two days of his classes had been cancelled due to picketing and one teacher refused to teach while the halls were taken over by anti-war protesters.

Matt smiled. "Are you going to take control and try and do something about it?" he asked hopefully.

Lana almost blushed underneath her olive skin. "That is not something I have been considering but I am concerned. And by the way, even the loyal supporters here, Chaz and Jack, are afraid the original noble ideas are drifting into the background." She leaned back and stretched her long legs under the coffee table. "I want only to return to my spiritual home Iran and somehow correct the injustice the CIA has perpetrated there. It will take a long time."

There was a little silence and then Jack said helpfully, "You know the CIA deposed the rightfully elected prime minister, Mossadegh, and installed the dictator in 1951, right?"

Matt shrugged. "That's not something they taught us in history class. Um, I'm sorry."

Lana tossed her head. "Pahlavi was not even one of us. His family came from Georgia. They were Cossacks. I am a Persian. Ours is a real culture, one of strength and beauty for thousands of years." She brooded. "Reza comes from horseshit." Everybody paused to consider that image.

"You know, Matt," Jack said to break the silence, "the Polity has many practical applications. It builds community with the entertainment, the sports, the various programs Lana is creating . . ." He raised his glass to Lana, who looked at him darkly over her glass and then smiled. Everyone seemed relieved.

"The Polity controls the entire sports budget," Chaz pointed out. Matt said he'd heard that.

Jack picked up the thread. "We try to spread the responsibilities out among the various dorms, as long as there's someone interested. Every dorm gets three representatives, and B dorm is down one."

Matt got the distinct feeling this discussion was not entirely accidental, and he was a little flattered by it even in his annoyance. "You know, guys, this is all . . . interesting," he said, realizing that they were all listening, even Lana. "But I'm really here for the academic side of things. My father wouldn't be all that happy if he thought I was spending all my time on sports and student government."

Jack sat up straight. "Don't let your parents oppress you."

Matt bristled. "My parents don't oppress me."

"They do," Jack insisted. "You just said so. Your father is telling you how to live your life. But it's *your* life. You should live it how you want. Jerry Rubin says that the first step is to kill your parents because they're the first oppressors."

Matt finished his drink. "The Yippies are a little crazy, I think. Look, I fight with my father all the time. He's wrong about a lot of things, but he's just trying to make sure that I don't waste my time and his money horsing around. I'm not going to give him the satisfaction of saying 'I told you so.'"

Lana stood up and put her hands on his shoulders. "Jack, stop now. You are oppressing yourself. Stop telling Matt what to do. You have made your point." Jack's head drooped, but then Lana said, "And we admire you for it."

Jack held up his hands in a gesture of surrender and smiled up at her. "Okay, okay, maybe that was a little out of line." He looked up and smiled. He turned to Matt and said, "Look, I'm sorry. I get carried away sometimes. I know I do. Don't let me prejudice you against us. We're doing our best."

Matt stood up and smiled at him. "Okay, no harm, no foul. I'll think about it. I think I'm going to crash, but maybe we'll talk some more later." Lana put her hand out to shake, and Matt shook hands with each of them in turn and went downstairs. He looked in on the television watchers. The late-night news was on and the screen showed the latest body count from Vietnam. More than 5,000 so far this year.

On the first floor, the music was still going. *Get back*, the Beatles told him, *back to where you once belonged.* He wasn't sure where that was.

7

ALMOST DESPITE HIMSELF, Matt decided to go to the Polity meeting, not telling himself it was because Bonnie would be there. At the student union, somebody at the door said, "Polity meeting? Down the hall and on the right. You'll see the sign," and handed him a sheaf of mimeographed papers. In the room, about ten Formica tables were arranged in a big square with a lot of uncomfortable-looking plastic chairs. Most of those chairs were full, and Matt figured they were dorm representatives who had been elected last year. He was surprised to see Wit at one of the chairs, but after a minute it seemed to make perfect sense and he was glad to see him. Wit gave him a quick salute and gestured to a nonexistent empty chair behind him. Matt waved him off and went to the chairs around the wall, which seemed to be where the observers sat. There were a lot of people there, including the blind Frisbee player—*What was his name? Sam*—and his dog. *Captain.* Matt waved at him and immediately felt foolish, hoping nobody saw.

He didn't have a very good view of the front, but he could see Kashman walking around in the front talking to the other officers—Jack Appel, Lana Harananinan, and Dorman. There was another person at the front and then he could just see Bonnie—he recognized the curve of her hair first—sitting at the side, but right up front.

Kashman moved to the center of the table, and said, "Okay, look, we should get started." There was a general settling and some rustling of the papers. Matt started looking through his papers, one of which said, "Agenda." Another said, "Bylaws." "Ah, a few latecomers,"

Kashman said and smiled broadly, "welcome, come in, sit down." Matt was having trouble holding all the papers in order.

A voice near him whispered, "Excuse me, is this seat taken?" He looked up at Nicky and his mouth dropped open. He'd mentioned in class that he was probably going to the Polity meeting but had no idea she was going to come too. She was wearing enormous dark blue velvet bell-bottoms, a peasant shirt, a big floppy newsboy's cap, and a leather jacket against the cold.

He stuttered, "N-no, I guess. I mean, there's no one there." He involuntarily looked to see if Bonnie had noticed, but he couldn't see her.

Nicky looked at him, bemused. "Do you mind if I sit here?"

He could feel his face turning red. "Oh, no. Of course not, Nicky. It's good to see you. Outside of English class, I mean."

"I know. We're all so different out of uniform." She took off her coat and cap and ran her hand through her hair. *Pixie cut* popped into Matt's mind. She curled into the chair and brought her other leg up so that she was sitting cross-legged, her foot about three inches from his leg. She had on little sneakers with a pattern on them.

Matt wondered how she could fold herself up that way, but said, "How, I mean, I didn't know you were interested in student government."

She smiled, looked to the front, and then raised one eyebrow at him. "I come to bury Caesar, not to praise him." Matt stifled a laugh. "But don't worry," she said and looked toward the front of the room, "I can't stay long. I have a date."

Matt felt the strangest knot start to form in his stomach. He looked straight ahead and said, "Oh."

"Well, you know, I have all this free time since I'm not working on your English paper with you. Shh, they're starting."

Kashman opened the meeting, explaining the agenda and that there would be time for questions later. The long-standing members groaned when Kashman discussed an audit that was planned for the end of the semester by the comptroller of the university. The groans got louder when he explained the paperwork each budget chair would have to fill out. "Look, I understand," Kashman said. "I'm trying to show them that it's bullshit. Give me a little time."

After that he launched into an enthusiastic description of the Polity rally for freshmen at the beginning of the semester, calling on Jack and Lana and Dorman to reprise their part of the show. Luckily nobody talked too long. When they were finished, Kashman looked out into the audience, and said, "And the meeting had a bang-up ending provided by one of our outstanding freshmen, Matt Aymer. I think Matt's here—yes, Matt, why don't you stand up?"

"As if you can't see him sitting down," Nicky giggled and moved her leg out of his way.

"Don't worry, you don't have to make a speech tonight," Kashman laughed. "Come on."

Matt, now fully red in the face, stretched himself out of the chair and stood up. He brought up both hands in a small double wave. Bonnie flashed him a peace symbol and smiled. He sat down, absurdly pleased that he didn't do anything stupid. Or anything at all.

"Thanks, Matt, and we hope to see you here all the time." Kashman went on to suggest that anyone who wanted to be on the Polity should think about filling out the candidate forms and hand them in by the end of December. "Elections are next semester, and the results are announced around March with the exact date to be determined. So if you're interested, don't wait. You can fill out the forms now. They're really simple."

The meeting turned to old business, which wasn't anything Matt knew anything about, and he mainly listened to Nicky's commentary. She had a way of skewering people that was funny and stopped short of being outright mean, but it was clear she didn't see student government as her future. After a while, she looked at the microscopically small gold watch on her wrist, and said, "I better go. See you in English class."

They looked at each other as if there was something else to say. Matt suddenly felt himself getting hot. He whispered, "Yeah, okay."

A little louder, he said, "Have a good time on your date." Nicky did a funny thing with her mouth and looked sad. "Don't stay out too late," Matt said. Nicky crossed her heart and slipped away. The knot in Matt's stomach was still there and he missed a lot of what followed, annoyed with himself for reasons he couldn't or didn't want to put into words.

When he refocused, the meeting was coming to a close. Kashman was saying, "Okay, that about wraps things up. Except if there's anything else anyone thinks the Polity should consider this year. Anyone, please. We want to make the university the best place it can be. We're seriously into suggestions." He looked around and then looked at Matt. Nobody said anything, but Sam's dog barked, and everyone laughed. "Can anyone translate that?" Kashman joked.

"Yes, I can." Matt's smoldering aggravation at himself propelled him out of his seat. There were some more laughs, and he could see Bonnie sit up in her seat. "He said that he wanted to thank everyone for letting him speak to the meeting. Despite his species." A few more chuckles. "But he also wanted to point out that for some people on campus, like people in wheelchairs or on crutches, or otherwise hand-icapped, those people often have a very difficult time on our campus." The room was quiet now and Matt felt he had their attention, to his own surprise.

"You can imagine, he says," Matt nodded in the dog's direction, "how difficult it is to go up stairs without some kind of ramp. But the people on campus who put those temporary ramps out aren't always around, or they don't do it." Matt started to gain steam, and he went with it. "And those ramps are pretty precarious sometimes, like when it's raining—or snowing, for god's sake—and so they can even be dangerous." He didn't know if this was true, but it was worth bringing up. "So I think we should petition the university to start, um, a program for building permanent ramps to make our buildings accessible. More accessible."

There was some applause, which picked up steam after people realized he was finished, and then Sam said loudly, "And install elevators in buildings where you can't put in ramps." There was more applause and the dog stood up and barked some more. People applauded loudly. Bonnie was smiling and for some reason, Matt felt guilty.

When the meeting ended, Matt was torn between leaving as quickly as he possibly could and waiting to see if he could talk to Bonnie. He had his jacket half on when Jack Appel caught his arm. "That was so, so—cosmic," he said, his eyes wide. "We totally forget about . . . some people. Like the way Blacks were downtrodden by southerners, ignored or condescended to by northerners and the entire government monolith. Well, it's time we expanded our consciousness and began to accept that not everyone is made the same."

"Well, I didn't really think of it on—" Matt started and then he felt some heavy breathing on the hand that was in the jacket sleeve. It was the blind guy's dog. "Captain," Matt said, scratching his neck.

"I just wanted to thank you," Sam said. "That was cool."

"I just . . ." Matt hesitated, not sure what he was just doing.

"Gimme five," Dorman said, reaching in past Sam. "Out of sight."

"Look, everybody," Matt protested, "this is Sam, and he's really the person who made me see the problem. Um, well, not see. Sam, what do you say?" Jack Appel took Sam's hand in both of his and shook energetically, asking him if he'd like to head a committee. Dorman, irrepressible, asked him if he could sense people around even if he couldn't hear them. Sam introduced everyone to Captain, who sat and accepted admiration patiently.

Matt was edging away from the crowd, hoping to sneak out, but Kashman came up beside him. "Excellent, Matt," he said. "You've already made a difference here."

"No, really, Sam was the one. I was just talking to him on the quad a while ago—" For a split second, Matt looked at the door and saw Neut, who touched two fingers to his forehead and slipped away.

"So now you understand how things happen," Kashman said, nodding. "One person talking to another. But one person has to stand up and take a stand. That's how things happen. And you made that happen tonight."

Matt considered this, peripherally wondering if Bonnie was still here and if she'd seen him sitting beside Nicky. "I guess I see what you mean," he told Kashman, thinking, *What else did I make happen? Too many things are happening way too much right now.*

"Of course you do," Kashman said. "Be sure to pick up one of those registration forms for the January election though. Talk to me. I can help you out, getting you on the Polity."

"I'll think about it," Matt said, seeing Bonnie coming in his direction.

Kashman snapped his fingers. "We can make it happen like that. Talk to me. Peace," he said and turned to another person who was leaving. He leaned in and whispered something in the guy's ear.

Bonnie slipped in behind him and smiled. "That was very cool. I don't think I'd ever thought about wheelchair riders on campus," she said.

Matt shrugged. "Really, Sam is the one. And Captain. That dog knows how to make a point."

"He's a great dog. Those seeing-eye dogs are incredible." She looked at Captain for a minute and then turned back to Matt. "You know, Bill Moyers is speaking here next week. He was LBJ's press secretary, but he quit in protest and now he's the publisher of *Newsday*. He brought in Pete Hamill."

"Oh yeah, I like him."

"Maybe you'd like to come. We could meet there."

Matt tried to keep his mouth from dropping open. He had no idea who Bill Moyers was and didn't care. "Oh, that'd be great. I've always wanted to hear . . ." He desperately tried to figure out where to go with that. "A presidential press secretary."

Bonnie smiled with half her mouth and said, "I just bet you have. That's great. Not as great as help for the handicapped, but great."

"Next he'll suggest they have their own track meets," Wit cracked, walking up behind Bonnie.

Bonnie looked at him. "That's maybe not a bad idea either." Matt was simultaneously glad that the focus was off him and mad that Wit seemed to have upstaged him. Bonnie turned back to Matt and said, "Two new ideas tonight. Not bad for one evening. Maybe that makes us even." Matt worried that she'd seen him with Nicky. "Anyway," Bonnie said, "I have some reading to do for tomorrow. I'd better get back home. I hope you had a good time tonight." She pulled her jacket on over the black turtleneck she was wearing. "Night, Wit. See you both in class tomorrow."

"Got that right," Wit groaned. "You going back to the dorm, Ribs?"

"Good night, Bonnie," Matt said. Then, "But I don't know about even," he called after her as she walked away. She waved a hand at him as if to say, *Your choice* and waved good-bye.

"What was that about being even?" Wit said as they walked out.

"Oh, nothing, it was just, you know, she helped me out at registration and . . ." He trailed off.

Wit looked at him for a few seconds. "Yeah, I think I see." He shivered a little in the cold. "Probably need sweats for practice tomorrow." They walked back to the dorm, not saying much, but when they got to the floor, Wit said, "You did all right, tonight, Matt. You should think about getting on the Polity."

When Matt got back to his room, he found Mel bent over a fat textbook, taking notes. "Hey, Mel," he said, "I went to that meeting, the Polity meeting. It was—"

Mel didn't move. "Fuck that."

"That wasn't on the agenda." Matt leaned down, tried to see Mel's face. "Everything okay?"

"I'm fucked. Lyndon Johnson is keeping me out of med school."

"Wow. Did he pass a law against you?" Mel looked up as if considering how to decapitate him. "Hey, I'm sorry," Matt said quickly. "Bad joke. I take it back. What's going on?"

Mel explained that the professor of his chem class, "which is the foundation of the premed course requirements," was refusing to teach while the constant protests went on. The chanting and drumming and shouting was too much for him. "So Prof Dickhead says we have to learn all the material on our own. He assigned reading for the next two weeks, said the next class would be after that, and threw us all out. If this war wasn't going on, there wouldn't be any protests, and I'd have a perfectly normal, ballbuster chem class."

"Damn, what a jerk. Do you think he's really serious?"

Mel leaned back in his chair and sighed. "He's really not so bad, but yes, I know he's serious. A bunch of us went up to talk to him. He's sympathetic to the anti-war movement and students having more control of their destiny, but he says he's here to teach, and he can't do that. He had to sneak into the building the back way yesterday when the protesters were sitting in the hallway chanting 'No more war research,' and he just decided to call it quits for a while. As he was packing up, he said, 'Look, I know this makes it tough on you guys, but you serious students have to decide whether you want protests or an education.' The student body has to demand that the disruptions stop." He looked over at his chem book morosely. "Meanwhile, I'm fucked."

Matt shook his head. "I don't know what to say. That's a total downer."

"Well, next time you go to that meeting, you can represent those of us who are here for an education. Tell them to get their act together."

"I might just do that."

———

When Matt walked into the calculus class two weeks later, he was surprised to see the guy from registration, Randy Silverstone, standing at Professor Wolf's desk. Matt wondered if he was going to jump it, but Randy threw a piece of paper down on the desk and turned around with the same heated look he'd had at registration.

As Randy strode up the stairs of the lecture hall, Professor Wolf walked in and started madly writing away on the blackboard. Before long, equations stretched eight feet long and probably four feet vertically. Practically the only sound in the lecture hall was the special Morse code of chalk on slate—tap, swish, tap, tap, swish—over and over again. Matt could see pencils in the room gradually hit the dust: dropped, let fall, thrown, stuck in the teeth. There were murmurs that

Professor Wolf ignored, if he even heard them. Someone called out, "Professor Wolf, Professor Wolf! I have a question. Professor Wolf!" It was Randy. Wolf didn't respond. Some others took up the appeal and it gradually synchronized into a chant: "Professor Wolf. Professor Wolf. Prof—"

Finally, Wolf turned around, obviously annoyed at the interruption. There was silence for a second. Wolf turned back and finished the equation he had been writing, then looked back at the classroom before the chant could start again. "Yes?" he said.

Randy stood up. His face was a bright red, but Matt had the feeling that it wasn't from embarrassment, but rage. That seemed to be Randy's specialty. Professor Wolf looked at him over his glasses. Randy took a breath, then bellowed, "Where the *fuck* did you get that?"

The classroom erupted in laughter. Matt could see Wolf's eyes narrow and his lips tighten. "Get what?"

Now Randy looked uncomfortable, but he wasn't giving up. He marched down to the front of the room. Matt felt like applauding him. When he reached the board, he stabbed his finger on one of the many, many lines of equations and said, "*That!* Where the fuck did you get that?"

Wolf looked at the board, looked up, looked down, put his hand on his chin for a solid minute, and then peered at Randy as if he were hard to see. He said calmly, "I'm having trouble answering your question because it seems so obvious to me. Perhaps you can elaborate on your confusion." He turned to the class. "Or perhaps someone else is equally obtuse."

Randy took a deep breath and held it as if he were going to explode. Instead, he turned on his heels—*pretty snappy*, Matt thought—and headed up the stairs for the door. When he reached the exit, he turned around and said, "Well, who else? Anyone who's feeling obtuse, join me outside." He walked out.

A girl—Matt was surprised again to see Beth—stood up, folded her notebook, and walked up the stairs from her front-row seat. As she passed the rows of seats, others followed her. After a minute, Matt stood up to go, and then looked down to the front of the room. Wolf was methodically writing equations on the board as if nothing was happening behind him. The only ones not leaving were the Asian kids in the front. One of them turned around, looking confused. He focused on Matt, who was still standing. Matt just smiled and shrugged, picking up his backpack.

As he walked up the stairs to the exit, he felt strangely giddy, that elevator start-up feeling. The door to the outside looked far away, and Matt thought that he might turn around except that there were some guys still behind him. So he didn't. He kept walking, through the door and out into the fall sunlight. He took a deep breath, let it out, and suddenly laughed out loud.

He wasn't the only one. The scene was like the celebration after winning a big football game. "Great start to the weekend partying even if it is only Wednesday!" someone yelled. "Where's the beer?" People were slapping palms and dancing around. Randy was standing smoking a victory cigarette, surrounded, being congratulated as if he'd just scored the winning touchdown. Matt was exhilarated, amazed at the sense of freedom. As a group, they had power. In fact, as an individual, he had power. When the professor was being an asshole, he could just walk out of class. He didn't even have to go to class.

Matt worked his way to Randy. "Man, that was so cool," he said. Randy grinned and reached to shake Matt's hand. A hand reached in past the crowd to shake Randy's hand and Matt recognized the voice.

"I heard what you did in there, man," Kashman said. "That is some of the coolest shit around. What a great idea, amazing. You are the man today. What's your name?"

Randy told him and Kashman went on, "Collective action is so powerful. We're so much stronger when we work together and you are living proof of that, Randy Silverstone. I bet there are lots of guys who would do the same thing if only someone gave them the idea." He nodded for a second, and then said, "I wouldn't be surprised if there were more walkouts. You have discovered a world of power today. I congratulate you, man. So cool. Keep it up. We'll talk more." Kashman finally took a breath and looked around. "Matt! So you were part of this too? That's great, just great."

"Oh, I was just part of the supporting cast. But I was glad to be here."

"Be glad. Enjoy it." He reached out and grabbed Matt's hand to shake it. "Pass it on. Radiate the power. Look, I gotta go. Great to see you at the meeting. You're coming to the next one, right?"

"Well, I, I guess so."

"Great. First Wednesday in November. Meet at seven in the student union. See you there." Kashman hustled off like a man in a hurry. Some other guys jostled their way past Matt, laughing and pounding Randy on the back. Matt gave him a half-salute and said, "Go for it. Enjoy. Radiate the power."

Matt found himself standing next to Beth, who was still writing in her notebook. She was wearing another flannel shirt, over beat-up-looking overalls and a T-shirt. Matt said, "Hi." She slapped her notebook shut, stuck it in a back pocket, and looked up at him. He said, "I don't know if you remember, but Dan Dorman introduced us a couple of weeks ago."

Her face relaxed into a smile, and she said, "Sure, I remember you. I was wondering when you'd say hi. I didn't know if *you* remembered *me*."

"I never forget a flannel shirt." Beth laughed, and Matt did too. "Besides I don't know that many people. But anyway, that was an incredible scene back there. I've never actually walked out of a class in protest before."

"We should all be protesting more," Beth said firmly. "The people who are supposed to be in charge of this world are screwing it up. If we don't take charge, it'll just get worse. I mean, I know Weatherman talks about building an anti-imperialist youth movement—"

"The weatherman?"

"Yes." Beth looked at the confusion layering Matt's face and corrected herself. "No, not the weatherman on TV. *Weatherman.* They've been like part of SDS, but now they're getting more radical."

Matt nodded. He'd heard about SDS of course. They'd been around for a while, and he always thought Jill had kind of a crush on Tom Hayden. Not that he could understand why.

Beth was racing ahead. "SDS was really retrograde about women's rights, you know, and anyway Weatherman split off from them. You saw that they blew up that statue of the cop in Chicago last week, right?" She raised both hands and made fists. "That was really something. That got everybody's attention. Then today, they're going to march in Chicago, and there are like thousands of pigs trying to stop them."

"Uh, oh yeah," Matt said. "Chicago is full of pigs, that's for sure." Beth nodded grimly, and Matt was disappointed that she didn't seem to get the joke. He was also a little embarrassed to admit that he had no clue about what she was talking about. It was hard to keep track of the alphabet names: SNCC, SDS, WSA . . . Every protest group had initials and sometimes you couldn't remember which cause was associated with what initials.

"They call it the 'Days of Rage,' and they're going to fight in the streets to bring the war home. The military fights in Asia. We have to fight here."

"Oh, I'm not very political, really," Matt said with a smile. He was surprised where this conversation was going.

"It's not about politics," she said with a conviction that was surprisingly convincing. "It's about saving your spirit. It's about living the life you want to live rather than letting people do shit to you and just lying down taking it. Being free. We all get beaten down in school, at work, at home. We shouldn't do that, shouldn't let that happen." She shook out her long brown unruly hair and took a deep breath and let it out. "I just want everyone to have a *real* life."

It took Matt a moment to know what to say. She was so serious and at the same time so anguished that he was stopped in his tracks. Finally, he managed, "That's cool. I wish, I mean, that would be great."

Beth ducked her head, and said, "I know I can get a little freaky about it. It's just something I really believe in. I want to do that. You know, like if I have a job, I want it to be about that."

"I hope you do," Matt said earnestly. "I really do." They were silent for a moment. Matt said, "But, um, you're taking a math class? Is that going to, you know, get you where you're going?"

Beth looked embarrassed. "Oh, yeah. Well, I'm not really taking the class. I'm just, um, auditing it."

"You're auditing *this* class?" Matt was astonished that anyone would voluntarily sit through hours with this professor.

"Well, not exactly auditing. I'd heard about Wolf, and I wanted to see for myself. What he was really like, I mean. It's worse than I thought."

"It was out of sight today, right? Randy, he stuck it to Wolf, that's for sure."

Beth's eyes widened. "Randy? Is that the guy who called Wolf out? Do you know him?" Matt said he sort of did, and Beth practically jumped up at him, asking, "Can you introduce me? Is he still here?"

Matt made the intro and Beth took over, asking Randy if she could talk to him about what happened later and where did he live, and when would he be free, all of it sounding like a little more than just a member of the fan club. Randy was happy to be the center of attention and readily agreed. When they were done, Beth said she had another class, "but it was really nice to talk to you. We'll do it again sometime, okay?"

Randy nodded. "Sure thing."

Matt walked away, back to the dorm, thinking that sometimes college was even stranger now than it had been when he started. Over the next week, there were six more student protests against faculty. Most of them were known for poor teaching, but one seemed to happen for no reason at all. The class just decided to walk out. At all of them, Zoo members showed up, cheering and jeering.

8

MATT COULDN'T WAIT for the following week's calculus lecture. He kept imagining different ways it would start. Wolf would send a pack of wolves in the room and lock the door. He would bring in the president and Dean Devin and the class would be lectured about the proper way to behave and the importance of learning and that they were all suspended for the year. Matt would stand up and demand that there be a separate meeting where the students would give their side of the story. The president would tell him what a profound and brilliant idea that was and immediately stop the class for a private meeting. Bonnie would ask him out for a date.

When Monday came, he was up early and had a full breakfast, in case he was on bread and water for the next six weeks. Most of the students were there early and the room vibrated with excitement. Matt sat down next to Beth and they just nodded to each other. Matt looked around and found Randy, who gave him two thumbs up from the back of the room. He was beaming.

Professor Wolf walked in without looking at the class and began to scribble equations as if nothing had ever happened. Beth started writing in her notebook, but it was full of abbreviations of words. She wasn't writing equations. She stopped after a minute, put her pen down, and waited.

A student off to the right—not Randy—said, "I have a question." The professor ignored him, but then the student to the left of the first student said, "I have a question." The professor ignored this one too, but the next student in the line of desks said the same thing and before long the entire class was chanting "I have a question" over and over. At first, it was just a jumble of sound, but gradually, they began to sync up, and eventually it was a unified chorus: "I have a question. I have a question."

Professor Wolf finally quit writing equations, looked around at the highly self-satisfied students, put his chalk down, and walked out of the room, shaking his head. Matt thought, *Well, I guess Professor Wolf is in charge of his own life too.*

Beth and Matt agreed that there would be another round. "It's just like the Parisian students at the Sorbonne last May," Beth smiled be-atifically. Matt wasn't sure that was the model they wanted. He hadn't followed it all that closely, but it seemed pretty chaotic. "Remember," Beth said as they were leaving the classroom, "Wednesday is the Moratorium." Matt looked blank. "About stopping the war," Beth said testily. "No regular classes, but we'll do teach-ins about colonialism and passive resistance and Communism. There's a list of events at the student union. I'll be going to the information/communication seminar."

———

Pretty much everybody took the Moratorium day off, but Matt felt like he was doing something wrong. Woodbell had announced that there would be a teach-in on the history of revolution and Marxist thought moderated (that was the word he used) by a different professor, Alex Smith. Bonnie made a note and Matt decided maybe he would drop in. He also really didn't know what a teach-in was, but it made him feel like he was doing his duty. He went to class because that's what he was supposed to do. And that was okay, wasn't it? Anyway, Mrs. Devin had said freedom was dangerous, and it was good to stay away from danger, wasn't it? After one thought chasing around the other in his head for a half hour, he got tired of it and went to breakfast. Neut was the only person at the B-3 table, reading the newspaper, and not just any newspaper, the *New York Times*. Matt kind of preferred the New York tabloids because they had fun covers and good sports coverage.

"You going to class?" he asked Neut. Neut nodded and went back to reading his newspaper.

"I was thinking about going to one of the teach-ins," Matt said, somehow feeling that he should make conversation. Neut nodded again with an expression that said going to a teach-in was a perfectly reasonable thing to do. "What about you?" Matt said.

Neut thought for a minute, and then actually spoke. "I was going over to the Taj Mahal. There's a guy there I want to talk to." Matt was surprised that Neut was going there and didn't respond right away. Then actually Neut spoke again. "Are you interested in the Polity?"

"Well, yeah, I-I kind of am," Matt stuttered. "I think . . ." He trailed off, not sure what he was thinking, beyond the picture of Bonnie at the head table.

"I think that's a good idea," he said. "Kashman has to be stopped."

This was getting stranger and stranger, Matt thought. "Oh? What do you know about him?"

Neut had already turned to leave. "Hey, it's almost nine. I gotta go. Good to talk to you. Here, take the newspaper if you want."

"Yeah," Matt said. "You too. Thanks." He wasn't sure what he was thanking Neut for. Encouraging him to run for the Polity? Acting like a normal human being for a change? The newspaper? Anyway, he was gone and Neut's weird responses seemed to be par for the course.

Matt looked at the newspaper, which had a lot of type and not a lot of pictures. The sports section seemed pretty thin.

Matt looked into the gym. There were a lot of cushions and blankets on the floor, and he was trying to decide where to sit when he recognized the brown-haired girl sitting near the front. He didn't want to sit up front in case he got bored and wanted to leave, but he couldn't resist walking up to Bonnie. Kneeling down, he asked, "Is this seat taken?"

She turned, pulled her hair off to one side, and smiled. "Matt! Well, look at you here! So great. Sit, please." As Matt was trying to figure out how to fold his legs onto the floor, he said, "I'm surprised not to see Wit."

She raised her eyebrows. "Yeah? Oh, because we always sit together in class?" That wasn't really what Matt meant, but he just kept folding until he managed a sitting position. "Between you and me," she said, making Matt smile, "it's just as well. He'd probably just make snide remarks, but I think this is going to be really cool."

"Yeah? Um, are you a Marxist?"

She thought for a minute and Matt was impressed that she didn't automatically reject the idea. "I don't think so," she said at last. "I'm not entirely sure what a Marxist is. That's why we're here. But I know that the Poor Players are one of the best political theater companies around. Maybe one of the best theater companies, period."

Matt was feeling overmatched again. "I don't know much about theater. My parents took us to the Rockefeller Center Christmas show. They went to see *The Sound of Music* once, but I think my father fell asleep in the second act."

Bonnie nodded. "That takes some doing in that musical. But the Poor Players aren't like that. It's more like . . . ," she thought, "like Kukla, Fran, and Ollie for grown-ups."

"It's a puppet show?"

"For grown-ups."

Matt really didn't know what to make of that, but he had a thought. "Did Kukla have to get a job? Join a union?"

Bonnie pretended to be shocked. "Maybe he became a Marxist," she whispered. Matt thought now that Bonnie looked a little like Shari Lewis. But then he remembered she did a different puppet, Lambchop, best sock puppet ever. *That time Lambchop got drunk, too good.*

"I heard that. But Howdy Doody was spying on him. Reporting to McCarthy." Matt had heard that name a lot when he was a kid. His father hated McCarthy.

Bonnie looked shocked. "Joe McCarthy? The senator?"

"No," Matt said, as seriously as he could at the moment, "Charlie McCarthy. But you know who was pulling the strings?" Bonnie was holding back a laugh and just shook her head. "Pinocchio!" Matt said triumphantly.

Bonnie pushed him over and looked up toward the front. "I think we're going to start. I hope you like it."

Professor Smith had walked to the chair in front of the audience. There wasn't really a stage, but people dressed in black stood at the sides and the back as if standing at the edges of a platform. Matt looked around and saw that the audience had grown substantially and he was glad he came early and that Bonnie came even earlier. Smith was wearing a rumpled grey suit and had wild red hair that stuck out in multiple directions. He said good morning and ran his hand through his hair, succeeding in plowing new directions.

A person wearing a giant papier-mâché head appeared behind the stagehands and walked over behind Professor Smith, holding one hand to his head as if thinking very hard. The head looked almost as big as the body, and it was ringed with a full corona of hair and beard. The person was wearing a wrinkled black suit.

"Karl Marx," Professor Smith began, "was the child of a reasonably comfortable family in Prussia, now Germany, in 1818." The Karl Marx puppet person strolled jauntily over to a sign that had been hung on the wall: BONN. There he was joined by a number of people carrying poles that had other, smaller heads on top, heads with long hair and caps. "He studied law and philosophy at the University of Bonn, where he joined the Poets' Club, a group containing political radicals that were monitored by the police. He also joined the Trier Tavern Club drinking society, rising to become club co-president." The audience cheered. Somebody asked if there was beer.

"Marx was involved in a duel there, and when his grades deteriorated, he went to the University of Berlin—" Marx now hunched over and scuttled to a sign that said BERLIN. The crowd of "students" moved off. "At the University of Berlin, Marx wrote a thesis demonstrating the superiority of philosophy to theology—not a popular idea, and after threats by the administration, Marx decided to move to Cologne." Marx, pulling a sheaf of papers out of his suit coat, was chased out of Berlin by more heads on poles, but these had academic-looking hats and monocles.

"They do a lot with a little," Matt said, laughing. Bonnie nodded enthusiastically and Smith continued.

"Marx received his degree and returned briefly to Bonn with a friend, where they scandalized everyone by getting drunk, laughing in church, and galloping through the streets on donkeys." More older-looking heads now took up the chase after Marx, who now fled to a sign that said PARIS. Some stagehands brought out a café table where another big-headed puppet, with a thinner face but a longer beard, sat down, smoking and writing furiously in a notebook.

"Marx moved to Paris where in 1844 he met another German, a socialist named Friedrich Engels. With Engels he began to seriously study economics and political philosophy." Marx joined Engels at the table and they began an animated, if silent, conversation. At another café table, a group of people with large puppet heads, some with top hats and some with helmets, sat down and leaned toward each other conspiratorially. "The authorities," Professor Smith said, "were not always comfortable with these new political ideas." The "authorities" started to look up, one at a time, toward the table where Marx and Engels were talking and gesturing.

To one side of Professor Smith, several stagehands brought on a large frame, maybe six by eight feet, that held what looked like chain-link fencing covered in burlap. Smith looked over at it. "The industrial revolution, the breakdown of aristocracy, and increasing urbanization were changing the patterns of work in the world," Professor Smith said, shaking his head, "and Marx saw the dehumanization of people who had once watched their crops grow from seeds until they wound up on their dinner table. Now these people took up individual tasks, each of which accomplished nothing in themselves."

Professor Smith stepped forward and gestured toward the frame.

"Anyone in the audience who would like to be a factory worker can step up to the loom," he said, "as we represent it here."

"Let's be workers," Bonnie said, rising to her knees and grabbing Matt's hand. She stood up and pulled him up, leaning back until he was able to struggle to his feet. She let go of his hand and led the way to the workers. A few were performers, but as more audience members joined the group, they gave up their hold on the large frame. Matt and Bonnie and the others were shown by gestures that they should hold on to the edge of the framed rectangle, which indeed held chain link. Threaded through the chain links were strips of burlap from one end to the other and from top to bottom. There was something inserted in the chain link's gaps underneath the material, not everywhere but in some kind of pattern that Matt couldn't figure out.

Performers now dressed in tunics and pants walked around the workers, holding sticks that they shook in the direction of their "employees." One directed Bonnie, who was in the bottom-right corner of the rectangle, to pull out some of the burlap. After she did, the manager did the same to Matt, pointing to the next strip of burlap. They continued this way across the bottom of the rectangle, but they uncovered nothing.

Professor Smith explained, "Marx believed that the workers would eventually become disaffected by repetitive, unproductive tasks." The Marx character wandered past the workers, shaking his great shaggy grey head, and then sat back down at his desk in Paris. The workers continued stripping away the burlap from the rectangle. After another row, they started to uncover the objects underneath, which Matt was surprised to see were just plastic cups with the bottoms sticking up. When the third row was done they had one long series of cups, then a space, then two more cups, then a space and two more cups, a third space and a third set of cups, and finally another long row. "It's like Morse code," Matt said to Bonnie. "Dash dot dot dot dash."

"What's that mean?"

"No idea. SOS is three dots, three dashes, and three dots. That's my entire Morse code dictionary."

She nodded and took her turn pulling burlap out of the chain link. Nothing.

"One of the many, many . . . ," Professor Smith shook his head like a maniac, ". . . many things Marx did was to change philosophy from an abstract science to a practical one. With what he called 'historical materialism,' he drew conclusions about philosophy from history, from past experience. And he believed that the workers' experience would be the engine of revolution. This was implicit in *The Communist Manifesto* of 1848, written when Marx was thirty years old. The established order did not like these ideas and chased him out of town."

The fat cats with the top hats and helmets rose up in a group and hustled over to Marx at his desk, making him flee from the sign that said PARIS to the sign that said BONN.

"Marx hoped that the revolution would first start in Germany, so Marx moved back to Germany, where he was accused of fomenting armed rebellion and forced to flee to England, because he was barred from Belgium and Paris." The hats and helmets again chased Marx, who ran with papers flying behind him, to a sign that said LONDON.

Matt and Bonnie and the others were about halfway done, and now they could see that the plastic cups were spelling out letters. Professor Smith described Marx's life in London and his work for newspapers—"He contributed for years to Horace Greeley's *New York Daily Tribune*—and wrote his masterwork of economic theory, *Capital*—in German, *Das Kapital*. His perception," Smith said, his voice rising in pitch, "was that in the modern world, as it was, each worker produces nothing of value in itself. It only has value as a part of something, which only has value as part of something else, and so forth. There is nothing, *no time* when the worker can say, 'I made this, it is the product of my work.'"

By now the workers had nearly finished the rectangle and saw what they were making. Professor Smith looked over at them and waited, saying, "Marx believed this was an intolerable situation and the workers would eventually reject it, fighting to regain their honor and dignity. So the most famous phrase in *Capital* is: Workers of the world . . ." He turned to the workers and gestured at them to hold up their rectangle. They did, and now the audience could see the single word written in plastic cups, which Smith called out: "Unite!"

Matt and Bonnie realized they were standing in front of the "E" and dropped down, but Matt's head was still in the way so he bent it down and wound up next to Bonnie's shoulder. It smelled nice.

The audience had jumped up and were cheering, and a chant began: "Unite, unite, unite." After the chant had continued for a couple of minutes, Professor Smith looked out at the audience and raised his hands for quiet. When there was some, he said, "The Poor Players are taking their leave. Please give them, and today's workers, the appropriate thanks."

The audience applauded and cheered again. Matt was exhilarated. All the workers shook each other's hand, and Matt had the feeling that they should all sit together. As he watched the others move back to their seats, Bonnie pushed him playfully from behind, and said, "C'mon, big guy, don't hog the spotlight." Matt turned back, then bowed to the audience and let her lead the way back to their seats. As he turned to sit, he saw Dorman at the back, standing and applauding with arms raised. Next to him, Lana and Beth were smiling and laughing as they applauded not so demonstratively. Matt was surprised to think that other people he knew would be watching him perform and it gave him a good feeling.

Professor Smith took over the teach-in by himself now, and he was almost as much a performer as a teacher. Gesticulating, shouting at times, wandering through the students sitting in the gym, he managed to make economic theory and European history almost entertaining. Not quite *Laugh-In* funny, but worth listening to. "Stalinist communism has about as much resemblance to Marx's ideas as a warthog to a warbler. Marx was an idealist. He envisioned a world of equals, with everyone working together in a harmonious chorus. 'To each according to his needs, from each according to his abilities.'

"Stalinist Russia was a brutal, autocratic society. Quite apart from the purges," he raised his arms and shook his fists, "that killed *hundreds of thousands*, if not millions. Stalinist communism has essentially imprisoned its peasants in state-owned farms and factories. While all receive education and health care, such as they are, provided by the state, it is still a society oppressed by its rulers." He told stories about visiting the Soviet Union in the thirties and that some speculated that it had carried out assassinations in the United States. After the professor had finished, there were questions for an hour, whether Marxism could work in the United States, if the United States should have gotten involved in Vietnam.

Not even Professor Smith's theatrics could keep Matt completely focused on the history, especially with Bonnie sitting next to him. She was rapt, and actually asked questions that showed she knew something. There was a final burst of energy over whether the Vietnam War was legal, or moral, or even a necessary evil. One student said indignantly, "If democracy is such a good form of government, why are we in this fucking war?"

Smith thought for a minute. "Winston Churchill said that the Americans can be counted on to do the right thing," he paused, "after they've tried everything else." Then, more thoughtfully, "Eisenhower warned us, as he was leaving office, against what he was the first to call 'the military-industrial complex'—that the money and power embodied in the military and the arms makers would have a pernicious effect on society and government. Maybe he was right." Smith left it there. Finally, there was a moment when things seemed to be winding down, but Smith was standing right beside Matt and Bonnie. Matt looked up and asked, "So what would the best form of government look like?"

Smith looked down at him and started to say something, but then paused and stretched out his arms to encompass the entire gym. "What would it *look like*? It might look a lot like this: people getting together to discuss their problems and learn from each other. The best government is one in which people take part. Well, our allotted time is up and then some. Thank you all for coming. Let's do it again sometime."

There was applause and the usual commotion. One student leapt up and shouted, "There will be a meeting about the march on Washington, D.C., next Tuesday. Right here! Eight o'clock!"

Matt and Bonnie stood up and helped gather the cushions and stack them in the corner. "Wow," Matt said, "work, work, work. I didn't know utopia would be so tiring. Are you hungry?"

"Starved. Want to get some lunch?" They walked across campus to the dining hall. It was the first time they had ever actually talked to each other at length, Matt realized, though he felt like they were old friends. Though she was several inches shorter than Matt, she had a long stride that kept up with his. She was from Garden City, and her father was a lawyer. "That's a, um, nice place," Matt said uncertainly.

"Oh, it's very *nice*," Bonnie said and laughed without a lot of humor. "Everything about it is *nice*. We have all the right things. A garbage disposal, a barbecue, a swimming pool. You know how in *Camelot*, the song goes, 'July and August cannot be too hot, and there's a legal limit to the snow here'?" She half-sang in a pretty contralto, as Matt's mother described her own voice. "That's how I felt about growing up," she continued. She'd always done well in school, she said, although never quite as well as her father wanted. Matt got the sense that her mother tried to make her feel better, but it never quite worked. "I took dance classes. And piano, but I hated it, so I demanded . . . Well, I convinced my parents that I was better at dance."

"So did you really dance?" Matt asked. "You look like . . ." She looked up at him with a question in her eyes and Matt got tongue-tied for a minute, then said, ". . . like you would be a good dancer."

She nodded. "I was pretty good. But you can only go so far with it, you know. Unless you want to sacrifice yourself." She frowned and then made it go away and looked at him. "And you? Did you play on a team?"

"Oh, yeah," Matt said. "I was the pole in the pole vault." She laughed and the tension left her face. "I was a baseball pitcher," he went on. "I was pretty good too. Up to a point, at least." She looked sympathetic and Matt found himself telling her about his last game and how much it had meant to him, how much it meant to lose. "I felt like I had let each one of twenty-five, thirty people down."

"Oh god, Matt, I'm sorry."

They walked for a bit, nearing the dining hall. "But the team . . ." he finally said, "they were great. They thanked me for getting them that far. They gave me the ball and they all signed it. I have it in my room."

Her eyes shone a little when she smiled and said, "How wonderful that must feel, Matt." He nodded and she said quietly, "I envy you that." They got in line for lunch. Matt watched Bonnie pick up a salad and soup, while he debated between a grilled cheese and French fries and a hamburger and French fries. It was a close call, but he went with the burger.

They ate in silence for several minutes, while people said hi to Bonnie and she waved back and gave them a smile that, Matt thought, probably made their day. They sat well away from the usual B-3 table, and Matt felt relieved. He didn't want to go through the razzing about his love life.

"What about the March on Washington?" she asked him after she'd finished the soup.

He chewed, trying to decide how to answer. He went with the truth. "I haven't really thought about it. It's soon though, right?"

"November 15. There are a bunch of people going. We're actually going to get a bus. The Polity appropriated some money, but anyone can go. I think Jack Appel has found a place for us to crash. The city is opening its arms. So it won't cost anything except food."

"Plus the cost of renting body armor."

"It's a *peace* march, you know."

"'S what I was saying," Matt said around a mouthful of hamburger. He swallowed and said as casually as he possibly could, "So . . . are you bringing anybody? To the march?"

Bonnie looked confused. "Bringing anybody?"

"Yeah, you know, like . . . bringing someone?"

She frowned, and then said, "Oh! You mean . . . No, I'm not *bringing* anyone." She looked away. "I guess I can be pretty intense sometimes." She laughed, shaking her head at the same time. "A lot of guys don't seem to like that. I mean, they don't get it that I can be more interested in Paris than the Yankees. And I can't understand why they aren't."

Matt picked up a French fry. "You know, one thing I've *always* wondered is why they're called *French* fries."

"Well, maybe because they invented them."

Matt was thunderstruck. "You're seriously telling me that McDonald's didn't invent French fries? Come on."

Bonnie looked at him, her face struggling between surprise and amusement. Then she looked down at his plate, snatched a French fry, and took a bite. "You're right," she said, pointing at him with the remains. "McDonald's did invent *these* fries."

Matt frowned and wondered where he could study up on the history of fried potatoes, wondering if he hadn't shown off his ignorance again. They were quiet for a moment, then Matt said, "So do you think the March on Washington can really accomplish anything?"

Bonnie looked away. "There are people dying in Vietnam every day. I think . . . people here should be able to put themselves out for one day to speak up for them. The bureaucrats in Washington shouldn't make all the decisions." Her voice was low but steely. "This is going to be history. It may never happen again. And if we don't say anything, it's like we're saying it's okay to invade a small country. It's okay to bomb them to the Stone Age and burn up all their forests *without ever declaring war*." She turned to look at him straight on, her brown eyes burning. "The country is run by an oligarchy that is funded by Congress and cheered on by the arms manufacturers. The powers that be are sending young Americans to their death for no reason. It isn't right. It isn't even a smart way to use our power. The Europeans hate us. The French spent ten years fighting there and got beat. They think we're idiots."

Matt held his hands up in surrender. "The last thing I want in the world is to fight in Vietnam." Bonnie tossed her hair and looked away again. "So," Matt said, "is it a Greyhound or one of those yellow school buses? I really like to be able to recline my seat. And the suspension on those school buses—pathetic."

Bonnie looked back without smiling. "Don't do it on my account."

Why not? Matt thought. He said, "I like being part of a team. Sounds like the biggest team since the French Revolution." Lame as it was, he was glad he could use the course. "We're not going to behead anybody, are we? Should I avoid taking a bath?"

She turned back to him and shook her head. "You're a one-man disarmament agreement, aren't you?"

"You're pretty agreeable yourself. Want a McDonald's fry?" He held one out to her on a fork.

"No. Thank you. And yes, it's a nice bus with padded seats that recline. A little. Revolutions don't happen in Cadillacs."

"You think I should run for the Polity?" he said, covering his tracks.

Bonnie took a deep breath. "It's like Smith said, the best government is the one you take part in. I think you would be good on the Polity. I think Kashman is trying to stack the Polity with his followers."

"You didn't tell me what *you* think."

Bonnie shrugged. "I'd like to see you on the board." She looked at her watch. "Hey, I've got another teach-in. 'Susan B. Anthony and the Suffragist Movement.' Interested?" She laughed.

Matt raised his eyebrows. "Oh, I've got a lot of marching practice to get in. Besides, maybe I'm taught-out. I'm a bear of very little brain."

Bonnie made a mouth. "I don't believe that for a second."

"No, it's true." They picked up their trays and dumped everything that wasn't flatware into the garbage.

"Okay," Bonnie said, "have a good day. Football practice, right?" Matt nodded a little sheepishly. "Boys will be boys," Bonnie said, and glided away.

Matt wasn't sure he liked that last comment. *Who says he was still a boy?* He looked at his watch and realized that English class was about to start, if it was going to start at all. *Maybe I'll just drop by*, he thought. *I've got some time to kill before practice.* As he walked there, he imagined telling Nicky about the teach-in, but he felt odd about either including Bonnie or leaving her out of the story.

Nicky wasn't there. Matt stayed as long as he could. He liked Professor Meadows. But he had a hard time focusing; his mind kept straying back to the teach-in and the Poor Players. *It was exciting*, he thought. *It was cool to be part of something. A little like football. Maybe the march would be like that.*

"No, we have attempted to control political revolution," Professor Meadows was saying, "and replace it with social evolution. There are times when evolution is not enough, however, and then we turn to social movements and political coalitions. The March on Washington, for instance, coming up in November—that's our way to demanding change in the government outside of elections."

9

"DEAR MR. AYMER." Matt stood in the middle of his room and read the first letter he'd received on campus that wasn't advertising. He hadn't even thought about getting mail for a couple of days, and the letter was dated two days ago.

> You are required to attend a meeting of the Disciplinary Committee on November 14 at 10:00 AM. This is an informal investigatory meeting to evaluate the events of October 15 during a Calculus 101 class with Professor Abraham Wolf. Please attend alone. The results of this meeting will be announced at a later Disciplinary Committee meeting no less than one month later. If you have others who are able to speak on your behalf, please give us their names and we will contact them.

He was speechless for several minutes. Mel walked in, took one look at Matt, and said, "Hey, you're white as a sheet. What's the matter?" Matt handed him the letter, which he read, turned it over, and gave it back to Matt. "Jesus fucking Christ, you really don't get any breaks from this school administration, do you? This is about that walkout? From the math class?"

"I guess." Matt was recovered enough from the initial shock that he could start to feel miserable. "I wonder if the whole class got the letter. I don't really know anyone else in it. That guy named Randy was the one who started it all." He threw the letter on the bed and picked up his baseball. If he got thrown out of school, he'd have to get a job. That was after his father killed him. If he got thrown out of school, he wouldn't have a student deferment. He might get drafted. Then he would get killed. "This is horrible," Matt moaned, "a disaster. I'm fucked." He realized he was squeezing his baseball hard enough to make his fingers hurt. He threw it to Mel, who sat down on his bed opposite Matt.

"Wait a minute, just a goddamn minute," Mel said. "The whole class walked out, right? And that other guy started it, right?" Matt nodded. "What are they going to do to you anyway? For cutting one single class?"

"I didn't cut it!" Matt barked. "Why should they do anything to me at all?" Then he thought that the one class walkout seemed to inspire the next six walkouts only a few days later. "Hey," he said to Mel, "this could be more serious. There were all those walkouts after that."

"Tell me about it," Mel said. "My chem test got cancelled. See, I told you this idea of grading teachers wasn't going to be just a fleeting idea with no consequences. What's next? What graduate school wants a student from Anarchy University?"

"But what if they think I started those too?" Mel rolled his eyes.

––––––––––

Professor Wolf was late to the class, which gave Matt time to look for Beth. She was in the second row all the way on the right, in a red flannel shirt, T-shirt, and jeans, as usual. As usual, Beth was writing in her notebook, which she slammed shut as soon as Matt said hello. Still she gave him a big smile, so he sat down next to her. "Look, I need to ... Have you ... ?" He realized he didn't know what to say. She sat there expectantly, her dark brown eyes matching her dark brown hair. Finally, he said, "I've been called into a disciplinary hearing about what happened with Randy, a couple of weeks ago. I don't know why. I don't know what's going on."

"God, that's for shit," Beth said. "I'm so sorry. You didn't do anything different from anyone else. I didn't get a notice, but then I'm just auditing. I know that Randy didn't get anything. He was kind of expecting to. Kind of hoping to, I think."

Matt slumped back in his chair. "I'm getting a little tired of being the poster boy for administration fuck-ups."

Looking concerned, Beth said, "These hearings don't usually go anywhere. They tell you not to do it again and slap your wrist with a ruler."

Matt was also a little tired of people telling him not to worry. "How do you know?"

Her eyes did a little dance around the room, but then she said, "Lana was in one last year. Also, I'm interested in how they handle academic things here. I've talked to a lot of people about hearings. I mean, no one really looks at the system from the student's point of view, do they?" The class was starting to talk about how late Wolf was, and there was some laughter. Someone said something about him being scared off. Beth raised her voice. "I think that it's time we began to have a voice in the management of the campus and evaluation of professors, and what courses are offered. The whole thing, all of it. *This is our life.*"

Matt was impressed with her enthusiasm. "You ever talk to Kashman about this? He might—"

She cut him off. "I don't talk to him."

Matt could feel the cold spreading from her frown. Surprised, he said, "You were at the—"

"Lana wanted to go," Beth said, biting off the words. "I thought I should be . . . be aware of the first . . . It was technically a mixer for the whole school, you know, supposedly. That's a laugh! Just another big plus for Kashman, using our money to have fun." She folded her arms and folded into herself. "And sell drugs," she muttered.

Matt wasn't sure he'd heard her right and wanted to ask her what she'd said, but Wolf stomped into the classroom, the door banging behind him. He walked over to their side of the classroom with a stack of papers in his hand. Matt shrunk back, afraid he was going to unload on him, but all Wolf did was to give Beth the stack of papers and say, "Pass them around."

Beth and Matt looked at the stack. At the top of the top sheet was written CALCULUS 101 FINAL. They looked at each other. The semester wasn't over for another six weeks. Beth took the top set of papers, handed the rest to Matt, and quickly reached for her note-book. "NO NOTES," Wolf yelled, or at least it sounded like yelling in a classroom that had become dead quiet. "*Take everything off your desks,*" he continued, only a little more quietly. "You have one hour." A student started to protest that they'd be late for the next class, but Wolf demanded silence. There were some murmurs and rustling of paper, but that died away quickly as everyone looked at the test. There were groans. "What?" somebody said. "What's that?" Some of the test looked like it was written in a foreign language, there were so many symbols, variables, and Greek letters.

Beth whispered to Matt, "This is intolerable. This is abuse."

"Quiet!" Wolf said. "No talking!"

For the rest of the hour, there was no sound except for pencils scratching on paper and slide rules hissing. The test was a real final. It covered material that hadn't been presented in class. It sketched out complicated real-life situations that required creative solutions. The multiple-choice answers seemed to dare you to choose one over the others and laugh at you when you did. Even the Asian students looked puzzled sometimes. Wolf's eyes never left the students, panning slowly from one side of the room to the other. Matt knew with certainty that he wouldn't pass the test, and when he surreptitiously surveyed the room, he could see heads down on desks in surrender. Exactly 60 minutes from the time he started the test, Wolf barked, "Pencils down!" The Asians were practically the only ones still working, and they reluctantly laid their pencils at the top of their papers. "Pass your papers to the right," Wolf ordered, and when they were all collected, Wolf went up the steps, and snatched the stacks, starting with Beth's.

There wasn't much discussion as everyone filed out of the class-room. All Beth said was, "Try not to worry too much. They don't want to throw you out." She put her hand around Matt's wrist. "I'll ask Lana about that disciplinary hearing. Look for us at lunch today. We'll be there around noon. We always sit by the door."

That's reassuring, Matt thought sarcastically, but all he said was, "Thanks. See you at lunch."

Matt almost always ate in the dining hall except when the floor ordered pizza. There was the usual grilled cheese and fries. There was mashed potatoes and corn kernels sitting in what Matt hoped was water. There was mac and cheese, ham and cheese sandwiches, and since it was Thursday, cheeseburgers. There was tomato soup, which came with parmesan cheese.

"Do we have a special mission to support the dairy industry?" he asked, sitting at the B-3 table. The table at the back left of the dining hall might as well have had a RESERVED sign on it, since almost no one outside the dorm ever sat there, except maybe at the beginning and end of lunch.

"America was built on the backs of cows," Brain said. "Steaks, beef, milk, cheese."

"It's what's for dinner," Monster said. "Serious lack of steak here, though. Bring that up at the next Polity meeting."

"And fish, don't forget fish," Fish said. Everybody looked at him. "I'm from Maine," he explained.

"You can't build anything on the back of a fish," Matt pointed out. "And I'm not on the Polity. But maybe we should have better food. Hey, Mel," he said, as his roommate arrived. "As a medical expert, don't you think we should have healthier food here?"

"Greetings, warriors of the sports field." Dorman strolled up to the table in a white T-shirt and white jeans. "There will be an action at the draft lottery. Be forewarned, or alternatively, join in. Planning session at the Taj this Friday. Also, the March Against Death next month in D.C. It's time for the war to end."

"I've been against death almost from the beginning," Mel said, getting snickers of appreciation. "I didn't know I had to say anything about it."

"Silence is agreement," Dorman said.

Matt turned to Brain and said, "The sound of silence." Passing words, phrases, whatever down the table had become a regular thing, a game they'd invented by accident.

"Hello darkness, my old friend," Brain said, and looked at Fish.

"I've come to talk with you about that—again," Fish said and looked at Monster. He got a thumbs-up for creativity.

"I'm a rock," Monster said. "I'm an island." He looked past Neut, who for some reason was always allowed a pass on the game.

"No man is an island," Barry said without looking up from his clipboard.

"Wait, is that fair?" Mel asked.

"'Scarborough Fair,'" Matt said.

"All's fair in love and war," Brain added.

"Stop!" Mel screamed.

"In the name of love!" Monster said, and the whole table broke up.

Neut sat quietly next to Dorman. "I hear that the Zoo guys might try to counter-protest the protest at the draft lottery." The lottery would determine the fate of a great number of students, unless Nixon or Kissinger somehow managed to stop the war in the next six months. Anybody who didn't have a student deferment and was nineteen would be eligible for the draft and therefore service in Vietnam, and therefore a possible death sentence. The university had agreed to set up chairs in the student center lobby with multiple TVs positioned around the room.

"I know nothing about the frat boys' plans," Dorman replied, "but I'm surprised they would have any plans beyond next Friday's beer."

"Some of them are pretty heavy-duty for the war," Neut said.

"Some of them are indeed heavy," Dorman agreed.

"He ain't heavy—" Monster started, but Mel cut him off by throwing a breadstick at him.

"Brothers all," Dorman announced, "I must leave you and continue, like Paul Revere, to alert the sleeping hamlets. But I leave you with Mr. Blue, who can make you see many colors. Or red, if you're a Puritan. Mr. Blue, halloo."

The long-hair with the briefcase from the Taj party nodded conspiratorially to Dorman. "My man. You're all good, right?"

"I am outstanding. The last batch was perfecto."

Mr. Blue continued nodding, like one of those wind-up toys of birds. "Right, right," he said. "Next delivery on Tuesday."

Dorman bowed slightly. "Azure leisure. I take my leave, with your leave." And he floated away.

Mr. Blue nodded to the table. "The B-3 boys. Is there anything I can do for you? Pep pills? MDMA? I guarantee you can get tackled and not feel a thing. Need to pull an all-nighter? Got just what you need."

Neut raised three fingers a few inches off the table and Mr. Blue nodded at him. Matt wondered if he didn't get dizzy doing that all the time. Brain said, "I'll do a dime bag." When heads turned, he looked around and said, "What? Everyone needs to relax now and then. Sherlock Holmes did cocaine."

"Did I hear 'cocaine'?" Mr. Blue said. "How much? I can probably get you some." Nobody answered and Brain passed a ten-dollar bill down the table. "Right, right." Mr. Blue nodded, looking at a piece of paper. "Delivery on . . . Friday. Five p.m. Not me; I'm just the sales rep. Fulfillment will be a guy in a blue hat. Watch for him. No refunds."

Matt stood up. "I've got to go to class. Be cool. See you at practice." He caught up with Dorman, who was alerting yet another table, and said as quietly as the lunchroom bedlam allowed, "Have you seen Beth? Or Lana? I was supposed to meet them at lunch today."

"Those girls," Dorman shook his head, "thick as thieves. Beware, they'll steal your heart." Dorman pointed them out at a table near one of the exits. They were sitting next to each other, their heads nearly touching. Matt walked over. Lana was sitting on the aisle, one leg sticking out, wearing jeans that didn't look like they'd been worn before and fitted her like a glove. Beth was still in her flannel shirt. She turned to see Matt and gave him a big smile. "Recovered from that exam yet?"

Matt shrugged dolefully. "I think calculus is a fatal disease. Hi, Lana." Lana smiled back and said hello, still using his full name. Matt thought she could make quadratic equations sound flirtatious—all those as on top of bs going into cs—but he did his best to act cool. She was wearing a sweatshirt that said, "California Southern University," no place that Matt had ever heard of but he didn't say anything. He tried not to stare at her chest anyway. "So Dorman just came over about the lottery and the march and stuff. Are you going to Washington?"

"I think Washington is very chilly in November," Lana said. Her hand came up from underneath the table and stubbed out a very small, hand-rolled thing that was obviously not a cigarette. She waved both hands over the residual smoke, which confirmed to Matt that no tobacco had been harmed in its production.

"You do that in the lunchroom?" he said, more than a little surprised.

"We try to be discreet," Beth said. "Does it bother you?" Matt shook his head, impressed at their nonchalance.

"Matthew, do you know that most of the workers on the line are stoned?" Lana said. "Their jobs, like so many others, are tedium from one end of the day to the other. It is the only way to survive." She took out a small purse and extracted a pack of Virginia Slims cigarettes from it, offering the pack to Matthew, who refused. She didn't offer one to Beth, and Matt figured they knew each other well enough that she didn't have to.

Lana lit her cigarette and took a pull on it without drama. "If I drew a low number in the draft," she said meditatively, "I would go to Bimini." The name rang a bell with Matt, but he couldn't remember why. "It is lovely there. I traveled there many times with my father when I was a teenager. He owned something there, I forget what. I met that congressman, Adam Clayton Powell, there."

"You were also the center of attention," Beth broke into his thoughts with a sly look at Lana, who waved her off. "You can imagine what Lana looked like at sixteen. And her father was not the only man on the boat." Lana looked away, and Beth said, "So she gained a lot of experience."

"I was a skinny coquette of a young girl," Lana said, "and I paid for it. Try to imagine what it is like when some man who seems to be made of unbaked bread dough presses himself up to you and looks down your bathing suit. And the hairy chests! Disgusting. I cannot tell you how many penises were offered for my admiration. Some almost too small to see. But I learned how to defend myself in those summers on the yacht." Lana put an arm around Beth's shoulder and said, "And I try to help others do the same."

They looked at each other until Matt began to feel that he was a fifth wheel. But Lana looked up at him, and said, "Beth told me that you are appearing before a disciplinary committee." Matt told her his situation and she nodded. "It is a predicament," she said. "I experienced something similar."

"Except you started it," Beth laughed.

Lana said that she had stood up in the middle of a history class in freshman year and protested that the professor was not allowing the students to participate. "I was still new to this public side of education, having spent so much time in private schools."

"Four of them, right?" Beth said.

"Well," Lana huffed, "they were all based on the authoritarian model, and it was similar here. I objected that your Mr. John Dewey and of course Maria Montessori had already long ago introduced democracy into education."

"And the professor objected?"

"Well, not to that precisely," Lana said. "But he showed no inclination to change his style. When I understood that, I could see I needed to mobilize support." Matt waited for her to go on, but she seemed to be somewhere else.

"So she led a walkout of the class," Beth said helpfully.

Lana shrugged with one shoulder. "I simply asserted that unless there was negotiation, I could no longer be a part of the process. I perhaps suggested to those around me that they should stand up for their rights. I could only be surprised when so many followed me. Of course, it was a very fine day outside too. The sun was restorative." She inhaled her cigarette and smiled, almost closing her eyes to remember the day.

"That was when we met, really," Beth said shyly.

After a pause, Matt asked, "So they called you up before a disciplinary hearing?"

Lana opened her eyes and came back to herself. "Yes, it was ridiculous. They repeated all the things that the professor said, and I repeated all the things that I had said to the professor. They asked me to apologize to the professor for disrupting class and I asked that the professor apologize to me for retarding my education. I had to once again explain John Dewey to them." She looked wistful. "His was the only book on the boat in English except for Harold Robbins and pornography. That was why I read it. Anyway, they had no response to counter my assertion of educational principles." She drew deeply on her cigarette and exhaled with satisfaction.

"So they let you off?" Matt asked, hope blooming in his head.

Lana tossed her head, sending dark hair flying. "Like any repressive society, they remained rigid. I was given six months' probation."

Matt collapsed inside. "Six months' probation," he repeated mindlessly.

"She got a little aggressive with them," Beth said, seeing Matt's disappointment. "Didn't you call one of them, what, 'a cancer-ridden ground worm'?"

"It is the brittle branches that break," Lana said. "I pretended to be a good girl for the rest of the year . . ."

"In class," Beth giggled.

". . . and I determined to uproot the tree from within. You should do the same," she said, pointing a slender finger at Matt. "That's why we need you on the Polity."

"I don't want to uproot anything," he objected.

"You can plant a new tree," Beth pleaded. "You have four years. Just don't compare anyone to a sick invertebrate."

———————

"What's the matter with you today?" Nicky said. "You look like the Ancient Mariner. Or the albatross."

Wearily, Matt explained his situation with the disciplinary hearing. When he finished, she said, "When's this meeting?"

"November 14."

"Almost the ides of November."

"I hope they're not going to stab me."

"That would be a drag. Matt, there's one thing you know for sure."

Matt braced himself for more uncomforting reassurance. "What's that?"

"Whatever happens at that hearing," Nicky said, "I'll still be your friend."

Matt didn't know what to say and would have had a hard time saying anything with a catch in his throat. She was looking at him, waiting. He smiled, and she smiled back. "Thanks, Nicky. That . . . that means something." He mustered up enough courage to ask a question he wasn't sure he wanted an answer to. "How was your date?" She looked confused. Matt made himself try again. "You know, after the Polity meeting."

"Oh!" She looked away, looked back. "Oh, great! I learned all about glycolosis."

Matt thought this seemed unlikely. Or was some code for sex. Or at least there wasn't a lot of studying going on. "Glycolysis?"

Her mischievous grin came back. "You know, hungry pirates pick all the greatest pickled pumpkins ever picked."

Letting the hammer fall if it was going to, Matt said tensely, "You and this guy picked pumpkins?"

Nicky ducked her head, and then looked up at him with a serious face. "I'm sorry, Matt, I was teasing you. I couldn't resist. So, I was helping my roommate study for her biochemistry midterm. Glycolysis is how cells break down sugar or something."

"Your roommate?" *Maybe Mel was right*, he thought.

"'Hungry pirates pick all the greatest pickled pumpkins ever picked' is a mnemonic for the process," she explained, talking very fast. "All the initial letters are about phosphates and a bunch of things that end in '-ase.' I forget them all. But I remember the hungry pirates. I'm a hungry pirate."

"And this was helping her?"

"You bet. She had to explain everything to me. That's the best way to learn anything. But then after a couple of beers we were the pickled ones." Nicky looked suddenly embarrassed and put her hands in her lap. "She's premed," she said quietly, as if that explained something.

Matt stifled a laugh, not sure what exactly was funny, but he felt better than he had in two days. "Really? You know, my roommate is premed. Maybe they should study together."

"Well, aren't you the matchmaker." She was quiet for a minute then quickly looked up, her blue eyes wide, as if she'd just remembered something. "I know. I know what you need."

"What?"

"A good home-cooked meal. Why don't you come over for dinner?"

"Come over?"

"Yes," she nodded enthusiastically. "We cook in the room all the time. We have an electric skillet and a hotplate. Who can eat all that barf food in the dining hall? It's full of fat and calories and a bunch of other stuff that's totally destructive to your body." Matt hadn't minded a steady diet of grilled cheese, French fries, meatloaf, and fried chicken. He'd put on ten pounds and nobody had noticed. Nicky was still looking at him, her smile fading. Matt didn't want that to happen.

"That sounds great, Nicky." Her smile returned and she leaned back in her chair, looking like a cat curling up after a meal. Matt suddenly realized they were still in class. "I just have one question, though." She turned quickly to look at him, eyebrows raised skeptically. Matt grinned. "What's the professor talking about?"

10

Matt went to the Polity meeting, restless and distracted, but feeling that it was better to do something rather than nothing. The room was buzzing when he came in, people were talking in small groups, and Kashman had to pound on the table and yell to call the meeting to order. "We've got a lot to get to tonight," he began, "so the fucking audit is going ahead, excuse my French. I have gotten most of the paperwork from the budget heads, and if anybody has a problem, I'll talk to them separately, outside the meeting."

Martin, a skinny math major with long hair who headed the concert series, said, "I'm having a problem. The numbers the auditors gave me don't match—"

"Like I said," Kashman interrupted with controlled fury, "I'll talk to you outside the meeting. See me after."

"But—"

"It won't be a problem," Kashman snapped. "See me after." Martin nodded but seemed annoyed. Kashman hurriedly moved on. "More important, there's a quick update from the Curriculum Relevancy Upgrade Development Committee."

"Oh—the CRUDs," somebody next to Matt snickered. This was Kashman's personal project, a complete overhaul of the curriculum and who decided it, and it seemed that a lot of people thought it was either too difficult to set up or too crazy to even bother with. The idea seemed to be for the students to decide what courses would be offered and what the requirements would be for graduation.

Kashman looked around and said, "I know progress has been a little slow, but I think it will definitely move faster now that we have had nearly ten walkouts in the last few weeks. We're making things happen!"

The representatives from the Zoo pounded the table and stomped their feet. Matt remembered Kashman talking to the Zoomen during the protest march the first day of the school year. And saying to Randy that there could be more like the one in calculus. Matt thought he'd ask Bonnie about it all, then saw Wit lean toward her and say something. Wit shook his head and Bonnie covered her mouth to laugh. Then she noticed Matt, his head several inches above every other head at the back, and smiled at him. His smile back was tight, and she tilted her head with a questioning look. He just shook his head.

Jack Appel took over the meeting next with a long description of the plans for the March on Washington. Wit interrupted him almost immediately to ask if it was appropriate for the student government to be involved in supporting a protest. Appel looked indignant. "As our own local government," he said emphatically, "it is imperative that we stand up for our beliefs. Tricky Dick just talked about a silent majority in favor of continuing the war. We have to stand up and be heard against it."

He went on like this for a while, and when he stopped to take a breath, Kashman stood up and held up a hand. "We should make every effort to ensure their safety during the trip and as far as possible, during the march and the protest. The executive committee felt that the smart thing to do was to investigate the cost of buses to take people down there, and the possibility of finding places for them to stay where they can be safe."

Then Dorman and Lana made a mysterious preview of "an action" for the night of the draft lottery. "We are planning the most incredible piece of performance art," Dorman crowed. "It will blow everyone away. No pun intended! Ha ha. We need volunteers for it, though! If you want to volunteer, see me or Lana after the meeting."

The rest of the meeting was mostly business, and it went quickly. When it was over, Matt hung around, telling himself he wanted to talk to Wit, who was striding out of the meeting room like his tail was on fire.

"Greetings, comrade." He heard Bonnie behind him, and turned around, almost bumping into her. "Oops!" she said and then, "Are you okay?"

"Well, I may be working on the assembly line at Grumman Aircraft soon, but other than that, sure, fantastic." She raised her eyebrows questioningly. She was wearing a brown turtleneck sweater that exactly echoed the color of her eyes, and Matt thought how easy it would be to fall into them and stay there. "I, uh, well, there was this protest in the calculus class. We all walked out, but now I've been called to a disciplinary meeting, hearing, about it. So, I don't know what's going to happen. Lana got six months' probation when she was called up for a disciplinary hearing."

"Lana could get herself six months' probation for jaywalking," Bonnie said. "Whereas you can get hit by a car just standing on the corner, at least at this university. I bet that if you just be yourself, they'll invite you to be on the committee."

"There's something else," Matt said. He told Bonnie about Kashman and Randy and Kashman and the Zoomen and the walkouts. "You think he could be organizing these walkouts?"

Bonnie's eyebrows rose. "Wow. Why would he do that? Just to create chaos?" Matt nodded. Bonnie thought for a minute. "What if I just asked him?"

"He'll deny it."

"Only if he's guilty."

"Guilty of what? Improving the quality of teaching?"

"No, I mean if he feels he's doing something wrong, he'll deny it. If he feels he's doing something good, he'll take credit for it."

Matt held his head in his hands. "This spy vs. spy stuff is making my brain ache."

"There is something different about him this year. He seems to have his finger in everything and I am beginning to think not all of it is great. Joe fought his way up and didn't take any prisoners when he was climbing, from what I can tell." Bonnie threw her hands up. "I'll just ask him if he thinks they're being organized. But I need a cover story." Her eyes widened. "When is your hearing?"

"Couple of weeks, November 14. Why?"

"Wow. Great timing. The day before the March. They wouldn't have thought about that. You *are* going to the March?"

"I was going to," Matt said, and Bonnie looked concerned. "But what with this hearing and all . . ."

Bonnie laid a hand on his arm. "I understand. I don't think you have a problem, but that doesn't mean it's easy to cope with. And I think that helps me. Give me a minute." Bonnie walked away and sidled her way into the group around Kashman. Everyone smiled and Matt thought that pretty girls definitely have some advantages in life. She took Kashman aside and had a quiet conversation. He looked up and over at Matt, nodded hello, and then said a few words to Bonnie.

When she came back, she said, very quietly and very quickly, "Kashman said, and I quote, 'Matt's not the organizer . . .'" Matt started to interrupt, but Bonnie talked over him, "which means that if he didn't organize them, he knows who did." It took Matt a minute, but then he understood what Bonnie had done. "And I told him you wanted to go to the March and he said he could help you with the hearing. Which means that he knew about it already."

Matt didn't like the idea that it was being broadcast around the campus, but before he could say anything, Bonnie leaned in and whispered, "He's coming over. Watch your back." Then she stepped back and smiled at him. "I can't watch it for you every second."

"I knew something was missing when I was taking a shower."

Bonnie rolled her eyes. "Look, I don't think you really have a problem with the committee. So there's no point in paying for a slap on the wrist with a big IOU to Joe. That's all I'm saying."

Matt frowned. "I'd like to hear more about that sometime. After this."

"Okay, I'm out of here. See you."

"Sounds good to me." When she turned to go, Matt was reminded that she had been a dancer. Maybe still was. He'd have to ask. Kashman said good night to her a little more loudly than necessary and she waved.

Kashman watched her go and tilted his head, gesturing in Bonnie's direction. "She's a very controlled person. I never really know exactly where I stand with her."

Matt shrugged. "I hardly know her. She helped at registration when there was a mix-up. And she's in one of my classes. With Wit."

Kashman considered this. "Well, she's on your side of the line, that's for sure. Let's go talk in my office for a few minutes."

They walked to an open door that was an office with two desks. One had some papers and a pen on it, the other had a blotter and a desk calendar, but otherwise looked unused. Kashman sat down at that one and motioned for Matt to take the chair next to it. Matt noticed that the calendar was turned to September 3 as Kashman said, "As Polity president, I'm told about most of the actions taken about students, usually before they happen." He grinned. "Not about drug busts, unfortunately." Matt tried to smile back, but it felt like a Halloween mask. "I just wanted to let you know that I can help here. If you want, of course."

"Help? What do you mean?"

"I can put in a good word for you. You know you're allowed to have people speak on your behalf. I can vouch for your character, you being level-headed, like that. And how much you've contributed already to the Polity. What a shame it would be for someone like you to have that black mark on their record. I may even be able to have the whole process disappear from your file."

Matt felt a wave of relief wash over his defensiveness. "Wow. Really? Completely gone? You can really do that?"

"Of course. That's what I'm here for." Kashman looked Matt in the eye and reached out for his hand. "Let them know I'll be weighing in and we'll stomp 'em."

Matt laughed out of sheer relief and shook Kashman's hand energetically. He went back to the dorm hardly noticing how cold it was. He checked his mail, which he now did religiously, and there was a piece of paper, folded over. He opened it up and read, "Friday, November 7. 6 p.m. D-312." Underneath that was an "N." Things were looking up. Now all he had to do was get Mel to come.

Upstairs, he found Mel in Wit's room, sprawled over the one easy chair in the dorm. Wit was sitting cross-legged on his bed, his wrists on his knees. Mel looked up at him nervously and when Matt smiled, Mel's eyebrows shot up. "What's going on?" Wit said in a no-nonsense kind of voice. Mel just looked at Matt.

Matt hesitated. All he had so far about the protests was guesswork. "Well, there's good news and bad news," he started. "I'm just not sure which is which." Matt explained Kashman's offer. "I think that's the good news. I'm grateful, but it just seems kind of off. Everybody says these hearings aren't a big deal. So why is the president of the student body coming to mine?"

"I still think he's a rattlesnake," Mel sneered.

"There's a lot of talk about Joe Kashman," Wit said. "Pro and con."

"I knew it," Mel crowed. Matt thought back to what Bonnie had said, while Mel demanded, "So now it's your turn, Wit. Spill, like you said."

Wit rose out of his chair and started to pace his room, which didn't take very long. Mel had to move his legs out of the way. "I shouldn't have said that," Wit said. "I don't like to talk about people."

"You're going to flake out on us after that tease?"

Wit ran his hand through his short hair and looked frustrated. "It's just that nobody knows exactly who he is. It's like he tells a different story to everyone. Or no, not different, just not exactly the same. He comes from Long Island or maybe the Bronx or Manhattan. I mean, he doesn't say he is from any of these places, but he talks about them like he lived there. His family had money but he wasn't a good student, so he wound up at this new university. Or his family doesn't have any money, but he was a great student. He's not political, but he's president of the Polity. He always seems to have money, but he doesn't have a job. Everyone around him at the Taj does drugs like there's no tomorrow. The Zoo guys are always around him and they instigate a lot of shit on this campus. It's just hard to figure. I don't know if I like the guy or not, because I don't know that I know the guy."

Mel grunted. "So that's the bad part of the good news. What's the good part of the bad news?"

"The bad news is that I'm still rooming with *you*," Matt deadpanned. "The good part is that there's beer left. Race you." They ran back to their room and pulled the beer in from the window ledge, where they stashed things to keep them cold.

They clinked bottles to toast each other. Sitting down on his bed, Matt said, "So . . . you're always trying to get me to introduce you to girls."

"Just one." He took a pull on the beer and sat down across from Matt.

"Well, I know one to introduce you to."

"You're joking." Mel could tell when something was fishy.

"It's like this. You know Nicky, the one you saw after the football game."

"The skinny little blond lollipop. She's all yours."

Matt picked up his baseball. "Well, a little thin, maybe, yeah, but she's got this roommate—" Mel raised one eyebrow. "—and she's premed too, wants to be, and so we're going to have dinner with them on Friday."

"You know I don't eat dinner."

"But it's really—" Matt did a double take. "You don't eat dinner? Of course you—"

"Ha. Gotcha." Mel finished his beer and threw it in the wastebasket. "So what's the roommate like? Is she drop-dead gorgeous? Does she put out?" Matt threw the baseball at him, which Mel caught.

"Okay, I'll do you the favor. But I'm not making any promises." He threw the ball back.

"You won't have to eat that barf food in the dining hall. And you'll be surrounded by girls. Literally. Nicky said her roommate would really like to meet you."

"She did?"

"Well, not in so many words . . ."

"How many words exactly?" He held up a hand. "Never mind. It's cool. But you owe me one."

Matt smiled, thinking he'd have to start a list of the people he owed.

———

The one thing that was going really well for Matt was football. The B-3 team had gelled around Matt. The games were so frantic that it was hard to say that any team was truly disciplined, but the B-3 attack was more coordinated than anyone else. Since there were only seven on a team, blocking was secondary to being able to just keeping moving, and Mel was the fastest player on the field and Wit and Matt were usually the tallest pair. They were 6-0, and the only other team that was undefeated was the Zoo team—even against stronger competition. It was inevitable that the two teams would meet for the championship.

So on top of all Matt's other stomach-churners, now he had to talk to Barry. Barry roomed alone because no one was able to stand living with him. Matt looked in. Barry was hunched over his desk, writing furiously on graph paper. Matt saw columns of numbers beside names; Barry was doing the statistics. The walls of the room were covered with graphs, charts, and lists. The bed and desk that his roommate would have used were covered with notebooks and one or two textbooks. Matt knocked on the doorjamb.

"Yeah," Barry said without looking up.

"Hi, Barry, it's me. Matt." Barry kept on writing, so Matt asked, "You got a minute?"

Barry looked at his watch and asked, "Right now?"

"Um, well, actually yeah, now would be good. I don't want—"

Barry turned around in a rolling swivel chair, obviously not college issued. "Okay, what's up?"

"I just wanted to let you know ahead of time." Matt stuck his hands in the pockets of his jeans. "I'm going to miss the football game on the fifteenth."

"No, you're not," Barry asserted, then frowned at Matt. "Why would you do that?"

"Well, I have this meeting with the, a college committee the day before—"

"I know. They're not going to tar and feather you. Or you can play if they do." He swiveled back to the desk.

Matt took a breath and crossed his arms on his chest. "Well, actually, ah, I'm going to be out of town."

"Why? Is your mother going to die? That's the only reason enough to make you miss the game."

"Oh, yeah, I mean, that would usually be right." Matt hesitated. "But no, not my mother, but a lot of people are dying every day."

"That's their problem, not yours."

Matt realized he had to go all the way. "Actually, I'm going to the march, in Washington." He paused. "D.C."

Barry swiveled back to Matt. "You're not," he said in surprise. Matt nodded emphatically, not trusting his voice. "Well, I'll be damned." Barry got up and went over to one of the charts on the wall. "We're playing I Hall. Buncha pussies. Except that they're five and one. Easiest schedule so far." He thought a minute. "We'll just delay the game until Sunday."

Matt shifted from one foot to the other. "Well, I don't know when I'll really be back. The bus comes back sometime Sunday . . ."

"What about a plane?" Matt just looked at him in amazement until Barry said, "Oh, okay, never mind. Maybe would take too long anyway, the drive from the airport. If you went to the Islip airport—"

"Barry. Can't they just reschedule? I'm sure other people will be going to Washington—"

"Never happen. Every team would have to agree. The Zoo would want our necks. Never agree. Look, just don't go. Why are you going? What's so great about being one of a hundred thousand people tromping around the Mall? You're a standout here."

Matt was beginning to feel a little sick to his stomach. He wasn't used to making choices on principle. "Wit can quarterback. And Mel will be there." His hands wanted to do something and he wished he had his baseball. Until this moment, he hadn't realized that, as much as the team and football gave him a place to stand and to stand out, it was part of a smaller world than the march. "People are going to remember this march for decades. I want to be part of it."

Barry looked at him for a while, then twisted up his mouth, thinking. "You say Wit isn't going? Mel neither?"

"Wit for sure not. Pretty sure Mel isn't going. But I bet other people are going, from other teams. They should just reschedule the whole day."

"Maybe. I've heard some talk among the coaches," Barry muttered. "All right. Have a ball. Don't hurt your arm throwing bombs."

Matt and Mel walked up to the girls' dormitory. Mel stepped on his cigarette and popped a mint into his mouth. "Okay, ready as I'll ever be." The guard at the door, a middle-aged woman about five feet tall and three feet wide, asked Matt and Mel who they were seeing. "Nicole Watkins," Matt said, "and Liz . . ." He realized he didn't know Liz's last name, but it didn't seem to matter. The guard turned around and led them up the stairs to the third floor. When she got to the hallway entry, she called out, "Visitors! Male visitors!"

"Jesus," Mel muttered.

"It's the rules," the guard said. Nicky's head popped out of a door and she told the guard it was okay, she should let them in. Then she stepped out, waving them in, and said, "Hi! Come on! No one, absolutely no one, bites." She was wearing grey pants that were like overalls but only came up to her waist, and a black turtleneck that made her hair look blonder than ever and big shiny bangle earrings.

Nicky showed them into her room. "Wow," Mel said. "Looks like home." They had actual curtains on the windows and spreads on the beds. One of the beds had a beat-up plush dog and the other had a doll that looked about as old as its owner. One poster was of Mick Jagger and the other was evidently about some French nightclub that probably didn't exist anymore. There were four folding TV tables sitting in between the beds and a chair on the ends. Inevitably, James Taylor was singing about going to Carolina. An electric skillet was snickering on one of the desks, flanked by an electric pot.

"This is Liz, and Liz is the cook," Nicky said. "Otherwise you guys might not survive the evening." Liz was taller and darker and fuller than Nicky, with a head of dark brown, very curly hair. She and Mel could look each other directly in the eye. Matt introduced Mel, and Liz said to him, "Nice to meet you. I have to say, I'm glad you're not as tall as Matt."

"I move a lot faster, though," Mel said.

Liz flung up her hands, palms flat. "Watch it, I know karate," she said, with exaggerated seriousness. Mel looked sheepish.

"He didn't mean it that way," Matt said.

"It's just because we're on the football team and I'm the halfback, so I run a lot, open up the defense . . ." He gave up, realizing it wasn't getting better.

Liz laughed and said, "Yeah, but Matt's the one making passes." Everyone relaxed a little. Liz said, "It's okay, Mel, I've actually seen you play and you *are* a lot faster." Mel was obviously pleased that she'd seen him play.

"I drag her to the games," Nicky said, "kicking and screaming. You should see the bruises I have." They leaned into each other, giggling.

"It's really a great bunch of guys," Matt said.

"Kind of like a team." Mel held out a palm for Matt to slap. "Mucho thanks to this guy."

"I wish there were more sports for girls," Liz said. "I mean, field hockey, for heaven's sake."

"Yeah, not yet an Olympic sport."

"Neither is football," Liz pointed out.

"What's for dinner?" Matt asked, a little worried that it would be something exotic that he wouldn't like.

"Chicken fricassee," Liz said, lifting the skillet's lid, "with corn and peas." She poked at the skillet's contents with a wooden spoon and then pointed to the pot with it. "And brown rice."

Matt said with relief that it sounded great, even if he'd never had brown rice, and Mel pulled the six-pack out of its bag. There was already water and hot tea. Mel was amazed that they could cook actual meals in their room.

Liz looked at the chicken again. "We're almost ready here. Sit."

Nicky pointed Mel to the farthest chair and Matt to the bed with the plush dog. "Matt, you can sit next to Roger. He is very good company. I know because I've had him since I was four." Liz sat on the bed with the doll, and Nicky put rice and chicken on stiff paper plates and served everyone. She sat nearest the door and Matt noticed there was less on her plate than anyone else's. There were plastic cups for the beer and smaller ones for the water that Liz and Nicky were drinking. Nicky raised her cup and said, "Here's to hungry pirates," then explained the joke of it for Mel's benefit, while Liz added color commentary about what it was like to study with Nicky.

"She's like a four-year-old. More questions than a quiz show. 'Why is pee yellow?'"

"That's what you get for asking a future English major to help you study biology," Nicky said. Mel started to explain exactly why urine was yellow, and Nicky said, "Can we switch to fart jokes now? Or, Mel, where are you from?" They exchanged family stories for a while and ate. About every ten minutes, one girl or another would pop her head in and say, "Hi! Oh! You've got company," and Liz or Nicky would introduce the guys. After a few more practiced sentences, the girl would leave. After a while, Mel started to keep score. The music changed, got a little darker. It was a song about a guy who loved his dog as much as his girlfriend.

"Who's this?" Mel asked.

"His name is Cat Stevens," Nicky said. "Amazing guitar player. He could be as big as Paul McCartney."

"Put on *Abbey Road* after this, okay?"

Nicky put her hands together and bowed over them. Matt asked Nicky what she'd done on the day of the Moratorium, and she said she'd stayed in the room mostly and read Camus. "I'm in love with Camus," she said, her eyes sparkling. "I think he's the bravest man. He wasn't afraid to wonder whether life has any meaning." That quieted everybody and Nicky hurried to change the subject. "You know that he lived through a war, like Vietnam. I think that's why we're all looking for new ways to live and do things, because of the war. It makes you think. I really admire all the people who are protesting." She closed her eyes and shook her head. "I can't do it, but that doesn't mean I don't think it's important."

Liz talked about going to a teach-in about medical advances in the Vietnam War, and after his second beer, Matt mentioned that he was thinking of going to the March on Washington.

"Really?" Mel was amazed. "You're going to miss the game?"

"I already talked to Barry about it," Matt said defensively. "It just seems important. It seems like it's going to be a real event that people will remember. The Polity arranged for a bus—a lot of buses, evidently—to take people down there and back. I just kind of wondered what it would be like." Mel wanted the particulars about where he'd eat and sleep and what he'd do. Matt worried he'd ask who else was going, but he didn't.

Nicky shuddered. "I think that's great, Matt. I wish I could. Just my own special, personal brand of paranoia. I don't want the war to go on or you guys to have to fight in Vietnam, but I just can't imagine being trapped in a huge crowd like that. All those people and communal living makes me feel claustrophobic." She smiled at Matt, but he thought there was a haunted look in her eyes that she tried to blink away. It made him think about a television special his sister Amy had made everybody watch. It was about Twiggy, the incredibly thin English model who had taken the fashion world by storm. But there was a shot of her toward the end of the show where she was being shepherded through a crowd by her manager and bodyguards and entourage. She turned to the camera for a second looking panicked, terrified even. Nicky's face was a different shape, heart-shaped, but there was something the same in the look.

The dinner over, the conversation slowly came to a natural close. Matt noticed that Nicky mostly moved her food around the plate, and he asked her if she wasn't hungry. After a while she had shifted over to the bed "to take care of Roger" and sit next to Matt. He asked if she had had enough to eat.

"Oh, I'm just stuffed. I had plenty," she said. "There are a couple of legs left over, though. You want them?" Mel said they would absolutely find a good home at B-3 and then said he had to go to the john. Liz said she'd guard the door while he went down the hall.

Matt stood up and stretched. "I had a great evening, Nicky, thanks."

Nicky stood up on the bed. "Now you'll have the strength to fight down those disciplinary jerks. I know you'll be great." She walked on the bed until she was standing facing Matt. "I'm as tall as you are," she smiled.

"Taller, even."

She put her arms around his neck and kissed him. "And faster," she whispered.

Matt said, "I need to work out more." He put his arms around her and kissed her back. When he didn't stop, she wrapped one leg around him, and then the other. His arms went completely around her body and he thought he could count each rib. It took him a minute to realize how light she was because his mind was elsewhere, but eventually she slid down him and put her feet back on the floor. They heard Liz and Mel talking in the hall, saying good night.

"That was an out-of-body experience," Nicky said, and leaned against him.

"Careful," Matt said, worried that there was barely enough of her already. "I'd like to keep all of you in one piece." He put his arms around her again.

"Doing my best," she said and smiled hopefully up at him.

"You about ready, Ribs?" Mel said at the doorway. Nicky quickly let go of Matt.

"I'm fantastic," Matt said, and Mel rolled his eyes and started to walk down the hall. Matt said thanks again to Liz and to Nicky. "See you next week in class?"

Nicky nodded happily. "Good luck next week, with, you know," she said. Matt crossed both fingers on both hands and Nicky did too, then blew him a kiss with the right ones.

On the way back to the dorm, Mel said, "Three blondes, four brunettes, and one African American girl."

"Liz seemed cool," Matt said.

"Yeah, guess so," Mel answered. "Did Nicky get a lick? That girl really needs some nourishment."

11

MATT MEANDERED down the hall of the administration building, looking at the numbers above the doors and hoping they didn't go as high as 220, where he was supposed to appear for the disciplinary hearing. He wondered why buildings don't skip the number thirteen for rooms the way they do for floors. If they did then, wouldn't room 220 really be room 219? *Did I pass room 213?* He was trying to remember when he heard his name called out.

"Mr. Aymer? Are you looking for us?" Mrs. Devin was sitting in a room at the end of a big table, flanked by two men. "We are the disciplinary review committee." Matt, frozen in place, nodded. Mrs. Devin waited a beat, then said, "Please come in."

Matt walked in and took a chair at the foot of the table. He'd brought his baseball in the pocket of his parka, and he shoved a hand in the pocket and gave it a squeeze. The faculty members looked far away. The room was basically featureless except for the table and an ashtray. There was a green board, blank, behind Mrs. Devin, who was at the head of the table. Although she was noticeably shorter and smaller than the two men, they both looked to her to take charge. The room was cold, and Matt shivered. "I do apologize for the temperature of the room," Mrs. Devin said sincerely. "It's a cold day for November, and we don't use this room all that often." Matt nodded again. "But I don't think we'll be here long."

Matt couldn't decide whether this was good news or bad, but he started the defense that he'd turned over in his head about a thousand times. "First of all," he said, "I didn't—"

Mrs. Devin held up a hand. "Excuse me, Mr. Aymer, we have some formalities required of us, and since they are for your benefit, let me recount them." Matt nodded again, and Mrs. Devin explained the purpose of the hearing, that Mr. Forsythe (on her right) would take minutes, and Mr. Reynolds (on her left) would witness them, as would she. She said that everything Matt said was confidential, and that they were not there to mete out judgment, as she put it, but simply to gather facts. She asked if that was agreeable to him.

Matt nodded again, and said, "I didn't really—"

Mrs. Devin held up a hand again. "If you'll allow me just a few more minutes, I'll finish my remarks and then you may speak. Is that agreeable to you?" Matt nodded again, keeping a tight grip on the baseball. "What brings us together today is that one of Montauk's students has anonymously told the dean's office that you were responsible for instigating a walkout of Professor Wolf's class on October 15."

"I didn't start it," Matt protested, "I—"

"We know," Mrs. Devin said.

"—walked out when everybody . . . You know?"

"Yes," Mrs. Devin smiled indulgently. "Professor Wolf has confirmed that it was not you who instigated the walkout, but another student. Isn't that correct, Mr. Reynolds?"

"Affirmative," Mr. Reynolds affirmed. He adjusted his horn-rimmed glasses.

"Then," Matt began, but stopped to think what he was going to say.

"Moreover," Mrs. Devin picked up a piece of paper, "Student Polity President Kashman has written a quite . . . glowing letter on your behalf, praising your responsible nature, regard for your fellow students, and—as he put it—'all-around cool.'"

"Oh." Matt could feel himself turning red. "That's great."

"Yes. Nonetheless," Mrs. Devin continued, "a walkout by an entire class is a notable event, and not one that we can condone. However, we do not consider it an event requiring discipline, or even a memo to the files. Everyone in the class will receive a letter warning that repeated events of a similar nature might well result in disciplinary action, but no such action will be taken at this time."

Matt sat back. Then he sat forward again, and said, "That's great, but if you're not going to do anything, why . . . I mean, excuse me, but what am I doing here?" Matt was getting a lot warmer. "Is anybody else from the class being called in? This was, you know, not a lot of fun to look forward to." He sat back and folded his arms.

It was Mrs. Devin's turn to nod, pursing her thin lips. "Yes, and I regret that, Mr. Aymer. To answer your question, no one else is being called, but that is because you were the only student singled out by name."

"Anonymously," Matt said truculently.

"Yes, that is correct. We do want to hear your version of events, however."

Matt went on to describe how another student was incensed by the poor teaching and that ultimately led to that student walking out with the whole class following. Matt had no idea why he was singled out. He didn't mention the other student's name.

Mrs. Devin thanked him for his summary and then said, "That brings me to the second reason we wanted to have this hearing. That reason, however, need not take up the time of Mr. Forsythe and Mr. Reynolds." She turned to one and then the other, and said, "Mr. Forsythe, if you will write these minutes up for my signature in your admirably brief fashion, I would appreciate it." He nodded and smiled. "Gentlemen, thank you both for your time." They rose and left without adding to the single word they had spoken. Mrs. Devin rose from her chair, so Matt did too, but she just walked to his end of the table.

"Mr. Aymer, if I could have just one more minute of your time. Please, sit down again. Unless you'd prefer to do jumping jacks or the like to keep warm."

Matt sat down again, as did Mrs. Devin, who then leaned forward and placed a hand on the table. "Mr. Aymer, I think perhaps the more important part of this meeting is that I'd like to pose a question to you that you should not answer. It is not, however, a rhetorical question." She paused.

"Oh," Matt said. It took him a minute to fit together each part of those sentences. Then he took a breath and let it out. "Okaaay."

She looked Matt in the eye. "Do you think you have any enemies on campus?"

Matt's eyes widened and he shook his head to make sure he'd heard right. "Enemies?" he said.

Mrs. Devin waved a hand. "I don't mean to suggest that you are in physical danger, but as I look at this sequence of events—an accusation so easily disproven, submitted anonymously, this curious letter from the student president—"

"But it was a good letter, right? I mean, said nice things."

Mrs. Devin sat up straight and cocked her head. "Yes, a good letter, but rather unusual for Mr. Kashman to become involved in something that he had to know was . . . ," she paused and slid her eyes toward the door. "You did not hear this from me, if you know what I mean." Matt nodded energetically, putting a fastball grip on his baseball. "He had to know this hearing was inconsequential, yet he felt the need to sit down and write a letter on your behalf." She drummed her fingers on the table. "You'll pardon me for sounding like a JFK conspiracy theorist, but these events suggest to me that there is something going on behind the scenes, so to speak. That someone is making an effort to make your life difficult in a way that brings you to the attention of the university. That someone, in brief, is setting you up for reason or reasons unknown." She looked at him.

Matt was dumbfounded at the idea. He opened his mouth but nothing came out and Mrs. Devin continued talking anyway.

"No, I don't want you to name a name. I don't want you to accuse anyone, and I hope I don't make you look over your shoulder. What I do want is for you to be aware that not everything that happens to you is a, your fault, or b, in your best interest."

Matt felt strange, as if he'd walked into the wrong room, or someone else's life. "Um, it's a little hard for me to believe that somebody's out to get me." His mind raced. *It doesn't have to be Kashman. Could it be the Zoo wanting to get rid of B-3's quarterback? Randy trying to put the focus on me for the walkout? He probably still hates me.*

Mrs. Devin smiled. "I hope that you are right and I am wrong. But from what I have heard, you have—by accident or inclination—" Matt waved his hands no, but Mrs. Devin just repeated, "by accident or inclination, found yourself in the public eye. Whenever that happens, it will have good repercussions and bad. Not 'could have' or 'might have' but 'will have.' That is all I can say now."

Matt thought about this. Mrs. Devin was saying he'd better get control of his life. She stood up, but Matt said, "Just, if you don't mind, there's just something I wanted to say." Mrs. Devin nodded and sat down, crossing one leg over the other. The crease in her slacks was razor sharp. Matt cleared his throat. "Professor Wolf, he's not, you know, like not a great teacher. When R—"

"No names," Mrs. Devin warned, waving one finger.

"When the class walked out, it was because no one was learning anything. We just wanted a chance to learn the damn material."

"Excuse me," Mrs. Devin interjected. "How did it feel? Walking out."

Matt was surprised at the question, and he thought back. "It felt strange. I felt like a cheat. I mean, it was powerful, but it felt like we were cheating. But it seemed like the only way we were going to get the point across to Wolf, Professor Wolf."

"And did it work? Did you get your point across?"

Matt thought about this for a minute. "Well, yes and no, I guess. I think our walkout was the reason other students walked out of classes a few days later. But, really no. I am not sure what we actually accomplished. He gave us a test the next week. On material we hadn't even covered. I don't think most people did very well."

Mrs. Devin raised her eyebrows. "I see," she said, although Matt wasn't sure what she saw. "Thank you. Mr. Aymer, please put all this behind you now. Draw from the incident—the whole of the incident—what you can and move on. Thank you for coming and good luck with everything." She stood and Matt quickly stood up too. "Are you going to Washington tomorrow?" she asked.

"Yeah, I guess so, now that this is done."

"Well—and again, you didn't hear this from me—give Nixon the finger on my behalf. You know, Matt, why don't you stop by my office sometime and fill me in? I would like to also continue this discussion if you would like to do so as well." With that she left the room.

Matt was relieved and puzzled at the same time. He left the building to go back to his room but decided to stop by Nicky's dorm. She was out, the matron said, but said Matt could leave a note. She gave him a little piece of paper and a chewed-up pencil. He wrote, "The almost Ides of November have passed with no wounds. Thanks for dinner and everything. See you next week, I hope." And he signed it "M" and thought how they made consecutive letters, *M* and *N*. He liked that thought.

———————

"So what happens at a peace march?"

The bus wasn't exactly as comfortable as Bonnie had advertised, but Matt was on a high after the disciplinary hearing. Not that he wasn't bothered by Mrs. Devin's warning, but the farther the bus went, the farther away the problem seemed. He was sitting at a window seat with Dorman next to him and Bonnie in the aisle seat across. A girl named Annette sat beside her in the window seat. Matt had tried to get the aisle seat but Dorman already had it. Beth and Lana were sitting together a few seats up and Chaz and Jones were near them. Kingman was carrying a sign that said "Free Bobby Seale," which was different from the other signs, which were mostly about the war. Jack Appel was sitting with a clipboard, complaining that the bus trip on top of the preparations for the draft lottery was making his life hell. It was obvious that he was loving it. The bus wasn't completely full but there were enough people to make it loud, and Chaz was playing a guitar, "The Times They Are a-Changin'," and some people were singing along.

"What do we do? We be," Dorman said.

"What?"

"We be—we be peaceful, we be outraged, we be there," Dorman said as if that explained everything.

Bonnie looked over and smiled. "Actually," she said, "that's sort of right. There'll be speakers and I think that some folk singers will be there. Dave Dellinger. Dr. Spock."

"So we stand around and listen to people talk? And sing?" Matt laughed uncertainly. He was beginning to wonder what it was really all about. He didn't know the first person Bonnie had named and that the famous baby doctor was a big anti-war guy seemed weird.

"It's kind of hard to explain if you haven't done it," Bonnie said. "Do you remember the big civil rights march a few years ago?"

Matt had only been eleven. "Yeah, kinda. Where King spoke?" He was proud of himself that he remembered that much.

Bonnie looked off into the distance. "I thought it was thrilling. So many people, all kinds of people, all thinking the same thing, doing the same thing. We go there to join with thousands of other people to show the government and the country that opposition to the war isn't just from 'radicals'—" she added the air quotes, "—or minorities who are disproportionately fighting the war, but from all kinds of people—younger, older, white, Black, Latino, mothers, fathers—all kinds of people."

"Not to mention draft-age kids of all makes and models," Dorman added.

"Wit thinks it's pointless," Matt said, "he said the government's going to do whatever it wants with the bodies of its people. Always has, always will. We did just elect Nixon, after all. Isn't voting how we're supposed to show how we feel?"

Lana came up as Matt was making his case. "If Nixon and Johnson and the military machine were telling us the truth, the vote would have real meaning. But they have lied to us from the beginning, saying that this is the war against communism."

Bonnie nodded. "Martin Luther King said, 'Freedom is the bonus you receive for telling the truth.'"

"I feel like I'm on a quiz show," Matt said, "and I'm losing."

"Anyway," Dorman said, "Nixon only won by point oh seven percent of the we-the-people. Five hundred thousand votes more than Humphrey. I'd say that's not exactly a landslide victory."

"And Humphrey was gaining ground all the fall," Bonnie pointed out. She sighed. "I just wish McCarthy hadn't waited so long to endorse him. And then do it so half-heartedly." Matt could never figure out Gene McCarthy. He seemed to be winning and then he wasn't. He seemed to be the hero and then he'd step back. Then with Bobby Kennedy shot and McCarthy sulking, McGovern just seemed to confuse things more.

"Yeah, I thought McCarthy was kind of an asshole about that," Annette threw in. "Poor Bobby. He would have won. God, that was a horrible night."

"Why did that guy shoot him anyway?" Matt asked. "I was never really clear about that. Or why he had two names the same."

"It was about Israel," Bonnie said. "Sirhan Sirhan was an Arab and he objected to Kennedy's support of Israel. The funny thing was that he was a Christian. I think he was a little off his rocker. First he said he was guilty, then that he wasn't. Then he asked to be executed."

"If we could have voted, Humphrey would have won," Annette said.

Dorman snorted. "I could never vote for that marshmallow man. He's like my father, full of hot air. We're voting with our bodies now because we don't get a chance until next election."

"Not me," Matt said. "I won't be twenty-one. I miss it by two months."

"They're talking about lowering the voting age to eighteen," Bonnie said, "you might be able to yet."

They were quiet for a few miles. Dorman said they were passing Philadelphia. Then, "I'm going to see if that guy knows more than two chords." He got up and went to Chaz's seat and began to talk to him. Bonnie reached over and grabbed the arm of Dorman's seat. "Move over here. Tell me about the hearing."

Matt moved over, glad to have the chance to stretch his legs out. "It was kind of a non-event. It was what happened after *that* was mind-boggling." He told Bonnie about Mrs. Devin's warning. "It was like being in a spy novel."

Bonnie breathed in sharply. "She's pretty sharp to put all that together. I don't know what game Kashman could be playing though." She thought for a minute, pulling on a strand of hair and chewing on it. "Is it driving you up a wall?"

She looked so concerned that Matt thought that maybe he wasn't understanding his situation. Then he shook his head. "I haven't had much time to think about it. But no, not really. Kashman has always been friendly to me. It could be someone else, maybe it's football related, say from the Zoo for example. I wonder what kind of person would cook up a scheme about me."

"When I was in high school," Bonnie said, "this other girl decided she hated me. She was always spreading rumors about me, lies, bad-mouthing me. I finally asked her what gives. She called me conceited and mean and all sorts of things that amazed me. I'd barely ever even spoken to her. She'd created this person she thought was me. For a while I was really worried that that was how I came off to other people."

"No, just the opposite really. You're smart and thoughtful and . . ." He caught himself short of saying "beautiful."

Bonnie frowned. "And what? You were doing so well, don't stop there." The bus bounced across some potholes and Bonnie's coffee came out of the cupholder. She caught it.

"And you have quick hands."

"That's not what you were going to say."

"I was going to say that you have so many good qualities that that girl couldn't stand it, so she made up all those lies about you to make herself feel better."

"All right, people, listen up!" Jack Appel stood up at the front of the bus. The guitar quieted. "Okay, first thing." He paused and looked up and down the rows of seats. "I'm really proud of you for being here. The future of the country depends on you." There was a little nervous laughter. "No, I'm serious," he protested. "Whether you're against the war or just wanted a trip to Washington, you will be the backbone of the country in a few years. I think if you're here, you're the kind of people who care about where the country stands then."

Jack went on for a few minutes, about where they'd stay and when they'd go to the March. He pulled a bunch of bandanas out of a bag on the seat next to him. "I want everybody to take one of these and keep it with you at all times."

"So fashionable," Lana said sarcastically.

"Maybe not," Jack said, "but useful when there's tear gas. What you have to do is wet the bandana a little and tie it around your head so that it covers your nose and your mouth."

"And try not to breathe, I guess," Matt said, a little worried at what he was getting into. Even apart from Chicago last summer, there had been violent demonstrations on campuses around the country. The police were jumpy. Sometimes the National Guard was called out.

"But don't worry," Jack said. "All of the organizers want this to be the parade for peace. So we shouldn't have to fight the pigs. But still, they'll be out there and they'll be ready to beat us down. Remember Chicago!"

"Free Bobby Seale!" Kingman said.

"Right on," Jack agreed.

Matt had heard enough that he knew Bobby Seale was a Black American who was one of the Chicago Eight, and that they'd chained him to the witness chair and put tape over his mouth because he talked too much and then tried him separately so that the Chicago Eight became the Chicago Seven. In fact, from what he could tell from Dorman, they all talked too much. Dorman had somehow found out that the PoliSci department was showing clips from the trial. He said he watched them for hours. It was really kind of crazy. They talked during the trial. They wouldn't stop talking. Abbie Hoffman did a radio show at night after the trial. No one was supposed to do that. It just kind of turned all the rules on their head. That was why the judge, who was a really, really buttoned-down, stone-faced kind of guy even for a judge, got mad at them. But somehow, chaining a guy to a witness chair didn't seem like it could make for a fair trial.

Dorman came back. "I got him to update from folk music to Buffalo Springfield. Like the song says, battle lines being drawn." Annette said that Bob Dylan wasn't exactly folk music and Dorman retorted, "My ears were saying 'folk music' and they are never wrong." He waited for Matt to move, but Matt pointed out that he needed the aisle seat for his legs. Dorman looked from him to Bonnie and nodded. "Leg room, yeah. Okay, move 'em so I can get in. I prefer the window seat anyway." He plopped down in the seat and said, "Kingman says that troops are being flown in. Nine thousand soldiers." Matt made a face. Dorman said, "Oh, they probably won't have live ammunition. It's more about crowd control."

Matt was worried. "Um, do you think we'll get jailed?"

"Matt," Dorman soothed, "you have to give up this idea of control. It's only an experience. After that experience, you'll have other experiences. Ask yourself, What's the worst that can happen? That you'll spend a night in jail?"

"That my parents kill me."

"Apart from that. First of all, there are going to be a million people there. Are the pigs going to arrest every one of them? No. Suppose you annoy them and they lock you up. Do you think the pigs are going to call home? No. You'll sleep the night in the jail, they'll let you out in the morning and you'll go home. Back to school."

"Dorman, you are not reassuring me. Have you ever been arrested?"

He thought for a minute. "Not for doing anything moral and honest like this, no." He went on to describe what sounded like a horrific night when he had his parents' car and was higher than the moon. The police stopped him, took one look, and locked him up for his own safety to sleep it off. Matt had nothing he could compare that to. He looked over at Bonnie, who seemed to be sleeping. He watched her for a minute. He tried on the idea of being a revolutionary. Bonnie opened her eyes, looked around, then at Matt, and smiled.

"I was just thinking," Matt said, "about George Washington and Thomas Jefferson and those guys. Taking a bus to go to a demonstration. Whether they worried about getting arrested."

"They were tall, like you. Their legs would stick out into the aisle too."

"They were lucky, they had horses then. But when you think about it, they did kind of the same thing."

"Jefferson and Washington lived in the country. Sort of a different world. But the Adams cousins would have. Gone to demonstrations, I mean."

"And worried about getting shot."

"I think you're right."

"Probably not about whether there'd be portable toilets."

"I think you're right again."

Eventually they got to Washington and the Methodist church where they were staying. It was late evening. They unloaded backpacks and such off the bus and took stock of where they were going to spend the night. It was strange, sleeping with about a hundred other people, but also thinking that even though you didn't know them, they were all there for the same thing. "Kind of like Disneyland, but with politics," Matt said to no one in particular, thinking that Mel would have liked that.

"Disneyland is politics," Jack said. Even Bonnie rolled her eyes. There were quiet conversations that came and went, as if it were just one conversation that traveled around the church basement randomly. Lana said she would look terrible in the morning and told Beth not to look at her then. Jack went over and over the schedule for the next day until Chaz told him to shut up already. Gradually everybody settled down.

"Did you ever go to camp, Bonnie?"

She laughed quietly. "I did. A bunch of times. But the last one was maybe the biggest mistake my parents ever made."

"How so?"

"I don't know how it happened, but they sent me to this camp in New Jersey that was run by a socialist."

"Wow. Were you forced to harvest crops and eat gruel?"

"No, dork, not a Stalinist, a socialist. He believed that everyone was equal. He even had Black people at the camp. I'm not sure my parents knew that. But it was a strange combination of leaving you free and taking care of you. Of how you felt."

"Like you're actually a human being."

He could see her smile in the dim light. "Exactly. It was the first time I realized that I was an independent person separate from my parents."

"Sounds dangerous."

"Beginning of the end."

"How old were you?"

"Twelve. I loved that place."

"Did you go back?"

"No. I begged to go back, but they said I was too old for camp now and I could take tennis lessons that next summer."

"And piano lessons."

"And piano lessons." She was quiet. "And you? Did you go to camp?"

"I went to baseball camp a couple of times. What I remember was about being aware of the people you were with, becoming part of something bigger."

Dorman said, "Do I get to tell you about my summer camp, or shall we get some sleep?"

"Dorman," Matt growled, "take a pill."

"I did. Several. Want one?"

"If I had a pillow," Bonnie said, "I'd throw it at you."

"Good night, Matt. Good night, beautiful."

"I have a pillow and I'm throwing it at you."

———————

Much later, Matt woke up, maybe like three in the morning. The church was dark and his watch was in his duffel bag so he couldn't be sure. He didn't feel like sleeping anymore, so he quietly got up, eyes all groggy, and walked to the door of the church, which led to a big entryway. Streetlights gave it a cool illumination. To his surprise, he saw Bonnie curled up in the corner of the entryway, serene and into her thoughts.

"Bonnie," he whispered, "are you okay? Want some company?" She didn't say anything but motioned to him to sit beside her. He sat against the wall next to her. "Are you okay? Couldn't sleep?"

"I guess I'm okay," she said not very reassuringly, looking out onto the empty street.

Matt was surprised to see her not so cool and in control. "It's not the March, is it?"

She shook her head. "No, I'm actually looking forward to tomorrow. But it's the war, our country, Black against white—and don't get me started on women's rights." They heard a noise like something out of a movie and a few minutes later two mounted policemen trotted down the street. They both involuntarily shrank back into the shadows.

"Before we left this morning," Bonnie said, "my parents called and told me that Johnny Stivers, a guy I knew, died in Vietnam last week. He," she choked back tears, "he really wanted to serve. He was . . ." She broke off and cried softly for a while, her head in her arms on her knees.

Matt realized, "He was your boyfriend."

She raised her head a little and nodded. "When he left, we said that we . . . that nothing was certain. He said he loved me, but he couldn't promise . . ." She trailed off again, then said, "Anything."

"Oh, god, Bonnie, that's awful. I'm so sorry." Matt wanted to hug her, but didn't know if it was right. He put a hand on her arm and she laid her head on it, then picked it up.

"What was he doing in Vietnam at the age of twenty?" she said fiercely. "Did he believe the BS that he was fighting to keep communism from spreading? He didn't have to die. The thought of it makes me so angry, I could scream." Matt could see tears on her cheek shimmer in the dim light.

"Bonnie, that's why we're here, isn't it? We have to do something. I have to admit that before I came to Montauk, I didn't have a deep thought—I was into myself. Now I don't recognize myself anymore—and that's good. There are things I know I don't understand. I mean, I never understood them, but now at least I *know* that I don't." Bonnie turned her face to him, asking for more. "Bad things happen to good people. Why? Is it just fate, is it just random? If I follow all the moral rules, do I stop bad things from happening?" Bonnie started to say something, but Matt held up a hand. "Beating yourself up won't do any good. We learn from the good and probably even more from the bad and we need to move on."

He stopped for a minute and Bonnie started, "Matt, I know that ..."

"And you're one of the great things. I've learned so much from you." Bonnie turned her face to him and he could see another tear sliding slowly down her cheek, but he kept on. "Anything I can do to be a partner with you in taking some kind of action, I will. We just learned we all need to unite."

Bonnie looked away again, very serious. "Matt, I'm so glad you didn't try to tell me that everything would be okay, to patronize me that easy way. You're genuinely you. You don't try to be someone you are not. That's what the existentialists admire, you know—authenticity."

Matt held up his hands. "I guess I just can't help myself."

Bonnie started to laugh. "You just can't stop yourself from being yourself, can you? That first day I met you, when you talked the table-jumper off the ledge, something hit me about you. Your sense of right and wrong and your genuineness. That's why people love you."

Matt shrugged. "It's a curse."

"We'll just have to live with it." She leaned over and kissed him on the cheek.

"I'll never wash my cheek again."

She pulled herself up on her knees and pointed a finger at him. "You're assuming I'll never do it again. Beware of false premises." She punched him playfully in the arm and said, "Let's get some more sleep."

12

THEY GOT A FEW more hours of sleep and woke up achy and excited. They got some breakfast on the way—there were carts all over the place—coffee and a bear claw for Matt, herbal tea and a cream cheese bagel for Bonnie, hot chocolate and three glazed donuts for Dorman. "I need an energy boost," he explained. Matt said he'd never had tea, and Bonnie said she'd just discovered how many different kinds of teas there were, but coffee was just always coffee and usually pretty bad. As they walked toward the Mall, they joined the stream of people going the same direction. "It's like going to a World Series game," Matt said. "Only more so."

They could see that all the neighboring streets were just as crowded. There were hundreds of signs. Other people had guitars or small drums. There was what looked like part of a college marching band, with trumpets and trombones and a bass drum. Three people were dressed up like the famous picture—a boy with a drum and an old guy also with a drum and a third guy with a bloody bandage on his head playing a flute. "A fife," Bonnie corrected.

It was cold but sunny, a beautiful fall day. The crisp air was energizing, along with the electricity of the people. Everyone seemed to feel it as they gathered around the Washington Monument. Chaz looked up and said, "You know, that thing's pretty cool." Already people lined the hill.

The speeches seemed to go on and on, but they were interrupted by the singers—Peter, Paul, and Mary, Arlo Guthrie, the cast of *Hair*.

They sang songs everybody knew or could get into one way or another, humming, dancing, or just swaying to the music. Dr. Spock spoke, but no one could remember exactly what he said except everybody cheered every sentence.

Matt hadn't actually listened to most of the speeches, partly because Bonnie was filling him in about the history of the Vietnam War. Ho Chi Minh—who had just died—came to the United States for help in gaining independence from the French, but the French were U.S. allies and President Truman kind of ignored Ho's letter and so he went to the Communists. The Vietnamese actually hated the Chinese because the Chinese had subjugated them for hundreds or thousands of years. But China wanted to help the war because they didn't want Russia to become allies of the Vietnamese and get a foothold in Southeast Asia. At least partly. Matt got a little confused here. And then there was all the infighting among the South Vietnamese and the influence of the American military and President Eisenhower had warned against the military-industrial complex, which was somehow part of the buildup.

"Bonnie, you know way too much about all this stuff," he'd said, joking. They were lying on the grass during a break in the program. There were a lot of breaks. It seemed like it was hard to organize all the different factions that had combined to put the march together.

"That," she said, "depends on your point of view."

"You could teach a course in it."

"I don't want to teach," she said with a fierce toss of her head. "I want to do it. I want to be a diplomat."

Matt had never thought of being such a thing. "Is that hard to do?" Dorman was dancing with Lana and Beth to "Hair," which Lana was especially fitted for. Her long black hair looked like a flag. Matt was afraid Dorman would break his neck, he was waving it around so much.

"Sort of. You have to take like a nine-hour test and be interviewed here in D.C., and I don't know what else. The whole diplomatic corps is a male chauvinist institution. But we're going to change that."

"We?"

"Women."

"The revolution, huh?"

Bonnie pursed her lips and frowned. "I don't see why it's a revolution in America to have equality."

Matt looked at her for a while. Then he said, "I didn't mean it. I mean, I meant it as a joke."

Bonnie looked back at him with an expression he couldn't decipher. "I understand, but too many people think it's just a joke." She looked back up at the sky. The wind had picked up and the clouds were moving fast. "Anyway, diplomats can make a difference. They can help people."

"You want to work within the system." It was the big debate, whether you could change things from within or you just had to break it and start something different. "Oh, it's great to work for individual projects—" She stopped. "Do you know what an NGO is?"

"Um. National Grievance Organization?"

"Never mind. Anyway. Diplomats are like people-to-people demonstrations." She was practically shining with excitement. "They can urge, they can suggest, sometimes they can even coerce other countries. But it's about person to person. I want to make a difference that way, person to person." She smiled a little, then looked away, as if she'd said more than she meant to.

They were silent for a moment. Matt finally said, "I think that you'd be good at that. Person to person."

She looked away, then back and with a half-smile. "You're not so bad yourself." They both looked up at the sky, which was getting a little shading on the eastern side. The mid-November light was fading. After a few more songs, she said to him, "I've been thinking."

"Wait a minute, you're getting ahead of me. It's my shift for thinking."

"Okay." She waited, looking at him. Her huge brown eyes looked almost black. She waited some more.

"Okay, okay," Matt said, "I'm done. You take the wheel."

"Mrs. Devin thinks Joe is using you. Or something."

Matt almost laughed. "You're . . ." He stopped just short of saying "crazy" and instead managed, ". . . kidding. He was helping me out."

"But he was helping you out when he didn't *need* to. You would have been fine. And he knew that. He didn't need to write a letter for you. He didn't need to do anything. You would have been fine."

"But why? I'm just a freshman. What could he . . ." Matt couldn't even finish the sentence.

"Matt, he . . . ," she hesitated. "It's like he collects people. You've seen that gang that hangs around him."

"Yeah but why would he want to collect me?"

"Matt . . . ," her mouth twisted a little, as if she didn't want to say the next thing. Finally she said quietly and very quickly, "You've got something that people like."

Matt didn't know how to take this and looked at the stage. A skinny guy who was old, but younger than Spock, came on with a guitar and started to talk. "That's Pete Seeger," Appel said. At first no one could hear him because he had kind of a reedy voice. He even joked about his voice, that if he could sing, all of the people there could sing too, and that's what he wanted them to do.

He told a story about America and how it was built on moments like this when people came together to make their government into the government they needed. "And what we need now is for the government to listen to us. So you all need to sing. It's a simple song, you all know it. It's by that fella John Lennon—not the other Lenin, the musical Lennon. So here goes and you join in now."

He launched into "Give Peace a Chance," a song Matt didn't think was all that interesting. All the words of the verse were hard to understand, especially in a crowd that size. But Seeger made sure that the chorus was front and center, and with hundreds of thousands of people singing "give peace a chance," the music washed over the crowd and lifted them up like a tidal wave. Seeger's enthusiasm and outrage were energizing, his singing made you believe that you could do it too, and his belief that this march, this day, and these people would make a difference magnified every second. Different parts of the crowd would sing some words differently, with different emphasis, and then join back with the others, like the bubbles in boiling water. There were peace signs everywhere. Some people had it on their faces —a big circle all around, a line down the nose and two angling off. There were peace signs on shirts and pants and American flag clothes. While people sang, "All we are saying . . . ," Seeger looked over to the White House and shouted, "Nixon, are you listening?" And everybody sang, "Give peace a chaaaaaance. All we are saying . . ."

Matt found himself singing along with everyone else and believing with everyone else, that together they could change things, that all this blood was being shed pointlessly because if the two sides just stopped and talked for a while, they could work things out. At the same time, he knew that his father would have sneered at the idea. But here, singing, people could turn to each other and just laugh for the sheer joy of the moment. In the middle of the crowd it felt warm and everybody was swaying together and repeating, "Peace."

—————

They left a little before it ended, not that it really ended. They started walking in the direction of the Methodist church, or what they thought was the direction, and turned a corner. In front of them was a line of police in riot gear—helmets, body armor, dark reflective masks, and even gas masks. They were all holding an odd-looking kind of rifle and standing casual but alert.

Lana didn't hesitate to walk up to one of them and demand directions to the Methodist church. The cop responded, but the words were garbled by the gas mask. "I'm so sorry," Lana said sadly, "I can't understand you with all this, this . . . paraphernalia on you. I'm sure you are much more handsome without them." She smiled prettily. It was hard to resist Lana. The policeman looked around uncertainly. Then Dorman started to laugh, really loud.

"Dorman, what's your problem?" Jack said acidly.

"It's just that joke," Dorman said. "You heard it." They'd all heard it. It was very simple.

What does a pig say when he meets another pig?

Hey, nice gun!

Jack growled, "Dorman, don't. Just stay cool."

The cop pointed his gun at Dorman. Matt instinctively stepped in front of Dorman, which was really dumb, but fortunately, the cop was so startled he lowered his weapon. Matt said, "Officer, I apologize for my friend, he was just carried away. We'll leave now. We just want to get back to the church."

The cop took off his mask. He looked to be maybe in his early twenties. "The Methodist church is over there, two blocks up and one over. You should get going. I don't know what's going to happen here."

All of them turned in the direction the cop had pointed and walked steadily away. Bonnie looked at Matt, her eyes wide and shining. Dorman thanked Matt profusely. All Matt could say was, "He wasn't going to shoot you."

Inside, Matt was thinking that he was lucky the cop showed restraint. Suppose he hadn't? Matt might have ended up in the morgue—for what? He always worried about unintended consequences of actions. He'd known that the March could turn into a riot, but he went anyway. His instincts just took over. As he thought about a 22-year-old with a rifle pointed at him, he realized that the unthinkable can become reality. *Boy*, he thought, *life can turn ugly in a second.*

––––––––––

Sunday, after the long ride back, everybody got off the bus, hugged each other, and said good-bye, so overwhelmed by the whole experience that they couldn't really talk about it until they had relived it, processed it, put it into the river of their lives, as Dorman said.

"Man, I owe you my life," Dorman said to Matt, grabbing him by the shoulders.

"That guy wasn't going to shoot you," Matt said again, but he returned the hug. "As long as you didn't tell the joke."

"You're a hero, man. People will be amazed."

Matt put his hands on Dorman's shoulders and looked him in the eye. "Not a word, Dor, not a word. I don't want anyone to hear about that. If I find out you told anyone, I'll . . . I'll take away all your drugs."

Dorman raised his eyebrows and shivered in the cold evening. "Damn, man. Why not?"

Matt wasn't even sure himself. "That's just how I want it. Do me the favor, Dor."

"For you, man, anything." He thought for a minute. "How about if I change your name?"

Matt shook his head. "Not a word. Nothing. Tell that to Lana and Beth and the rest." Bonnie came over to hug Matt as well and he said the same thing to her. She nodded her understanding and flashed the peace sign as she walked back to her dorm. It was already dark when Matt walked back to B dorm, thinking. Thinking about existentialists and whether courage was talking to a cop like a person or whether it was facing up to the uncertainty about . . . everything.

He shook his head to clear it and saw he was walking by shattered glass. Some of the dorm windows were boarded up, and there was a heap of garbage in the middle of the quad. *What the fuck happened here?*

"Hey radical, how much government did you overthrow?" He turned around to see Nicky skipping up to him.

"How did you know I was . . . ," Matt babbled, and trailed off. He was tired. He had spent a weekend in another world with Bonnie and here he was back in the middle of a wrecked quad. "Well, look at you here," he said. "What happened here?"

"Boy, did you miss a scary couple of hours. I'm okay now, but for a while . . . ," her voice trailed off but then she went on. "There was this anti-war demonstration that started out peaceful but then got completely out of hand. Some new speakers, I don't think they were students—"

"Outside agitators," Matt said. He'd heard about them at the March.

"Yeah, anyway, they really roused the crowd and before you knew it there were fires, and rocks thrown, and fights. I huddled up in my room and fortunately they didn't trash our dorm."

"Are you okay now, Nicky? That must have been really frightening."

"It was bad. But I'm okay now," she repeated and stepped in closer to him. She was clearly downplaying what had happened. "Take me away from all this. Tell me about your adventure. I'm sure it was a mind-blowing experience. More peaceful than here, I think."

"It was . . . It wasn't all that exciting," Matt said, not quite sure of the ground underneath him.

"Oh, you're a terrible liar," Nicky said.

"Guilty as charged," Matt smiled.

"Your zentence is to take me up to your room and tell me everyzing," Nicky said in her best Colonel Klink voice. "Everyzing! Do you hear?" She paused. "But just the facts."

His resistance was absent, or perhaps ignored. They went upstairs to B-3, which was strangely quiet. Matt opened his door, inventing several different explanations as to why Nicky was with him, and then saw the note that Mel had gone home after the game which B-3 won. He was just tired enough that he didn't fight his natural inclinations about Nicky making herself at home, which she did mostly on his lap. When he stretched and leaned back, he saw that his clock said 12:15 in the morning. "I'm supposed to be in class at nine o'clock tomorrow," he pointed out groggily.

"Yeah, me too," Nicky said, reaching up around his neck and pulling his head down. She was a fierce kisser, she didn't want to let go, and Matt acquiesced happily. "I'm glad you're back," she whispered, during a break.

"Yeah," Matt said, "I'm glad you didn't go away," he added, thinking of Mel.

Nicky sat up. "What was that?"

Matt reached out to her, realizing. "I mean, I'm glad you're here. With me."

She had changed, Matt wasn't quite sure why. "You're tired," she said, accurately. "I'm going to let you sleep."

Matt was not nearly conscious enough to figure out what to do next. "I am tired. And Mel's gonna be back."

Nicky stood up. "Okay, I'm outta here. You rest up. You going home for Thanksgiving?" Matt said he was, but he had to be back for the last football game Sunday before break. "So I might see you again some time?" she said, anger oozing out of her in small drips.

Matt pulled himself together and stood up next to her. "Nicky, it was a long, strange trip, but this is the best welcome home I've ever had." She put her arms around his waist and buried her head in his chest.

"I'd like welcome homes too." Matt thought it was a strange thing for her to say, but he was too tired to figure it out. He walked her out to the entrance, an arm around her in a way that was familiar and even comfortable.

———————

"You did what?" his mother squealed, passing the mashed potatoes. "You could have been killed at the March!" Matt thought, *She doesn't know how right she is.*

"I never do anything cool like that," Amy said accusingly.

It was the usual start to Thanksgiving dinner, although Matt wasn't usually the focus of the outrage. Amy was. "Nobody even got a sunburn," Matt protested. "It wasn't about doing crazy s—stuff. Everyone was totally mellow. In fact, it seems like it was more dangerous to be on campus than in Washington."

"I don't believe it," his mother said.

"What do you mean?" his father said, eyes narrowing at Matt.

"The campus had a mini-riot in protest to the war—windows smashed, buildings graffitied."

His father stuffed a hunk of turkey in his mouth and chewed fiercely. "Those damn radicals. What do they know? We need to keep our country free and destroy communism. It's everyone's duty to fight and do the honorable thing—"

Matt cut him off and was about to rage at his father when he got some control. "Look, Dad," he said tersely, "you don't know what you're talking about. This is a civil war and the government is lying to you. I'm not going to fight with you, but I have no plans to fight in this war, period."

He could see his father was about to take off on him when his mother put a stop to it with a plea to have a nice Thanksgiving dinner. Matt thought to himself, *Another casualty of the war, father against son.* He turned to his mother. "Really, Mom. And there wasn't a lot of radical talk like you hear about. There were some speeches—I didn't really hear most of them—and singing and we marched down the Mall."

"Were there a lot of girls there?" Amy asked.

"Uh, well, there were guys and girls, yeah."

"Uhhh-huhhh," Amy said.

"Was there a lot of talk about revolution and destroying the country?" his mother asked.

"Oh, I don't, that wasn't . . . it was a *peace* thing." That seemed hard to get across. He also didn't tell his parents about the incident with the cop.

"Do you want another helping?" his mother asked. "Once you go back to school, we'll have more than we need." She held the plate of turkey remains under his nose.

"Oh, I can't," Matt said. "Stuffed. I have to make room for dessert." His mother started to collect plates and glared at Amy until she grudgingly did the same.

"You know," Matt said, "I'm thinking of running for student government."

"You?" his father said. Matt looked at him until he got an answer. "I mean, that was just never really your thing."

"Yeah, but, um, some people have said I should."

"Oh, I think that would be wonderful, Matt," his mother said, bringing out a pumpkin pie and setting it in the middle of the table. "There's apple crumb too."

"Well, I didn't, like, finally decide yet, but I'm thinking about it. I think it would give me, like, a new perspective on being in college."

"Huh," his father said.

13

MATT WALKED INTO the gym and shook the snow off his parka. It was bitterly cold, totally nasty outside, but the gym was feeling overheated. The Polity had gotten three really big TVs, 26 inches, spread out left, right, and center on tables at one end of the gym. There were folding chairs set up in what had been rows, but people had moved them into groups. It wasn't like it was going to be all that interesting to watch. Visually, it was a non-event, a bunch of old guys picking little blue plastic capsules out of a small barrel. The plastic capsules reminded Matt of the things you'd get out of gum machines—put in a nickel and you might get a plastic ring or some other little toy. Except that these plastic balls held the future of the guys in the gym and millions of others.

Anyone who was graduating this year was about to have their fate determined by the draft lottery. Every date of the year was entered on a slip of paper and put into a large drum. The head of the Selective Service System would pull each day out of the drum. If that was your birthday, it would determine how likely you were to be drafted. If your birthday was picked as one of the first 195, you were probably going to Nam. All the 19-year-olds and up knew that their lives could be altered forever by this fateful day. Matt wasn't eligible this year for the lottery, but he would be next year. There was a big blackboard beside the television, and Chaz was going to write the dates in order and numbered on the board. There were campus cops at all the exits.

Matt saw Wit sitting with a group of guys up toward the front and made his way there. The air was filled with tension and cigarette smoke. If he'd ever wanted to smoke, this was his chance. All he had to do was inhale. He came up behind Wit and one of the other guys looked up at him like an intruder. He smiled tentatively. "Hey, Wit," he said.

"Matt," Wit said, his voice flat. "Guys, this is one of the guys in my dorm. The Joe Namath of the year in touch. Taking his team to the championship." It was a credential that was worth something even to these guys. Wit reeled off their names, which Matt immediately forgot, and they smiled and reached up to shake his hand. "Grab a chair," one said, "watch the ducks go down."

"You too can die for your country," another guy said. It was hard to calculate your chances of surviving. There were stories, on the news and repeated from supposedly firsthand accounts, of the danger and insanity of the war. You never knew where the Viet Cong were. In the jungles and forests, they could be anywhere and they knew the terrain better than anyone. The rice paddies were reported to be littered with booby traps that could cut through your boot and your foot before you knew what happened. Arms and legs were blown off. The medical corps was so good they could helicopter you out even if you were bleeding to death, but you were still crippled for life.

Almost as bad were the people who survived the war but came back permanently damaged. Victims of night terrors reliving the fear and uncertainty of the war. Depression that invited suicide. Guilt over your friends who had been killed while they were standing beside you. Guilt that you had a cushy job at a base camp and had to watch decimated platoons come back out of their heads. No one seemed to escape being scarred by the experience unless you started out crazy.

Among the upperclassmen, there was anger, fear, and resentment. Matt wasn't all that concerned for himself—he was deferred as long as he stayed in good standing at Montauk. Nixon was insisting that the war was winding down, and even if peace talks were going nowhere, this plan called "Vietnamization" of the war meant that the

Vietnamese would do all the fighting. How long they would last was anybody's guess.

"So, if keeping Vietnam free is in our national interest, why are we making the Vietnamese do the work?" John said. "If it's not in our national interest, what were we doing there in the first place?"

"Fuck if I know," one of the guys said. "Goddamn gooks. I'd like to blow some heads off."

It was just after 7:30. The lottery would start in 30 minutes. Matt looked around. The gym was filling up, and while most were boys, some of them had girlfriends with them. "What the hell's that?" Andy said.

A person draped in black from neck to toe entered the gym playing a drum draped in black, like at the March on Washington. He beat a slow, funereal cadence, and was followed by a figure wearing a black sheet with a skeleton outlined on it. A few feet behind the first came another skeleton, and then another, and another, and so on. They marched slowly and lined up around the walls of the gym. The security people tensed up.

"These are the Polity people, right, Matt?" Wit asked him.

"Yeah, some of them, and some others, I think. People who are against the war."

People started hissing "Shhhh" as loudly as they could and someone turned up the television set. There was a CBS logo and the announcer told everyone that *Mayberry RFD* would not be shown that night. People booed. There was a little talk by the head of the Selective Service System about the rules, which sounded a lot more complicated than they really were. Then another old guy in a suit, a congressman, was brought up to pull out the first number.

Every guy in the entire gym leaned forward and the place became astonishingly quiet. The congressman pulled out a blue capsule and gave it to another guy at the desk. That guy read out, "September 14." The first skeleton fell over and lay flat on the floor. The place stayed quiet, then there were a few murmurs. Everyone was safe so far.

Another guy took over pulling out the numbers, and when they pulled the second one, April 24, someone groaned, "Oh, no," and stood up. The second skeleton fell over. The guy who'd stood up, looked around, and said, "Okay, good-bye. That's it. I'm done for," and he walked out of the gym. The third number was called, and the third skeleton fell over. There were three now, all facedown, parallel black lines of death. Some people walked over to take a look and the fourth number, February 14, Valentine's Day, was called and the fourth skeleton fell over.

The guy whose number it was jumped up, pulling his girlfriend up with him. "You said you would! You promised!" he yelled. She looked embarrassed and mouthed, "Not here," but the guy hugged her and pulled her toward the door.

Wit chuckled, a little bit sad. "Ah, I know him," he said. "He made her promise that they would screw all night long if he had a low number. So his roommate's got to stay the hell out. They get the place to themselves, since he was born on Valentine's Day and all. You ask me, I don't think it's the first time anyway. She's a honey."

As the numbers were called out, guys screamed or groaned or just sat there in shock, and the skeletons fell over. Matt looked around all the sides of the gym and figured that they didn't really have 366 skeletons. Supposedly, after number 195, it was extremely unlikely that you would be drafted, but Matt didn't think they had got even 200 people to be skeletons. He wondered how they would make up the difference.

A few minutes later, the guy called out "December 10," and Andy said, "Goddamn," and threw down his cigarette.

Wit said he was sorry and stood up and hugged him around the shoulders. "If there's anything I can do, feel free to ask."

"Wit, I appreciate that but I'm going to make a call to my daddy and tell him to wake up his lawyer. Gentlemen, it's been—well, I wouldn't call it a pleasure, but not due to the company. Good night to y'all." He strolled out of the gym.

The first student Matt knew whose number came up was Martin

Bader, one of the B-3 gang. Matt didn't know him very well. He was a kind of creepy figure but harmless. The guys in the dorm had given him the nickname "Master"—which while cruel always made Matt smile. Matt could see him through the crowd, his head down in his hands and his shoulders shaking. Bader was in tears and for good reason. His life as he knew it was over. He left the room, almost running.

"We got some extra medication back at the dorm for the low numbers," Wit said quietly to Matt. "Enough to anesthetize the pain, at least for a while."

It settled down into a chillingly monotonous night, as the numbers were methodically, idiotically drawn out of the barrel as if they didn't represent human lives. Among the double-digit numbers, guys reacted in all sorts of ways. Some were angry, some quiet, most just walked out. Someone nearby said that one of the bars near campus was filling up. The skeletons continued to fall, and when they got to number 65—May 10—the last one fell. With the next number—66, November 12—the very first skeleton stood up again, and that continued around the gym until they were all standing. It was kind of mesmerizing, Matt thought, if you weren't petrified about the army.

The utter boredom of the process made people drop their attentiveness some. Matt started to think about all the work he had to do for finals when a voice behind him said, "Matt Aymer, peace marcher!"

Matt stood up and shook his hand. "Your number come up yet?"

Kashman made peace Vs with both hands and then crossed the fingers. "Not so far. Where are we? About one hundred?" Wit said, "One oh four," and Kashman congratulated him on being out of the game. "You served your time honorably, sir." Wit said he had to take a leak, and when he'd gone, Kashman leaned into Matt and said, "Could I just talk to you for a second? Out of the crowd?"

He and Matt walked toward one side of the gym. More of the skeletons were standing back up now, and Matt wondered what would happen when they were all upright. "Hey, thanks for the letter," Matt said, "to the disciplinary committee. That was great."

"Cool, I hope it helped. I understand that you got off." Matt said that it wouldn't even go down on his record and Kashman tried to give him a soul shake, but Matt didn't know how. They laughed at the flub. "Say, my man, I wanted to ask you if you had thought any more about running for the Polity."

A skeleton fairly near them stood up. "As a matter of fact," Matt said, "yeah. I thought . . . I'm going to run."

Kashman grinned from ear to ear. "Outstanding, outstanding," he said and gave Matt a palm to slap. "That's terrific. I'm sure you'll be elected." Matt stuck his hands in his pockets and shrugged. "And look, of course I'll help with that. And I was thinking that you should take over as treasurer of the athletic fund, and maybe the concert and speaker fund too. Assuming you win." Matt's mouth dropped open and Kashman told him quickly what the treasurer would do and that he was combining the entertainment committee with the athletic committee to streamline, as he called it, the organization. Matt didn't take it all in, thinking about what was going on and watching skeletons get to their feet. Almost all of them were standing up again.

Finally, he said, "Wow. God, I'm, um, honored. I guess I can do it." Kashman reassured him and said he would help Matt figure it out. "But, um, aren't you . . . ? Won't there be a different president after the election?"

Kashman looked away for a second. "That's been, ah, the tradition." He looked back, straight into Matt's face. "But traditions get old. It's time for a change." Matt was reminded of how Napoleon had taken over without firing a shot. "I'm concerned this year," Kashman went on. "What with all the uncertainty about President Thomas and all the disruption—"

Matt had seen the boarded-up windows and the entrance doors that had been smashed. "Yeah, I heard there was a, a—"

"Riot. Yes, really a riot. I tried to stop them. I had hoped that

President Thomas would come out to speak to us. I'm sure that he would be able to calm people down. But he didn't come. So the crowd became . . . restless. So it started from there and just got out of control." He shook his head and rubbed a hand across his face. "It was so preventable. A shame."

"Damn. I had no idea."

Kashman clapped a hand on Matt's bicep and said, "Well, that's not your problem. But so you see, it might be better if the tradition was broken. What's the point of doing something just because you've always done it that way, right? Revolution, evolution." Matt thought about it for a second, but Kashman kept on talking. "But none of this is finalized, so best not to tell anyone. Not to Wit, not to, um . . . your roommate, okay? Swear it."

They walked back to where Wit was sitting. "Wit," Kashman said, "the Taj is serving beer after the lottery. Come on over if you feel like it." Wit said thanks but he was going back to B-3 to commiserate with the prospective conscripts. Kashman left, saying he'd be in touch with Matt, who wanted to ask about President Thomas, but didn't get a chance. The first skeleton fell over to start the third round of dates, the 133rd, May 2. "*Goddamn it!*" A guy stood up. "No! No! Shit! Shitshitshit, mother*fuck!*" He stomped away, followed by a girl who looked almost as mad.

"It's almost worse now," Wit said. "You're beginning to hope that you'll miss the cut entirely. You're feeling close to the escape hatch. Then it slams down on your fingers." Wit had no skin in the game anyway. "Hey, Matt," Wit said, "I didn't get to hear about your hearing. What happened?"

Matt gave him a quick summary of the hearing and a longer one of Mrs. Devin's thoughts. It seemed like a year ago. He almost told Wit what Kashman had just said, but he didn't want the whole world to know about it.

Wit shook his head. "I'm glad I'm not a part of that scene. That free-for-all after the anti-war march was a total bummer."

"Yeah, I'm glad I was at a *peace* march," he said.

"I hear that President Thomas wishes everybody had been in Washington. Some guys were saying that the board isn't very happy with him." Wit said that evidently a lot of the directors of the university thought Thomas was too laid-back about controlling the campus. They were worried about repeats at Montauk of some of the really violent demonstrations that had blown up around the country.

Matt said that he'd heard that Thomas refused to come out and speak to the demonstrators. Wit shrugged. "Dunno. I didn't hear that. As far as I know, nobody asked him. Thomas really believes in freedom of speech and hearing all ideas. He wanted Malcolm X to speak on campus, but the man was killed before they could book him. And he believes in government by the people. What I did hear is that Kashman was the one who started the riot. Got some of the Zoo people high and made breaking windows seem like a good idea. That's what he wanted tonight, too, I bet."

"Kashman's going to run for president again," Matt blurted out.

Wit blew a long plume of smoke and sighed. "I was afraid of that. And I'm afraid, buddy, that that's your problem. You and maybe Bonnie and the other good people in the Polity. I've served my tour of duty, I'm almost done with academia, and I just can't fight that battle."

"Yeah, well, I understand," Matt said, feeling like he was watching a ship leave the shore. "He also said that he wanted me to be in charge of the money for the sports teams and entertainment activities on campus."

"Be careful what you wish for," Wit said. "People get pretty intense about how that money gets used. And paranoid. I remember Barry did it for a while, but he quit because it was too much of a hassle. You might want to talk to him about it."

The tense group at the beginning of the lottery had broken up into smaller groups, some of them downcast, others talking and joking. There were still people focused on the drawing of the little blue capsules, but now that it was near the magic number, there weren't so many. Matt thought, *If I were nineteen and drew a low number, maybe I wouldn't care about Kashman or the Polity or Montauk.* He caught himself. *That's totally weird. For a moment that's what I wanted—to be drafted. How did I get in the middle of all this?*

The guy on television picked up the 195th little blue capsule, September 24, and there was a change in the gym, as if everybody was just waking up, trying to shake the sleep out of their eyes. The last skeleton fell over. When the next birthday was called out they all rose—one or two had to be woken up, looked like—and turned toward the central exit. They began to sing as they marched out of the gym:

Well, it's one, two, three,
What are we fighting for?
Don't ask me, I don't give a damn
Next stop is Vietnam

And it's five, six, seven,
Open up the pearly gates.
Well there ain't no time to wonder why.
Whoopee! We're all gonna die.

When the last skeleton left the building, it took all the excitement too. Though the draft people were still droning out numbers, people started to pack up and go. "Hey!" Jack Appel yelled out. "Clean up after yourselves! Pick up the beer cans! Everything in the trash."

There was one last student, his eyes fixated on the screen. He was stoned out of his mind, but he was euphoric he hadn't heard his birth date, December 4, yet. He knew he was out of the woods by now. He had been celebrating with his friends, waiting to hear the date, relishing the moment.

When the last date was announced, he was puzzled. It wasn't December 4. The panic was instant. *Shit, shit, shit,* he thought. "Wait a minute," a friend said. "Maybe it was after the 195 cut-off. Go check on the board that guy was keeping with all the numbers."

The guy ran to the board, frantically searching for his birthday. When he found it, he screamed. "One-sixty-one! Nooooo!" He ran out screaming with his friends close behind.

Wit watched him run. "Man, to go from high as a kite to the most depressed person on earth in a second. Could it be more insane?" He shook his head. "I'm going back to the dorm, see if I can help. You coming?"

Matt said he might come by later but didn't say he was actually thinking of going by Nicky's dorm. It was still early, after all. The whole process had only taken about an hour and a half.

———————

When he got to her dorm, he asked at the front for Nicky's room, but the matron wouldn't let him up. "Miss Watkins is unavailable," was all she would say. Matt went outside and yelled up at her window. Finally, after several women told him to shut up, Nicky's head came out of her window. "Matt, I'm sorry, I can't see you. I feel . . . rotten. I'm rotting. I'm a rotting hungry pirate." Matt said he was sorry to hear that and asked if she'd be in class tomorrow. "I don't know. I don't think so. I'm sorry, Matt." She blew him a kiss, then smiled weakly. "Liz was asking about Mel. But don't tell her I said so. Good night."

The window closed as Matt said, "Feel better." He thought it was a strange conversation. *A rotting hungry pirate.* He was turning away back to B dorm when he heard his name called out.

"Matthew. I thought it was you I heard bellow." It was Lana and, inevitably, Beth. "We wanted to talk to you," Beth said. "We must discuss Kashman," Lana said. It was like one person who had two bodies.

"Oh! That's . . . good," Matt said, and shivered. "Where do you want to talk? It's pretty damn cold out here."

"We can't use the lounge in our dorm," Beth said. "People are studying. And they'd have to throw you out at ten."

"We could try our lounge," Matt offered. "Nobody's ever studying there. I mean, they study, just not there. And everyone headed for the local bars to get completely shit-faced."

"I am certain," Lana said skeptically.

They found the lounge empty and, as he saw it through Beth's and Lana's eyes, not much to look at. While the women managed to keep their lounge looking clean, B dorm's lounge needed a litter patrol and some air freshener. Well, they could open the windows in a few months. Lana moved some chairs around into an oval and Beth gathered up the trash. Matt felt like the host. He put the backpack on some shelves and asked them if they wanted something to drink. A beer? Lana said no and pulled out a joint. Beth pulled out a notebook and said yes, so Matt had to go up to the room and ask Mel if he could borrow some beer. He knew Mel would be studying despite the momentous night.

"You can't borrow it, but you can have it. What's going on?" Mel said.

"Oh nothing, just some girls," Matt said, feeling totally cool. "Lana and Beth."

"The tall skinny one and the short pudgy one?" Matt nodded. "Not Nicky? Liz?" Matt shook his head. "Wait, is this more politics?"

"Um," Matt said, realizing that he actually didn't know what they wanted to talk about. "I guess so. There's some strange stuff going on with Kashman."

"No surprise there. If you're gonna take him down, count me in. I'm serious."

"I might take you up on that. Come down later if you finish. I'll hold a beer for you."

When Matt got back to the lounge Lana and Beth were already talking, heads together in neighboring armchairs. Matt gave Beth a beer and sat across from them. They already knew that Kashman was planning to run for president again. "It's a coup," Lana pronounced. "We have to stop him."

"But in a democracy, he should be voted out of office," Matt protested.

"Is it a democracy if one person can manipulate the vote?" Lana sneered. "I believe that we should include Dorman in this discussion. He knows things about Kashman, I think. That might be useful to us. Matthew, why don't you run over to the Taj and get Dorman and see if you can find Bonnie?"

"It's cold out there," Matt objected.

Lana leaned forward and smiled sweetly. "That is why you will run, Matthew."

Matt sighed, shrugged himself into his jacket, and ran across the quad. He kept an eye out for Kashman, and it only took him a couple of minutes to find Dorman, who was sitting cross-legged in his room, wrists on his knees, listening to some strange kind-of-guitar music. Matt roused him and told him that Lana wanted to see him.

"Then I needs must hie to her side," Dorman said. Matt figured that was a yes and asked about the music. "Ravi Shankar," Dorman said, pulling on a sheepskin coat that Matt envied. "A genius. Not of this world."

Matt couldn't find Bonnie but left a note under her door. On the way back, Matt explained the situation. Dorman just listened, then said, "Did you see the stars? It's an amazing night." Matt thought maybe the cold air would straighten him out. He wasn't sure Lana had had such a great idea.

When they got back to the B lounge, Beth was sitting curled up in the armchair, looking both scared and angry at the same time. Lana was pacing back and forth in the lounge in her form-fitting jeans. Matt found it extremely distracting. Dorman went up to her and hugged her, leaned over Beth and made a gesture as if blessing her, and asked if there was more pot. Beth gave him a joint.

"You could run against him, Matthew," Lana said.

"Run against him? I don't know anything about being president. Why don't you run against him?"

She stopped and put her hands on her hips defiantly. "The male chauvinist pigs on this campus would find that offensive," she said. Then she smiled. "So it must be an outstanding idea." Curling her hands into the most elegant fists Matt had ever seen, she announced, "I will do it. I must do it." Beth applauded. Matt did too. As Lana stood there, her expression changed from smiling determination to inquisitiveness bordering on suspicion. "And who do we have here?" she asked.

Matt turned around to see Neut coming into the lounge. He stopped and announced, "Kashman is running for president again."

"This is not news," Lana said. "What would be news would be to tell us who you are."

Neut raised his eyebrows. It was the most reaction Matt had ever seen in him. "Lana," he said, "this is Neut—I mean, damn, Neut, I've forgotten your real name."

"John Riley." Beth wrote something down in her notebook.

"Right, of course. Lana, he's one of us."

"Yes, but is he one of *us*?" Lana sauntered over to Neut. "Or are you a spy, Mr. Neut?"

Neut had regained his usual stoneface. "He can be stopped."

Lana folded her arms. "Yes, I am going to stop him. I am going to run for president."

"I think there are other ways," Neut said hesitantly and licked his lips. "Maybe better."

She's really thrown him off, Matt thought. He said, "Neut's okay, right, Neut? You don't want Kashman to run things again, right?"

Neut turned to Matt, and his face congealed. "Damn right," he said. "Bring Kashman down."

"Music to my ears." Mel stood in the doorway, surveying the scene.

"It's a party!" Lana said, exasperated. "Who else can we invite?"

"I think Bonnie would be a good addition," Dorman volunteered.

"Yes, an excellent idea," Lana agreed. "Mattheeew?"

"No," Matt said.

"I'll go," Dorman said. "I can finish the doobie."

Mel stepped aside to let them pass and said, "So what's the story, morning glory?"

Matt explained, "A lot of suspicion and fewer hard facts but here it is in a nutshell. Kashman's using the Zoo to cause trouble on campus—the riots during the March on Washington, the walkouts after Wolf's class."

"Why?" Mel barked.

Matt shrugged, but Beth suddenly said, "Weatherman."

Mel rolled his eyes. "Because it's cold?"

"No," Beth said, "it's the Weatherman strategy. Destabilize. Bring down the establishment by blowing up the foundation of it. Kashman wants to bring down the school."

Neut said, "And throw in that he has moved from weed and pill dealing to harder, more dangerous stuff, and we have to do something. I don't care about the weed or pills but hard drugs kill people." As he said that, Bonnie walked in with Dorman.

Lana pressed, "How do you know for a fact what he's dealing?"

Neut just said, "I know." Then, "You can't beat him in an election. He's got a death grip on most of the guys in the Taj and also in the Zoo. He's their supplier." Neut's voice had taken on an assertiveness that surprised Matt. There was more to him than it seemed. For sure, he was serious about Kashman. "And given that he's already been president, people who don't know him are going to vote just on the name. He'll win, no matter what."

"I don't disagree with anything I've heard," Bonnie said. "What still confuses me is what has happened to this guy. Last year he was all about the ideas. He even used some Polity money with a lot of donations from outsiders to fund a child-care center on campus for the workers at the U. He raised money to fund poll watchers in the south. What happened to *that* Joe?"

"Well," Lana said, "power corrupts and absolute power corrupts absolutely. And regardless of the reason for his behavior, if he is elected again, it will only be worse."

Neut strode out of the lounge, leaving everyone slightly amazed. "Maybe he's a narc," Mel said. Lana nodded. They added a couple of chairs to the circle, and Beth sat down and leaned forward. Lana sprawled in the chair next to her and Dorman stood beside Lana's chair, too twitchy to sit down. Mel sat next to her and Matt next to him.

It looked to Matt that Bonnie was still piecing things together but wasn't ready to share. Matt said, "Want to let us in on your thoughts?"

Bonnie shook her head. "No, not yet. Let's stay focused. How do we defeat him? When I joined Polity it was for the ideas and hopefully the ability to make real change. Now I see nothing but chaos. It seems that on this campus, only one person is benefitting and that is Joe Kashman."

"So you guys are, what, planning a coup d'état?" Mel asked. "A coup de school? Cool."

14

"BEAUTIFUL LOSERS is a masterpiece," Nicky gushed, "and Leonard Cohen is one of the great writers of the English language. He wrote it on a Greek island while he was high on speed."

"Anybody can write a great novel if they live on a Greek island," Matt objected, a little jealous. It was one of the rare nights when her roommate Liz was gone and Nicky invited Matt to her room. "Even I could, maybe. No, on second thought. But I bet you could."

Nicky laughed and put her arms around his neck. "Okay, let's go." Then she laughed harder. "Oh, I wish I had a picture of the look on your face just now. Don't worry, I won't buy tickets. But wait, Cohen's a great musician too." She put on an album that had a dark, sulky-looking guy, which made Matt more jealous. Matt thought the songs were kind of moody and obscure—who was Suzanne anyway?—but they made Nicky romantic, so Matt was pretty okay with that.

She'd been kind of hard to get hold of these last few weeks and a little freaky when he did see her. She'd either be real quiet and distant, or she'd say she was "sooooo tired" and lean her head on his shoulder. Both sides of her made Matt uncomfortable. But then they'd meet for ice cream, and she would be a complete hoot, cracking about other students, and herself, and scarfing down three helpings of Rocky Road before she ran off to do her reading.

And she did read—she told Matt the stories of what she was reading in a way that was fun even when Matt had no interest at all. She was in love with this novel about a guy who was obsessed by a Mohawk Indian woman. She was so excited by it that Matt was envious.

They were sitting on the floor in her room and Nicky curled up in his lap. Then they messed around for a while, making themselves frustrated in a nice way, but then the album was over, and Nicky sang in a pretty soprano, "Hey, that's no way to say good-bye," said it was time for him to say good-bye because she had work to do. Matt couldn't remember when they'd spent more than an hour together, now that he thought about it. They weren't exactly a couple, but he knew that's the way people thought of them and he wasn't sure how he felt about that.

––––––––––

The following day Matt was with Mel in the room and Neut walked in and closed the door. When he walked in, Matt said he had been looking all over for him. "Do you *really* know stuff about Kashman? Or is it just a hunch? What gives with you?"

Neut got a very patient look on his face. "First, I'm not a narc, but I am very close to the people that want to eliminate the dangerous drugs—coke, mescaline, PCP, and heroin. They don't want to devote their energy to low-level marijuana dealings. Too many people using and it's not hurting anyone at this point."

Neut explained that he was the son of a campus cop who had been killed in a car accident two years ago. The kids driving the car were strung out on PCP—"stardust," he called it, really dangerous—and they ran a red light and smashed into his car.

"My dad lived long enough to be in agony," Neut said in that strange neutral voice. They weren't really close, Neut said, "but I can't erase the memory. It was like having a wall of the house knocked down. Suddenly there was nothing between you and the outside. And the weather was bad, all the time."

"Sounds pretty hairy," Mel said.

"We went through a rough time. We got some money from insurance and my father's pension account with the school, but my mom didn't have a job then. She went back to work and with loans, here I am."

"Got to do something to you, your father being killed. Especially like that," Mel said, shaking his head. "Was Kashman in the other car?"

"No. Two of the kids in the other car were killed and the third was hurt pretty bad. Anyway, that's not what put me on to Kashman. Last year a kid I knew in high school came home from Montauk in the middle of the year, completely strung out on drugs. OD'd—*twice*—but they were able to save him and get him into rehab. I spent a lot of time with that kid. It was like being with your grandfather. The kid was kind of slow, and kind of weak. It would take him a while to answer a question, and there were whole times, like weeks, that he just couldn't remember. I'm not sure he'll ever really be able to live on his own.

"*That* was Kashman. He fed him the drugs, let him buy on credit—he took the kid's whole bank account, he sold his stereo and his car . . . It was a total wipeout."

"So you decided to go here?" Mel wondered aloud.

"I'd already applied—remember, my dad was a cop here, so people knew me. I mean, I was smart enough to get in anyway, but it just felt good—for my mother, mainly—to know that I had people who would watch out for me. God knows, I wasn't going to get into drugs, but still."

"Always nice to have friends in high places—or with the cops."

"Yeah, especially with all the riots on campuses and stuff. In case that happened here, they wouldn't bash my head in or anything." He turned and left. Mel and Matt just looked at each other. Nothing more needed to be said.

————————

Matt had to focus on finals for the next two weeks. Of course he figured he'd failed the calculus final, so he needed to do really well on the rest of them. He was worried about Woodbell's final too because it would undoubtedly emphasize abstract concepts, not facts. That had never been his strength, but he hoped Bonnie would help. Over the next week he locked himself up in his room to study and fought the noise and the chaos in the dorm. He thought it was the lesser of the two evils: noise in the dorm or demonstrations outside at least three university buildings.

He finished mid-December. He wasn't sure how he'd done on his finals but at least they were over. He vowed next semester he would keep up with the coursework and do less cramming. He couldn't afford to flunk out, of course. That was a pretty good incentive to keep his grades up. He figured *fighting the war on campus was better than fighting the war in the jungle.*

With finals over, he could resurface and face the world. He was a little worried about Nicky. She was under the weather and during finals study week he didn't have the time to connect. It was cold, the wind sharpening the cold, but Matt didn't want to run the gauntlet of the iron maiden and all the girls checking him out on the way to Nicky's. *The girls are worse than guys.* Some of the windows had Christmas tree lights up. Lurch had written "Santa here! Giving out Kisses for Free!" in fake snow on his window. Matt looked up at the window he knew from the curtains was Nicky's and called her name. To his surprise, her blond head popped out almost immediately.

"Matt! Don't move! Wait right there! I'll be right down!" And she was gone. Matt stomped his feet and rubbed his hands together to keep warm, wishing that she'd asked him to come in. In about a minute, she came flying out the dorm's front door, barefoot, and leapt down the steps straight to the sidewalk. She was wearing a yellow T-shirt and tight jeans and charged toward him, arms waving, looking like a twelve-year-old, until she came to a halt and threw herself at him. "Matt, I'm so glad you came over," she said, talking into his chest.

"I guess I am too, now. I wasn't sure you would . . ."

"Oh, I know, I've been a total creep. I just haven't been feeling so great, and I hate for you to see me like that. It just drives me insane."

Matt wrapped his arms around her, turning right and left a little, thinking, *It's hard not to like this.* "It kind of drives me insane too. When you disappear."

She looked up at him. "Matt, Matt, Matt. I'm soooo sorry." She put her feet on his shoes, still holding on to his waist. "I was just sitting up there, getting ready to leave—my parents are coming in an hour or two or something—and I was thinking I wasn't going to see you, and now I really need to see you."

"I'm—"

"I mean over Christmas," she said, shaking her head. "I can't bear not seeing you for two weeks. You're not, like, going to Washington again, are you?"

Matt got that weird feeling in his stomach again. *Did she know about Washington? What was there to know?* "Hey," he said, "you're the one who disappeared. I thought maybe your parents had given you an all-expense-paid trip to the Greek islands."

"Oh, no. No, never." She looked up at him so serious that he felt wrong about saying anything. "I would never do that." She let go of him and put her feet on the sidewalk again, hopping from one foot to the other while she dug into her jeans and pulled out a piece of paper that had been folded and folded and folded. "Here, here's my telephone number. My home number. Please please please call. Anytime. Don't worry about my parents, they're cool with my . . . friends."

"Boyfriends?"

She smiled a little sheepishly. "Yes, my boyfriends. Such as you." She picked up his hand, put the piece of paper in it, and folded his hand back over it. "You're blushing."

"Just the cold makes my cheeks rosy red," Matt said. "Like yours."

She put her hands to her cheeks and then folded them under her armpits to keep them warm, still hopping from one foot to the other. "What's your phone number?"

"I didn't bring a pen, or paper . . . ," Matt started, patting his pockets as if he'd magically find them.

"Doesn't matter, just tell me, I'll remember it." She fixed her eyes on his face while he gave her the number, then closed her eyes and after a few seconds, nodded. "Okay, got it. Okay, I'm freezing. Gotta go," she said, but looked up at him, waiting. It started to snow, and she reached up to wipe a snowflake, or a tear, from underneath her eye.

Matt leaned over and took her head in his hands and kissed her, meaning to say that he would call her and that he was worried about her, and that he was open to taking their relationship further. But he didn't say any of it.

She stepped back and said, "Okay, I'll take that." She turned and started to run back to the dorm.

"Hey!" Matt shouted. She stopped. "Hey," he said again, "that's no way to say good-bye. I'll call." She ran back to him, kissed him again, and ran into the dorm.

"That's better," Matt whispered to himself. He started to walk back to B-3, whistling. Life was complicated, but not without some benefits.

———————

Matt hoisted his duffel bag onto his shoulder and asked Mel if he was ready. "It's not 11 yet," he complained. "I still have a few things to get together."

"Right, it's 10:55. I'm going." The hallway was noisy with the B-3 gang's preparations for going home, and Matt yelled out, "All right, you guys. My bags are packed; I'm ready to go."

"Good-bye, Ruby Tuesday," Fish said.

"No Rolling Stones," Barry ordered. "Not after what happened at Altamont. It's a disaster, a disgrace, the end of the sixties." The Hells Angels, doing security work for the Stones at a California concert, stabbed a drugged-up Black guy to death. It was the last piece of bad shit in a day that had been one bummer after another. Three other people had died, cars had been stolen, and Mick Jagger got punched in the head before he started the Stones' set. "Anyway," Barry turned to Matt. "Have a cool Christmas. Good-bye, Columbus."

Monster said, "I got a feeling that you're gonna hear from us." He scratched his head and shrugged. He didn't know what he meant either.

"Walk away, Renée." Neut was staying another few days.

"Hit the road, Jack," Brain said. "And don't you come back no more." He wrote on the back of his hand UNTIL 1/19/70.

Wit leaned against his doorjamb. "You say good-bye, I say hello." He was staying on campus over the break, except for the holidays, to work on his thesis. Matt slapped palms with everybody and yelled to Mel to get going.

As he walked into the common room, Bonnie said, "Hey, stranger." She uncurled from one of the armchairs and stood up. "We don't have class, I don't see you."

Matt's feelings were trampling over each other like annoyed elephants. He was glad to see Bonnie and wishing she would run up to him like Nicky had. He felt guilty thinking of the two of them at the same time. He felt stupid for feeling guilty. "I guess it's a good thing Lana wanted to have this meeting then." Actually, he'd suggested it to Lana. "I still don't know what room you're in, so I couldn't leave a note. You haven't been around much."

"Yeah, I know. I had some things I had to do before the break." She walked over and said, "Put your duffel down." He did and she put her hands on his arms and kissed both his cheeks. "Before the others get here, I wanted to wish you a Merry Christmas. Why is it so cold in here? Why would Lana have a meeting in this dorm anyway?"

"I don't know, maybe they turned the heat off already." She was wearing a big furry hat that was almost the exact color of her hair and a sheepskin coat that wasn't far off either. "You look like an acorn," he said.

She folded her arms. "You're a little nuts yourself."

"Merry Christmas and Happy New Year. It's going to be a new year for me, for sure," he said. "I don't know exactly how I got into all this. Just lucky, I guess."

"I don't know about luck. But we're in it together."

"I'll count that as lucky." They smiled.

A "MERRRRY Christmas!" exploded from the door as Dorman walked in. "We've got snow! Snow is the greatest!" He bustled over and slapped Matt on the back and grabbed Bonnie in a big hug that made Matt envious.

She extricated herself, laughing, "Merry Christmas, Dor."

"I *love* Christmas," he cheered. "What could be better than an old fat man flying around the world giving away toys? What were they on when they thought that one up? That's the job I want to have when I grow up."

Bonnie gave him a look. "The question is, what are *you* on?"

"Black beauties," he said, looking very satisfied with himself. "I had to have something to get up after Altamont."

Bonnie frowned. "You're not driving, I hope."

"Nah. I got a ride with a guy who lives near me. I'm cool."

Lana and Beth arrived together of course, and Mel was on their heels. "Okay, our agenda is short," Lana announced. "Over the break we will think about strategies to get me elected president of the Polity," she smiled. "And get Matt elected."

"And a plan B," Mel said, walking in.

"Yes, although the optimal plan is to have myself elected," Lana said.

"You are so full of it," Beth said.

"Perhaps. But," she smiled at Beth and put a finger on her nose, "it would be a benevolent dictatorship."

"Main thing," Matt said, "is to focus on Kashman and figure out any point of weakness." Even with all the advantages Kashman had, he himself had built weak spots into the system. "And most of all," Matt announced, "everybody have a Merry Christmas and a Happy New Year." He put his hand out, palm up, and one by one they all put a hand on top of his.

15

MATT SPENT the first three days of Christmas break sleeping. Once he'd topped off the sleep battery, he felt aimless. His father was at work for another week, his mother was busy with the housework and getting ready for Christmas, and his sister Amy was at school until the afternoon. He felt completely different from the way he had at Thanksgiving. Now he felt like he was morphing into a child again. He kept feeling like he should be doing homework, like in high school, but he didn't have any for Montauk. He spent some time putting the lights on the gutter of the house, and then asked if he could buy more lights so that he could outline the entire roof, which he'd seen on a neighbor's house last year.

He knew he had to call Nicky, that he wanted to call Nicky, but something held him back. After a day or two, he realized that he was afraid of the unknown. How weird would it be to see her? Maybe she was a different person when she was home. Worse, maybe *he* was a different person.

He thought about shopping with Amy after she got home. He was thinking he had to get something for Nicky, and he hoped Amy would have some suggestions. But then he'd have to tell her that he was going out with a girl and then it would be all over the house. So that was out. Finally, he figured that he couldn't go wrong with earrings or a bracelet or something like that, and he went to Macy's and asked the woman behind the counter if she had anything from Greece or about Greece. She pulled out about a dozen sets of earrings and

Matt was instantly overwhelmed and confused. While he was looking all of them over, the woman got bored or had to help someone else who knew what they were doing or something and left. Matt lost focus and left, thanking the woman. He wandered the mall for a while until he walked past a jewelry store that he guessed was more hip than Macy's and in the window hung a pair of earrings that were swords, like pirate swords. So he bought them.

That did it. He felt prepared. It was like going up another step in the relationship ladder. He dialed the number. It rang a couple of times, and a voice he didn't recognize answered. That was okay, he'd rehearsed that. "I'm a friend of Nicky's from Montauk—"

"Oh, Matt. Yeah, Nicole said you might call."

He twisted the coiled phone cord around his hand, worried that "Nicky" was a mistake. "Okay, yes, that's good. Um, is N—she there?"

"Wait a minute." There was a little shuffle and the earpiece was muffled and the person who was probably Nicky's mother said something in a loud voice. Then a little silence, and a "What?" and the phone hit something hard. A half minute later, she came back on. "Nicky's going to call you back."

"Do you need the number?"

"Oh." Then from a short distance, "Nicole, do you need the—?" Another rustle. "No, she says she has it. Okay, it was nice to talk to you. We may see each other soon."

"Okay, thanks." See you soon? He hadn't thought of that. He hung up the phone and it rang. "Hello?"

"Hi there," she said, purring a little. "Say your name."

He wasn't sure what to make of this, but he said, "Hi, it's Matt."

"That's good to hear. I wanted to make sure I've been hearing it right in my head. Now I want to see your face. Do you wonder if you can remember what I look like? I mean *exactly* what I look like?"

Matt laughed a little. "I guess I hadn't thought of it that way." There was a little silence and Matt felt his mistake through the wires. "I mean I can remember the way you look a dozen ways. I remember what you looked like that first day in class. And when you said you'd be my friend—"

"Before the hearing."

"Yeah, before the hearing. And I remember the snowflake on your face last week. And your toes on my shoes."

She giggled. "My toes don't count. The others, they count. I remember—there was a girl down the block that I played with, like, every day when I was six, seven, eight. For years anyway. She was my absolute best friend. Then she moved away and now I can't remember what she looked like. That makes me so sad. I hate it. Do you think you'll remember what I look like twenty years from now?"

"That's a trick question. Like 'When did you stop beating your wife?'"

"Oh, I see what you mean. Hmm."

"You could give me a picture of yourself. Then I wouldn't have to remember. Do you have a Polaroid?"

"I can't help myself from playing with the chemicals before I put the fixative on. It's my own personal art form. But I have a great picture of myself from when I was four. That was my best year. After that, well. After that, I changed."

"That's hard to believe. That it was your best year. Given how you look now. You must have been a knockout at four." Matt started to relax into the call. Nicky was herself, a person he liked. She talked about being home and how difficult it was. Her mother was so worried about her being at college. "I've gotten myself into some bad scenes, for sure, in high school. I always worked, so I always had money and so, well, I got into trouble."

"I'm surprised to hear that."

"Well, I can't tell you all my secrets at the same time. You'd never speak to me again."

Amy walked by. "I doubt that," Matt said, watching Amy. She went into the kitchen. "Anyway, I'm not going to get you into trouble."

There was a little pause. "We'll see about that. Didn't you ever get into trouble?"

Matt had to really think about it. "Oh, sure, when I was a kid, you know, I broke things, and . . . and . . ." Amy walked by again. "Hey, Amy, I'm on a private call here. Give me a little space, for god's sake."

"I'm not *listening* in on *you!*"

"I hear you're not alone. Who's there?"

"My creepy little sister."

"*Not* so little! *Not* creepy!"

"That sounds pretty normal," Nicky laughed. "When can you come over?" They agreed on the next Saturday night, Matt would come at six and they'd get something to eat and see a movie. Nicky said she'd like to see *Butch Cassidy and the Sundance Kid* and Matt agreed. "You'll have to come in and meet my parents. They demand it. It's a leftover from the bad times. But they're not going to, like, interrogate you."

"I'll wear body armor, just in case."

"You do that. Just remember what I look like."

———————

Nicky's house was an ordinary ranch house in the suburbs. Matt rang the bell, and the door opened to a woman in pants and a blouse with big swirls of blues and purples. "Hi, you must be Matt Aymer," her voice neutral. Nicky was a few feet behind her, like she'd been racing her mother to the door and had lost by a hair. "I'm Julia Watkins. Please come in. Oh, and here's Nicole."

"I'm pleased to meet you," Matt said. He was wearing the most acceptable outfit he could find in his limited wardrobe: chinos and penny loafers and a checked shirt and a sweater. "Hi, N-Nicole. It's great to see you again. You look nice." She had on her navy-blue sailor pants with all the buttons in front and a top that was all-blue geometric patterns. He didn't think he should hug her right there and Nicky seemed to be thinking the same thing, keeping a little distance.

A very large man strode up with a scotch in his hand. It wasn't all the time that Matt met someone he could look straight in the eyes, and it looked like four of Nicky could have fit in him. He had a big confident smile and stuck out a hand to shake.

"Dad, this is—" Nicky started.

"Dan Watkins, Matt. Pleased to meet you. Come on in, want a drink?" He lifted his scotch and lumbered back toward the dining room table.

"Thanks, but I shouldn't, I'm driving."

"Right," Dan Watkins said as if he hadn't thought of that. He picked up a martini that was on the table and gave it to his wife. "That's smart. Maybe just a beer then?"

"No, really, I'm fine." He looked at Nicky, who had an impatient look on her face.

Mrs. Watkins took a sip of her drink and said, "Maybe he'd like a Coke, Dan."

"Sure. Whatever he wants. God, you're skinny. Like her. Play sports?" Matt said he'd played baseball in high school. "How about those Mets, huh?" Mr. Watkins said. "One day we're really gonna have a subway series. Have a seat. Wacha doin' tonight?"

Matt looked at Nicky, who'd perched herself on the edge of a chair at the table, ready for a quick getaway. Her father stood behind her chair, looming over her. Matt sat down too. From where he was sitting he could see the living room, which had a big easy chair and a La-Z-Boy and another armchair facing a television set. There was art on the wall that looked like stylized flowers. Nicky said, "We're going to get something to eat at Frattelli's and then see a movie. *Butch Cassidy.*"

"Be sure to eat something, Nicole," her mother said, and Nicky nodded once, sharply, about a subject that was evidently an old one. "I'm surprised you haven't seen that movie yet," Mrs. Watkins said, and took a satisfied gulp of her martini. She fished the olive out and ate it.

"We don't get much of a chance to see movies at Montauk," Nicky said. "The closest movie theater is miles away, like I told you. Right, Matt?"

"Oh, yeah. Besides, we spend a lot of time studying."

Mr. Watkins gave out a hearty laugh and moved over to sit down. "I'll bet you do. Hey, Matt, what position did you play?"

"I was a pitcher."

"Good one?"

"He was great."

Matt twisted his hands together. "I was eight and one my last year. But the one was the championship game."

"Oh." He drank some scotch. "Still, that's damn good."

There was a little silence. "Your house is very nice," Matt said.

"Pretty good," Mr. Watkins said. "I'm in construction, you know, so I could do some improvements for a good price. Kind of gave Nicole her own wing, didn't we, Nicole?"

She nodded her head quickly and put her hands together. "It's really super, Dad."

Matt smiled and nodded his head up and down and Nicky said brightly, "Say, you know, we should probably get going. The movie could be crowded."

"Yes," Mrs. Watkins said. "Have a good dinner." She took another sip of her martini and stood up. "Well, you kids enjoy yourselves."

They all stood and Nicky said she'd get her coat. "Yeah, have a great time," Mr. Watkins said, raising his glass to Matt and finishing it. "We'll see you later tonight, right," in a tone that was more advice than a question.

Matt nodded and Nicky came back. "Of course," she said. "Like always." Mrs. Watkins patted her shoulder and then Mr. Watkins gave her a hug. Matt winced involuntarily, fearful that she wouldn't survive it. But she smiled up at him.

Once they were outside, Nicky put her arm around Matt and said, "Like always, they'll get bombed and pass out in front of the television." Matt laughed. He had the earrings in a box in his coat pocket but wanted to wait until the right moment. At the Italian restaurant Nicky suggested, she picked at a Caesar salad and Matt had lasagna. Nicky was quiet, for Nicky, but asked him what it was like to be home now that he had a real place in college. She got him talking in a way that surprised him. Suddenly she looked at her watch, and said, "Oh god, we should go, we don't want to be late. Here, my parents gave me money for dinner, take what you need." She ran off to the bathroom while Matt got the check and paid it. By the time she was back, he had her coat and put it on her, hugging her from behind. She turned around and smiled and hugged him back.

They watched the movie mostly in silence, Nicky leaning against Matt, seemingly enraptured by the movie. On the drive home, they agreed that it was a great movie. "Didn't you love it," she said, "at the end, when they just jumped off the cliff? I just got this feeling of floating and freedom."

"Yeah, and that line about him being afraid of jumping because he can't swim and Butch says, 'Don't worry, the fall will kill you' was hilarious. Kind of like the way things are now."

When they got back to Nicky's house, Matt assumed that he would drop her off at the door with a little smooching, but she said, "Come in a second, I've got something to give you." She opened the front door very carefully and looked inside. Satisfied, she pulled Matt in by the hand and they snuck by the living room. Evidently Nicky was right. Her parents seemed to be asleep in front of the television, which was showing a cigarette commercial. Nicky led him down a hall and around a corner, into her room. She closed the door and turned on a lamp by the bed. There was a poster on her wall of Janis Joplin.

"Take off your coat. Have a seat." The only place Matt could see to sit was on the bed, a double bed with a blue blanket and bunches of pillows and Roger. He put his coat on a hook and sat down on the bed and Nicky went to a bureau and reached deep into the top drawer. She pulled out something small and covered it with her hand. Holding it behind her back, she kneeled on the bed next to him.

"I've got something for you too," Matt said, happy that he'd found a gift for her.

"That's sweet," she said and kissed him on the cheek. Bringing her hand out from behind her back, she gave him a small square of foil. "Hold this," she said.

Matt looked at it. "What's this? A condom?"

"Yes," she said, "I'm your Christmas present." She slid off the bed and took off his loafers and socks. Matt, dumbfounded, just watched her. When she was finished, she crawled up his legs until she was on the bed again. She pulled off his sweater and said, "Take off your shirt." She pulled off her top. Her breasts were small but perfectly round, like cherries. She put her hands underneath them. "The French say they should be just big enough to fill a champagne cup. Which makes me perfect. You're not getting anywhere with that shirt." She started to work on the buttons.

"Nicky . . . are you sure . . . ?"

She put her hands on his shoulders and leaned against him. "Matt Aymer, is this your first time?" Matt tried to find an answer that was better than just "yes," without success. Meanwhile she unbuttoned his shirt and pushed it off his shoulders. "Well, that just makes it all the better," she said contentedly. She pushed him down on the bed and reached over to turn off the lamp. "Maybe that will be more comfortable."

Matt wiggled out of his shirt while Nicky started unbuttoning her pants. There was a little light coming in through the window blinds, enough that he could see her, her blond hair glowing in the light and the planes of her pale skin shifting. He felt himself getting erect despite the surprise, fear of her parents in the other room, and his own inexperience. He was amazed at how thin she was. Her ribs were as prominent as his. With her pants off, she pulled his down, getting his underwear and chinos off in one motion that he was happy to help with.

"Give me that condom," she whispered, and he heard her unwrap it and felt her grab his penis. She kissed it and worked the condom over it, making sure it was completely covered. Then she lay down on him, her legs on either side of him, and started kissing, softly, tenderly, steadily up his body until she reached his mouth.

After a few minutes, she said, "I am *completely* ready. You?" He kissed her and she reached and put him inside her. He gasped and she breathed in and out, slowly. She climbed on top of him and kept both of them going, speeding up and slowing down, sometimes with a laugh that was all hers, something she was feeling inside that she didn't want or need to tell him. There came a time when neither of them could stop. Matt came first, but Nicky bore down on him until she shuddered and gasped and fell down on his chest. She lay there and made small noises. Matt thought, *I hope she's as happy as I am.*

They drifted for a while, and then she turned from one cheek to another on him and started to shake a little. At first Matt thought he was sweating and then he realized that there were drops falling on his chest, not coming from perspiration. She was crying.

"Nicky, what's the matter? Are you okay?" He tried to raise her head to see her face, but she wouldn't let him.

"Nothing," she whimpered, shaking her head so that he could feel her hair brushing his chest. "Nothing. Everything. Matt, this was great. You're great. But you've got to stop seeing me."

This was like the way a lightning flash changes everything for a second. Matt thought maybe he'd heard her wrong. He laughed tentatively. "I thought you said I can't see you anymore."

"Yes, no, no, you shouldn't. You can't." Her little body shuddered, and Matt could feel more tears on his chest. He put a hand on her head, and she cried very quietly for a while.

"The thing is," she finally said, "I'm just so fucked up. And you're not."

He looked up at her head in the soft light. "What do you ... ?"

"Matt, I'm bulimic." He thought this was the beginning of a joke, like "some of my best friends are bulimic" but he didn't know what "bulimic" meant and said so. "It means I throw up. I make myself throw up. After I eat. Give me a Kleenex. On the night table. Thanks." She blew her nose and threw the tissue on the floor. "You remember I said that I was at my best at four? Well, after that I got fat. Fat and fatter. I was a little butterball. I didn't want any pictures taken. By the time I was ten, I weighed twice what I do now and I kept on going from there. By the time I was twelve, the school nurse was calling home to say that I was obese and had to lose weight."

"I didn't know people did that."

"Yeah, well, those people did. 'Obese' is like a code word for them about how your weight is screwing up your health. So my mom was all over me about it for years and I tried diet pills—boy, did they make me manic. You think I'm hyper now. I hated myself, hated how I looked, hated that I couldn't control myself. That kind of started the trouble. Boys didn't mind some fat if they were getting what they wanted, surprise surprise. Then I discovered I didn't have to actually, like, take on all those calories if I could get rid of them right away. Like by making myself throw up. I tried laxatives, but they made me feel rotten."

"Jeez, Nicky . . ."

She shook her head, mad, not wanting to be interrupted. "So I thought I had it all planned out. I had a strategy. I got into Montauk, 'cause I'm not, you know, dumb . . ."

"No. No way."

She looked down at him, her eyes wet and shining. "And then I met you. And you were so cute and you didn't know about all the horrible things I was—no, don't say anything—" She put a finger on his lips—"and I thought *I can make this guy like me* and *I can be normal too*. You were so *normal*, so fucking *normal*, and I wanted to be that way, for once, again, like I was at four. I wanted that. I wanted it so much, I thought it would rub off on me, I'd absorb it, like with osmosis. But it didn't happen. I'm still the same fucked-up child that I was before, making myself heave after every meal."

She rolled off him and settled in underneath his arm, her hand on his chest. "But after a week, a couple of weeks, I could see it wasn't working. I'm never satisfied, and I'll suck you dry with that. I'll make you as crazy as I am, and I don't want that."

Matt thought about all this and realized she was talking about a world he didn't understand in any way. But he knew how it felt to be defeated. "Nicky?" he said. "I might not be all *that* normal."

She laughed and reached her hand up to caress his chin. "Wrong. You are *all* that normal. And I still want that, or some of that. So, listen, I decided." She raised herself up on one elbow, unconscious that one small breast was against his chest, which he liked a lot. "I'm going to drop out of school." He raised up to look at her in surprise. "No, I mean I'm going to take some time off and get straight. Then I'll come back. I told you, I always worked. I have some money."

"Your parents will be okay with that?"

She fell back on the bed. "Oh, yeah, sort of. I was always Daddy's little girl, you know. And Mom goes along with what he says." She thought a bit. "There was a time when they fought a lot. I think I felt guilty about it. But now I think maybe they were just fucked-up in their own way and they got past it." She looked up at him. "That's kind of weirdly encouraging."

Matt smiled at her, feeling a little bit sick and completely unsure about what to do next. "Nicky, there's one thing you know for sure," he said.

"What's that?"

"When it's all over, I'll still be your friend."

She brought her face up close to his. In a deep voice she said, "Just the facts, sir, just the facts."

"That's a fact."

She kissed him hard on the mouth for a while, then said, "Now you should go. Before they wake up." She looked at the clock. "It's not even eleven yet. They won't think we could have had sex already."

"Nicky . . ."

"No, really, don't say anything. Let's just say that time stops between us here until it starts up again. Okay? Is that okay? Okay."

They turned the lamp on, got dressed, and Matt picked his coat off the hook. "Oh. Um, Nicky." He pulled out the box. "Merry Christmas." He felt his eyes start to tear up.

She clasped his hands and the box in her hands, then picked it out of his palm and opened it. She smiled, her cheeks wet. Wrapping her fist around the earrings, she said, "I'll keep these until I'm not a hungry pirate. Then I'll wear them and I'll see you. I'll be a pirate for your love."

They snuck downstairs to the front door. Nicky got her mischievous look on and made a lot of noise opening the door and stamping her feet. There was a snort from the living room, and her mother snapped up from the armchair. "Nicky, is that you?"

"Yeah, it's me," Nicky answered. "Matt was just saying . . . good night."

Mrs. Watkins fell back. "Yes, Matt. Nize to meet you."

"Oh, yeah, g'night, Mrandmrs Watkins. Good night, Nicky."

Nicky gave him one more hug. "Not good-bye. I hope."

"Me too."

16

MATT CAME BACK to Montauk in the middle of January because the group had decided to meet on the 16th to plan election strategy. Anyway, Matt was tired of sitting around the house watching old movies and getting all his mental exercise from *Concentration*, the game show. He kept replaying his night with Nicky in his head and feeling like there was nothing he could have changed. *Only so many times you can watch the same movie*, he thought. So he was happy to get back.

As soon as he walked in the room, he had second thoughts. Or rather his first thought was about seeing Nicky and the second was that he couldn't do that. Mel was back but left a note that he was getting something to eat. Restless, Matt threw his duffel bag into the closet and decided he'd take a walk.

As he got to the landing, Matt saw about twenty guys crowding around an open room. But "open" wasn't exactly accurate. John, a junior, was standing at the doorway, clearly furious. It took him a minute, but once Matt understood what he was looking at, he couldn't believe what he was seeing.

The doorway was crammed with newspaper. John put a hand on it and pushed. It moved in about an inch. "Hey," someone said, "go around and look at it from the outside! Totally blocked!"

Evidently the room was completely filled from wall to wall, floor to ceiling, door to windows, upper-left-hand near corner to lower-right-hand far corner, with crumpled-up newspaper. You couldn't see the windows or anything but the newspapers. They filled the entire cube of the room.

Matt was impressed. "Who did this? This is genius."

No one wanted to take credit but one of the seniors with a devilish look said, "I have absolutely no idea. But I can tell you it takes a while to gather this many *New York Times*es and crumple them up to fill the room. I don't know, but I've heard it takes about a week to find the papers—with a little help from the delivery guy—and then a few hours for about five people to crumple up the papers. Of course, that's just a guess. But I think that about sums it up."

"Why would anyone go to all that trouble?" Matt asked.

The senior looked at him. "Didn't you see the look on John's face?"

Matt said, "But now John has to spend hours cleaning up."

There was a chorus of objections. "No, not really," the senior said. "I suspect there's a clean-up crew ready to help. They somehow happen to have a box of those giant garbage bags ready. I hear."

"Very clever," Matt said, and then in his best Inspector Clouseau voice, "But zese perpetrators. Shall we ever know who zey are?" Lots of heads shaking no. "Zey are very clevair. And we are fortunate zere are no smokers on ze floor. One match and kabloom!"

That was a trip, Matt thought as he went on his way. *Things are better already.*

As he walked out the dorm, he went by his mailbox to see if there was anything in it, which seemed unlikely. Maybe there was an explanation of the calculus grade. He'd sort of prepared his parents that he wasn't going to do well in calculus because the professor was such a dork and anyway, he probably wouldn't be a math professor. But somehow or other he'd gotten a B. Made no sense. He got a 45 on the exam and it was a B? *I hope the surgeon I may need someday didn't get a 45 on his or her final surgery exam.*

Surprisingly, there was a note squeezed into his mailbox that said, "Matthew and Mel, I do not know if you are on campus but if you are, you must meet us in the lounge in G dorm immediately!!!!" There was no name and no date, but it wasn't hard to figure that it was Lana. He turned the paper over, and on the back, there was: "That's January 13 at 3:00. If you can come. Beth." *The dynamic duo*, Matt laughed to himself.

He found himself at G dorm. There weren't any guards on duty, or they were taking a break, so he walked into the lounge. He had a few minutes, so he could warm up.

Bonnie was sitting there, her head down reading a book and twirling a strand of her hair. He just stood there. He could almost see the fireplace and the cat that would make the picture complete and utterly enviable. Every once in a while, Bonnie would put the strand of hair in her mouth and make some notes in the book with a pencil. Then she looked up and saw Matt.

"Well, Happy New Year, fellow sufferer of the Kashman regime." She stood up and they walked up to each other. Matt wanted to hug her, but she beat him to it with the two-hands-on-the-shoulders hug. "How was your Christmas?"

"Oh, okay. I guess it's not the same when there aren't toys," he shrugged and tried to grin, but it didn't come off so well. He wanted to talk about Nicky with someone. He didn't know if Bonnie was the person. He didn't know how to start.

"Oh, that doesn't sound good." She looked at him. "How were your grades?"

"They're fine. I got a B in history. Thanks to you."

"I was just the conduit." She smiled, then frowned. "Fight with your parents?"

"Actually, no fights with anybody. Not a fight, anyway."

"Mmm, that leaves one thing. That blond girl you were with? You broke up?" Shocked that Bonnie knew about Nicky, Matt was speechless and embarrassed. Bonnie tried to suppress a smile. She took his arm. "Come, sit. I'm sorry to hear it. I thought she might be good for you. Get you out of your shell a little." They went to sit on the couch, Matt still trying to reorient his world with its new dimensions of Bonnie knowing about his love life. Bonnie drew her legs up under her and asked, "She break up with you or vice versa? You don't have to tell me if you don't want to."

Matt didn't know what to do with his hands and wished he had his baseball. "Uh, she decided that, uh, we shouldn't see each other for a while." Bonnie waited patiently. "Um, she had, has, a physical problem."

Bonnie shook her head. "That poor girl. That's a shitty problem to have. She was so skinny, she practically advertised it." She patted her stomach and Matt wondered what that would feel like. "I have the opposite problem. Is she going to get help?"

Matt took a deep breath. "Yeah, that's her idea. She's dropping out of school. For a while."

"You'll miss her."

Matt looked at Bonnie and felt his eyes tear up. He wasn't sure if it was because of Nicky or because he could talk about Nicky, but he really, really didn't want to cry in front of Bonnie. "I will. But, you know, she . . . it was hard. She'd disappear for days at a time. I was never really sure when I'd see her."

"When she felt ugly and disgusting—not that she really was, she just felt that way—she didn't want people to see her. *Especially* not you, you of all people."

"Because I was her, her friend."

"Because you were her *boyfriend* and she wanted to look and feel her best when she was with you and didn't want you to see the bad—what's her name?"

"Nicky."

"The bad Nicky. She's hardly the only person who ever felt that way, but that doesn't make it any easier for her." She paused a second. "But when she was the good Nicky, she wanted to be with you."

"That's right. I never saw her down, almost never. She was always up. Not from drugs, just from whatever she was doing that day. She was interested in everything. Books, music, art. Reading. She loved to read."

Bonnie sat up. "I like to read too."

Matt was thinking about the Nicky he never saw. How could he be so close to her and not see what was such a big part of Nicky's life? What else was he missing? "Do you ever feel that way? Like you're worthless?"

Bonnie looked surprised and sat back against the couch. She pulled the strand of hair again. "Sure, I've felt like a loser. Plenty of times. I guess I never felt I had to hide the feeling. It's the one good thing my parents gave me—I never felt I had to hide anything from them."

"Well, you're not a loser, either." He smiled at her. "And you don't have the opposite problem, either."

She laughed. "If the freshman ten turns into the sophomore twenty, I will have." She twirled her hair. "How about you? Do you ever feel like a loser?"

"Oh, god, yes. When I lost that last game . . . You know, losing the game was bad enough, but then I had to face everybody on the team. I had to apologize."

"And you did."

"I did."

She put a hand on his arm. "It takes a big person to do that. I so much admire you did that. I know you'll be sad about Nicky, but she didn't break it off because there's anything wrong with you. In fact, it's more like there *isn't* anything wrong with you."

Matt laughed sadly. "She said I was too normal."

"That's not the way I'd put it, but I get the idea."

Suddenly there was an explosion of sound and bustle, and Lana and Beth walked into the room in the middle of what sounded like a ferocious argument. Bonnie and Matt leapt off the couch together and turned to look at them. "Well!" Lana said and smiled. "*What* have you two been doing here?"

Matt felt himself turning red, but Bonnie said, "We have solved the world's problems, so we're ready to take on yours."

"Hah! We'll see about that," Lana huffed genially. She turned to Beth. "Come, give me your coat. You are pigheaded, but I will hang up your coat for you."

Beth said, "No, I'll hang yours up. You just think about why I'm right."

Lana rolled her eyes. "All right, we will compromise. You hang up my coat and I will hang up yours."

Beth thought about this for a second and burst out laughing, which spread to everyone else. The two of them went to the coat closet in the corner of the room. Matt leaned over and whispered to Bonnie, "Thanks."

She smiled. "Anytime, Ribs. That's what they call you, right? Ribs?" She poked him in the ribs and then gave him a quick hug before he could do anything to react. Beth and Lana came out of the coat closet and Matt went to pick up his coat. Bonnie marked her place in her book and went to sit at the table in the front of the room. Lana paced around everybody, the tiger in her cage.

"First," Beth said, opening up her notebook and taking out a pen, "we have to have a manifesto."

"A what?" Mel yelped as he and Dorman walked into the lounge. Matt thought that there was no other reason in the entire world that these two people would be doing the same thing at the same time. Mel was so solid that he never seemed to lose contact with the ground, no matter how fast he was moving. Dorman seemed to hover about six inches off it, propelled by small jets of moving air. Neither of them needed a manifesto, a word Matt had learned only in the history class with Bonnie.

"A manifesto," Beth repeated, writing in her book. Matt sat down next to her, curious as to what she was always writing in that notebook of hers.

"What are you writing?" Mel asked.

"I'm just writing down who's here. We should keep a record."

"That's fine, dear," Dorman said, "as long as you're not reporting to Kashman."

"Or the FBI," Mel said, and the two of them laughed and slapped their palms together. Mel pulled out a chair and asked again, "What's a manifesto?"

"It's a document that explains why you're doing what . . . ," Bonnie began and at the same time, Beth said, "It tells people what you stand for." Dorman took a seat next to Bonnie.

Circling around Bonnie, past Dorman, and heading toward Mel, Lana said, "Bonnie is right, but in any case, a manifesto is not what we need."

Matt had the feeling that this was the argument they had been having when they came in and he tried to head it off or at least get in the way of it. "But don't you have to tell people what you want to do as president? Your ideas about governing?"

Lana stopped behind Beth and put her hands on her friend's shoulders. "Ideas, of course. I have multiple ideas. Many more than Joe Kashman. And I will explain them in detail. But what we need is a plan to make people vote. My people. To speak plainly, the women."

"Don't you want the guys to vote for you too?" Mel said with a little edge in his voice.

"I'll vote for you," Dorman said.

"Thank you, dear." Lana smiled.

"But we're not sure if you count," Beth laughed, "as a guy."

"Speak for yourself, girlfriend," Dorman said sweetly.

"So you want us to focus on getting out the vote," Matt talked over the sniping to Lana.

"Yes. I have been talking to Jack Appel."

Matt raised his eyebrows as Lana walked past him, back on her circuits of the table. "I thought he was one of Kashman's people."

"Jack has become disenchanted with Kashman. Besides, he has flirted with me extensively, though I have been very clear I have no interest." She smiled across the table at Beth.

"Men think 'no' means 'in a little while.'" Beth nodded.

"So," Lana continued, "I bought him a few beers in return for his thoughts about how someone else might win an election against Kashman." Lana explained at great length how Appel had outlined winning against Kashman. It mainly involved making sure that all the women voted for her along with various appeals to the commuter students, who usually didn't vote, and special interest groups, like Sam.

"And his dog," Mel said.

Lana was not to be diverted. "In other words, our work will require serious effort. But look, there are boys who won't vote for me no matter what I say. Fuck them. There are boys who will vote for me because they dislike Joe, but they are probably a small number." She said there was a squadron of women who would go door to door to get out the vote. "And they are not afraid of flirting."

Bonnie was taking notes on what Lana was saying. *She doesn't wear any makeup*, Matt thought. *I wonder if her skin was always perfect like that.* So was Beth, but she was like the recording secretary. Mel was drumming his fingers on the table, really listening to Lana. If there was one thing he liked, it was a challenge. And he hated Kashman, always had. Dorman was, well, Dorman. He liked doing anything with people he liked and he liked almost everybody. Suddenly Matt heard his name.

"No, Matt should act like he's going to vote for Kashman," Bonnie was saying. "Besides, he's got to campaign for himself."

Matt sat up. "Sorry, what? I was spacing out there a little."

"Space, the final frontier," Mel intoned.

"I'm the space cowboy here," Dorman objected.

"We were saying." Lana cut them short. "You should not let it be known that you are with us in any way." She pointed her long arm and finger at him directly. "You will be our eyes and ears on Joe's campaign. And perhaps even spread some disinformation for us." She smiled mischievously.

Matt frowned. The idea of lying bothered him a little. "What would I be doing?"

"I will think about that. Bonnie, you think too. There are historical precedents perhaps."

Bonnie looked at Matt and gave him a half-smile. "I'll see if I can focus on that. I have to campaign too."

Dorman laughed. "Bonnie, people would vote for you twice if they could."

On the Monday that classes started, as on most Mondays, waves of people went to lunch around noon, so a very large percentage of the school was surprised to see a large sailboat parked in the visitors' circle of the school. Painted on the sail was "Cruise with Lana" on one side and "Lana for President" on the other. The candidate herself stood on the bow in a fur coat, since it was sixteen degrees, calling out, "Vote for me for president of the Polity" or just "Hi! I'm Lana! For president!" Little puffs of vapor floated away from her mouth as she talked, as if she were a steam engine. A guy and a girl stood on the stern sailing paper airplanes toward the students walking by.

Matt and Mel stood watching. "Where'd she *get* that?" Mel said.

"Her father owns a boat company. I mean, he sells boats. Hey, check out the flyers. They literally are flyers." Mel retrieved one and opened it up. Large letters at the top said, "Hi! I'm Lana Harananinan and I'm running for president of the Polity. Don't worry! You won't have to spell it to vote for me! Just remember Lana!" There was more about her ideas, coming down heavy on more equality, especially for women, changes in curriculum, how student money was spent, and campus issues. At the bottom, large type demanded, "Stop investment in war and killing machines! Out of Vietnam and the military-industrial complex!"

"Covers the bases," Matt said.

"Yeah, but the boat is what makes it," Mel pointed out.

After a few minutes, campus police drove up, parked in front of the pickup truck pulling the boat, and two cops got out of their car. The person driving the pickup leaned out of the cab and yelled to them, "Hello! I'm just dropping my daughter off for the semester! Can you direct me to the G dorm?"

The campus cops were not amused. "Why the boat?" one growled.

"We sailed up," Lana's father answered cheerfully.

"You're a little late. The semester's started."

"We had headwinds!"

Lana leaned over the side of the boat, and yelled, "Donald! How very nice to see you again!"

The cop heaved a sigh. "Hi, Lana. Come down off the boat and let your father get back home."

"We were just going to the dorm. Daddy! Turn around the circle and we will go down that street, over there. Donald, could you move your car so that we can leave?"

The cop shrugged and directed his partner to their car. When they drove off, the sailboat followed and both drove down the campus perimeter road on the way to G dorm as if the cops were providing an escort. Kashman walked up in jeans and a worn leather bomber jacket, frowning. "Where'd she get that?"

Mel said, "Her father owns a boat dealership." He surreptitiously nudged Matt. Kashman, still watching the cop car and the boat proceed down the road, said, "Whaddya think, Matt?"

Matt shrugged. "She's a hot chick. I wouldn't push her out of bed, but voting for her for president?" Kashman just nodded, still frowning. "Come on, Mel," Matt said, "let's get some lunch." They left Kashman still glaring down the road.

"Listen to you," Mel snickered. "'Wouldn't push her out of bed.' As if she'd get in yours." Matt was silent. "Hey," Mel said, "I'm sorry about Nicky."

"It's okay," Matt said. "I mean, not, but I hope it works out for her."

"She was sweet," Mel said, "but a little psycho."

"Are you still seeing Liz?" Matt asked, changing the subject. "She's got a bed free this semester."

"I see her. But we're not, like, a couple or anything. I'm hungry."

On Friday, the lunchroom was buzzing. It was the day that the student newspaper came out, the election edition. It led with an article about Kashman running for a second term, carefully pointing out that there were no rules about a junior running for a second term.

Ominously, it also pointed out that neither did the rules specify that the president had to be an underclassman. There were other articles about the basketball team, new courses that were being offered that semester, profiles of President Thomas and Dean Devin, horoscopes, and lots of ads for yearbooks and prom outfits.

But what set people off was another newspaper, a four-page broadsheet that gave a very different story. Its main headline, in big type, said, "Woman Challenges for Polity Presidency." A second article, with smaller type, said, "Polity Faced with Unprecedented Power Play," about Kashman running for president. That article also listed the requirements for running for the office, pointing out that no one had ever succeeded themselves and that no senior had ever held the office. It went on to point out that there were good reasons why seniors might not, or even should not be, president of the Polity.

The article on Lana told Matt things he didn't know about her.

Lana Artemisia Harananinan grew up in Kings Point in Nassau County, when her family emigrated from Iran when she was six years old. They left Iran after the CIA overthrew the democratically elected leader Mohammad Mossadegh and installed the Shah because Mossadegh nationalized the oil industry.

Harananinan was the treasurer of her high school class and was named Miss Nassau in a talent contest. She had a high B average throughout high school and is currently intending to major in Politics.

Her platform for Montauk is based on the goal of inclusiveness and equality. She is in favor of a curriculum that is less hidebound but still based on the great body of knowledge that is our heritage of the Greco-Roman–Middle Eastern world. She envisions a curriculum that embraces both the achievements of human beings from all parts of society—from the thrones of kings to the looms of weavers and the fields of grain and livestock that keep all of us alive. While there is always room for change, she says, it is shallow to tear down the great tower of knowledge that the world's people have built over so many years.

As fun as it was to learn more about Lana, Matt was even more interested in the article on Kashman. Sketchy as it was, it answered some questions and asked as many more.

Joseph L. Kashman is listed as living in Riverdale, the Bronx, although the mailing address for his grades is in Bensonhurst, Brooklyn. Known as a sharp dresser, Kashman often speaks of growing up in an Italian neighborhood amid perils of the gangs who controlled the streets, often street by street. "Only the Mafia provided any security," he has said, describing this as "a joke," when asked about it since he has become president of the Polity.

At the same time, he also describes long vacations in Europe during the summer with his father, who was traveling for business. He has described these trips as "amazing," "boring," and "educational" to different people. It is said that his parents are divorced.

His high school academic record is unknown. He does not seem to have held any office in high school. He says that he only became interested in holding office recently, inspired by the civil rights movement and John F. Kennedy. He is currently majoring in Business Administration.

Kashman has presented a program for curriculum change, which he calls Curriculum Relevancy Upgrade Development, that would place all curriculum development in the hands of a committee of students and faculty equally. New courses would have to be approved by a majority of the committee and new faculty hired as necessary.

Kashman has also supported an increase in the intramural sports and entertainment budget. He believes that it can be increased without asking the students for more money, but through economizing and eliminating waste.

On the inside, *The Broadsheet* also had articles about women's sports including hockey and soccer, a call for birth control information and pills to be distributed at the health center, the need for more bathrooms for women, and a women's literature section in the library. There was an article reprinted from a magazine that everybody read but only a few people talked about. It was really called, "The Myth of the Vaginal Orgasm," but in *The Broadsheet* it was called, "The Myth of the Va**nal Orgasm." You could always tell when somebody was reading it because the table became real quiet.

"This is Beth, right?" Mel muttered as they sat at the B-3 table. "Is she going to get in trouble for this?" She was hiding more or less in plain sight. The main editorial was signed "Elizabeth Winstead," and it said plainly that the writer had a personal connection to Lana Harananinan, and that the newspaper was "unapologetically and unequivocally" in favor of her for president. It also pointed out that the campus newspaper was no less prejudiced, despite its "façade of comatose fair-mindedness."

"Probably. But there aren't any four-letter words or naked girls."

"Wait until next week. Naked men. Wonder where they got that stuff about Kashman?"

"From his FBI file, probably." They laughed.

Toward the end of lunch, a couple of Zoomen came in with big garbage bags and started picking up *The Broadsheet*s and throwing them in garbage bags. Almost instantly, a dozen women converged on the men, yelling at the top of their lungs, "Lana! Lana! Lana!" They grabbed at the garbage bags until they tore, and the papers spilled out. Finally the guys turned and marched out, yelling that they'd be back. When they left, the entire lunchroom cheered.

"This could get ugly," Mel said. "You know that it's Kashman pulling the Zoo's strings. They're as bad as he is."

One day Matt was walking toward class when one of Kashman's minions, Rocky, caught up with him and said, "Joe wants to meet in the office. He wants you to come."

Matt thought, *Right, Agent 007 on my way. Where are the girls?*

There were about a half-dozen people in Kashman's office. Jack Appel was there, although he was sitting off to one side as if only halfway involved. The guy named Rick was there—Matt remembered seeing him at the first Taj party. He was passing around a joint. Matt didn't really know the others or had forgotten their names. "Matt, I'm glad you could come," Kashman said. "I think you know these people. This is a strategy meeting. Lana's got a lot of ideas and she's a hot chick. That's a problem. How do I attack a chick?"

"Hey man," Rick said, "what's to worry? You've got the Taj and the Zoo in your pocket." He took a drag on the joint and talked it out. "The rest will split. The commuters will vote for you because they know your name and they don't know hers. Can't even pronounce it. Hairy Nan Nan? Come on, man, it's a lock."

Kashman was not convinced. "I didn't get to be president by taking things for granted."

They discussed tactics and strategies in such detail that Matt started to space out. Then he heard Kashman saying, "Yeah, Beth Winstead. She is a real troublemaker. I know she and Lana are doing it. Anything we can do with that?"

Rick laughed again. "I don't think the dyke vote is very big here."

Jack Appel suddenly spoke up, warningly. "Joe, I wouldn't push that too hard. About Beth."

Kashman made a face. "Yeah, okay. But *you* can."

Appel gave a noncommittal shrug.

Kashman urged one more time. "Remember why we're here. Our

work is not done. If we want to change this campus, I need to be reelected and you need to get me over the finish line. Let's make sure all my people vote and vote often, if you get my drift."

Matt wondered what it was all about, but he also didn't want to get any more involved than he was. *Was Kashman just drunk with power or did he really want radical change? This double-agent thing sucks*, he thought. He settled in to listen as they mapped out tactics to stop Beth from issuing the next edition of *The Broadsheet*, to attack Lana personally with a whisper campaign, and to focus on Kashman as the best person to change the campus. "We Are the Revolution" was going to be the slogan. "One last thing," Kashman said. "Anyone who says they'll vote for me—let'm know they'll get a jay—a couple of jays— from me."

"How are you going to know if they really did?" Matt asked.

"Doesn't matter," Kashman laughed. "The thing is, most people are actually honest. Amazing." He looked around. "Okay, everybody, we've got a lot of work to do. Get ready to blast off." He clapped his hands and the group started to get on coats and go. As Matt slipped out the door, he suddenly found Kashman at his elbow.

"Matt," he said, looking concerned, "everything okay?" Matt shrugged and put on a smile, but Kashman said, "You still seeing that girl? Nicky?"

Matt shook his head. "No. We broke up. Anyway, she's not at school this semester."

Kashman put a hand on his arm and led him down the hall a ways. "Man. Bummer. I thought you were looking down. That can put a damper on anyone's life. Look, I can see you cared about her, and that's there, that's a part of you. But there are other parts of you too. You're a good athlete, a good guy, you've got friends in B-3. I'm your friend. It will hurt for a while, for sure. But it will also get better."

Matt thanked him, confused that the cutthroat politico in the room could sound like a guru here in the hall. He walked back to the dorm, trying to figure out what to do with what he knew. He wished he knew how to get in touch with Bonnie right away, then worried that it would be out of line, then gave up on the idea. He got to the third floor and heard a mournful song coming out of Brain and Fish's room: "Many rivers to cross . . ." Brain was sitting there reading and Matt asked him who was singing.

"Jamaican guy," Brain said, "Jimmy Cliff. Really cool sound. They call it ska, or reggae. They are very spiritual people, these musicians. Rastafarians believe that the music and the musician can change the world. I don't really believe all that very much, but the music is incredible."

Matt listened some more, thinking that it sounded like folk music, but with something else. "I merely survive because of my pride," the man sang. It felt like a challenge. Matt moved on down the hall. It was after ten now, so things were mostly quiet. Mel was studying, as usual, and Matt blew in and flopped on the bed. "I'm beat," he said. "Listen to this." He told Mel about Kashman's meeting and the tricks they intended to play on Lana. "And Beth," Matt said. "I had no idea it would get this batshit. It looks to me like Kashman is desperate for some reason."

"Hey, you have to work on your own campaign."

Matt groaned. "Don't remind me. Why did I get into this again?"

"To get the girls?"

He talked to Bonnie in the European history class and she said she'd alert Lana and Beth about Kashman's plans to steal *The Broadsheet* and even stuff the ballot boxes with the Zoo's help. After class they walked over to the lunchroom and sat together. It was still early, so none of the B-3 guys were at their table. When they had lunch and were going to sit down, Matt started to go one way and Bonnie a different way. They looked at each other and Matt said, "How about over there? Halfway between?" Bonnie grinned and agreed.

There was one thing Matt had been uncomfortable about saying in the classroom, but he took the plunge now. "Kashman also said they were going to make an issue of Lana and Beth being, you know . . . together."

"Gay," Bonnie nodded. She sighed, "I guess that was kind of inevitable. I think Lana can handle it, but I'm a little worried about Beth."

Matt swallowed some hamburger. "They're so different. It's kind of surprising that they . . . that . . ." He didn't know what he wanted to say.

Bonnie raised her eyebrows and smiled a little. "Maybe they're good in bed together." She smiled some more. "That can make up for a lot. You don't have to worry about birth control, for one. But two women aren't any more different than a woman and a man. I'm sure you've known odd couples."

"Oh, sure," Matt said. "Even my—" he stopped.

"Your girlfriend in high school?" Bonnie prompted. "What was she like? Was she like Nicky?"

Matt felt totally screwed talking about his love life with Bonnie. It took him a while, then, "No, not like Nicky. Nicky was . . . Jill was a real go-getter. She was smarter than I was, and really involved like with school activities. She could talk to anyone, anytime." He laughed, "I just was along for the ride."

Bonnie smiled. "The ride to the state championship. Were you two the senior prom king and queen?"

"Um, no." Matt reddened. "Homecoming."

Bonnie smiled. "Knew it," she said, as if she'd won a bet with herself.

"What about you? You must have had boyfriends in high school."

Bonnie looked away for a moment, then ate some soup. "There were some sweet guys. And some pretty intense guys. There was Johnny, of course. But I never felt that I wanted anybody's ring. I knew since I was twelve—"

"Martin Luther King."

"You remember. Yes, so I was always kind of looking ahead."

Matt felt an undercurrent in that. "Are you still?" he asked. "Looking ahead?"

Her face went through a couple of changes, a frown and then that little thing she did with the corner of her mouth. Then she focused on Matt. "Sometimes. Not right now."

Matt felt that she could be maddeningly elusive and completely open at the same time, but somehow she'd made him feel like he was interesting. Worth being interested in. "You're ahead of me," he said, "I can barely even look ahead to running for the Polity."

She leveled a finger at him. "I've been meaning to talk to you about that." He met her finger with his finger, but just smiled and let her talk. "You should be starting now," she said. "You already have some recognition around the school—and what you did in Washington, you know, it got around."

Matt frowned. "That—do I have to talk about that? It was just . . . you know, a spur-of-the-moment thing."

Bonnie nodded. "Oh right, that kind of spur-of-the-moment-risking-your-life-to-save-a-friend thing. Happens every day." Matt had to laugh at himself, and Bonnie went on, "Anyway, like I said, word got around. But you can't coast on that." He raised his hands in surrender and said he wasn't sure where to start. "No problem," she said. "Come around to the dorm lounge on Sunday and I'll help you get started. You're going to be busy as hell for a couple of weeks, you know. You're sure you want to do this?"

"Absolutely," Matt said. All his doubts suddenly seemed puny.

———————

The next two weeks were a blur. Protests against the war went quiet. Henry Kissinger continued to act like he was conducting private diplomacy that would fix everything as long as everybody stayed out of the way. There were bombings, including a really horrific one in Manhattan that revolted almost everybody, but these were strange and distant events on campus. Classes started and Matt had to adjust to not seeing Nicky in his English class. Wit and Bonnie were in the continuation of the European history class. Matt realized he knew even less about European history in the second half of the nineteenth century up to World War I than he did about American history in that period, and that was saying something.

Lana was everywhere and never around. She organized the door-to-door election coverage. One night, a woman came through B-3, to the general amazement of all the guys. Her pitch was very simple: it was time for somebody new, Kashman was not going to help anybody but his cronies, and he might destroy their education. There was a buzz on campus. People were actually talking about the election, and Wit said that hadn't happened in his experience—at least not talked *seriously* about the election.

―――――――

The next issue of *The Broadsheet* came out with a special section on how women were treated on campus. Women were seduced against their will. There was talk of rape, but no names were mentioned. Most of the girls were afraid of being shamed or even thrown out of school. "No matter what, it's always our fault," one of the women said. Some of the stories shocked even the administration, and they called Beth into a meeting. Beth refused to say who had written the story, who had been quoted in it, or who was alleged to have committed rape. She was told these weren't proper journalistic standards. "They can take journalistic procedure and shove it up their asses," she muttered to Matt. "There's a new journalism in town. I'm doing these stories."

When he saw that Lana was gaining ground, Kashman found another woman to run for president—a girlfriend of one of the Zoo animals, who was as middle American silent majority as any of Nixon's supporters. He hoped he could split off some of the women to vote for Nancy. But after a week, he began to hear that some of the guys who would vote for him were curious about Nancy. They were a small group—against drugs, against revolution of any kind, extolling the virtues of homework, housework, and child-rearing.

"I'm worried that she is going to take votes away from me as much as from Harrigan." He said that "Harananinan" was too long for him to bother saying.

Kashman fought back against the sailboat with a golf cart that had a banner on it: VOTE FOR SPECIAL K! It didn't hurt that "special K" was also the nickname for very high-quality marijuana from Kauai, Hawaii, that had arrived on campus. No one knew for sure that it was from Kauai, but they did know that afterward they didn't exactly know where the night went.

The cart drove around campus, legally or not, playing the Beatles' "Revolution" repeatedly and that was the sum of Kashman's pitch: he would bring the revolution to the campus, put the students in charge, make the school come out against the Vietnam War. Kashman even got one of the faculty, Joel Sanger, a psych professor, to talk at a rally he held. They called it a teach-in, so it was held in the auditorium, but it was packed with Kashman's crew, including Matt.

Bonnie helped him get his election flyers together. "My propaganda," he called it. Matt had shelled out $50 for postcards that he and Mel would give out at the dorms. Matt looked at the empty card. "How about one of those *Peanuts* cartoons about Linus running for president?" Bonnie wrote a couple of paragraphs for him when he pleaded he couldn't do it. "I can't write about myself," he claimed. It was true, but he also wanted to see what she'd say.

"'Matt Aymer comes to the Polity with an openness and a fresh eye,'" he read. "'He has been a leader in every organization he's joined.'" He looked at Bonnie. "Right, all two of them."

"Keep reading," Bonnie said.

"'He has advocated for students without a voice and changed the way campus makes itself accessible. And he fights for those who are baselessly attacked.'" He looked at Bonnie dubiously.

"Randy, remember? First day?"

"It's a good thing you're here," he said. "If I didn't know me, I'd almost vote for this guy."

"I can introduce you to him," she said and leaned forward. "He's worth knowing."

"Wait, I got it." He picked up a postcard and a pen, wrote a few words in big block letters, and handed it to Bonnie. "That should be all I need."

"'Bonnie says vote for him,'" she read slowly, as if to a child. "With an arrow pointing to a stick figure. Are you trying to get my endorsement?"

"I'll give you mine if you give me yours." She cocked an eyebrow at him and smiled. "Bonnie, this—" he held up what she wrote, "—is terrific even if it's barely true. Thank you. Thank you. It seems like I keep owing you, no matter what I do."

She nodded sagely. "That's right. You're in deep now." She held out a hand and they shook, not letting go of each other for an extra beat. "Look at that paw," she said. He turned his hand up to let go but she kept her hand on his as if comparing sizes. "No wonder you can throw a football." He grinned. "Okay, now go type this up and get it printed tomorrow. I'll see you in class." He watched her go, thinking, *This is where I say I won't wash my hand, right?*

————————

Lana's big moment was a rally in the gym a week later. Lana's theme song, "All You Need Is Love," played in the background, and women with signs were marching back and forth in front of the stage. There was LANA FOR PRESIDENT naturally, but also IT'S OUR TIME NOW and WOMEN ON TOP. Lana strode onto the stage in a spangled red, white, and blue vest that caught the lights like a disco ball. There was a sustained, high-pitched cheer while she walked from one side of the stage to the other. Matt found Bonnie, who was obviously enjoying the vibe, so he just said hi and watched.

Lana began with the basics of the platform she'd laid out in her literature: more classes on topics important to women, more sports for women, divesting stocks that were related to the military-indus-trial complex, more input from students about classes. "Evolution, not revolution," she said.

Then she moved on, urging more personal topics about men and women. "Some men—not all, but too many—use us to feel they have power. They want to have sex with us so that they can feel attractive. They want us to vote for them so that they can feel in charge. They want us to listen to them so that they can feel intelligent. If we take those things away from them, they will feel unwanted, powerless, and stupid. Let us take what is ours!"

Matt shifted his feet, starting to feel uncomfortable. Bonnie looked at him and raised an eyebrow that seemed like a question. Matt leaned over and said under the cheering, "Is there a target on my back?" Bonnie shook her head.

Suddenly there was a loud fake cough with "fuck you" garbled in it. From another section, a fake sneeze sounded a lot like "bullshit." The Zoo had planted guys in different sections, each taking turns to interrupt Lana's speech. People were turning around and shouting, "Quiet, shut up!" Bonnie frowned up at Lana, who kept on and even amplified the rhetoric. "Agitation for specific freedoms is worthless without the preliminary raising of consciousness necessary to utilize these freedoms fully," Lana said, now really into her speech. "We must put our own interests first, then proceed to make alliances with other oppressed groups. We must demand a piece of the pie before we have to serve it to them!"

There was more shouting at the back and a group started to chant "Special K! Special K!" Some of the women were trying to shove the men out and Matt thought things were getting bad. He recognized some of the guys as part of Kashman's Zoo allies. They knew he was part of Kashman's "team," as they called it. Suddenly one of the women screamed and there was a thud when she hit the gym floor. Matt worked his way back to the guy he thought was probably in charge of the harassment.

"Hey, Murphy," he said.

The guy turned to him and grinned. "We'll break this shit up, right?"

Matt shook his head. "Look, if someone gets hurt here, it's gonna go down on Joe. Some girl breaks an arm or a leg and you're in deep shit. I'd cool it."

Murphy argued with him for a while, but Matt pretended to have Kashman's authority behind him. "He said to me, 'Make sure no one gets hurt. Knock her off her stride, but don't knock her on her butt.'" Finally, Murphy agreed. "Look, lead the chant out of the gym. Take control here. You the man."

Murphy looked sullen but went over to another Zoo guy and

talked into his ear. The guy looked surprised, but Murphy just nodded his head toward the door. The Zoos formed a ragged line and wound their way to the door.

Lana was still going, but he thought she was wrapping it up. He slipped back toward the stage and saw Bonnie wave to him. "What did you do?" she asked.

"I was just fighting for those who are baselessly attacked," he said, deadpan.

She looked serious. "I see. Oh . . . ," she smiled and reached into her purse.

"Here." She handed him a folded card with a heart on the front. Inside at the top line was, "Lana says" and below that another heart inscribed "Be Mine." Bonnie said, "It's a Lanatine. Or maybe a Haraninatine. We haven't decided yet. But the Saturday before the voting is Valentine's Day. We're going to pass these out. Maybe with those little candies."

"Sweet," Matt said, and they winced simultaneously. "Can I keep this?" he asked.

"I wanted you to have it." She looked around. "Say, if you're all done here, maybe we can get some tea or hot chocolate or something. We really have to talk about what Joe is doing to disrupt Lana's campaign. It is obscene."

Matt had never heard Bonnie use that word, but it seemed to be an apt description. "My schedule is clear," he said.

They went to the student union and found a quiet corner. Bonnie reminded Matt that the voting would start in a few weeks. She wanted to talk to Kashman in person. Matt asked her what good that would do. "I want to read Joe's body language. I just don't understand him. Why is he so ruthless? Why isn't he focusing on the changes sorely needed on the campus? Is the dangerous drug dealing true? We can't be a part of this if god forbid he should win again. I want to find the right time to talk to him. I will find the right excuse to confront him next week. Stay tuned!"

"I'm a radio."

17

Matt, having run out of underwear, had his head in the closet, gathering up clothes to do laundry. "Mel, I think we need some room freshener in here." Mel, studying at his desk, didn't answer. "It kind of stinks," Matt said, a little louder.

Mel didn't look up from his book. "Yeah, you should do your laundry."

Barry poked his head in the room. "Matt, Mel, you've been honored—or perhaps sentenced is a better word—to become an official member of the B-3 Inner Circle. Get ready for lots of fun a week from Saturday."

Mel threw up his hands. "I've got exams coming up."

Matt tried to avoid thinking about that paper he was supposed to write for English and that he would miss a few days of campaigning. "Barry, what's your draft number?" he asked.

"Two seventy-six. Why?"

"I was hoping you would be preparing to go to basic training," Matt said.

Barry ignored this and sketched in the details. They were going to a resort on Montauk Point. "It's really cheap in the winter, so your part is only $25. We'll take care of your food and lodging for that. And don't worry. Nothing is life-threatening, at least as life is generally understood. But they will be novel experiences." He walked out.

Matt and Mel had heard rumors about an initiation from the upperclassmen. "Humiliating" and "gross" and "upchuck" were used freely. Matt couldn't figure out why he should participate or what the point was anyway. Plus, no one would tell him exactly what would happen. "Mel," Matt said, "what's your take on this initiation shit?"

Mel turned up from his biology textbook. "I think it's kind of a really cool idea. I really want to be part of something and I like these crazy guys. I think this may be Barry's way to solidify the team for the playoffs, to make us all want to kill for each other." He paused. "Sorry for the four-letter word."

"Huh?"

"'Kill.'"

"I thought you were against fraternities and pledging?"

"That's just the point. This isn't a fraternity. This is just a bunch of guys."

Matt thought about this for a while. He was worried that things could get out of hand and someone would get really hurt. He knew that the B-3 guys would never deliberately hurt anyone, but sometimes bad things happen. On the other hand, the best time of his life had been with the high school baseball team. They were there for him, even after the . . . game. That meant a lot to him. The entire country was so polarized, but not these guys.

Just as he had rationalized that everything would be okay, Wit popped into the room with a fishbowl containing four goldfish. Wit had been carrying these fish for weeks, saying all kinds of things to the fish, like they would enjoy their time in Montauk . . . up to a point! He wanted the freshmen to see and hear the banter. "Hey guys, got extra changes of clothing? The water at Montauk Point is very cold this year. Don't forget barf bags. And oh, maybe some iodine, just in case." He said nothing about the goldfish.

Mel made a face. "How about splints and sutures? Just in case."

"Hey, great idea," Wit said. "Mel, I think you're our first premed. Could be a great addition." Wit walked out without a word about the fish.

"What's with the goldfish?" Matt was more than a bit concerned. "Do you think they would really make us eat them? I can't imagine that." *Would they really do this? Make their star quarterback sick? If I back out—that would be too weak, too embarrassing. Shit. Why do I want to be part of this?*

Mel didn't seem to be concerned. "Let's take it one day at a time."

Twenty-five dollars sounded like a lot, Matt thought, but he didn't really mind the money. He was more concerned about time. He had to get real serious about running for the Polity, which meant signs and stuff around the dorm. Wit had decided not to run—he had to write a thesis next year, and he couldn't stand Kashman's bullshit anymore. He'd stand out in front of the dorm to meet people, campaign for Matt.

Bonnie said she would stand with him and Matt figured it wouldn't hurt to have a cute girl on his campaign. *Kind of weird to even think the word "campaign."* He'd never been elected to anything except captain of the baseball team. But he'd enjoyed that, even when people came to him with problems. It made him feel great that the younger players looked up to him. The sourness of the final game had eaten away at that feeling, but he was realizing that he missed it.

He also missed the touch football games, but it was still a little too cold to play now. The league would start up again in a few weeks as spring neared. Then the playoffs would be on their doorstep. Matt figured things would be calmer by then. Maybe Kissinger would make a peace deal with the North Vietnamese. Now that they'd agreed on the shape of the table, which had to be the stupidest argument ever. Bonnie had explained the reasons for it, but that didn't make it any less idiotic. It was all so depressing and awful, why would anyone keep it going? There were more and more rumors about soldiers fragging their officers or other soldiers. It had to be total batshit craziness to blow up your own guys.

He threw his packed duffel back on the bed with a grunt, which made Mel turn around. "Hey, that sounds heavy," he said. "If you need someone to help you carry your load, I'm sure Barry can find someone." He snickered.

Montauk Point is at the far end of Long Island with miles of beach and an unobstructed view of a lot of ocean. In the summer, it's a popular place for cheap vacations and summer rentals. There are lots of places to get hamburgers and hot dogs and fish, served mostly by Irish teenagers who come for the summer. No one is quite sure why the Irish.

In the winter it is ten miles of completely deserted beaches with cabins directly off the road.

Matt and Mel found that the other initiates were Neut and a guy named Bill, who really had been a tremendous blocker. He wasn't sure why Neut was there at all. The drive took about three hours on a two-lane highway that was mostly empty. In the summer you could spend an hour to move a yard, but now they had no competition on the road. They stopped regularly for gas and bathrooms and beer. "We don't want to buy too much at a time," Fish said, "looks suspicious."

"Yeah," Matt said. "Like nobody'll guess now." There was also a very substantial stock of weed, Matt noticed, and even the normally calm upperclassmen were starting to get some strange looks in their eyes. Even Brain's demeanor seemed to change. "Hey, Matt," Brain said, "you don't want to bring this up at the Polity. You know that psychology study about people who were told to give electric shocks to subjects and it got out of hand?"

"No," Matt said with a frown. "Inflicting pain is not my thing."

"Well," Brain laughed, not listening, "this'll hardly be like that at all."

They drove up to a red-roofed one-story motel that stretched along the beach. It looked like it needed a coat of paint and a good carpenter. "Calling this place a resort," Matt whispered to Mel, "is like calling me an all-pro quarterback." It was about three in the afternoon and the sun was already heading down for the ocean. They parked in front of the office, which was flanked by the rooms. "Okay," Barry said, "Inner Circle members on the right. Pledges on the left."

"These are all winterized?" Mel asked.

"The ones on the right."

Mel gaped. "So what do we do?"

"Sleeping bags in the trunk. You'll be warm as toast. At least until you take a shower in the morning. Hot water can be iffy."

"I'll pass."

"You might rethink that when we're done," Barry said ominously. Then he called the pledges to attention. "All right, we are going to dine in the finest fashion this evening, and drink to our heart's content. At least we are, but you guys need to get some exercise for us so that we can do that. Everybody down and give me a hundred push-ups."

"Are you kidding me?" Mel said with heavy sarcasm. Lurch ran up behind him and swatted him with a boogie board. "Ow!" Mel said, more out of surprise than pain. Lurch drew the paddleboard back again. He was so much taller than Mel it looked like the paddleboard could wind up on his head. "Okay, okay," Mel said and got down on his hands and toes.

"No hurry, gentlemen," Barry said. "You can do them in parts. If you need to rest, just call out, 'Takin' a rest here, boss,' and one of us will come over and hit you with the paddleboard until you're rested. Wit, Brain, Lurch, and I will keep count. Beer here! Neut, you can get me a beer before you start. Lurch, hit Jack with the paddleboard to teach him what a straight back feels like."

Mel started doing push-ups like his arms were springs, and Matt quickly realized he couldn't keep up. He got to 30 push-ups, and just lay on the sand for a while until he got hit with the board. "And one more for not calling himself out," Barry yelled, and Matt got another whack.

When they were finished with their push-ups, Barry had them unpack all the brothers' clothes and lay them out on the bed. They were timed for speed, or really, not timed, just whacked. No one did it fast enough, so more paddling. The initiates were sent to their cabins while the brothers prepared a dinner for themselves. As they wobbled away, Wit said, "Take this opportunity to write a will, if you haven't already done so." There was some nervous laughter. "It's not like the ceremony is going to kill you, but you might want to commit suicide after."

Matt and Mel lay down on the bed, quickly realizing that there was no way to get comfortable. "Remind me why we're doing this," Mel groaned.

Matt thought about that for a while. "For the greater good? So we can become one with our brothers? Because nine out of ten doctors recommend it?"

"I think that's Camels."

"Well, we should get one last cigarette."

"Good point." He rolled over. "And if you comb your hair just right, nobody will notice it."

"At least I'm not so short that it pokes people in the eye."

"Are you going to start with the short jokes now?" Mel asked.

"Just one more," Matt chuckled.

"Okay, I'll bite."

"Okay. Did you know Mel uses a ladder to get up on the bunk bed?"

Mel played along. "What's so unusual about that?"

"He has the bottom bed!"

They both laughed. "Better than Mel yells 'two' on the golf course instead of 'fore!'"

So much time passed that they dozed off, until there was a ferocious banging outside the cabin. Lurch was walking by hammering a frying pan with a metal spoon and yelling, "Everybody up! Dinner! Our dinner!"

They were all driven into the common room, where the brothers had pushed together four or five card tables and set places with paper plates and plastic utensils. The initiates sat in the folding chairs that faced the table. "You're going to really enjoy this," Barry said. "It's not often you'll get the chance to see your B-3 Inner Circle have such a fine dinner. Let's see . . . Mel, here, you can pour the cocktail." Barry produced a bottle of scotch and directed Mel to fill the plastic cups that were set at the table. If he poured too much or too little, which of course he did every time, he was whacked with a foam baseball bat.

Neut was told to put out a beer at every place, and then to bring out the food. The first course was lasagna that filled the air with a sweet, warm smell. "I'm truly sorry that you can't enjoy Mrs. Di Santis's lasagna and her vegetables," Barry said. "Richie's mother is a truly wonderful cook. But don't worry, you'll have your dinner in a while." Richie Di Santis was a senior and Matt knew he had a real low number, so he always seemed kind of tense now. He'd had a couple of scotches and at least a couple of the beers.

Matt could feel himself getting hungry. A fancy mini stereo system was set up in the corner, playing reel-to-reel tapes that the brothers must have put together. "The music is the traditional accompaniment to our task of educating you," Barry said, as they heard, "That's the sound of the men working on a chain gang . . ."

The diners praised the lasagna loudly and often, occasionally calling for more beer while the initiates watched, smelling something else cooking in the kitchen. When they were done, Barry ordered Mel to pick up the plates and wash them. Matt was told to bring out the steaks. They were hot, fragrant, and juicy. By now Matt was really hungry. "That steak looks really good," he muttered to Mel.

It was clear to Matt that the Inner Circle was going to humiliate them as much as possible. Each diner continued to deliberately drop food and drink on the floor. Each time the initiate had to bend down to clean it up, they were paddled. Matt thought that he picked up food and wiped up spills on the floor at least twenty times. It was surprisingly tiring and humiliating and the fact that the meal looked and smelled so great was torture. As the meal progressed all the way to chocolate cake and ice cream, the Inner Circle managed to find multiple ways to smear the initiates with samples of their food. It wasn't exactly a food fight, since Matt and the guys couldn't fight back. Matt had chocolate cake on his clothes and lots of ice cream in his hair. The other initiates weren't spared either.

Finally, they were done. It was now the initiates' turn to eat but first they were ordered to clean the table and themselves.

Wit sneered, "Initiates, you wouldn't go to a dinner party looking like this. Clean yourself up and return in five minutes."

"Now's our chance to escape," Mel grumbled.

"Yeah, why are we doing this again?" Neut asked.

"Because there's nowhere to go," Matt pointed out. "They have the keys to the cars. Besides, under normal circumstances, they are sane. Even funny sometimes."

"Oh, yeah. I forgot," Mel nodded. "Can't imagine why."

Matt found himself wondering why they were going through all this. It hadn't really been fun so far, but the guys weren't really pounding them. It was more about the humiliation. The push-ups, the food on their clothes and in their hair, the paddling and overall subservience were just stupid. Maybe it was like the sociologist they read in history said, people become a lower form of life in a crowd. But they also have heroism and bravery in a crowd that they might not have alone. That made him think of Bonnie, and he wondered what she would think about all this. Would he be embarrassed if she were here? Would she think it was a hoot? She said that the French title of the book was like "The Psychology of Fools" or some French word that sounded like "fools." She'd enjoy that part of it.

Just as Matt was losing patience, an unusual feeling for him, they were called back into the main room. As they were standing around the table not knowing what to do, Barry yelled from the kitchen area, "Ta-da!" and the brothers walked in single file, wearing formals—tuxedos, shiny shoes, stiff white shirts, the whole nine yards. A couple of them peeled off and went into the kitchen. They brought out a tablecloth, fine china, silverware, and glasses, just like a fine restaurant. The initiates watched as they set the table and invited them to sit, all in complete silence. *At last*, he thought. *Were things going to be normal now? Is this their way to pay us back for being their slaves? For the humiliation? Or are they going to feed us the goldfish?*

He glanced at the spot where the goldfish were and they were still happily swimming in the bowl. He didn't know what to think but he hoped the humiliation was over. Of course, it wasn't.

When they were seated, each was handed a menu and his hopes faded instantly:

Montauk Point
Special Pledge Dinner—1970

APPETIZER COURSE
Pâté de Frog Gras
Crudités

MAIN COURSE
Hominy Grit Soufflé
Potato Au Rotten

DESSERT
Gelatin Rouge

Wit was the maître d' for the night. Standing behind Matt, he clapped his hands twice and commanded, "Let the first course be served!" The brothers acting as waiters walked in from the kitchen carrying silver serving plates with domed silver covers. "Where'd they get those?" Mel hissed to Matt.

"I think they're just those aluminum bus pans that were in the cabinets," Matt said.

With absolute precision, the platters were placed in front of each pledge. The one in front of Neut moved a little after it was put down. "What the fuck?" Mel said nervously. Neut raised his eyebrows, then frowned. Matt wondered if he should do anything. He tentatively picked up a fork.

"Gentlemen," Wit said, and the waiters all came to attention beside the diners. "One. Two. Three!" and the waiters, quick as could be, pulled the covers off the plates. The initiates froze in astonishment. Matt looked down at a frog staring back at him, its throat pulsating.

Everybody else had the same, except that as soon as the covers were lifted, the frogs realized they were free and started to hop away. The brothers shouted and cheered and whooped. Wit yelled, "Initiates! Your dinner is hopping away. Go!"

The initiates scampered after their appetizer, running into each other as the frogs nonchalantly evaded everyone. One of the frogs jumped up onto Wit, but before Matt could catch it, it jumped off. Wit whispered to Matt, "Don't try too hard, idiot. We don't care if you actually catch them." That was just the appetizer.

The main courses could only be described as vile. No one could eat more than one bite before gagging. Anchovies and concentrated onion juice were the only recognizable ingredients, combined to be perfectly disgusting. The ones that were not identifiable were much worse particularly when added to half-baked hominy grits, Robitussin, jalapeños, and molasses.

The initiates managed to get through the main courses but the pain on their faces said to the brothers that maybe they had hit the breaking point. "Okay, everybody, just one more course, dessert. Gelatin Rouge," Wit said.

"I hope the army food is better than this," Richie said, opening another beer. "I don't want to die on an empty stomach."

Wit put his arm around Richie's shoulders. "Richie, stay with us. Have some fun. Enjoy the day, each day." Wit toasted him with the beer can, but he didn't look happy about it.

The main meal was bad enough but Matt knew that dessert would probably be the worst yet, given what had transpired so far. Matt was even more worried that they would have to swallow goldfish, one of the weirdest hazing rituals in the fraternities. There were people who swallowed dozens. There was even a *Guinness Book of World Records* entry for swallowing the most goldfish, 257.

Are they alive or dead when you swallow them? Matt thought. Then he realized that maybe it didn't matter. But he hoped they were dead. He didn't want something swimming in his stomach. *Do I have to chew them? God, I hope not. They can throw me out. I'm not doing it.*

"And now, gentlemen," Wit said, interrupting Matt's thoughts, "we provide for you the conclusion to your meal, Gelatin Rouge, the crowning touch, the *pièce de résistance!*"

"The what?" Mel said.

"I took French in junior high school," Jack said proudly. "I think he said, 'piece of resistance.'"

"I had a girlfriend like that once," Brain said sadly, laying a plate in front of Matt.

It was a shimmering red cube of gelatin with some stuff inside. Matt wasn't sure what the stuff was, but he thought that worms was a possibility. "What flavor Jell-O is it?" he asked.

"Not Jell-O," Wit said scornfully. "No multinational company involved. This is our own creation."

"But what flavor is it?" Neut repeated.

"Clam juice," Wit said gleefully. "Ornamented with onion and garlic."

Matt's stomach heaved. "I can't." All the waiters brought foam baseball bats out from behind their backs. "Can I have the sick-up bowl again?"

One bite of this and all hell broke loose. Each of the initiates took one bite and spit it out on the floor. Mel picked up the paper plate of gelatin, looked around the table, and everybody got the same idea at the same time. The gelatin went flying in all directions while the brothers ducked and dodged. Suddenly there was a roar and Rich Di Santis started pummeling the initiates as hard as he could with his foam bat.

"Eat it!" he yelled. "Don't you know this is the greatest day of your lives?" He was chasing Mel. Wit lunged at him but missed. Di Santis kept on yelling, "You'll have four years of this, these great guys, and I'll be lying in a rice paddy!" Wit caught up with him and wrestled him out the door. "Enjoy it, motherfuckers!" were Di Santis's last words. The room got completely quiet and there was a sound of retching outside, then silence.

Everybody looked at everyone else. "Well," Brain said, "to paraphrase Joe Cocker, he's not feeling too good himself."

"An angry young man," Neut commented.

"But at least he's hiding his puke in the sand," Mel said.

"Getting better all the time," Jack said.

"Easy to be hard," Matt said. They all looked at him. "Couldn't think of anything else."

Wit came back in. "He's gonna sleep it off," he said. "He said to tell you he was sorry, he just lost it, and we should finish the initiation and have fun."

"Easier for him to say than us," Matt said.

Brain raised his beer can. "A toast to Rich Di Santis. He brought us the lasagna." They all raised their beers solemnly and drank as much as they could, then threw the cans into the fireplace.

"Okay!" Wit said. "We have one more event on the program, the grand finale. Let all the initiates await their trial by fire in the next cabin."

"Goldfish," Mel whispered. "It's gonna be the goldfish."

Matt shrugged. "Some Goldfish would really raise the level of the cuisine so far."

After about fifteen minutes, Wit came into the cabin, surveyed all the initiates, then brought out the glass bowl with goldfish in it. He held it up for everyone to see. "Okay, it's time," he said, turning the bowl around. "One, two, three, ah, four. Hmm. All present and accounted for." He put the bowl down on the table by the door. "Do you have any last wishes?"

"How about a good dinner?" Mel suggested. Wit laughed. "Last cigarette?"

Wit shook his head. "You don't want to ruin your taste buds, do you? Okay, let's go. Neut, how about you? Into the common room." The remaining three breathed a sigh of relief. The fishbowl was still in their room. Wit came back a minute later and said, "Sorry, I forgot something," and grabbed the bowl. Everyone groaned.

The three initiates waited. Five minutes passed. Screaming and raucous laughter came through the window. Then there was a chant:

"Go! Go! Go! Go! Go!" and a very loud cheer. Then nothing. "Well, I guess he did it," Matt said.

"Should we notify his next of kin?"

The first pledge didn't come back to the room but was placed in a post-ritual holding room.

Wit came back for each initiate one at a time. And each time, the same sequence: quiet, the chant, the cheer. Matt's turn was last. When he entered the room, it was almost completely dark. The brothers had lit candles all around the room, and all around the fishbowl, which was sitting on a table in the center of the room. The brothers were lined up in a circle around the table. "Please," someone—Brain, maybe—said, "step into the Inner Circle."

The circle parted slightly to let Matt through and he walked up to the table. Even in the dim light, he could see that there was only one fish remaining. He knew what he was supposed to do and took a step toward the table. "Wait!" someone commanded. Matt stopped and looked around, confused.

"Are you prepared to do anything to become a member of the B-3 Inner Circle?" a voice said. Matt answered yes.

"Do you pledge to support your brothers?" Yes.

"Will you follow any plan, any goal, any insanity that the brothers create?" Yes.

"Brother, can you spare a dime?" Matt chuckled and said yes. *Maybe they're really just kidding.*

"Do you regret that you have but one life to give to your brothers?" Matt thought a moment but said yes. *What the heck.*

"Which is better? Cheetos or Goldfish?" Matt knew there was only one right answer to this question.

"Goldfish."

"The acolyte is ready." Someone stepped up behind Matt, sat him down, and tied a blindfold around his head, so big that it covered his nose. For the first time, Matt truly understood that he was going to have to swallow a live animal and let it flop around in his stomach until he threw it up or shat it out. Of course, by then it would be dead. Which kind of made it worse. And worst of all, all the pledges before him had passed! If he didn't do it, he'd be shamed forever.

"When we say 'Ready,' open your mouth and tilt your head back. We will slip that sucker into your mouth, so close it right away. And when we yell 'Go!' take one hard swallow. It will be over before you know it."

Matt nodded, thinking, *Why would anyone in the world ever think of eating raw fish?*

"Ready!"

He swallowed and opened his mouth very wide. *Maybe they'll throw it all the way back and I won't taste it.* He felt something salty, slimy, wet, and cold land on his tongue and he closed his mouth and swallowed almost before they could start the chant of "Go! Go! Go!" but they didn't seem to notice and kept chanting anyway. Finally, Matt stretched out his chin and gulped in the most exaggerated way he could do. They cheered and laughed. He'd done it! He was now a full-fledged B-3 brother! Part of the Inner Circle!

Somebody took off the blindfold and Matt looked at the fishbowl. Empty. The B-3 guys came up to him, slapping him on the back and giving him a beer and saying congratulations. Finally, he was ushered into the other room with the other initiates. The room was buzzing, and Mel, Neut, Bill, and all the others shook his hand and described how they heroically swallowed that disgusting piece of fish shit that was as big as Moby Dick. You could feel the pride in the room.

Wit interrupted their celebration and began, "Oh, brothers, this is the story of a brave pledge group that weathered the gauntlet and the eating of the goldfish."

He paused, and Brain held up a fishbowl and said, "You mean *these* fish?" Four blasé goldfish were swimming in it.

There was more laughter and cheering and the initiates all looked at each other like *what the fuck?* "No, brothers," Wit went on, "you thought you were eating goldfish, but we spared you. What's important is that you were willing to humiliate yourselves—indeed, make fools of yourself, sacrifice yourselves and possibly the entire contents of your stomach, for the sake of B-3. That's what's important." And he raised his hands and applauded again, along with all the other brothers.

"Wait a goddamn minute," Mel yelled. "So what the hell did we eat?"

"Elementary, my dear Watson," Brain said. "Lurch, bring in the fish!" Lurch went into the kitchen and they could hear a refrigerator door open and close. He came back with a platter that still had a bunch of mushy, wet-looking things. Along with some whole pears.

"Those were *pears* we ate?" Matt said.

"Yep," Brain smiled. "We just put some cooking oil on them to make them more slippery and salted them down because for some reason, the initiates think that goldfish—even though they live in fresh water—should be salty. Works every time. Never gets old."

Wit handed Matt a beer and said, "Okay, Lurch, bring out the food." They were ushered into the main room and a minute later, Lurch came out with another big tray and a huge aluminum pan of lasagna. More beer came out and the remains of the scotch. In a few minutes, the initiates were able to forget how they'd been fooled, as the older brothers remembered their own goldfish trials. By the time the lasagna was finished, everybody was tired, drunk, overfed, and laughing. Matt stopped for a moment and thought that this was a feeling he'd been missing, and he raised his beer high. Mel noticed and did the same, and gradually everyone in the room was standing with their arms raised, and Matt said, "To B-3!"

Matt could see that Mel was deep in thought. "What are you thinking?" he asked.

Mel said, "This whole thing seems incredibly planned. Think about their psychological torture back at the dorm with the fish, the two cabins, the barf meal, the menu, the fish on display, the food fight.

"Hey guys," Mel turned to the upperclassmen. "Who planned this? It is really well organized."

Wit said, "I didn't think you would notice." He tossed him a binder that detailed every hour planned out. Mel was shocked.

"Boy, you guys really have the psychological torture down to a science."

Wit replied, "We will take that as a compliment."

Matt understood now. In their own way the guys were very special. Quirky, certainly, but a refreshing alternative to the seriousness and the chaos all around. He wanted to be part of a team, no matter how eccentric. They liked him, he liked them, and he could just be himself. Whatever that was.

18

MATT AND BONNIE electioneered together and they both won a seat on Polity. Bonnie hadn't found the right time to talk to Kashman yet but she said she would do it in the next couple of days for sure. Though Matt was elected to Polity and survived Montauk Point, the high didn't last because Lana lost. Matt had never felt depressed before but he suspected that was what he was feeling. Kashman was still in charge. The university would go to hell.

He decided to try to take up Mrs. Devin on her offer to talk and walked over to her office. It was March now, and with the warmer weather, the construction crews had reappeared. *What, did they go south for the winter?* They were out in force now.

To his surprise, Mrs. Devin was not only in, but free, and she waved him in. She put down her glasses and said, "I believe a typical greeting is, 'How's it hanging?' Is that right, Matt?"

He smiled for the first time in a week. "I guess some people say that. How are you, Mrs. Devin?"

"Troubled, Matt. Oh, where are my manners? Congratulations on being elected to the Polity."

He nodded. "But Lana lost. After all that work, and even when everybody was saying that they were voting for her . . ." He shrugged and shook his head. Matt knew he was telling Mrs. Devin something that she already knew perfectly well, but the hurt of it was still so fresh that it stopped him cold.

What made him colder still was the way that Kashman had

instantly consolidated his victory even before the next scheduled meeting. He had replaced all the committee chairs, moving Lana, who had been elected to the Polity separately, and Dorman out. And he had made Matt head of the extracurricular committee, which now included concerts and speakers along with intramural sports. Matt wasn't happy with this added responsibility but Kashman sold it to him as a great way to get closer to all of the campus groups, not just sports nuts. Kashman told him that Martin, the prior head of the extracurricular committee, was going to focus on his difficult math courses so Matt wasn't taking the chairmanship away from him unwillingly.

Matt wanted to think there was a way that he could use the chair to everyone's advantage, but then he realized how tied up he was by it. If he screwed up, the whole world would know.

Worst of all, losing seemed to make everybody spin off in different directions. Lana was nowhere to be found, and Beth was spending most of her time trying to revive *The Broadsheet* as what she called "an opposition newspaper." Mel was studying a lot, which wasn't new, but he seemed to do it at the library more. Matt suspected that he was with Liz but Mel wasn't telling him because of Nicky. Bonnie seemed preoccupied with something that she didn't want to talk about, and Matt couldn't help but think she had a boyfriend.

Mrs. Devin looked at the clock on her desk and said, "Matt, I was just going out for a late lunch to my favorite hiding place. Want to join me?"

Matt didn't know what to say at first. He'd already eaten lunch at the dining hall, but that was no bar to another lunch. The thing was no teacher had ever invited him to a meal. He'd had a lot of pizza with the coach of the baseball team, but that wasn't the same. This was like an adult meal. Finally, he said sure and they headed to the parking lot where they got into a VW Bug. Matt thought to himself, *Of course she drives a Bug. Does she have lunch at Steak 'n' Brew?*

They stopped in front of Lassiter's Bar and Grill. Since it was two in the afternoon, it was completely empty. "Hi, Dr. D," the bartender shouted out and reached across the bar to shake her hand. "The usual?"

"Probably, but let me first talk to my friend before we order." She motioned Matt to a table in the back of the bar. He wondered how many of the students were friends of hers. He thought maybe a lot. "I often come here only in the afternoon when no one is around. It gives me time to think away from the madding crowd."

"I guess your job can be maddening," Matt said. She raised an eyebrow and he quickly added, "That's a joke. I saw the movie."

She indulged him with a smile and said, "Yes, Julie Christie is a knock-out. I think we should order first. They have a great cheeseburger here if you like that. Would you like a beer?"

Matt stammered that he was fine, thinking, *If she downs a whiskey with a beer chaser, I am going to freak out.* The bartender came over and Matt ordered the cheeseburger, fries, and a root beer. Mrs. D said she would have the usual—which turned out to be a steak sandwich and a glass of red wine. She was razor thin and could probably down a million calories a day without gaining weight.

The bartender brought the drinks and Mrs. Devin raised her glass to Matt. "I realize I am not supposed to know, but you should be aware that despite your attempt to cover up your heroic act at the march, there are people who know about this now on campus. They will probably not say anything, just look at you differently. Many people do not know how to respond to selflessness. But I suspect it had much to do with your being elected, even if that was no part of your goal."

Matt just gulped. "I have no idea why I did that. I think that was insane of me. I just thought—not even a thought, really—I didn't want anybody to get hurt. I tried to keep it quiet. I don't want the attention."

"Besides escaping a bullet," she laughed, "how was the march?"

"I am really glad I went. It made me think about a lot of things. I never thought about the war before this year, not really. I never thought about poor people, about Black people, or people with, you know, physical problems, and what their lives are like."

Mrs. Devin smiled at him. "These are the most extraordinary times and you have to go back to World War II to find events like these that are threatening to change young people's lives forever. Life and death decisions are a lot for an eighteen-year-old to have to face. I don't think it is unusual to have lots of thoughts that aren't yet connected or resolved. You shouldn't beat up on yourself."

"It's funny, when Bill Moyers was here, Bonnie . . . I happened to be with him after his speech and he was talking about Ronald Reagan."

"Yes," Mrs. Devin frowned, "no friend of education. He cut the University of California by ten percent across the board. Only California would elect an actor to be governor."

"Yeah, well, Moyers said this funny thing about Reagan—'Deep down, he's shallow.'" Mrs. Devin looked at him quizzically and waited for Matt to go on. "And I thought, during the march, that's me. I never really thought about what I'd do with my life. I don't think I had an abstract thought until now. And all around me were these people who were totally invested, totally involved. They cared about it so much . . ." He stopped and thought about talking with Bonnie during the trip. "And the people I went down with, they knew so much about the history of the war and even, like, the U.S. and Asia . . ." He trailed off for good.

Mrs. Devin gave him a sly smile. "Why do you think this is called 'an institution of higher learning'?" Matt laughed as she went on, "You will find that much of what you gain here will come as readily from your fellow students as your teachers. How are you feeling right now?"

Matt had never been very introspective and until now he'd been able to ignore what was going on inside of him. He thought that both Nicky and Bonnie, in incredibly different ways, had made him think in ways he'd never had before. Nicky had made him think that he mattered to someone, so much that she had to stop seeing him. What did that even mean? But he cared for her. Bonnie had made him think that the world mattered to him. And he cared for her.

Mrs. Devin was looking at him and he realized that he mattered to her, even if he was just one student among thousands. Mrs. Devin seemed to want to know what he was feeling, not to tell him what to think or how to live. "Um, hopeless. I feel like I don't have any control over my life. I don't want to fight a war that makes no sense. I don't want to die because a government I didn't elect sends me out to do their bidding. I never really thought much about equal rights for women, or Blacks for that matter. I didn't even know until Montauk that they wanted to be called Blacks, not Negroes. My town was all white—at least the parts that I went to. I've been so blind to it all. Totally oblivious to the hurt around me. That my people caused."

The Beach Boys' "Surfin' Safari" came on in the bar. Matt shook his head. "I used to love that song. Now it seems like . . . an oldie. From another world when we didn't have to care about anything. That's the way I was. Now I see the caskets being unloaded at Andrews Air Force Base on Walter Cronkite and I can't help but feel that these poor guys fought for nothing. How do their parents feel? How could all that money be wasted on bombs and equipment instead of helping poor people, starving people here? And why don't my parents get it? They think that if the government says something, it must be true. I have to say I lost a lot of respect for them, but I don't want to feel that way." Matt had run out of gas. He sat there, toying with the straw in his root beer.

"If it makes you feel any better," Mrs. D answered, "you are not as alone as you think, but most people aren't willing to deal with it just yet. The first year in college is hard for everyone and this year has been particularly hard. I haven't seen this much antagonism between one group of Americans and another in my lifetime and I'm 70. No doubt it was there, but I didn't see it. As to your parents, don't be so hard on them. They grew up during the Depression, lived through an apocalyptic world war, and were rewarded with the greatest economy that the world has ever seen. They don't want to give up what was so hard won. And they want you to have it too—unchanged, comfortable, comforting."

Matt considered this for a minute. "I hadn't thought of it that way," he finally said. "But does that mean they're right? That the country shouldn't change? That Black people should still be hurting? That kids should die for a war they didn't want?"

Mrs. Devin laughed gently. "Change is constant. We either ride its wave or fall behind."

"Surf it?"

She laughed again. "Yes, that's it. Your parents are trying to keep the tide from coming in. It's up to you to surf the change into the future."

Matt grimaced. Mrs. Devin asked if he'd like another soda, which he did. They were quiet until it came and then Matt said, "The last few weeks I have had a hard time getting out of bed some mornings. I thought if Lana could defeat Kashman at least there would be some normalcy around here. Surfing is way beyond me. I don't even know how. Some guy tried to teach me one time and the tenth time I fell off the board I gave up."

"Oh dear." Mrs. Devin looked concerned. "Let's see what, if anything, can be done to lessen those feelings. Suppose we start at the beginning. Why did you come to Montauk?"

Matt was taken aback by the question. Everybody had always just told him that he had to go to college, and so he did. He took a long pull on his root beer. "Mmmm. I guess, let's see, well, I wanted an education. I knew that was important for getting a good job. I was thinking I wanted to be an engineer, so I'm taking math. But then I got into this history course and it's, um, interesting."

"How are you doing in these classes? Any feelings that you may not be up to it?"

"No, I'm doing okay, but I wonder. Is it hopeless? I mean, will it just go to waste if I get drafted, go to Nam, and get killed?"

With a truly sympathetic look, Mrs. Devin replied, "If you spent the time sitting in your room worrying and moping, would that be less of a waste?"

Matt winced. "Whoa. Killer. So what do I do?"

"Stay in the present."

"You sound like Dorman."

"Dan Dorman, for all his excesses and eccentricities, has learned—has taught himself, actually—some valuable things. But to my point. You can choose to act or not act. Each is a choice. Whatever you decide you are responsible for your actions and only you are responsible for the outcome. I suggest that you focus on the things you can control, the people you care about, the ideals that you believe in."

"Oof," Matt said. "That sounds like a lot of work."

The bartender called out to Mrs. Devin, "You ready for another wine?"

"No, thank you, Richard," Mrs. Devin said. "But I think I'd like a cup of coffee. Would you, Matt?" Matt nodded.

"Comin' right up," the bartender said.

"Actually," Mrs. Devin said to Matt, "those three things are all connected. And it is easier to change things you can control than, say, the United States government. The march was a valid and worthy effort, but what can you do here, now that you are on the Polity?"

Matt rolled his eyes. "Man, I don't know. Kashman is rolling ahead with his curriculum plan and he's got this clique of people who support anything he says."

The bartender set down the coffees. Mrs. Devin thanked him and stirred her coffee deliberately. "He has an ally in the administration, a rather excitable young professor named Sanger. And Mr. Sanger has lobbied very hard with the president." She frowned and said, "There is a certain movement to do something that might avoid the kind of violent demonstrations we've seen elsewhere. Not give up full control, but make some kind of accommodation. I am unsure as to the outcome."

Matt felt like he was being given inside dope that he wasn't supposed to know, which encouraged him. "The shutdowns seem linked to Kashman and we think he's dealing hard drugs. He just made me head of the extracurricular committee, but I'm not even in charge of it. I have to clear everything with him but he can do whatever he wants with the money."

"What is that committee responsible for?" Mrs. Devin asked.

"All the concerts, speakers, and intramural spending."

"Oh," Mrs. Devin said.

"Mrs. Devin," Matt said, "that 'oh' makes me wonder if I should ask if there is something I should know."

"It may be nothing, but I hear that the university is auditing the committee that ran the speaker and concert bookings. That makes me wonder." This conversation was becoming a roller coaster. *What if Kashman was somehow setting him up?* Matt felt chilled. He picked his head up from his coffee. "What can we do?"

"Think about what parts of your life you can control. I have some thoughts about the administration. Perhaps there is something that the Polity could do? Lana Harananinan developed a very effective organization. You know a number of people from your various activities. That new newspaper seemed to attract attention. The March on Washington effectively drew attention to the cause and a march here, albeit somewhat smaller, might do the same."

Matt shrugged his shoulders. "Lana's kind of played out now. And Beth. I don't know, a lot of people seem to be just sitting around."

Mrs. Devin leaned forward. "Matt, you may find that being a leader sometimes simply requires someone who will say out loud what other people are thinking. You stepped in front of a loaded riot gun in Washington. This is not as dangerous."

Matt tasted his coffee and wished he'd ordered another soda. Then he replayed the tape of what Mrs. Devin had said and did a double take. "Wait. You want me to be in charge of bringing down Kashman?"

She sat up straight in her chair. "Would you rather sit in your room and bemoan your fate?"

———

Matt didn't follow Mrs. Devin's suggestion immediately. He wanted to check a few things out. Additionally, football season started, and the team felt like home, the football field a backyard. After a few practices, despite the still-cold March air, their timing synchronized, their legs came back, and the game was pure pleasure. They played their first game the second Sunday in March and rolled over, 49–14. As they walked off the field together, Jones said quietly, "Hey, look, don't let on to those guys, but that didn't actually feel like a contest. We're going to need some damn competition before we hit the Zoo."

"Don't gripe," Barry barked. "That's coming. I didn't want you ladies to raise blisters on your delicate fingers the first time out."

"Why, I do believe our coach is in a good mood," Jones said. He looked up at Matt. "Hey, my man Matt. How's it feel to be part of the political establishment?"

Matt didn't know what to say at first, other than "shitty," but he didn't want to savage the good feeling. "I think I'm better at being a quarterback. Kashman seems to run the show from behind the scenes. You go to the meeting and everything's already decided."

"I been thinking," Mel said. There were some noises of surprise and doubt. "What you need is a political party."

"There you go," Monster said. "We can do that. We'll be . . . the Aymerocrats." Matt was surprised to hear real enthusiasm around him.

"How about 'Aymericans'?" Wit said. Groans all around.

"Bee-you-ti-ful . . . ," Brain sang.

"Oh, say, can you see . . . ," Fish warbled.

"I'm looking through you," Monster said.

"And we walked off to look for Aymerica," Mel said. "Let's eat."

There was a chorus of "right ons" and even though Matt thought he had mainly been joking, they were making him think maybe Mrs. Devin was right.

———————

At the April Polity meeting, Matt and Bonnie were both early and no one else was there. She had taken a seat about as far away from Kashman as possible, at the corner of the far end of the U that the tables created. Matt sat down next to her so that they framed the corner. She asked him how he was, and all he could do was grimace.

"Well, good morning, sunshine," she said. "It has started off kind of—how do you Americans say it?—fucked up, hasn't it?" Matt nodded and Bonnie looked away and then back at him. "Have you heard from your . . . friend? Nicky?"

Matt got a pang when he realized that he hadn't thought about Nicky for weeks. "Um, no. I haven't . . . I guess when she . . . if she gets right, she'll come back." Bonnie looked away and Matt added, "But, you know, thanks for . . . It was good to talk to you, that night. You helped."

Bonnie raised one eyebrow. "Bonnie Williams Relationship Counseling, at your service."

"Gee, I've always wanted to be able to do that," Matt said.

"What, get counseling?"

"No, raise one eyebrow on command." He grinned at her and pushed up on his right eyebrow with a finger.

"Here, let me help," Bonnie said, and put a thumb on his left eyebrow. He could feel her fingers on his skin.

"Oh, yeah, that's much better," Matt said. Bonnie pulled her fingers through his hair and put her hand on his arm, laughing. Matt paused and then said, "Maybe we could do it again sometime."

She looked puzzled. "Raise one eyebrow?"

"No, talk some more."

Her eyes brightened. "Maybe we could." She thought for a moment. "But, you know, I don't have any relationships to have a problem about, so we'd have to find something else."

"Oh, yeah, we'll definitely have to do something about that." Matt put a fist under his chin like *The Thinker* and looked across the U. Randy was sitting opposite them and caught Matt's eye. He saluted and Matt just grinned and held his hands up in surrender.

"Wasn't he the guy, on the first day . . . ?" Matt nodded and Bonnie smiled. "I guess he's on your team now. Wow, a serious face all of a sudden. What's the matter?"

"Oh, well," he started to shrug it off and then changed gears. "I think we should . . ."

"Do something about Kashman?" Bonnie interjected. The corner of her mouth turned up. "I talked to him. It wasn't a long talk, but I'm positive he's behind the walkouts. When I asked him if he was upset about the riot on campus, he said something like he can't control everything that goes on on campus, but we should rejoice, as he put it, that the students have risen up and are taking power. When I told him that there were rumors he was dealing bad drugs and I would hope he would try and squelch them, he gave me this look like *Who cares?* What he said was, 'Everyone is doing drugs and sharing them so what's the big deal?' He is up to his neck in all of this stuff. I feel like a fool. How could I have misjudged him so much?"

Matt reached over, put his hands on her shoulders. "Bonnie, you're not a fool. He's just a faceman. Whatever he says, I'd bet it's all about himself. He doesn't care if students have power, as long as he has the ultimate power. The drugs are just a way of controlling people."

"You didn't know him before. It's hard to adjust to the idea that he's just like Nixon." She reached up and put one hand on his. "What if you're not like what you seem, Matt?" Matt was thunderstruck and pulled his hands away, but before he could say anything, Bonnie said, "What if I'm not?" She took back one of his hands. "Remember Nicky. She didn't want you to see the bad Nicky. We all do that one way or another."

Matt looked down at her slender hand on his. Her skin was darker than his, so she always looked like she had a tan. "Is that . . . are you . . . ?" He shook his head. "I don't believe that for a second. I mean, I don't believe you're hiding anything. That there are other sides to you—that's different. I just need to know you better." She held his hand a little tighter. "I want to know you better."

She dipped her head and then looked up at him, smiling. "Me too you."

He wanted to kiss her so much that it was an ache, but there was a noise in the hall, and they both straightened up quickly. Kashman walked in with a bunch of his cronies and called out, "Matt! Matt Aymer! Come up here to the front table. I want all my committee chairs up front where people can see them." He smiled broadly and waved Matt up, nudging someone next to him to vacate the chair. Matt stood up. Bonnie rolled her eyes and smiled. "If he thinks he's insulting me, he can shove it," she said.

Kashman dictated every step of the meeting like a third-grade teacher telling the students when they could go to the bathroom. He passed along a statement for the athletic funds and Matt was stunned to learn that there was nearly $10,000 in the account. But that paled to the numbers he saw under Concerts and Speakers. It was nearly $100,000. He couldn't really read it closely during the meeting, but there were some other odd lines of where money was supposed to go. The intramural football program got a lot—about $3,000, but there were things like the ping-pong team and girls' field hockey, which got $1,000 apiece. Matt had no idea whether either of them existed.

After the meeting, Kashman turned to him and said, "I'll explain the budget to you. I have to go see somebody now, but come over to the Taj, let's say Friday, like seven or eight. Okay? Great." He was gone before Matt could even answer.

After Kashman left, Matt caught up with Bonnie. "Look, I need to talk with Neut. Whatever is up with Kashman, we need to stop him. Neut may know a weak spot."

"Go. Go for it." She nodded, brown eyes looking up at him, clutching her notebook against her chest, and waited for him to go on. "So I could, like, leave you a note about a time we could talk." She looked at him, waiting. A light went on in his head. "Oh! If I knew what your room number is, that is."

She gave him a half-smile. "You are the worst flirt in the world."

"That's a possibility. Although statistically speaking, I might have competition." She opened her notebook and wrote something, tore out the page and handed it to him. There was a room number and what looked like the dorm telephone number. "Thanks," he said. "Um, do you know if there's a ping-pong team? Or a girls' field hockey team?"

"Can't say that I do. But I'm not your sports gal." She smiled more, motioned for him to lean down, and whispered in his ear, "No, you don't have any competition." As he tried to decide what that meant, she turned and walked away, and then smiled back at him over her shoulder.

19

Neut wasn't in his room. Matt went to the library to see if he was there, but no luck. He walked over to the student union. It was a spring night and a lot of people were out, talking excitedly. Some were even shouting and Matt wondered if there was going to be another protest. *Maybe*, he thought, *we could organize a protest against Kashman*. The student union was mobbed, but he saw Lana and Beth sitting down and went to see if they'd seen Neut.

Before he could say anything, Beth blurted, "Did you see the news? We invaded Cambodia. Oh man, the shit is going to hit the fan now. This is going to make the Washington march look like a, a homecoming parade." The U.S. had been bombing Cambodia for months, arguing that the Viet Cong were moving troops and supplies through Cambodia to strike at South Vietnam. The army said they needed to stop those routes. "Nixon finally convinced Sihanouk to let him do it," Beth said. "They're calling it an incursion as if that makes it different somehow. Such bullshit."

Matt was vaguely aware of the geography of Southeast Asia— very vaguely—and that Prince Sihanouk ran Cambodia. He'd always wondered why he wasn't king instead of prince, but that was about the extent of his curiosity. He let Beth ramble on about the geopolitics for a while, then asked tentatively about organizing a protest against Kashman. Once he said it, he realized it was probably a weak idea.

"Oh, Matthew," Lana cooed, "I am exhausted and dispirited from the campaign. And now there's this invasion, incursion. Anyway, I don't see how a protest will have any effect on Joe. He is drunk with power. We need something that can take him down in one fell swoop."

"One swell foop," Beth giggled. "But Matt, if you are organizing a protest, tell me ahead of time. I've got to get out another issue of *The Broadsheet* on the invasion, but I'll cover anything you do. I'll take pictures and everything. I'll do anything I can to bring down Kashman."

Lana blew out smoke and raised her eyebrows. "Anything?" Beth looked uncomfortable and Lana patted her hand. "It was a joke. A bad one."

Matt wasn't sure what that was all about, and he told Beth he'd let her know about the protest. He didn't think the fighting in Cambodia would be such a big deal—the whole war was a stupid fuck-up, but Nixon wanted to get out. There would be protests, though, and it wasn't worth trying to compete with the anti-war activists. *Damn*, he thought, *got to find something else.*

Friday morning he was up early and went to breakfast. Neut was there, looking at the newspaper, the *New York Times*. The headline about Cambodia was huge. "Looks like this is going to be a big deal," Neut said, without saying hello or anything else. "Protests all over the country, especially on campuses. The faculty had a meeting last night, I hear. Talking about whether they should do something. Sanger wants them to shut down the school."

"No shit?" Matt said, munching on Cheerios. "Think that's going to happen?"

"No way to know, not yet." He continued reading the paper. Matt thought the paper looked incredibly boring. All that type. Even the pictures were boring. Not like the *News* or the *Post*, which always had great headlines, even funny ones, and good pictures. "Wow, weird," Neut said. "They fired on students at Ohio State. Tear gas, shotguns, the whole nine yards."

"Jeez. They didn't kill anyone, did they?"

"No. I don't think that's what they want. But the establishment is getting pretty vicious. Nixon eggs 'em on. All that law-and-order shit." Matt didn't know what to say. He felt that maybe it was time to actually do something about the war, not just say that he was against it. But he'd gone to the march—so many people had been there to say they didn't want this war—and not a goddamn thing had happened. In fact now it was worse than ever. But Mrs. Devin had said to focus on the things he could control, and he sure as hell had no control over Vietnam. Whether he had any control over the Kashman problem was another question, but at least he could try. As if reading his thoughts, Neut said, "I hear you want to try to protest against Kashman." Matt agreed he was thinking about it, but the news seemed to call a halt to it. "You ask me," Neut said, "I don't think a protest is the way. He's smart. He can co-opt almost anything. You need a crime."

"Neut, you know anything from your cop friends yet?" Matt asked, then hurriedly added, "I mean, I'm glad you know them."

Neut nodded. "No harm, no foul. Yeah, I know some things. I know you might be able to help. I'm just not sure you'll want to." He looked at his watch. "Hey, I gotta go. My parents are picking me up. Mom's worried about something happening on campus. But let's talk next week." He picked up his tray and was gone again.

There was talk all day about whether the school would go on strike, or classes would be cancelled, or nothing would happen at all. Matt felt lost. *Should I study? How many classes will be cancelled? Will we even finish the semester?* Before practice, Matt dropped off a note in Bonnie's mailbox asking if she was free on Sunday for coffee or something in the afternoon. There was a football game on Saturday, and he had to see Kashman at 7:00, so Sunday was the earliest. This would give him some time to think through what he should do next.

After dinner with the B-3 guys, he checked his mailbox and found a note from Bonnie. "I'm so worried about what's going to happen," she began. Sunday she was going to a rally set up by the Women Against Vietnam Aggression, WAVA, she wrote, but Monday afternoon would be great, if he could make it. They could meet in the G lounge, where she always got a table for studying. So on the way over to the Taj, he left her a note that Monday was great.

It was a pretty typical Friday night at the Taj, lots of the Rolling Stones, Santana, and the Doors. Jim Morrison had said they were bringing the band back after all his fuck-ups onstage. *Soft Parade* had been a big hit, but Morrison kept talking about retiring. "Roadhouse Blues" told Matt to keep his eyes on the road and his hands on the wheel. *I guess the Taj is like the roadhouse*, Matt thought.

He found Kashman in his room, at the end of the second floor. The end rooms were a little bigger than most, and Kashman had it all to himself. When Matt knocked on the door, which only opened a crack, there was a shout of "Wait a minute!" and some movement. Kashman came to the door and peered through the crack, and said, "Oooh, it's Matt." He turned to look in the room. "Okay, guys, never mind." Then he opened the door a little more and motioned Matt in. A bunch of guys were sitting around a table that had a little bowl with a heap of white powder in it. Even Matt knew it had to be cocaine. "Want a line?" Kashman said. Matt shook his head no and Kashman drawled on, "I kinda forgot you were coming. Where were we? The budget, right. Here, come in my office."

They walked into what would have been a bedroom if Kashman had had a roommate, but now had just a university-issue desk. There was a small refrigerator on the floor and a safe with a combination lock sitting on top of it. "How about a beer?" Matt said yes to that and Kashman pulled a Heineken out of the refrigerator and gave it to Matt. Then he opened up a file drawer and pulled out a manila envelope. "Look, this is pretty simple. You can pretty much do what the last guy did." Kashman went over the parts of the budget without explaining much. Matt asked about why the sports and concert budgets were now under one person. "Just works better that way. I didn't think the guy was doing a good job so I asked him to step down, or strongly suggested he step down," he said with a nervous laugh.

There was a shout in the other room, and music came on. Hendrix. "Boys are having some fun now," Kashman said. He put a hand on Matt's arm, and said very seriously, "This is an important year for the school. Lot of things are gonna change. I need your support, Matt.

We can do great things for Montauk, but we need to work together. This is really for your future. When we get that curriculum change pushed through, you'll be in charge of your own education and the lousy teachers will be gone. We can't trust the old people to do it. They don't know what they're doing. Look at this war. This government."

"Yeah," Matt said, enthusiastically, "now we're invading other countries. When's it gonna stop? Does Kissinger really care what happens to the Vietnamese?"

"Who fuckin' knows?" Kashman growled and then narrowed his eyes and grinned slyly at Matt. "I bet Bonnie Williams is keeping you up on all that. She is one fine piece of tail."

"Yeah," Matt said, uncomfortable. "She's . . ." he wanted to say "beautiful," but it felt dumb and romantic, so he tailed off with ". . . hot."

Kashman laughed loudly, and said, "Don't think that Miss Bonnie-Too-Good won't fuck you over. Get what you can when you can. Take it easy, but take it. You'll be part of the regular executive meeting, by the way. I'll let you know." He turned for the door to the main room but Kashman said, "One more thing. I'm gonna call a general meeting about the invasion and what the school should do. For some day next week. Give people a focus. I don't know how to use it exactly, but I'll get it together."

Matt thought it was odd to say "how to use it," but maybe Kashman was just stoned. The guys in the main room had acquired a couple of girls and were passing around a bottle of tequila. *At least they're not wearing togas*, Matt thought. He pulled the door almost shut again and walked down the hall to the main stairway. He was about to go down when he saw Mr. Blue standing in the other hallway. Matt hadn't seen him since that first week and thought he'd say hello. He headed down the hall and thought Mr. Blue looked a little strange. He was just standing there, with his briefcase, not moving at all, just staring into one of the dorm rooms.

"Hey, Mr. Blue, how's it going?" Matt said, trying to sound casual.

Mr. Blue turned to him very slowly. His stare was so frozen Matt wasn't sure that he recognized him. "That guy," he said, pointing into the room.

Matt looked inside. The light was pretty dim, but he saw a guy sitting on a chair, slumped over. The line of cocaine still on the table. Matt started to feel a little dizzy and he grabbed onto the doorjamb, afraid he was going to fall.

"I think he OD'd," Mr. Blue finally completed his sentence as if it was some riddle he wanted to solve. "Giving out some bad shit. K. That stuff isn't mine. This is not good. I can't be associated with bad stuff."

"What do we do?" Matt whispered.

"I gotta go," Mr. Blue said. He hoisted his briefcase. "I gotta go. Cops'll be here soon. I'll tell K."

He rushed down the hall. Matt wasn't sure if he'd said, "tell K" or "tell, okay?" Matt wanted to do something, but he stood stone still. *We can't just leave the kid as he is. That can't happen. Shouldn't happen.* He could go looking for the resident advisor or find the phone and call campus police. He was frozen in place.

He saw Kashman striding down the hall, some other guy following him. He pushed Matt away from the door and looked in. "Him," he grunted. "Jerkoff." He turned to the other guy and said, "Bob, call the infirmary. Tell 'em the room number. Don't tell 'em your name. Matt, get out of here. Bad shit happens, is all. Go, go on."

Matt waited outside Kashman's dorm and vowed that if an ambulance didn't show up in a few minutes, he would call, even though he didn't know where to find a phone. The ambulance did show up and he could see the medics reviving the kid. He heard one of them say "at least he isn't dead."

Matt drifted through the weekend. Friday night, he'd gone back to his room and started the six-pack of beer that he and Mel kept. By the time Mel got back, he'd had four and felt sick. He told Mel what happened, and Mel just said, "This is totally fucked up. Give me a beer."

On Monday, he had lunch with the B-3 guys and went to class. The overdose was the buzz around campus. Rumors were that the kid was in intensive care but would live. Matt didn't know if this was true but he hoped it was.

The OD took second place to the bombing of Cambodia. There were flyers all over campus about a general meeting to talk about the war and the school's actions on Tuesday night at 7:00 in the main quad. There were conversations about the war and the protests and jokes about how this could make it a lot easier to pass the semester, if classes just ended now. Matt hadn't slept well. He was tired and worried and confused about what to do, but he knew he had to do something.

He found Bonnie in the lounge just as she said he would. She was sitting there with a pile of books and notebooks in her hand, but she also had a transistor radio on the table. Her head was down, her face in her hands. Matt came up behind her and said hi, but she didn't immediately move, although her shoulders were shaking. He put a hand on her shoulder and said, "Bonnie, are you okay?"

She looked up at him with tears running down her cheeks. He thought they must be about the guy who'd OD'd, but then she said, "Oh, Matt. They killed them. They just shot them right there on campus." She put her face in her hands again and sobbed.

Matt had no idea what she was talking about, but he felt awful just seeing her cry like that. He squatted down and put an arm around her shoulders, and she turned into him and sobbed against his chest. She felt delicate and wounded and he hugged her. The radio was talking about the National Guard and ambulances and how the governor was calling for calm. Gradually Bonnie stopped sobbing and picked her head up to look at him. "It was a protest at Kent State. It's a college in Ohio, and they've been holding meetings and demonstrations over the weekend." Her breath caught in her throat. "And then today there was another protest, but the governor had called out the National

Guard. He said they were revolutionaries, or Nazis, or just about any awful thing he could think of. It was like he *wanted* them shot."

Matt took her hands in his. "It can't go on like this. Too many deaths." She looked at him strangely, but he went on, "It's like Mrs. Devin told me. We have to change what we can change. We have to do something where we can."

Tears formed in Bonnie's eyes. "It could have been me." She looked at him. "It could have been you."

He managed a wry smile. "Can't be you. I won't stand for it."

She laughed a little and sniffed and said, "Speaking of not standing, you're probably cramping up in that position. Here, get a chair." Matt pulled a chair close to her and Bonnie told him as much as she could about what happened. It made Matt even more dejected. Neither side listened to the other, but what the Guard did made no sense. At least the kids were just trying to make a point. Officially, the government said they'd disobeyed an order to disperse. "Is that something you should be shot for?" Matt snarled.

"I just don't understand why we always turn to guns," Bonnie said wanly. "JFK, Bobby, Martin Luther King—they didn't want to hurt anybody."

"I guess some people don't know any other way to object. There's so much awful stuff happening."

Bonnie dried her cheeks and looked at him. "Talk to me."

Matt took a deep breath. "I found the guy who'd OD'd."

"Oh my god." Bonnie put both hands on his shoulders and leaned her forehead against his chest. He told her the whole story, about the dope, and how Kashman had taken over the situation. "It was like he was looking for a garbage can to throw the guy in. He didn't care that he was near death. Or that maybe it was his drugs that killed him." Matt couldn't say another word, more affected now than he had been at the time, just seeing the guy slumped over the desk in his mind's eye, ashamed that he hadn't done anything. "Bonnie," he said finally. "Let's do something. We can't stop the war, but let's get rid of Kashman, however we have to do it."

She held a hand up, palm flat, and he put his hand against hers. "Say the word," she said. "I'm wiped out, but I'm with you. Let's do this again. Maybe Wednesday. Maybe it will be a better day." She gave him a hug and when he leaned down, she turned her face up and he kissed her.

Almost the entire student body turned out for the Tuesday rally. Mrs. Devin had agreed to speak. Matt thought that she probably didn't want Kashman to have the stage all to himself, though she was gracious when he introduced her.

"Thank you, President Kashman," she said, stepping up to the podium and onto a small box so the crowd would see her above the lectern. "It's important that we have this assembly. It's crucial." The noise from the crowd was deafening but when she tested the microphone, it diminished to a loud buzz. She was still the one everyone wanted to hear in the midst of the great turmoil. Matt stood with the B-3 crowd some distance from the stage and slightly to the left of center. The night was cool for early May and he was wearing his varsity jacket, glad to have his old baseball in one pocket for reassurance. He looked for Bonnie, but it was hard to find anyone in this crowd. When he turned around, he was surprised to see not only campus cops but local police and even Highway Patrol officers standing around the edge of the crowd. There were a lot of them, and Matt had seen police cruisers and vans in the parking lot. It didn't give him a good feeling.

"Montauk community," Mrs. Devin began, "my heart is sad today. I know you are grieving as well. Please honor the dead with a minute of silence." The crowd quickly became absolutely silent and stayed that way as she stood with her head down. When she looked up, she said, "How can anyone make sense of what has happened at Kent State, or this country's escalation of the war? How can we trust our government? You are asking, 'Why do I feel so hopeless while I have my whole life ahead of me?' I suspect everyone gathered here feels this way.

"There are no easy answers but I can assure you that inaction is not an option! Debating the state of our country is not sufficient. Even standing here at a rally for peace is not enough on its own.

"A word of caution. When I say this, I worry that many of you will leave here and promote violence. Please, please don't. None of you want to die fighting in a civil war in Asia and you certainly don't want to die on United States soil at the hands of a fellow American. Think about this: If actions lead to violence, you are playing into the hands of the government who will turn it into a focus on the violence and not the reason for the protest. Be smart!

"The Kent State horror tells us a lot. No one foresaw the out-of-control response by ill-trained police and National Guardsmen. Even one of our students had a gun pointed directly at him during the Washington peace march. We all want the same thing, so let's put peaceful pressure on the government to stop *now*. Our job is to make the government come to their senses and to realize they are out of time and options. America will come to its senses, but it will need you to make sure the madness stops quickly."

At this point the crowd chanted, "Stop the war, stop the war, stop the war." The chanting went on for quite some time, and Mrs. Devin broke in when the chant started to ebb.

"What can we do? First: organize. Science majors, do you want to stop war research? Picket the labs conducting the research. Lobby the funders of the research, apply economic pressure.

"Black students, women: work with the elected officials that are advocating for radical change. Collectively you have power. You have purchasing power, lobbying power—together you can make sure your voice means something. Go out and fight for the America that you deserve!"

She stopped, and there was a moment of quiet. Then a large, loud group at the front of the crowd started bellowing, "No school! No school!" Mrs. Devin said something no one could hear and Kashman stepped to the microphone. He called for quiet, but the people at the front went on. He looked annoyed.

Kashman started to talk about a kind of combination of memorial march for the Kent State "martyrs" and an anti-war protest, but the gang at the front picked up their chant again louder. Black Power advocates jumped on stage, then the women's rights group stormed the stage and they all wanted to take the library. The Zoo started their own chant, but it was drowned out when a chorus of other voices started repeating, "No more war! No more dead!"

The crowd in the quad kept pushing forward, and Kashman started to look more and more nervous. Some of the Zoomen climbed up on the stage and started jumping up and down, chanting. One of them grabbed the microphone and now the "No school" chant drowned out everybody else. More people got on the stage, some pushing the Zoomen and of course getting pushed back. A couple of people fell off the stage. A trash can blazed up in flames, then another. There were screams. Nobody seemed to know what they were doing and that only intensified the combination of adrenaline and panic in the air.

Matt looked to the sides of the quad and he could see police moving in. *Why are they doing that?* he thought. *That'll only make it worse.* They didn't seem to have guns out, but they had batons and they seemed to be trying to clear the students at the edge and move them out of the quad. One of them had a bullhorn and started yelling through it, but Matt couldn't really understand what he was saying. Evidently nobody else could either, or they weren't willing to listen, so the police started pushing more forcibly. Some students were knocked to the ground.

The Zooman with the microphone saw that and pointed to the police. He yelled, "Off the pigs! Off the pigs! No school!" People started pushing their way onto the stage, evidently trying to get away from the police, and that was when the stage crashed down. He and Mel rushed up to help as much as they could. It was total chaos, but they and the other B-3 guys helped as many as they could.

In the midst of trying to help people out of the wreckage, Matt kept an eye out for Bonnie. After he helped one guy to the ambulance, he saw Kashman near a lamppost grabbing a girl. One of the fires that had been set in a trash can lit them up as they wrestled with each other, and he saw that it was Bonnie and he really, really didn't like what he was seeing. Anger volcanoed up in him. Bonnie pulled away from Kashman but stumbled and fell. Kashman walked up to her and stood with his legs spread, talking to her. Matt pulled out his baseball and threw a straight fastball, hard as he could.

Kashman grabbed his crotch and went down like a rock, rolling from one side to the other. As Bonnie scrambled to her feet, Matt ran up to her, asking if she was all right. She leaned into him, saying that her ankle had turned, but she'd be all right. "I'm glad to see you, Tom Seaver," she said, grimacing a little with each step and holding on to his waist tighter. "You've got dead aim."

Matt held her waist a little tighter and said, "Actually, I was aiming for his chest. Can you walk?"

"Let's get out of here." Kashman was quieter now, but still not aware of what was going on around him. Matt held on to Bonnie, managed to grab his baseball off the ground, and helped her walk.

About 30 feet across the quad, the police and National Guard had circled the protesters and the counter-protesters and everyone else who happened to be in the courtyard at the wrong time. There were some thuds and smacks and screams of pain and kids were dragged to the police cars. The firemen were going around with extinguishers, and there was a hose drowning out the biggest fire in the doorway of the student union. Matt and Bonnie staggered behind the main building and went a back way to her dorm.

They went up to a second-floor room, and again Matt was impressed that the girls made their rooms like home while the boys made them look like a locker room. There were deep brown curtains in the windows and a rug on the floor between the two beds. Bonnie pointed to the bed with the light brown cover and a Che Guevara poster above it. Matt helped her sit down on it.

"This looks nice. Um, where's your roommate?"

Bonnie very carefully took off her moccasin and looked at her ankle. "She's with her boyfriend most nights now." She looked around.

"I don't see her purse, so that's probably where she is." She gingerly lay down on the bed. Matt stood awkwardly between the beds and asked, "Is there anything I can get you?"

"Aspirin and some water. The aspirin's on the shelf over there. There's a bottle of water over there somewhere."

Matt found the aspirin and water and knelt down by the bed. He helped Bonnie sit up, enjoying the feel of her body under the sweater. She swallowed the pills and drank and gave him the bottle. "Okay, that'll help," she said and lay down, looking at him and smiling. "Thank you," she said.

"Do you want to rest? You want me to leave?" Matt asked, not really wanting to ask either question.

"I want to relax. I don't want you to leave." Matt sat back on his heels. They were quiet and could hear shouts and people running out on the quad. There were still flickers in the window from the trash can fires, but even as Matt watched, he saw them stop. Someone, probably campus police, was yelling for everyone to get back to their dorms, there was a curfew, nobody could be out.

"W-e-l-l," Bonnie said, stretching the word out. "Looks like you're stuck here."

It took Matt a minute to realize that a curfew meant he couldn't go back to the dorm. His mouth fell open a little and Bonnie got a mischievous grin on her face. "Make yourself comfortable."

He looked around at the other bed, which was also made up. "No," he said, "I'll be okay. I'm sure I can sneak back to B-3. They'll want everyone in their dorm." He stood. She cocked her head and made that comma with her mouth. Not really wanting to leave, he asked, "Is there anything else you want?"

Bonnie looked around at the window ledge and pointed to a lantern. "I want you to light that. My father gave it to me. He said it would weather any storm. There're some matches there."

Matt had to lean over her to pull up the lantern's glass and light the wick. It gave off a good warm light. He looked down at her, admiring. "Cool," he said. "Anything else?"

She pointed to his jacket. "I want you to take that off," she said. He did, hoping against hope, and dropped it on the floor. She raised herself on one elbow and pointed to his shirt. "Now I want you to take that off." After he did, she looked at him for a while, then pointed down. He dropped to his knees and she reached up and ran her hand down his chest. "Oh god, I can feel each one of your ribs individually. Do you have names for them?"

"Names?"

"Sure," she said. "I have names for my breasts. Alice and Gertrude." She took her hand off him and levered herself into a sitting position, pinching at her sweater. "Now you can take this off and meet them." She raised her arms.

Matt couldn't move. "Are you sure you're all right?"

"I'll be a lot better when you get this off. It's easy, just start at the bottom." Matt bent down and his face nestled into her hair, then he pulled her sweater up over her head. She shook her hair back into place so that it framed her face. She pointed to his jeans and said, "And now I want you to take those off."

Matt instinctively turned his back to her as he pulled off his pants, thankful he was wearing clean underwear. When he turned back to her, she had taken off her bra and sat there, smiling. "Say hello to Gertrude and Alice," she said quietly. There was a shout from outside that bounced around in Matt's head.

"Hi," Matt said, even more quietly. He could barely catch his breath and felt himself getting erect. In the light of the lantern, her golden skin looked as smooth as cream. She looked down. "I'm afraid I can't show you my ribs, since I'm so fat, but you might be able to feel them."

"You're not fat," Matt said. She was slender but smooth, a silhouette so symmetrical that it was like somebody drew her as the example of how a woman's body should look. He couldn't take his eyes off her.

She took his hand and pulled. "You're way over there. Come here." The next thing he knew his arm was around her back and she was kissing him quietly but repeatedly. She stopped and smiled at him.

"We have a lot to talk about," she said, "but let's not use words."

"I was never very good at them."

"Perfect." She lay down, unbuttoned her jeans, and pointed at her feet. Matt gingerly pulled at the material on her hurt ankle, and she said, "It's okay. Keep going." Then he took off the rest of their clothes, feeling like maybe he wasn't a complete klutz. After that, he was so wrapped up in what Bonnie was doing to him and her unspoken guides about what to do to her that he didn't need to think about himself. He remembered what had happened with Nicky, felt bad that he was thinking about Nicky, but now he realized that with her, he'd only been thinking about himself. Now all he could think about was making Bonnie feel great. He kissed her and touched her until she purred and moaned and held him in place so that they went on and on. At last she cried out and laughed and he came, and she wrapped her arms around him and pulled him to her.

After what seemed like a very long time, Bonnie said she had to go to the bathroom and then she played guard while he went to the bathroom, and they cuddled back up in bed, blew out the lantern, and did it all over again. Later, when the campus seemed quiet again, Matt said, "I know we're not supposed to use words, but what was Kashman trying to do to you?"

"I don't really know," Bonnie said. "I mean, he said he just wanted to get me somewhere safe, he said, but . . ." She trailed off. "You can't tell anyone this, but he, I don't know exactly, he assaulted Beth. Last year. Right at the beginning. Beth won't say exactly what happened, but she changed completely after that. Started wearing those flannel shirts, gained weight—I mean, we all gained weight, but she, it was like she didn't want anyone to know she was a girl."

Matt was silent for a while. Then he said, "Wow. I didn't think . . . I like her. Not like that, but . . . she seems nice."

Bonnie nodded in the dim lantern light. "She's better now. Lana helped a lot. Lana swore me to secrecy about Beth, so you can't tell a soul."

"Cross my heart."

"Here, I'll do it for you." Matt felt her finger slowly cross his nipple and took the opportunity to pull her close. Then she said, "Matt, I have to tell you something, and it's something that I did and now things are completely different and that changes everything."

"Okay," Matt said, worried, "I'm listening."

"You know I want to get into international relations? Maybe the State Department?"

"Yes, I remember."

"I applied for junior year abroad. To intern at the EEC, the European Economic Community, in Europe. In Brussels."

"Wow." Matt started to work that through. "So you'd be in Europe next year?" He started to get a bad feeling in his stomach. "That would be really great for you, wouldn't it?" He could feel her nod against him. He swallowed. "I would really miss you." He felt her nod against him again. "But it would be the right thing."

"If I get accepted," she said as quietly as it was possible to say.

"Remember when Lana said that all relationships between men and women are power relationships?"

Bonnie giggled, "Oh, I felt the power."

Matt could tell he was blushing, but at least it was in the dark. He looked down at Bonnie and how beautiful she was, and said, "Well, thanks. But you were in charge. I liked it like that. Maybe Lana is right, but maybe it can go either way."

"If I were in charge, I would order you to stop underrating yourself." She kissed him. "But I'm not. And you're a wonderful lover." She snuggled into him a little more. "And a really good pitcher."

20

THEY SNUCK OUT of her dorm like conspirators, waiting until the hustle and noises of people going to first-period classes quieted down. When they walked out the door, they looked around in unison, then looked at each other and laughed. They felt like the only people in the world. The day was clear and sunny, still cool, but the world seemed quiet in a strange way. Paper and plastic bags were strewn around, sailing a few feet in the wind away from overturned garbage bins.

When they walked into the quad where the demonstration had blown up, damage was more apparent. Pieces of the stage remained in front of the admin building. There was graffiti and some scorch marks. The people who walked by were moving quickly, either late to class or upset at the lingering evidence of chaos and anger. As they came to the dining hall, a voice behind them called out their names. It was Dorman. They turned around.

"I hate to bear sad tidings," he began. But then he stopped midbreath. "Wait a minute." He looked at them both until Matt started to feel embarrassed. He put a finger to each temple. "Your aura has changed." He walked around them. "Definitely. Peace. Harmony. Love. So different from the world around you." He lowered his head and shook it slowly back and forth.

Matt and Bonnie worked very hard not to look at each other. Bonnie took him by the shoulders and said, "Dor, what's the matter?"

He raised his head dramatically and looked at the clear blue sky. "Mrs. Devin."

Matt felt a cold lump in his stomach. "What happened? Is she all right?"

He cocked his head. "That depends, I suppose." He seemed to think about it.

"Dorman, give it up," Bonnie said, annoyed now.

"She's been relieved of her duties."

"What?" Matt and Bonnie said it together. Then Bonnie said, "Why?" and Matt said, "What does that mean?" over each other.

"No one knows for sure," Dorman said, maybe answering both questions at once. "There are whispers about her losing control of the rumble last night. Also that Kashman organized it, but it got out of hand. Also that Sanger used the riot as an excuse to get people to move her out of his way."

"So that he and Kashman can ram that curriculum plan down everybody's throat."

"Is she okay, though?" The snowball in Matt's stomach was melting into heat. He was furious at the thought that Mrs. Devin might have been hurt because Kashman's little plan got out of control.

"Physically, I would think so. She left before things got really hairy."

"Dorman," Matt said, teeth clenched, "we have to stop him."

Dorman laughed. "Well, it seems like somebody stopped him, at least temporarily. Word at the Taj is that K is in the infirmary. He says he was trying to help some injured people last night and walked into a post or something in the dark. Hurt himself real bad, evidently."

Bonnie looked up at Matt and started to giggle. "Oh, that's too bad."

"Yeah," Matt said, "I hope it's not too swollen."

Bonnie said, "This is serious. Matt's right. We've got to do something to get Kashman out. I think we should all meet again." They agreed to meet in the lounge in G dorm at seven. Bonnie would tell Lana and Beth, Matt would get Mel to come, and Dorman volunteered to bring drugs. "I think Neut should be there too," Matt said. "I'll see if I can find him."

It was a subdued meeting. Lana was, for once, relatively quiet, leaning against Beth for support. "I don't know what we can do," she said. "We have tried democracy. Joseph was too clever for us. He knew too well how to manipulate the system."

"The system is corrupt," Beth announced.

Bonnie rolled her eyes. "Beth, I'm sorry, but we're not the military-industrial complex. We're just a small university on the eastern end of Long Island. Kashman is the one corrupting the system."

Lana put her arm around Beth and tried to change the subject. "I suppose, like the peaceniks, we could protest."

"We've been protesting Vietnam for years," Beth said, "where has it gotten us? Besides, the university isn't going to allow protests. Not after yesterday."

"Maybe we should try a real coup," Mel offered. "You know, get all the B-3 guys together and just go into the meeting and grab Kashman and throw him out the window." He smiled broadly.

"Mel, you have the makings of a true deviant," Matt grinned.

"Perhaps Joseph should have a little accident," Lana said mischievously.

"Matt tried that," Bonnie said, holding back a smile. Beth looked at her and then at Matt and started her own knowing smile.

"Anyway," Matt said, hurriedly trying to think of some alternate route for the conversation, "can we all agree that Kashman is a danger to this campus? He put Mrs. D in danger, he's going to ruin the academics, he's making a fortune selling bad drugs—"

"No harm there," Dorman said instinctively.

"Wrong. He's responsible for the kid who OD'd and is still in intensive care." Dorman looked at him in surprise. "I saw it myself." Matt told the story of the victim he saw in the Taj. It quieted the room. The despondent sound of "Long and Winding Road" floated into the room. *Let It Be* was going to be released officially the next day, but the songs were already everywhere.

"Sorry to lay that on everyone," Matt said, "but that takes it to a whole other level."

For the first time, Neut spoke. "He's a criminal. He should be treated like one."

"Neut, maybe you should tell people a little about what you've been doing. I know you don't like talking about it, but I think it's time. And I'll fill them in on the audit of Polity funds."

Neut looked like he was going to bolt, but he slowly, and only with the help of numerous questions, told the group about his father's death, why he hated Kashman, his work with the campus police about all the drugs on campus. The whole time, he seemed to be talking about someone else. Except about his father. He choked on that story more than once. He confirmed that Kashman was now buying and reselling more dangerous drugs, cocaine included, from a new supplier. Mr. Blue only supplied the weed and pills, but he was scared that he would get the blame for the kid who overdosed. When he was finished, Matt added, "And last but not least Kashman has been pocketing the cash receipts from guests to the concerts."

"The problem," Neut said, winding up, "the audit may get him, but cash is hard to trace, and it'll be one person's word against another's. Also, the school may not want to admit that their financial controls are nonexistent. I bet they would love to cover it up. We need to get him *actually* committing a crime. Drug dealing, most likely. But Kashman never does the deals himself. At least not that the police can nail him on. He uses other people to deliver the drugs and pick up the money—sometimes different people each time for each end of the deal. There are only a few people he lets get even close, and they're so close that they won't turn on him."

"Where do the drugs come from?" Beth asked. "Who supplies him?"

Neut spread his hands. "Buncha people. I mean, not a big number, but he spreads it out to a few. We're not going to bring them down, if that's what you mean. Besides, all I want is Kashman, to be honest. I—we—can't stop the East Coast drug trade all by ourselves."

Everybody thought over what Neut was saying. "Well, at least we know for sure he's a criminal," Matt said. "So, Neut, you're just saying you need somebody to do a deal with him so that the cops can nail him." Neut nodded.

"Well, if that's all you need," Lana said, "I'll do it."

"He'd never sell to you," Neut said. "And you know, you'll probably wind up getting arrested. Even if it's only for a night."

"Oh, I cannot do that. My father . . . I cannot do that to him."

"Look, I don't think he's going to sell to anyone here. Matt, you and Mel are too straight. Dorman, he knows you have your own supply. He's a suspicious character, and you supported Lana. He's not happy about that."

"Tell me about it. He'd sell me weed killer, hoping I'd take it."

More quiet. Finally, Matt said, "I think I know someone who can do the deal."

"Who?" Bonnie asked.

"I don't think I should say. Until he's in."

"Not even then," Neut said. "Best to keep it as quiet as possible."

"Besides, I'm not sure how to get Kashman to let his guard down."

"Loose lips sink ships," Mel said. Everybody looked at him. "I dunno," he protested. "It's something my father always said when he didn't want my mother to know something."

––––––––––

Matt went to see Kashman on Tuesday afternoon. He took a few deep breaths before he walked into the Taj. He was as nervous as the first time he asked a girl out on a date. *Maybe that's a good thing*, he thought. There were a bunch of people in the lounge who looked like they were playing a board game, Life. Someone spun a dial and cheered at the result. "I'm going to the moon!" he yelled, "and I get a half million dollars!" Everybody congratulated him and laughed.

Matt went on up and down the hall to Kashman's room. He and some of his lieutenants were sitting around the coffee table making lists. There were a couple of roaches in the ashtray. "Hi, Joe," Matt said. "How you doing?"

"Matt, hey," Kashman said. "Fine. We're just doing the books for

April. A good month. People need some relaxation from all this bull-shit going down. I guess war is hell but it's good for business." He laughed sardonically and the others joined in. "What's shakin'?"

Matt's nerves made his voice a little shaky. "Maybe we could talk privately?" He inclined his head toward the bedroom.

Kashman's eyebrows went up briefly, but he shrugged and said, "Sure, whatever you need. Take it easy, guys, I'll be right back." They grunted and nodded. One took out papers and some grass and began rolling a new joint.

In the bedroom, Matt was even more nervous. Kashman looked at him questioningly, and Matt said, "Um, well, this is a little hard to talk about . . ."

"I'm here for you, man, be cool."

"Well, see, I need some money."

"No biggie. What's up?" Kashman smiled a little and waited.

"Well, uh, it's like . . . I can't ask my parents for it, so . . . The thing is, Mr. Blue—you know Mr. Blue, right?—yeah, well, he just landed some killer new business—his biggest buy yet. And he says it's the best high yet. And so, like, I'm buying into it."

"Well, well, well," Kashman grinned. "We'll make a businessman out of you yet. How much?"

"Well," Matt hesitated, "like a couple thousand."

Kashman's bloodshot eyes got wider. "That is some money. But I can do it." He turned around and hid the safe with his body again while he dialed the combination. Taking out an envelope, he pulled out a bunch of bills, counted some out, and put them in an envelope that he held out to Matt. "Here you go. You say that you're buying into it. Is there more to buy?"

Matt nodded and looked around as if he were afraid a narc was in the next room. "Seems like it. Seems like a lot, in fact. He says a huge return on investment too."

Kashman frowned. "Huh. I'm surprised, I'm annoyed, that he didn't talk to me about it." He thought. "Mr. Blue has been a little strange with me ever since . . ."

"Yeah," Matt said. "Maybe that's . . ."

"Hmm. Look, Matt, I'll come in on this with you. In fact, I'll buy five large. But don't tell Mr. Blue that it's me. I want . . . to surprise him. I want to impress on him that I'm someone he should be talking to."

"Got it. Sure, Joe, thanks a million." Matt stuffed the envelope in his pocket and turned to go.

"Hey," Kashman ordered. Matt froze and then turned back to him. "Count the money," he said. "That's how you do business." Matt nodded and pulled the money out. He counted out loud and got to $2,400.

"Okay," Kashman said, "when's it going down?"

"Next week," Matt said. "After the game. We, uh, actually I was going to meet him during the party at the Taj after the game."

"Right," Kashman nodded. "Well, that's just perfect. I hope you win. But actually, either way, you win."

"Oh, yeah. Well, thanks. Thanks again."

"You bet. See you Saturday."

Matt had been so busy he hardly had time to think about the last football game coming up, the championship, between B-3 and the Zoo. Both teams were undefeated for the year but the Zoo was a bigger, stronger, meaner team.

No one really thought that the Zoo could be beaten. Except B-3.

Matt walked to the field with Mel, hanging a little behind the rest of the team. "So everything is still a go, right?" Mel asked.

"Yeah," Matt said. "We got the money. And we got him."

Barry caught up with them and for the hundredth time started reeling off plays, evaluating the Zoo offense and defense, and asserting that they were wimps. Matt and Mel just listened. B-3 was good, but their edge was discipline and planning. If the Zoo had B-3's planning and discipline, their physical skills would have overwhelmed B-3. They all knew that it was up to Matt. Their running game was good, but real yardage comes when the quarterback can throw effectively 15 to 20 yards downfield. In a nutshell, if he didn't have a good day they would lose for sure.

By game time, more than a thousand students and faculty were in the stands. The head referee called both captains, Wit and the Zoo captain, to midfield. "Congratulations to both teams. You both deserve to be here, and it should be quite a game. Please don't screw it up. This is the largest turnout ever. Do it for all those who play intramurals. Captains, I know you have been through it—you have ten players on each side represented here, correct?" They said yes perfunctorily. "Good. Shake hands."

Wit and Barry, as co-captains, handled the coin toss. The Zoo won and elected to receive. Matt was ready to upchuck, but he had to control his nerves.

B-3 kicked off to the Zoo. They were really in for it. While B-3 had scouted every game, every play of the Zoo prior to the championship, they never actually experienced their strength and speed. On the kickoff the Zoo halfback practically broke it for a touchdown. If he hadn't stumbled, he would have gone all the way. The next play, the quarterback dropped back to pass, spread the field, and ran himself up the middle for a touchdown. In less than three minutes the Zoo had the lead, 7–0.

The quarterback's smooth play made Matt even more nervous. When B-3 started their offense, Matt dropped back to pass on first down and missed a wide-open receiver by throwing the ball in the grass at his feet. His second pass was worse. *I could have missed the ground, that was so off target*, he thought.

Barry called the third play—a run. B-3 got a few yards but not nearly enough for a first down. The scene on the sidelines was chaotic. Everyone was shouting at no one in particular. Barry tried to calm everyone. "Stay in the game mentally," he said. "Get a grip. Stick to the game plan."

Matt said, "I don't feel right. The ball seems to be floating. I have to make some corrections."

Wit pulled Matt aside. "It's only the first set of downs. Don't over-think this. You don't need to make any corrections. You need to calm down. You were right on the money, just low. Throw a few to me now on the sideline and you'll be fine. These guys will wear themselves out with overconfidence and we'll get them in the second half. Throw me a few."

The warm-up on the sideline seemed to help. On the second series Matt called shorter passes and completed a few but not enough to get the team really moving. The Zoo took advantage of his tentative play and improved their field position on every possession, but the defense held them off.

In the second quarter, Wit made a miraculous defensive play on the goal line, batting down a 20-yard pass on third down to keep the score from going to 14–0. On fourth down, the Zoo lined up to kick a field goal. No one could believe this. A touchdown was worth seven points because the rules never contemplated that kicking would be a major part of the game. No one had ever tried a field goal the whole season, and a 37-yard kick wasn't easy even for a pro. Also, with only four blockers, it wasn't hard for the defense to stream in and block the kick. This was the Zoo's surprise.

The Zoo snapped the ball and kicked a low flying shot that just cleared the goalposts. B-3 was in shock. In a close game, this was as good as a touchdown—and it was even more devastating psycholog-ically. B-3 was totally outplayed in the first half and was lucky to be down only 10.

Barry always had a surprise for the team. Instead of just group-ing outside on the sidelines during the twenty-minute halftime break, Barry had reserved a room in the gym complete with oranges, water, and a chalkboard.

"Settle down, guys. We just had our asses kicked. But the second half will be different." Instead of criticizing his players' performances, he had real analysis and constructive comments. "First, guys, they are overpowering us because they know we're cautious. That's why you feel they're all over you. They've studied our plays and we have to make *them* a little more cautious. We have to use their over-pursuit against them." Barry's demeanor and confidence lifted the team. They broke from the room ready to score.

Mel went back into receiving position with Wit blocking. B-3 needed to get Mel somewhat downfield, so Wit would be behind for the lateral. When Mel caught the ball, Wit moved to block and pretended he was injured on the play. The defender instinctively abandoned Wit and headed for Mel, who heaved the ball to Wit, who got up in time to catch the ball and kick into high gear for the goal line before the fastest Zoo player caught up. The B-3 fans went crazy. The Zoo captain yelled at Wit, "What a chickenshit play."

Wit walked to the Zoo captain and pulled a piece of paper with the play diagrammed on the back. "Here's the play. We knew the cretin on your right flank would run to the ball. I know how stupid he is because he's in my history class. Maybe next time you'll get it right." With that Wit jammed the ball into the Zoo player's stomach and ran to the bench.

They were all flying now but even if B-3 held them scoreless for the second half they'd still need a touchdown to win. The rest of the third quarter was brutal. Matt started to throw much better but still couldn't move in for the lead. The Zoo came close, but Mel knocked a pass down at the goal line that would have been the clincher. In the fourth quarter players started to get hurt. B-3's number two receiver sprained his ankle. The Zoo's fastest runner hurt his collarbone and had to go to the hospital for x-rays.

B-3 was down 10–7 with one minute left. They called a time-out on their own 40 with the entire team resigned to losing. Barry came out to the huddle and called the play, BK right. It took Matt a minute to remember the play, but when he did, he thought, *The guy is a genius.* They had practiced the play, but never called it until now—the perfect time.

The team broke the huddle and Wit lined up on the left sideline. Barry, clipboard in hand, walked toward the right sideline and his usual coaching position. The other players lined up as usual.

Barry was almost off the field when he threw his clipboard over the sideline and stood on the field, lined up behind the line of scrimmage. At the same moment, Wit walked off the field. The two guys guarding Wit were stunned and didn't know what to do now that they had no one to guard.

Matt called for the snap as Barry broke for the end zone as fast as he could. By the time the Zoo realized they'd been duped, Barry was completely alone. Matt heaved the ball and hit Barry right in the numbers with the pass. In his anxiety, Barry almost dropped the ball as it hit him in the chest, but he hung on just as the first Zoo team member hit him hard in the end zone. Barry held on to the ball, stood up shakily, and looked down at the Zooman. "Dumbfuck," he said.

B-3 had a 14–10 lead. The crowd went nuts. The Zoo captain ran to the referee, screaming at the top of his lungs, "That play is not legal! They had too many people on the field." The captain was so mad he was spitting. "That twerp didn't play all game, he can't be eligible. This is bullshit."

Barry walked up and calmly explained, "First, we only had seven men on the field. I was also behind the line of scrimmage for at least three seconds to ensure no offsides. And just because I haven't played doesn't mean I'm not on the team." He pulled a piece of grass-stained paper out of his back pocket. "Here is our official roster approved by the league."

The Zoo captain tried one more time. "We had no notice you were checking into the game. You can't do this."

"Wrong again," said Barry. "There are no requirements to report who is going in or out. Only that we have seven men on the field."

The ref nodded. "He's right. They win."

B-3 celebrated in the middle of the field for what seemed like days. Girlfriends, friends, and Zoo haters all united to cheer for the good guys. Bonnie found Matt and hugged him. "That was amazing," she said. "They were so much better, but you managed to find a way to win. That last pass was incredible. You're a hero."

"Barry thought it all up."

"I told you to stop underrating yourself. Now you've done it a second time, so you have to promise me that you will stop."

"Okay."

"Okay, so now you have to show me that you are stopping. We are going back to my room."

"What about—"

"She's not going to be there."

Matt was drained from the physical and emotional stress of the last few hours. Bonnie and he lay down on her bed and both quickly fell asleep. They slept in each other's arms for about an hour, enough to recharge their batteries. When he woke up and looked at her sleeping, he thought he was the luckiest man in the world. Then her eyes opened, and invited him in.

"Hey, hero, you really missed an opportunity. I would have been easy. I always wanted to date the quarterback."

"Gosh, is this my last chance? Can I get a rain check?"

"Hmm, let me see." She reached down and stroked his penis, which was instantly hard. "Is that what you want?"

He nestled against her. "You know what happens tonight."

She let him go and put an arm around his shoulders. "What can I do?"

Matt felt a kind of gratitude that was new to him. "Just be yourself."

She hugged him. "We have to do this, right?"

The Taj was well into party mode when Matt and Bonnie and Wit arrived. The party was overflowing with students and non-students alike. Even the Zoo was there but of course they weren't in great moods. The drugs helped them get over their sorrow.

The music was loud, the smell of beer and pot thickened the air, and people were already beginning to get sloppy. They all got beer from the keg and tried to make small talk. Wit was as happy as Matt had ever seen him. Finishing his thesis, on the effect of war on the industrial economy, seemed to come in second to beating the Zoo. He and Bonnie argued about whether the UN or the EEC was more important to the world. Matt was tense and didn't add much to the conversation. Bonnie caught his hand and gave it a squeeze. As usual, Neut seemed to materialize out of thin air. "We're ready," he said into Matt's ear.

Matt nodded and looked around. "I don't see him yet." Neut frowned, so Matt added, "But I know he'll come." Neut gave him a dark look and sidled away, pointing to a doorway where he'd stand.

About ten minutes later, Matt saw Mr. Blue saunter in, without his usual briefcase, but carrying a backpack. Matt looked toward the hallway and Mr. Blue gave him a peace sign. "I've got to go," Matt said to Bonnie. She looked frightened for a second, then smiled and squeezed his hand.

"God, I hope this works," she said, standing on tiptoes so she could talk into his ear, which she kissed then.

"What's going on?" Wit shouted above the music.

Bonnie and Barry went up to the front and stopped the music. They made an unusual pair. Bonnie announced, "Since no one will listen to Barry"—the crowd whistled and howled—"I have an announcement. All of the B-3 folks should assemble outside to re-create the winning play." Barry held up a few duffel bags and said he was going to line the quad outside and yelled to all the B-3 folks to come outside.

The B-3 guys roared and started to move outside. The Zoo people yelled obscenities and continued to smoke and drink. The music was turned back on, blaring as loud as possible.

Matt caught up with Mr. Blue in the hallway. He looked nervous. "Okay. Is everything set?"

"You got all that stuff from Neut, right?" Mr. Blue hoisted the backpack and nodded, licking his lips. "And look, Mr. Blue, thanks for doing this."

He looked scared. "I'm going to get off, right?"

"Right. It's as solid as cement."

"Okay then. Things were getting hairy anyway. I'm looking at other business opportunities."

Matt shook his hand and went up to Kashman's room. The room

was hazy but cool from all the windows being open. Kashman was sucking cocaine up with a straw when Matt came in the room. "Hey," Matt said, walking into the room. "Everything's arranged."

Kashman gave him a smile. His head wavered a bit as the cocaine did its work. "Outstanding. Hey, have a snort. Relax a little. You deserve it. Hero of the day. How did that feel, when whatshisname did his thing?"

Matt said, "Outta sight. Totally cool."

Kashman gestured toward the bedroom office. "I'll get the greenbacks." He grabbed the arms of the chair, levered himself up unsteadily, and went into his office. He came out stuffing an envelope in his back pocket. "We really have to do this outside?"

"Mr. Blue thinks . . ."

There was a knock at the door. "Hey, Matt," Bonnie said. "They told me you were in there. Everybody's waiting for you."

"I'll be down in a minute. I'll meet you outside," Matt said, but Kashman brushed past him and opened the door.

"It's just that—" Bonnie stopped mid-sentence. "Oh, Joe."

Kashman smiled broadly. "Hey, Bonnie. I've been wanting to talk to you."

"Talk is cheap," Bonnie snapped.

Kashman waved his hands in front of himself. "Bonnie, I really think that there's been a misunderstanding. Let me explain . . ."

"You want to talk, come on down. I'm going. Matt, get done whatever you're doing here and come out to the front lawn. Everybody's there." She turned and strode off down the hall.

Kashman closed the door, his body tense. Matt said, "Come on, let's get this done before somebody else comes up after me."

Kashman nodded, turned around, and opened the door again. "Yeah, okay, let's go out the back," he said. "It's quiet and there's not much light. Nobody'll see me tear Blue a new asshole."

"Great. Let's go."

The party was still in full swing in the lounge. He and Kashman went out the back door and walked a little ways off the sidewalk and next to the building where there was a light. Mr. Blue was waiting there, standing on one foot, then the other. "Hey, guys," he said.

"Mr. Blue," Kashman said, drawing out the name. "Long time no see. You been hiding from me?"

"Fuck," Mr. Blue said. "Matt, you didn't tell me . . ."

"No, I didn't want him to," Kashman said. "I wanted to have a few words with you."

"What about?" Mr. Blue said. "Hey, Joe, I was going to talk to you about it. Look, I even brought extra in case you were interested. Same amount, same price as Matt's."

Kashman frowned. They all waited. Finally, Kashman reached in his back pocket and pulled out the envelope. Matt did the same. Mr. Blue took the envelopes and gave Kashman the backpack. "Here, you can check it if you want."

Without taking his eyes off Mr. Blue, Kashman reached into the backpack and felt around in it. Then he said, "Ah," and pulled out a gallon-sized zipper baggie that was filled with a white powder.

Suddenly a light lit up the baggie and then a dozen bright lights lit up everything else. Matt felt an arm go around his neck as he watched the same thing happen to Mr. Blue and Kashman. Maybe a dozen police surrounded them and handcuffed them, while Matt saw a phalanx of police running into the Taj. "Hey," he said, "that wasn't—" He was shoved against the brick wall of the building and felt his cheek scrape grit and mortar.

"Shut up, kid," a voice said while his wrists were caught and handcuffed. Kashman was down on the ground and the cops were checking his pockets. Mr. Blue had simply dropped the backpack and held up his hands, which were also cuffed in a second. Matt heard screams from the Taj as a dozen or more cops invaded the dorm. *Getting everybody outside was genius*, he thought. *Bonnie's in the clear.*

Matt and Kashman were drag-walked to a police cruiser and Mr. Blue to another. "Hey, I'm not part of this," he protested, his voice shaking.

"Shut up, kid," the cop growled.

His head pushed down, Matt was loaded into one side of the

cruiser and Kashman into the other. They were strapped in, and the car's wheels squealed as it took off, throwing them first one way and then the other. The siren went on and after a few minutes they were speeding down the main road to town.

Kashman looked over at Matt. "Your cheek's bleeding." He leaned forward a little and said, "Hey, this guy's bleeding all over the place back here. How about a rag or a Kleenex or something?"

Without looking back the cop in the passenger's seat said, "At the station, fuckhead."

Kashman nodded tightly, sat back, and stared straight ahead. Matt was suddenly more scared than he had been all night. *Why isn't he breaking down?* He didn't dare look at Kashman, but he could feel Kashman looking at him. Headlights came through the front windshield and passed by.

"Goddamn fucking sonofabitch," Kashman said, and laughed. "I have to congratulate you. I thought you were too stupid to pull off something like this. And by the way, that stunt to get the B-3 guys away from the drugs was very clever. Taking down my posse and the Zoo was a real coup." Matt didn't say anything. "So you're going to get off, right? And Mr. Blue too?" Matt said he hoped so. "You know Mr. Blue has sold thousands of dollars of drugs, right? He's my biggest supplier."

Matt started to get mad. "Your other supplier's product was bad. Mr. Blue was a businessman and you were going to kill his business. He wanted to get out."

Kashman snorted. "That's a laugh. You're right, he is a businessman. Better than me, really. He takes no pleasure in it. You getting this all, officer?"

"Shut up, fuckhead."

"But it's all right if we talk to each other, right?" There was no answer.

Matt started to feel vaguely human again. He wished he could wipe his cheek. He could feel the blood dripping down his neck onto his shirt. "So you mind if I ask you a question?"

"Fire away. I've got all the time in copland."

"How come you're so cool about this?"

"I've got a lawyer."

A lawyer? Who the fuck has a lawyer? "You know, people say a lot of different things about you."

"And you know what? They're all right."

Matt looked over at Kashman, who was looking into the middle distance. "Right about what, for instance?"

"I grew up in Riverdale."

"Nice place."

"Yeah, but then my parents divorced, and I went to live with my mother. She moved to Brooklyn, and then to Far Rockaway. She was a mess. Couldn't hold a job, couldn't hold her liquor. I'd wake up and she'd be passed out on the couch, drooling. You know what it's like to see your mother drooling?" Kashman looked at him and Matt looked away. "Anyway, finally my father found out about it and took me. He was, he is, a lawyer. He has some clients . . . maybe not the kind of clients your parents would approve of. But they have a lot of money. And even more, a lot of influence."

"You mean, like the Mafia?"

Kashman laughed. "That's a TV word, Matt. *The Untouchables.* Forget it. You know, one thing the radicals get right is that there are all kinds of 'mafias.' Like the Kennedys are a mafia. The Rockefellers. The country is run by mafias. They call themselves 'businesspeople' or 'patriots' or 'politicians' or shit like that."

"But there are a lot of good people too." Matt thought about his father and his mother.

"Those are the suckers."

"Oh, fuck you."

"Oops, sorry. Struck a nerve, did I?" Kashman was quiet for a moment. "You know, I liked you, Matt. I liked you and I hated you. There was a time when I wanted to be you, when I was a kid. Then I thought that I could make you into somebody who wasn't a sucker. See, that's the thing. You can be whatever you want. When I got here, to Montauk, I realized that my past, all that shit was *my past*. It didn't have to be *me*. I was free, I could be whatever I wanted."

"And you wanted to run things." Kashman shrugged, which made Matt madder. "I don't think I'm a sucker to want to get an education. From actual intelligent people. I don't believe I'm a sucker for wanting to know what Mrs. Devin knows. I don't believe I'm a sucker for standing up for what I believe. For acting on it, not just thinking about it."

Kashman considered this. "Righteous. I think we agree on that. I just don't think we agree on what to believe in."

"What do you believe in?"

Kashman thought for a moment. Then he said, "Whatever works." He looked at Matt just as Matt was looking at him. "Just like you do. That's why you planned this bust tonight. You tried to get me out with Lana. That didn't work, so you got me arrested. And you'll get off and Mr. Blue will get off. Congratulations to me. I did better than I thought. I just didn't see where it would lead."

———————

Bonnie lay back on the grass. It was an impossibly beautiful spring day, and she had on a T-shirt for the first time, as far as Matt knew. "So you spent the night in jail?" she said. "I thought maybe the cops would just decide to put you away, despite what Neut said he arranged."

"I had a few tense moments myself." Matt was on his elbow on the grass so that he could look at her. "I wasn't actually written up. Kashman and I were put in different cells and after a few hours, a cop came by and unlocked my cell and said I was free to go. I asked about Mr. Blue and the cop said he was out. I didn't ask about Kashman."

"Does what he said bother you?" She looked up at him and the earnestness in her brown eyes almost made him forget what he was going to say.

"Could you blink?" he asked. She blinked, which didn't help. He couldn't forget what she looked like in bed. He kissed her, which did help. "Yes, actually it does bother me. I—"

"We."

"We made a decision about what we thought was right. Were we right?"

"Yes."

"How do you know?"

"I don't *know*. But everything I *know*, everything I've learned, tells me that his kind of personal, imperial leadership is dangerous."

Matt decided he couldn't carry on a rational discussion as long as he was looking at her. He lay back on the grass. "I know that I'm glad he's gone. I wouldn't even mind if he gets off, as long as he doesn't come back to school."

"Oh god, you're too good. Are you going to run for president of the Polity?"

"Me, after a drug bust?"

She smiled. "That's probably a plus these days. After they arrested eighty people? What's important is that you made a difference."

Matt looked up at the sky. "I don't think I told you. Mrs. Devin asked me the same question."

She elbowed him in the ribs. "Creep! You didn't say anything about talking to her. Tell me everything you know!"

"No, she just asked me to come in. It was kind of a strange conversation. She couldn't say that I—"

"We."

"We had engineered Kashman's arrest, but she wanted to thank me."

"She knows *everything*."

Matt laughed. "Yeah, you're probably right. But I was glad that she was back."

"Me too."

"What I'm sad about is that you're leaving."

She was quiet. She'd told him that she'd been accepted to the junior year abroad program and was going to work at the EEC in Brussels. It was a punch in the gut. He'd expected it, but he couldn't say it was the wrong thing to do. "Matt?" she said tentatively.

"Yeah?"

"Look, if Nicky comes back next year, I'll understand that you want to see her. I think you should see her."

Matt didn't know what to say about this. He was almost angry. He thought they were together. "Why? I mean why do you want me to see her?"

She was silent for a while. Then she said, "Because it's the human thing to do. She cared about you." She was silent again, and then said quietly, "Because you should know whether you like her better."

Matt felt his eyes get wet. "I think saying that is a lot braver than anything I've ever done. Or maybe just better." It was his turn to be quiet. "I think I love that you are able to say that. It makes me even sadder that you're leaving."

"I'm sad too. I didn't know about you when I applied."

"I didn't know about me when you applied." She giggled at that. "I'm not sure what that means," he said. "Anyway, I would have told you to apply if you had known. If I had known."

"Next time," she said, getting up on an elbow to look at him, "we'll make that decision together."

"Oh, well. Yeah." It took him a minute but then he thought, *I like the sound of "next time."* "I like the sound of 'next time,'" he said.

"Me too." She leaned over and kissed him. "You know . . . ," she started, "you *could* come to Brussels. Like, for a little while. You wouldn't have to stay in a hotel, so it would just be plane fare. There are a lot of cheap flights."

"Well . . . ," he said, and stopped. *No hotel means . . .* Suddenly he realized that he was actually an independent person apart from his parents. It was his life. *Why the hell not?* They probably wouldn't even object. Or at least maybe not. He'd told them some of what went on, the sanitized version about how he'd helped the police stop a drug ring on campus. "You know," he said, "I'd like that a whole lot. Anything is possible."

She put a finger on his lips. "*Everything* is possible."

ABOUT THE AUTHORS

WALTER BODE is currently a freelance editor. He was editor-in-chief of Grove Press, a senior editor at Harcourt, and also worked at the Viking Press. The books he has edited have been awarded the Pulitzer Prize, the National Book Critics Circle Award for Fiction, the Casey Award for Best Sports Book, the Lambda Award for Best Fiction, the Whitbread Award for Biography (UK), and the Gold Dagger for Best Mystery Novel (UK). He graduated from Princeton University in 1973. This is his first novel. He lives on eastern Long Island with his wife Carmela and his two sons.

DAVID MAUER graduated from Stony Brook University in 1969 and went on to receive his MBA from Penn's Wharton School. He has since served as President/CEO of several consumer products companies including Mattel USA. As the father of grown children, he wanted them to understand how his life was influenced by the social revolution that had its roots in the Vietnam War and the long-delayed demands of Blacks and women to share in the promise of America. His experience at a large, newborn university in the sixties showed him firsthand how individuals could make a difference in the direction of society. Like many others of his generation, he found the freedom and possibilities intoxicating. This book is a fictionalized story of what he learned. The parallels to the events of the 2020s are both remarkable and predictable. Mauer lives with his wife, Freddi Greenberg, in New York City.

Momentum Ink Press is a cooperative advancing the work of writers unavailable through traditional commercial publishers. Each book is carefully reviewed by a collection of authors, editors, and designers ensuring an authentic artistic version of the writer's best work. By selecting and reading a Momentum Ink Press book you are joining and supporting a community of readers and writers committed to quality in literature. We hope you appreciate our books as much as we enjoy bringing them to you.